"Hi, Linc. Thanks for stopping by to collect me."

She got the words out before she looked at him properly. It was just as well, because when she did, she couldn't drag her gaze away again.

He had on a sleek evening suit in a dark pin-striped gray, a crisp white shirt and thin powder blue tie. Polished black dress shoes completed the outfit, and as he moved his arm slightly, she caught a glimpse of a gold cuff link.

Oh.

My.

Gosh.

Could any man look more handsome than Linc did tonight?

TEMPTED BY HER TYCOON BOSS

BY
JENNIE ADAMS

First Published in Great Britain 2016
By Mills & Boon, an imprint of HarperCollins*Publishers*
1 London Bridge Street, London, SE1 9GF

© 2016 Jennie Adams

ISBN: 978-0-263-91978-3

23-0416

Our policy is to use papers that are natural, renewable and recyclable products and made from wood grown in sustainable forests. The logging and manufacturing processes conform to the legal environmental regulations of the country of origin.

Printed and bound in Spain
by CPI, Barcelona

After years of living in a small inland city in New South Wales, Australia, **Jennie Adams** re-embraced the country lifestyle of her childhood. When she isn't writing, Jennie dedicates her time to promoting the natural wonders of her new area and encouraging others to visit and enjoy what now constitutes her back garden—large tracts of native bushland, flora and fauna reserves and wetlands. Jennie's family has grown to embrace in-laws (and outlaws, she always jokes), sisters, daughters and brothers of the heart. Find Jennie at www.joybyjennie.com.

For my dad. You were my first storyteller and you'll always remain the best to me. Love you.

CHAPTER ONE

'GOOD MORNING, CECILIA.' Linc MacKay spoke the greeting as he stepped between shoulder-height hedge shapes bursting from within with raised flowering displays. 'Your second-in-command told me I'd probably find you here.'

'Here' was the feature maze area of the Fleurmazing Plant Nursery on its acreage just outside the Sydney city limits. The Australian sun warmed the air, and the light breeze carried the scents of a summer garden.

Now it had also brought a handsome millionaire, stepping around a corner of the maze to an alcove where a statue of a sun goddess draped in gossamer folds reached her arms upwards as though to bless the world with her light.

Was it the soft look in Linc's eyes as his gaze moved beyond the sun goddess and lingered on her that made Cecilia's breath suddenly catch? A moment later the expression disappeared, if it had ever truly been there at all.

'Linc. Is it that time already?' She focused on projecting professionalism into her words and tried to push those discomforting questions to the back of her mind. 'I'm glad Jemmie was able to point you in the right direction to find me.'

Cecilia placed one final hedge trimming into the basket over her arm and walked towards the plant nursery's owner. If she didn't feel entirely calm she could at least act as though she were.

'This is my favourite part of the maze, to be honest.'

'I can see why.' His gaze took in the maze, its beautiful flowers every shade from creamy white to deepest violet and blue. But then he turned back and took in Cecilia, too, from the top of her honey-blond hair in its high ponytail, over her face, lingering on each feature, and quickly sweeping over the simple strappy sundress that showed off her curves to perfection.

She rarely dressed in her best girly attire for work but, knowing that today she'd be inside most of the day in the office, Cecilia had let her most feminine side have its way.

'It's stunning,' Linc finally said. 'The...ah...the maze.'

'Thank you.' She drew a slightly unsteady breath. 'I'm sorry I wasn't up front, ready to greet you.'

Cecilia glanced at the trimmings in the basket over her arm and hoped by doing so she would disguise her swirling thoughts from him.

'This is a never-ending job.'

'And a very important one at the moment, I can imagine.'

Why, oh, *why* did she have to feel suddenly oh-so-conscious of him? She had much better control than this. Usually...

Wasn't it enough that she'd mistaken his interest once before, years ago?

'The maze needs to look good. Fantastic, in fact.'

She forced the words out and told herself to concentrate on matters at hand. The Fleurmazing plant nursery was the third and most recent of Linc's Sydney plant nurseries that she had managed over the six years she'd been in his employ, but this one was different.

It was *her* brainchild—a holistic nursery that required greater upkeep but offered an enhanced experience for its visitors. At least in this aspect of her life she had it together!

She should keep her focus on that. Now, of all times, Cecilia needed to 'sell' the nursery's virtues to Linc at any opportunity she got. Noticing his character traits or wondering if his attention was caught on her wasn't part of that plan.

'We're logging hundreds of people every day, who all come here specifically because they want to experience the maze. Sales out of that alone are fantastic. And the maze needs to be perfect in time for the part we're playing in Sydney's Silver Bells charity flower show, so I'm giving it a lot of attention at the moment.'

'A masked ball in the middle of a plant maze is ambitious.' One side of his mouth kicked up. 'But I'm sure if anyone can carry it off it'll be you.'

'The Silver Bells organisers have put their faith in me, so I have no choice now.' She said it laughingly, but the importance of it was never far from her thoughts.

She wouldn't have had the opportunity if Linc hadn't agreed to let her take the risk.

'It'll pay off, Linc. Your whole chain of plant nurseries will get good attention out of our participation in the Silver Bells event.'

Linc owned a dozen nurseries across the city, along with bucketloads of real estate and a commodities trading portfolio that, on its own, probably ran into millions. He truly was the quintessential millionaire bachelor, with the world at his feet. They were more than poles apart, which had made her *faux pas* of throwing herself at him six years ago even more embarrassing.

He hadn't been interested. She'd mistaken his charming way for something it wasn't, and then— moments after he'd let Cecilia down as gently as anyone possibly could have—a woman had arrived for her lunch date with him. A sophisticated older woman.

Old news, Cee. Linc played the gentleman that day, apologised that he'd given the wrong impression and went off on his date with Ms Socialite while you went back to digging around in potting mix. And you got over it.

Cecilia had worked hard to impress him professionally since then, and she'd dated. Then she'd found Hugh, and that relationship had lasted almost two years. Linc had no doubt dated lots more versions of Ms Socialite, too, though Cecilia had not heard of him ever being in a serious long-term relationship since she'd known him.

'I appreciate you coming in for the business review. I know you're busy. Actually, I thought you might have sent someone to do it for you.'

'You've earned this opportunity, and I felt I owed

it to you to undertake the review myself.' Sincerity rang in his tone. 'I want to grant you that twenty per cent share in the nursery if I can, and no one else will understand your work here and your vision the way that I do.'

That was true. Even though the bulk of their inter-actions were over the phone, she'd always reported regularly to Linc.

And she'd negotiated—refusing bonuses over the years in favour of building up to this: a chance to own a share in the nursery. One day she wanted to open her own business.

'I hope the review proves my efforts worthy of your time.'

Linc might have rejected her overtures, but he had been her example since he'd first taken her on and let her manage one of his nurseries six years ago, with no experience and only her determination to get her through. He was proof that a person could achieve anything if they wanted it enough.

What would he be now? Thirty-four? Thirty-five? Still with the same deep timbre to his voice, the same way of wearing his work boots, jeans and chambray shirt with an authority overlaid with a deceptive dose of casual charm.

With a strong chin, short-cut dark hair, those gor-geous shoulders and a way of carrying himself that shouted, *Look out, world!* Linc MacKay was in all ways a force to be reckoned with.

Linc would be making the nursery his base while he undertook the review. They'd be spending quite a bit of time in each other's company. It couldn't be a worse time for that old awareness of him to resurface. Whatever had brought it back, she needed her interest in him *gone*. Now, if not sooner.

Cecilia began the return walk towards the equipment shed and the front office.

'I know I'll see good results here, Cecilia. With each new nursery you've managed, you've improved on the last.' Linc fell into step beside her in the maze. 'I *have* taken it all in, you know—including the way this one has exceeded all expectations. Bringing coach tours in on a daily basis, gaining that whole new layer of tourism clientele…that has shown real vision.'

His words made every moment of her hard work feel doubly worth it. Cecilia couldn't help smiling as she quietly thanked him.

'Our social media presence has made a difference, too. I'm blessed to have Jemmie here, with her skills in photography and videography. Her plants-growing-and-bursting-into-flower videos get a lot of attention online.'

'You found a good asset in her.'

His compliment pleased her, but it was his simple gesture for her to precede him through a narrower section of the maze that brought back that earlier flutter to Cecilia's pulse. It felt *intimate* to her. As though they'd met here for a morning tryst and were returning now to their 'real' lives.

How silly.

Planning for this masked ball must be messing with her brain. Cecilia couldn't come up with a more feasible explanation for her sudden case of hyper-Linc-awareness.

Or perhaps you've simply been out of your rela-

*tionship with Hugh long enough to open your eyes
and look around you?*

If so, she could cast her attention in some other
direction, thank you very much. Because Linc was
not for her and she'd accepted that fact and got over
caring about it a very long time ago.

She *had*, right…?

'Thank you, Linc, for the commitment you've
made to do this review.'

If the words were a little stiff and formal, that
couldn't be helped. Surely that was better than falling all over him, even if only inside her own thoughts.

'I know it's time away from the other demands of
your life.'

'I suspect some of those demands will follow me
here, but I'll do my best not to disrupt you.' A teasing smile came and went.

Cecilia ignored how that smile made her tummy
flutter. It had to be the kind of smile that one friend
might share with another, or a person who'd known
another person for years, or a boss who felt comfortable with his employee. And Cecilia fell into the lat-
ter category. Yes, she'd known Linc for years, but
they were work associates with a lot of *professional*
ground walked over in that span of time.

Therefore his smile must be a perfectly normal one
that meant nothing whatsoever outside those bounds.
He couldn't help it if he was cute.

Great avoiding of his appeal, Cee.

He went on. 'I don't want to make a painful time
out of this for you.'

'I'm sure it will be fine.' No matter the outcome,
she knew Linc would be fair in his assessment.

Whether she could eliminate the painful knowledge of her reawakened awareness of him was another challenge altogether.

But it was one that she had to achieve, and she could not let the rest of her life mess with her head, either, while she got through the review. That would be easier said than done, when one part of it gnawed at her ceaselessly and she was still stinging over another part.

Well, no-longer-interested-and-nothing-could-keep-me-here-now Hugh could go and trip over and fall into a duck pond, for all she cared. And the other thing just…*was*.

Cecilia drew a breath.

Her personal life might not be as calm as she would like, but she could manage—and Linc didn't need to know about any of it.

She detoured to leave her plant cuttings and basket in the potting shed, and then led the way to her office. 'Come on in. How long do you think the review will take?'

'Depending on how much I get interrupted, it shouldn't take more than a few days.'

His gaze searched hers just a little bit too keenly for her comfort.

'Great.' She gestured to where a second computer and desk sat at a diagonal angle to her own, and pushed those other thoughts as far back in her mind as she could manage. 'I don't mean it's great that you won't be here more than that. You know what I mean…'

Did he? Was he hearing her words falling over themselves in a way that was quite out of character after her usual modulated approaches to him?

So get over it, Cecilia. You've been to see him at his city office, where the staff all complain that he's hardly ever there but say it fondly, as though they're glad that he gives them the autonomy to do their best for him while he's out spreading his holdings even further. You've been to the warehouse home he shared in the past with his brothers. He's seen you at each of the nurseries you've managed. Multiple times, in fact. This is no different.

'The financials are all on there.' She used her best I've-got-over-it tone, which would at least make sense to her. 'Along with my strategic forecast for the business for the upcoming couple of years.'

The hand she'd been waving around now hid itself in a fold of her sundress's knee-length skirt.

'Thanks.' Again his lips curved into that hint of a smile. 'I'll jump straight in.'

'I'd best get on with my work, too.' Cecilia dropped into her chair. 'I have invoices to get into the system from the weekend's trade.'

She did *not* mention that she'd spent so much time ensuring that the outdoor aspects of the nursery were impeccable in recent days that she'd allowed that invoicing to get somewhat behind.

She'd known Linc would be here and that he'd want her around—at least to start with. This way she could work while she answered any questions he might have.

That's right. You weren't hiding out doing your favourite tasks just because they help you not to think about other things.

Cecilia had a major event coming up for the nursery. She simply didn't have time to think about anything else. Not family stresses, not her abandonment by Hugh and certainly not this morning's odd noticing of Linc in a way she had stopped herself doing for years.

Cecilia jabbed the start button of her Slimline computer. 'I'll be here all day in the office to be sure I'm available for any questions you may have.'

'I appreciate that you're so well organised for the review, even with a big event looming on the horizon.'

Linc MacKay murmured the words as his plant-nursery manager shuffled her bottom into her office chair and peered down her nose at the computer screen in front of her.

She looked beautiful today…a summery woman with golden skin. Her shoulders were bare but for a couple of spaghetti straps on the deep red sundress splashed with a bold floral design, and her lips were highlighted in a subtle lipstick.

Linc had rejected her innocent overtures six years ago, even though he'd felt a spark of interest at the time. It had never truly gone away, and he had felt that fact keenly today. Seeing her in the beautiful sundress, showing such a feminine side of herself, Linc felt as though he were seeing her in a whole new light.

And because that awareness wasn't acceptable to him, he forced his focus to her business acumen.

Cecilia was determined and motivated and very capable when it came to running a nursery. Her push to gain a share in this one had impressed him, and she'd earned that opportunity over the last six years.

She was an intriguing woman, Linc acknowledged silently, and his glance returned to her once again.

Slender, with shoulder-length hair every shade from ash to dark blond and eyes the colour of bluebonnets…

Where had he been?

Right. Her inner strength and drive impressed him. Linc told himself not to think about how sweet she looked, how he felt as though layers had been pulled from his eyes and he could see her clearly for the very first time.

'I'll review the strategic projections first.' He pushed the knowledge of her appeal to the back of his mind, where it had to remain. 'Those will form a solid basis for the rest of my review. They'll also help me to spot any areas where the business might not yet be living up to its full potential.'

'I'll be keen to discuss any weak areas with you.' Cecilia sat very upright in her chair. 'I pride myself on trying to keep everything strong. I've printed a copy of the projections document for you.'

She pointed to the pile of files beside his computer. The document sat right on top.

'I appreciate it.' He lifted the sheaf of pages and flipped through them before turning back to the first page and lowering his gaze so he could fully concentrate on it.

It took a while, but Linc did immerse himself in the work. Even if he *could* see acres of soft, delicately sun-kissed skin in the periphery of his view.

Cecilia focused studiously on her office work, but out of the corner of her eye she remained very aware of Linc as the hours passed.

She wanted to know how he felt about his findings so far, even though he would have only just scratched the surface at this stage.

Distractingly, she noticed the scent of his after-shave. It made her think about things that had no business being in her mind.

'Cecilia?'

'Yes. No. I mean—' Had Linc asked her a question while she'd been daydreaming about woodsy scents and clear grey eyes? She had no idea—and no business noticing his eyes. Or his shoulders. Or the way his strong nose perfectly matched the firm, sensuous appeal of his lips.

Concentrate, Cee! On something other than how gorgeous he is.

'I might get a bite to eat.' He glanced at the clock on the wall. 'It's getting to be that time of day. Would you like to join me, or can I pick up something for you?'

For a moment blank incomprehension filled her. She fought her way out of it and realised she *was* hungry—but a lunch date with Linc MacKay...?

'Thanks, but I have errands to run on my lunch break.' Fortunately, his invitation had been offhand enough that she didn't need to worry about causing offence by refusing it.

Exactly.

So why had her heart skipped a beat?

'Plus, I brought something to eat from home.' Something dull and ordinary that held no uncertain surprises and certainly wouldn't make her think back to a past time when she had wanted to know Linc better on a personal rather than a business footing. 'But I appreciate the offer.'

He gave a little nod and a half smile and went on his way—which quite put it into perspective, as she should have done from the start. Thank goodness she hadn't sounded as though she were turning him down in a personal way or anything like that.

Cecilia ate her home-packed sandwich at her desk, and then headed for the nearby mall. Her thoughts turned to her sister more and more with each step. Hugh might have dropped Cecilia like the proverbial hot potato when her family life had suddenly gone from slightly troublesome to really concerning, and that still hurt, but it was the rift with Stacey that remained as a constant source of heartache any time Cecilia let the thoughts surface.

Rejection seemed to have formed a bit too much of a repeat cycle in Cecilia's life lately. It was just as well that she had learned to bury her emotions in her work and that she was very *good* at that work.

'Next, please.' The voice of the man behind the counter at the postal outlet drew her from her thoughts.

'Hello. I need to purchase a money order, please.'

'Same name and amount?'

The clerk probably thought he was being helpful, asking that. Instead, it just reminded Cecilia of how many times she had done this. Every Monday for the past five months, and it wasn't over yet.

Not this guy's fault, and not your fault, either, so smile and be normal. Got it?

She was fulfilling a duty, and if that felt like a paltry thing to do, well, the situation wasn't easy—and doing this was a lot more than just duty. She had to continue to hope that things would improve.

'Yes. Thank you.'

Cecilia placed the money order into a pre-stamped envelope and mailed it.

As she returned to work she let her spirits find happiness again. She loved the nursery and loved what she'd achieved here. And if she felt a little lift, knowing she was about to see Linc again, too, that came from knowing that every moment in his presence brought the results of the review and his decision about her share proposition closer. It was that and only that.

If she didn't entirely believe herself, Cecilia ignored the fact.

Her peace lasted until she approached the office and heard Linc speaking.

'I can tell you really want to speak with her, but Cecilia is at lunch just now.' There was a pause. 'Are you in a position where you could call back a bit later?'

'Is that for me? I'll take it now.' She could hardly speak for the buzzing in her ears, and she saw Linc was ending the call even as she spoke.

For a moment after he'd placed the phone back in its cradle, she simply stood there.

'That was a supplier wanting to change an order.'

Linc seemed to be searching her face with a great deal of attention.

It was just a supplier, phoning on the office phone. Your sister only has your cell phone number. You haven't missed a chance to speak with her, and Linc hasn't found out anything about her.

Disappointment and relief fought for supremacy inside Cecilia.

They both won.

'The guy sounded old…grumpy.' Linc gave a what-do-you-do kind of a shrug. 'He didn't want to leave his name or number, only wanted to speak with you, and he ended the call quite abruptly.'

'I think I know which supplier that would have been.' She walked to her desk, sat down. Felt Linc's gaze on her and an added layer of awareness of her that she would swear, despite her admonitions to herself earlier to the contrary, was real.

Did she want to set herself up for further rejection? No.

Exactly, Cecilia. So get your mind back on your work. Now!

But trying to do that just reminded her that her heart had almost stopped for a second or two, and now she was fighting a renewed sense of sadness and loss that she tried to keep distant during work hours.

'I'll call the supplier back a bit later and let him know that a message would be welcome the next time, whether I'm here or not.'

Next time she wouldn't practically fall apart over a silly, perfectly routine, office-related phone call.

Cecilia ignored the reasons why she *would* panic, and why she now felt deflated and sad all over again. Because no cause for panic had actually ensued. She'd ignored the way Linc had made her feel today so far, too. If she ignored that for long enough, she would get it under control.

She turned her attention back to her work. In the end, that was where her focus needed to stay!

CHAPTER TWO

'IS THERE A chance we could move my tour of the facility forward and do it now? I have to disappear for a while later this morning on other business.'

Linc made the request as he and Cecilia met at the front area of the plant nursery the next morning. They'd driven into the staff parking area within seconds of each other.

'I'm sorry for the disruption to our review, but would that be manageable for you?'

'There's no need to apologise. I'm surprised you got through even one day without a disruption, to be honest. And the flower show management team aren't due here until eleven—so, yes, I can do the tour now.'

Cecilia's words and tone were calm. Yet in catching her unawares Linc had glimpsed what had looked like sorrow in her eyes, before she'd shielded her expression and the mantle of 'business manager' came down over her face.

There'd been an awareness of him, too. It had sparked briefly before that mantle had come down. It disturbed him that he had looked and hoped for that very thing. And it disturbed him that she had seemed sad.

He frowned, but a moment later Cecilia spoke with such enthusiasm and apparent focus on her work that he wondered if he had imagined that earlier moment of interest and its preceding sadness.

'It'll be a real pleasure to show you everything here in detail. Just let me stow my things, Linc, and we'll get into the tour.'

Cecilia quickly divested herself of her purse and her lunch, tucked her cell phone into the back pocket of her jeans, and led the way to the first part of the nursery.

She'd been an intriguing young woman at twenty, when she'd fought so hard to get him to let her manage one of his nurseries. With nothing but a community college course and some time spent in customer service in a small plant nursery behind her, she'd gone after her dream of managing one, tenaciously.

Linc would have been a fool not to employ her, so he had done exactly that. But not before she had let him see that she would have welcomed the opportunity to know him better as a *man*, not only as a potential employer.

Her interest then hadn't been one-sided.

And now…?

Now, for his sins, Linc had seen a whole new aspect of her yesterday, and that had not only refreshed the underlying awareness of Cecilia that had never truly left him, but had added to it. *Why?* Was it because there'd been no woman in his life at all lately?

Well, he'd been busy.

Too busy to pick up the phone and invite someone out or to say yes to any of the invitations that came his way?

Was he getting jaded? Or perhaps lonely? Wanting what his brothers had in their marriages?

That last thought came out of nowhere, and Linc shoved it right back there just as quickly. Ridiculous. He was perfectly happy as he was. He ignored any possibility that he might not be.

Linc's gaze was focused on the back of Cecilia's head as she walked along a curved pathway ahead of him, but all that did was draw his attention to her again.

A yellow sleeveless shirt contrasted with denim cut-offs, and both highlighted her soft curves. Today she wore her hair up in that ponytail again, and it bounced with every step of her work-booted feet.

The ponytail made Linc want to kiss her, and while the sensible work attire spoke of her determination, she looked equally as appealing to Linc today as she had yesterday—all feminine curviness and beauty.

Layers had definitely been peeled from his eyes, and Linc wanted to paste them right back on. He needed to do that, because Cecilia wasn't the kind of woman he'd date and forget—the type of woman he had always dated because it was easy to walk away.

He had to set aside this awareness of Cecilia—whether he'd suddenly noticed her on a whole different level or not.

Cecilia glanced over her shoulder. 'Shall we visit the cold storage first?'

'Yes. That would be…ah…great.'

They headed over there, and Linc forced his attention back to the tour. He noticed the amount of empty space surrounding the limited offerings of cut flowers.

'How's the cut-flower trade going?'

'It's going well.'

Her glance seemed only to calculate the empty shelf area. But her cheeks held a hint of pink that couldn't be attributed to their brief walk.

Was she feeling this, too? This interest and curiosity that felt fresh and new and oh-so-tempting to pursue?

'At the moment we're keeping our stock orders tight.' She waved a hand in the general direction of the shelves, and then shoved it into the front pocket of her cut-offs.

She's as aware of it as you are.

Maybe, but that didn't mean she wanted to pursue it any more than he did, Linc reminded himself belatedly.

'Any special reason?' He cleared his throat. 'For keeping the stock orders tight?'

She tipped her head on one side and seemed to consider him for a moment before she responded. 'It's because Valentine's Day is very close and we'll need the space for all the cut roses.'

'Right. It's good that you've thought ahead to make as much of that day as possible.' His voice was so deep it might have come from his boots. 'I should have thought of that straight away.'

'It's a very special day.' The pink in her cheeks deepened. 'For—for the customers, and very much for the nursery.'

And most of all for lovers.

She didn't say that. Instead, she drew a deep breath, as though to try to compose herself.

In Linc's experience women seemed to expect a

very emotional expression of love on that particular day of the year. To show a love that encapsulated exactly the kind of commitment that would never be part of Linc's own life.

He was grateful his brothers had found such love—that their lives had turned out okay in the end. However, Linc would never deserve—

'We'll be getting in red roses, predominantly.'

Cecilia's words drew him back from the dark thoughts as she led the way out of the cold storage area and, once he'd joined her outside, secured it.

'We'll stock other colours of roses, too. There's a growing percentage of buyers who will purchase something other than the classic red—particularly when purchasing for friends or family rather than—'

'The romantic loves of their lives?'

There. He'd said it and the sky hadn't fallen in.

'Yes.' She glanced at him and quickly away again. Her chin tipped up. 'Roses are lovely at any time of the year. My favourites are the creamy white ones. They have a beautiful, subtle scent.'

She led the way through a section of potted seedlings and, as he came to her side, gave him the benefit of a determinedly work-focused gaze.

'Hopefully this year's sales of roses will prove to be as lucrative as last—if not more so.'

The words made Cecilia sound as unromantic as they came, and she *was* a great businesswoman. But one who'd managed to bring romance right to the heart of her working life through her instigation of this year's masked-ball event. Not to mention all the flowers she stocked for Valentine's Day, and the flowering maze she had designed and nurtured to fruition.

'Given your track record over the last six years, I have no doubt that the Valentine's Day trade will exceed all expectations.' He made the comment matter-of-fact, but his thoughts were not pragmatic.

She'd been in a relationship a few months ago. His brother Brent had mentioned that it had ended.

So she's single.

Why would Linc even consider her availability?

She may be hurting and still love the guy.

'Thank you.'

For a moment Linc didn't know what she was thanking him for, and then he remembered. He'd paid her a compliment. A business one, about her ability to do a great job as plant-nursery manager.

Which was true.

'You're welcome.'

They moved between rows of gardening supplies, through arrays of flowering plants and herbs, potting mix and foliage. Linc began to find his focus again, and the colour in Cecilia's cheeks returned to normal.

So it was fine. He'd been foolishly carried away—imagining things, nothing more. Flights of fancy weren't Linc's style. He would make sure it didn't happen again.

Cecilia's love of her work shone through more and more as she talked avidly, explaining the progress and plans that related to each area.

'What's happening in that shed?'

He asked the question as they walked towards a shady path, far into the back section of the nursery. Access to the shed was gained through a locked gate. There were no customers to be seen or heard, and it truly felt secluded and private.

In fact, it was the perfect setting for a man to steal a kiss. Assuming that a man would choose to do something so unprofessional.

So much for him returning his thoughts to nothing but business.

'I'll show you.' Cecilia led the way to this final shed on the property and unlocked and opened the door. The tour with Linc had proved productive so far, but she had been oh-so-conscious of him the entire time.

This sharpened interest towards Linc needed to stop.

She felt a moment of nervous anticipation as she prepared to reveal this part of the business. It was working well, and she was proud of it, but what would Linc think of the concept?

'I hope you'll approve of this aspect of the nursery.' She tried to imbue nothing but confidence into her tone as she went on. 'This is where I work on my repurposing projects. I get some of my best ideas for the future direction of the business when I'm working here, too.'

With this statement carefully delivered, and avoiding the thought that she also came here when she missed her sister the most, Cecilia glanced about the area.

Sunlight streamed through skylights in the roof into a large open-plan area that housed projects in various stages of completion. Old boots with creepers growing out of them...a rocking chair that had been painted orange and black, its seat area filled with a large planter of pumpkin vine... Demand for this kind of repurposed item was growing.

'I didn't know about this.' Linc's gaze moved about the area before it returned to her. 'How long have you been doing this work? Where did you get all these items?'

He wouldn't realise it, but the sun coming through the skylight above had cast his profile into sharp relief. Every strong feature and every subtle nuance was there for her to see. Right down to the length of his dark eyelashes and the way they curled slightly at the ends. And the shape of his lips…

Cecilia struggled to remember his question. He'd asked something about where she got the items for refurbishment. It was one of her favourite aspects of the plant nursery, which showed how easily being around Linc could throw her completely off her guard.

'I find items in all sorts of places.'

She took a step to the side, to break that particular view of him. It was as though she'd jumped back through time six years and all her past awareness of him as a man had returned.

Actually, it hadn't—because she saw him now with a history of working in his employ for six years. She saw him with more maturity. With more certainty in her interest in him…

'I started this operation about four months ago.'

Soon after she'd realised she needed a distraction and a way of letting out her emotions, thanks to the implosions going on in her personal life.

She simply *couldn't* feel a renewed attraction to Linc, let alone a deeper one. Because—because business and that sort of pleasure didn't mix. Because she had enough to deal with in her life without trying to take on a romance. Because she'd learned the hard way, when Hugh had disappeared from her life without a backward glance, that you just couldn't trust romantic attachments once 'real life' interfered with them!

Most of all because Linc had rejected her overtures all those years ago. *Remember?* There was no earthly reason why he'd feel any differently now.

'Any time I'm out and about I visit garage sales and junk shops…thrift stores and car boot sales.'

Perhaps if she made herself sound like a lonely single girl with a craft obsession, she would embarrass herself out of being so conscious of him.

'All the items are ridiculously cheap to buy,' she continued, 'and people leap at the chance to purchase the end product—the repurposed item. There's good profit to be made, and the items appeal to the style of visitor who comes here to tour the maze. Jemmie features them online, as well.'

His strong hands lifted a pottery urn from the bench. It had a chunk missing from one side. 'So a buyer will pay top dollar for this?'

'Once the urn has herbs growing in it, or maybe some flowering cacti, you'll be surprised how quickly it will be snapped up.'

She took the urn from his hands, held it up to the light. She ignored her fanciful thoughts and how it felt to stand so close to him, to measure her smaller frame against his taller, stronger one.

Get over it, Cee. Get over it right now!

Cecilia went on to tell Linc about her repurposing timetable, and then led the way back through the nursery acreage to the maze, quickly showing Linc the upgrades she'd had done to the *fruticetum* at the centre of it. Its circular arrangement combined colourful blooming potted shrubs with evergreen native species.

'Clever work.' He made the declaration the moment they stepped into the central area. 'Those shrubs grouped all around the edges of the circular space will add to the air of mystery for the masked ball.'

She gestured to the picnic tables dotted around the central area as well as the edges.

'Currently, when folks finish touring the maze, they can sit for a while, enjoy the quiet and utilise the screens embedded in the tabletops to scroll through our available stock lists and place orders. They can either take them with them, collect later or have them sent to any address they choose. The night of the ball there'll be a raised dais for dancing. The central picnic tables will be shifted out to the edges of the area and the canopied dais will be assembled on-site the day before the event.'

Something she had told herself was mostly about commerce and exposure for the business suddenly felt quite personal to Cecilia. She could imagine herself on that dais, dancing with a handsome partner.

Well, a girl could buy into a romantic idea, couldn't she? Even if it *was* an idea she had germinated to increase the popularity of her business.

As for that vision of herself on the dais… The man who appeared in it with her looked remarkably like Linc.

Heat warmed the back of her neck. The middle of a working tour was not the time for such flights of fancifulness. Hadn't she allowed herself to be distracted enough by him this morning?

'Will it be an old-fashioned ball?' he queried. 'With waltzing and so on?'

Was his voice deeper than usual? Cecilia glanced at his face but couldn't read his expression.

'There will be waltzes and other simpler dance tunes. I want people at all levels of dancing ability to be able to participate,' she murmured, and then had to clear her throat and strive for a stronger tone. 'I hope to create a night to remember.'

His gaze met hers and, for one breathless moment, electricity seemed to charge the air between them.

'I'm sure you'll achieve that.'

Oh, Linc, do you feel this too?

'I hope you'll be there.' The words came unthinkingly, and the warmth that had started at the back of her neck now rushed into her cheeks.

Had she not learned the last time?

She rushed on. 'What I mean is, it would look good to have the owner here. For business. But I understand you may be busy. It's not an expectation.'

Cecilia *had* asked the question with business in mind. She had!

'I'll have to consider—' He broke off as his cell phone started to ring.

Yet not before Cecilia sensed the hesitation in him. So there. That answered her unspoken question.

Of *course* he wouldn't want to involve himself in a masked ball. She had never asked him to do anything like that before. Why should she start now?

Mortification threatened, because she did *not* want him to see her request as an overture. It didn't matter what she might or might not have felt towards him since his arrival to undertake this review of the business.

Her request had been about *business*, and she needed Linc to know that.

Cecilia ignored the little voice that suggested it had been a little bit about the man himself, as well…

A moment later he'd responded briefly to the caller. He turned to Cecilia. 'I'm sorry. That was the call I've been waiting on. I need to go.'

'You're fine. Go do what you need to do.' Cecilia waved him away as though she had some claim to granting him permission or not. 'And don't worry about my invitation. I understand if you can't make it or don't want to attend. It was a marketing-related thought. That's all.'

Another thought encroached. What if he *did* attend the masked ball and arrived with some beautiful woman on his arm?

Not her business—and she wouldn't care one way or the other!

Linc gave a quick nod and strode off.

Cecilia did *not* watch his departure until he was out of sight, nor did she stand there daydreaming, incapable of remembering what she should do next even though she'd just given herself a stern internal talking-to.

She merely took a moment to gather herself for her next job. Yes. That was what she did.

And that job needed to be a last-minute check of the maze before the flower-show committee arrived.

Cecilia forced her attention to her work. And it was as she inspected the perfect flowerbeds that Cecilia admitted to herself that she really did hope Linc would attend the masked ball.

But only for business purposes.

'You can go ahead and sell off two of the three apartment complexes as whole lots to those investors. It's a good time to do it, and you know the profit margin I'll be looking for.'

Linc gave his agreement over his cell phone to his property broker as he strode from his car to the entrance of Cecilia's plant nursery the following morning.

'The third is to be offered as individual units under the first home-buyer arrangement we have with our partner real estate firms.'

'You know that plan is neither time efficient nor as cost-effective as the investor option.' His broker's voice held the tone of an oft-repeated lament.

Linc treated the warning to the same response he gave it every time. 'Nevertheless, you know where I stand on this.'

'There are times when you're going to give back, whether it reduces your profit margin or not. Yeah, I know. I'm proof of that myself.' The other man gave a wry laugh and yielded the point. 'You gave *me* a great chance when you employed me, and I haven't looked back since.'

'You can fill the time while you're waiting for those units to sell by property shopping for me in Queensland,' Linc offered. 'How does that sound? I've been wanting to buy into that state for a while.'

He gave his broker—suddenly a much happier

man—his instructions, ended the call and set out to find Cecilia.

'She's in the office.' Jemmie, Cecilia's second-in-command, told him as Linc strode across the courtyard.

'Thanks.'

As Linc headed for the office, he acknowledged silently that he really *wanted* to see Cecilia. He *should* want to see her again to prove to himself that this recent and inexplicable sharpening of his interest in her had disappeared as quickly as it had made its presence felt.

Odd that he should feel a lift in his spirits as he approached the door of the plant-nursery office, if that was the case.

The office door stood open. As Linc drew closer, observing Cecilia's concentration and hearing the sound of her voice as she spoke into the phone, he silently acknowledged that she looked beautiful sitting there and that seeing her gave him a warm, happy feeling.

He could live with that without ever doing a thing about it. In a short span of time he'd be out of here and back to his regular world, anyway.

Out of the way of temptation?

'Linc. Hi.' She glanced up after ending her call and offered a welcoming smile.

For a moment Cecilia looked equally happy to see him. Happy and…*interested*? Linc couldn't take his gaze from hers. And blue eyes stared back at him—before she seemed to realise how long their glances had held.

She dropped her gaze. 'I wasn't sure if you'd be here today.'

He stepped over the threshold and let his gaze linger on her face, enjoying the lovely lines, the sweep of her lashes against her cheeks.

'The business with my property guy didn't take long.' Linc gave himself full points for sounding so close to normal. 'I wound it up a few minutes ago on the phone, actually.'

He brushed aside his travelling all over Sydney to inspect his property holdings as though it had barely impinged. Right now it didn't seem to matter. All he could focus on was Cecilia.

What the heck was going on with him?

'Besides, I've got this review to do for you. It still shouldn't take too long if I get a good run at it.'

As though to mock him, his phone rang.

'I think you may have spoken too soon.' Amusement crinkled the skin at the corners of Cecilia's eyes, and her mouth turned up into a soft smile.

Linc lost himself in her in that moment. His breath caught and, still stuck on that smile, he answered his phone absent-mindedly.

He had to run the caller's first few words back through his mind again before he could focus. 'Sorry, Alex. Which export law did you say is concerning you?'

Linc forced his attention to the call.

Cecilia turned her focus to her work while Linc spoke on the phone with his brother. It felt strangely intimate to be in the same room with Linc while he did that, yet she had learned from his brief time here so far that he would step outside if he wanted privacy for a call.

Maybe she should find a reason to step out, anyway. She didn't need to add any extra feelings of intimacy to her connection with this man. She was having enough trouble ignoring her awareness of him as it was.

She started to stand.

'Okay. Tell Jayne I said hi.' Linc's voice softened noticeably as he said his goodbyes on the phone. 'I'll stop by to see you both tonight on my way home.'

The man loved his family to pieces.

Cecilia's heart softened and ached a little at one and the same time. He must be close to his family. That was so appealing. Yet it made her feel sad because she, on the other hand, was experiencing a difficult phase with her sister.

But that was going to get better. It *was*!

Linc ended the call and glanced up just as Cecilia settled back into her chair. 'How did the committee's visit go yesterday?'

'It went well.' She welcomed the distraction from her thoughts more than he could know. 'The committee members were happy with the standard of the maze and with the area that will be used at its centre for dancing. There will only be a hundred guests. Tickets to the ball are being auctioned online, with proceeds going to charity. I'm relieved the committee were satisfied with my plans and with the site itself.'

If the nursery played its cards right, it might get a yearly event out of this. She would definitely hold more balls for special occasions…weddings. The possibilities were endless. Cecilia couldn't help but feel a little excited about the doors this first event might open up.

'It sounds as though you have things well under control.' Linc murmured the words as he sat down to recommence his review.

Cecilia laughed. She didn't mean to, but the sound escaped her. 'All except the fact that Valentine's Day is about to erupt onto my work horizon, whether I feel ready for it or not—and I'm leaning somewhat towards the "not" side of that particular equation right now.'

As Linc turned his attention to his work—with numerous interruptions on his cell phone, despite his desire for a clear run at the review—Cecilia refocused and settled in to finalise stock orders for Valentine's Day.

She worked hard, but she had to admit—to herself, at least—that Linc's proximity was corroding her concentration. He was just so *there*.

And she was so busy. Every time she tried to work on her orders, the phone rang again or a supplier called through directly on her cell phone. There were cancellations of previously established orders, stockists informing her that they'd oversold to other buyers and couldn't fill *her* order, asking if other blooms could be substituted.

Cecilia's answer was always the same. No, they couldn't!

This happened every year—it was part of dealing with this particular day on the nursery's calendar—but that didn't make it any less busy or any less challenging for her to ensure she reached her necessary stock levels.

On top of that the floor staff came in more often than usual, with odd questions that simply couldn't wait. The more that time passed, the busier it became.

'Linc, I'm putting this call on speaker. I'm sorry if it disturbs your concentration.'

She tried not to let frustration colour her tone as she jabbed at the settings on her cell phone. Once she had placed it atop the filing cabinet in the corner of the room, she began to riffle through the cabinet's contents.

'It's fine. I can see you're under pressure.'

Linc's words were calm. He had fielded numerous distractions of his own since he got here today, and he seemed quite unfazed. As though he didn't find Cecilia's presence and nearness at all disturbing.

Not that Cecilia felt agitated due to *his* presence. Certainly not in any personal kind of way. She'd had that conversation with herself earlier. She simply had to get over the nerve-racking, overalert, oh-so-conscious of him feeling.

And she was over it. She 100 per cent totally *was*. Her consciousness could just catch up with that attitude right now!

'Mr Sampson, I have your previous delivery docket, your invoice and a receipt showing a nil balance in front of me.' She gave the reference number, speaking towards her phone. 'If funds are outstanding to your company, they aren't owed from here.'

After a moment the man discovered a mistake at

his end. He agreed to finalise Cecilia's order for the next day and ended the call.

With Mr Sampson sorted out, Cecilia replaced the file in the cabinet and returned to her desk.

Time passed. And when a customer phoned with a special request for a particular style of repurposed item, and Cecilia happened to be able to match it, she decided to take the opportunity to head to the repurposing shed to collect the piece.

She replaced the desk phone in its cradle. 'You'll be okay for a few minutes, Linc? I'll put the phone through to Jemmie, out front.'

'Leave it. I believe I may *just* be able to manage without you for a little bit without having to disturb Jemmie.'

His wry smile brought out every gorgeous manly feature. It also undid every bit of Linc-ignoring effort Cecilia had put in today.

Before she could stop herself, she smiled back. A big, wide, pleased-with-the-world smile that brushed across her face and made Linc grow still before an enigmatic veil came down over his eyes.

Her breath hitched, and just like that it was all there again. The awareness. The *interest*.

She drew in a slightly shaky inhalation. 'Okay. I'll…ah… I'll leave the phone. I'd better go take care of this.'

Before she did something she regretted for the *second* time since knowing him.

Cecilia exited the office and gave herself a good talking-to while she was at it. She wasn't interested in Linc. Such an interest wasn't something she could allow to exist. Just because her boyfriend had dumped her when her issues with her sister had hit crisis point, it didn't mean she should try to pick up the next available—

Oh, get over yourself, Cecilia. And get over Hugh, too.

As if Linc would participate in that possibility, anyway. He was a millionaire, for crying out loud, *so* successful in life. *And* he'd already rejected her once before. Was she trying to line herself up for a second shot at that humiliation?

She wasn't. She just hadn't expected to feel this attraction to and interest in Linc again. It had surprised her. All she needed to do was adjust to that surprise factor and she would be fine.

In minutes she was back at the office.

'Item retrieved and left with the front staff ready for collection.' She spoke as she stepped over the threshold of the office space.

'Great.' Linc was in the process of putting down the office phone extension as he responded. 'I've taken a couple of messages. You'll know what to do with them.'

He didn't break into a big smile. She didn't, either. That earlier moment of blinding connection had passed. So why could she still not seem to be able to tear her gaze from him? And why did he gaze so intently at her? And had she not taken any notice whatsoever of her earlier warnings to herself?

Immersed in those thoughts, she was slow to realise that her cell phone had started to ring.

When she did realise it, she barely gave the caller's identity a thought. It would be some supplier again. However, she wasn't sure where her phone actually was.

Cecilia patted her pockets. Her gaze searched the desk. Then, without any warning whatsoever, the worst possible thing happened for her privacy, and perhaps the most heart-wrenching yet hope-inspiring thing for her emotions.

The phone's voicemail picked up automatically, went straight on to the speaker setting she'd left it on and a tinny prerecorded message from the caller's end began to play out into the room.

'Are you willing to accept a call from the Fordham Women's Correctional Centre? Your sister, Stacey Tomson, wishes to speak with you...'

The revealing words blared across the room as though trumpeted through a megaphone by the world's largest elephant.

'If you do not want to accept this call—'

She'd left the phone on the filing cabinet. She had received only two other calls like this, and questions filled her mind.

Why had Stacey chosen now to phone? Did it mean their rift might be ending or would they argue again?

So many emotions swirled inside Cecilia in that moment. Hurt. Frustration. Disappointment. Love.

Cecilia quickly crossed the room, grabbed up the phone and fumbled to take it off speaker.

One glance at Linc's face told her it was way too late to try and hide this, but she managed to change the setting and get the phone to her ear. She wasn't sure if he'd heard her sister's voice or not, but when she started towards the door, to leave the room, it was to realise Linc had beaten her to it.

The door clicked shut behind his receding back, and Cecilia could acknowledge both the joy and the pain of finally receiving this call when she hadn't known when or even *if* she ever would.

She said hello to her troubled, incarcerated twin.

CHAPTER THREE

'STACEY. HOW ARE YOU? I've been hoping you'd call. It's so hard not being allowed to call you. It's been such a long time. I've missed you so!'

Are you still angry that I said you needed to change your direction in life? I wanted to help you, and it needed to be said!

Cecilia didn't want the gap between them to widen even more, and yet if she hadn't challenged Stacey, who would have?

The man who'd disappeared and left Stacey to carry this punishment alone? Who'd appeared to do nothing but manipulate Cecilia's sister up to that point?

'Are you okay?'

She couldn't make herself say *Are you okay in jail?* Or even, *Are you okay in there?*

'Have you been getting the money orders for extra food and things?'

'Yes, I've been getting them.'

Cecilia thought she heard Stacey swallow hard before her sister went on.

'Thank you for doing that.'

'You're my sister.' Emotion rose in Cecilia's throat.

'Cee, I wanted to ask if you'd be willing to start visiting me again.' Stacey's words couldn't mask her emotion. 'I've missed you. I should have called sooner. I was angry, and it's tough in here. There's been a lot of adjusting to do—'

'Of course I'll visit again. I've been dying to see you.' So much relief coursed through Cecilia that she wanted to laugh and cry at once. 'We can talk about your future, when you're finally out of there.'

Surely that would be something they could both look forward to?

'We can.' Stacey sounded on the verge of tears before she spoke again. 'I don't want to not be talking to you. I guess I felt hurt at a time when I needed you to just love me. But there's been time for me to think, and to realise I've made some really big mistakes.'

'I'm really sorry, Stacey.'

Cecilia had thought she was doing the right thing in pointing out the bad pathway that Stacey had followed. For some reason she'd thought that because Stacey had been so angry at the time her sister couldn't possibly have been hurting. Tears sprang to the backs of Cecilia's eyes again. How could she have been so short-sighted?

'I should have found a better way to deal with your situation than I did.'

'You were worried about me, and with good reason.' Stacey sighed. 'I can't understand now how I was so blind. Joe seemed nice at first—a little rough around the edges, but charming with it.'

'And then the charm wore off.' Cecilia understood that. She'd been there herself with Hugh. At least in this she could try to rebuild some solidarity with her sister. 'We're not very good at finding great men, are we?'

Stacey agreed, and then sounded a little troubled and vulnerable as she went on. 'I need to tell you that if you start coming to see me it will help my chances of gaining parole, because I'll be demonstrating that I have a sound relationship with someone reliable. I want you to know that before you come in, so you don't think I asked just because of it. I've missed you and I'm longing to see you.'

'I believe you, and I want that sound relationship again.' Cecilia had longed for it over the past months. 'I'm so glad you phoned, Stacey.'

'I am, too. I'm *allowed* to have a sister.' Stacey's words were firm, almost defiantly so. '*And* to see you and have a relationship with you. I should have stuck up for that from the start.'

'Of course you are.' Cecilia frowned. 'Who's told you otherwise? Surely not the authorities there?'

'Joe did—constantly throughout my relationship with him and again quite recently before I finally woke up.'

Cecilia clamped her teeth together so she wouldn't speak without thinking first. Finally, she said carefully, 'I thought that after the armed robbery he'd gone underground. Wouldn't he be detained and taken in by the police if he visited you?'

'He found a way to get messages to me in here through another inmate who was about to be released.' Stacey admitted it in a low voice. 'At first I was happy. I thought there must be some explanation for Joe dragging me into what happened that day and then leaving me to pay for being an accomplice to something

I didn't even understand was going to happen until it was too late.'

'I'm guessing that's not what happened?' Cecilia wished she could give her sister a hug.

'No. He wanted me to tell him if I had any secret money stashed anywhere outside of here or any valuable jewellery.' Stacey made a disgusted sound. 'I sent a message back telling him never to contact me again.'

'That was horrible of him, Stacey.' Cecilia could only be glad that Stacey had cut the man off. 'I love you, sis. We've got through life up to this point, and we can keep getting through it.' Cecilia struggled not to choke up again. 'I just want to see you. When can I come?'

'Let me talk to the officers here and find out.' Relief filled Stacey's tone.

'You'll ring again?' Cecilia wanted that assurance before Stacey hung up.

'I will. As soon as I know when you can come.'

They said their goodbyes then, and Cecilia slowly placed the phone into her pocket. They'd never been cut off from each other before. At least now she could see Stacey. Relief and gratitude tugged even further at her teetering emotions.

But right now, somewhere on the other side of the door, Cecilia had to face Linc. What could he possibly think?

Stacey had been unhappy since they were teenagers, but this was the first time she had done anything actually against the law. No one knew about the jail sentence. In fact, no one here had even met Stacey. The sisters had tended to meet up after work, and then when Joe had come on the scene, Stacey had kept contact with Cecilia to a minimum. Cecilia understood why now.

The guy hadn't wanted anyone else to have influence in Stacey's life. Thank goodness her sister had finally sent the man packing.

Cecilia wanted to undo Stacey's history and get her out of there because she'd been tricked. Those wishes were unrealistic, and she knew it, but she hated it that Stacey's life had been impacted so deeply by this whole situation.

Well, for now it was time to face Linc. Cecilia didn't feel ready, but she had no choice.

She forced herself to open the office door and to speak to Linc, who lounged with pseudocasualness against a pillar partway across the courtyard.

'I've finished my call. Thanks for giving me privacy for that.'

'It was no problem.' He started towards her.

Cecilia didn't know what else he might have said. Anything, or nothing at all. But suddenly she couldn't stay there to find out. Not right now. Not until she could get her emotions under better control. If he was sympathetic she might fall apart. She couldn't let that happen.

'I need to do a few things in the repurposing shed.' She blurted the words and turned on her heel. 'I'll be back in a bit.'

She couldn't even speak to him about getting Jemmie to come out of the retail section and cover the office during her absence. Cecilia couldn't say anything more at all. But she had her back turned before Linc reached her, and she walked herself quickly far enough into the rear of the nursery that no one would see her until she could blink back the well of emotion that threatened to overcome her.

It wasn't perfect. She shouldn't walk out on a busy office. But she needed time to gather herself.

Cecilia walked on and set to work on regaining her control—because that was what she needed to do.

Linc wanted to go after Cecilia. To ensure that she was okay. Although clearly he couldn't ensure any such thing, because she wasn't. The heartbreak she must have tried so hard to shore up before she opened the door minutes ago had been etched on her face.

That had shouted more loudly than any voice could have done for her to be given privacy to regroup. Even so, it had taken all his resources not to stride across the courtyard and take her into his arms.

She had a sister.

That sister was in a correctional facility.

Linc hadn't known either of those things.

What had Cecilia's sister done to land her where she was now? How long had Cecilia been trying to cope with this reality?

'Linc, I could use your help.'

The request from Cecilia's second-in-command forced his attention back to his surroundings, to the busy plant-nursery office. He'd called in Jemmie to help out, and the phone still kept ringing. The rest of the world remained unaware of Cecilia's turmoil and wasn't about to grant any concessions.

Jemmie went on. 'Will Cecilia be gone long? I've got an enquiry about one of her orders, and the amount of money involved is too substantial for me to make the judgment call alone. Unless *you* want to decide, Linc?'

'She won't be gone much longer.' Linc would have to go and find Cecilia before he let much more time pass. 'What exactly is the problem, Jemmie? I may be able to resolve it.'

He did just that, but he had no sense of satisfaction—only a gnawing awareness of the passage of time.

Linc frowned, checked his wristwatch again and got to his feet.

As he did so Cecilia stepped into the office space.

'Thanks for helping out, Jemmie.' She spoke as though nothing were amiss. 'You can head back now.'

The office phone rang. Cecilia answered it as Jemmie left. Again, Cecilia's composure seemed rock solid.

Except she was pale, her beautiful eyes looked as though she'd been crying and she wouldn't fully meet his gaze.

Linc waited while Cecilia took the call. When it had ended, he spoke carefully. 'I didn't know you had a sister.' He hoped that by acknowledging this in some way he might help Cecilia to feel less uncomfortable. 'I'm sorry that I heard the start of your conversation. If I'd known—'

'Stacey is my twin.' She searched his gaze. 'I wouldn't have expected you to know anything. This whole situation has been...challenging.'

'I can imagine.' Linc took care to allow that search and to keep his expression as open as possible. Cecilia might feel comfortable enough to confide in him a little more—not because he harboured some morbid curiosity about her difficulties, but because he cared.

He refused to ask himself whether that kind of care should fall within the realms of an employee/employer relationship. It fell within *his* realm.

After a moment Cecilia simply said, 'We hadn't spoken for months. We went through a really bad patch. Both of us were partly to blame, but I—I can see now that I let her down, and I regret that so much. Today was the start of turning that around, at least.'

'I'm happy for you—that there's a chance for you to get things on a better footing with your sister.' His words emerged in a deep tone. Linc hadn't managed to be there for his brothers when they had needed him vitally. For Alex most of all. He'd never forgiven himself for what he'd allowed to happen. His heart squeezed for Cecilia.

He cleared his throat. 'If there's anything—'

'Thank you.' She spoke quickly and seemed to force herself to draw a slow, deep breath. 'There's nothing. And it's busy.' She turned to her computer. 'I should get on with this work.'

Linc conceded to her need to refocus her attention and did the same, but her situation and his own memories from the past remained in his thoughts.

He'd hated the orphanage so much—the discipline and the emotional darkness and the complete lack of love or hope. Alex and Brent had saved him—had given him their brotherhood and let him love them and be loved in return.

Except at one vital point in time when Linc had failed in that charter.

And for that he could not forgive himself.

Linc forced his attention back to his review.

He still wanted to take Cecilia in his arms, but today's revelations had only drawn more attention to the reasons why he must let go of just such thoughts.

He wasn't worthy of her.

He never could be.

CHAPTER FOUR

'LINC. I WASN'T sure if I'd see you today.'

It was the following morning—Valentine's Day—and Cecilia had arrived at the nursery well ahead of schedule. She had wanted to be certain everything was in order for this most lucrative day on the nursery's calendar.

She had wanted time to compose herself before facing Linc again, if he did come in today, but would that composure even be possible? Yesterday's phone call with her sister had brought joy. That was undeniable. But it had also left Cecilia feeling exposed.

Yet when she searched Linc's gaze now, she saw only acceptance and, as their gazes held, awareness.

Cecilia stood on the outside of her office space, and Linc stood on the inside. She tried to pull herself back to the conversation. 'Did you—did you resolve your business challenge so soon?'

Linc had received a call from his brother late yesterday afternoon and had excused himself to go and take care of whatever matter had arisen.

'The problem was a joint investment I have with Alex.' The words were gruff. 'I'm sorry I left so abruptly yesterday. I had to deal with it quickly otherwise Alex could have lost a sizeable chunk of his portfolio. It is sorted out now.'

'I'm glad everything turned out okay.' She was, but her emotions were still a jumble. 'I had better print yesterday's orders, ready to start checking stock.'

Cecilia grasped the edge of the door and prepared to push it wider so she could enter.

'Actually, I hoped we could talk.' As he spoke those words he, too, reached for the door.

For long, still moments Cecilia felt the touch of warm, strong fingers over hers. *Linc's* fingers.

Aside from a handshake, when she'd first met Linc for her initial job interview, they'd never touched. But now they were, and that one simple touch undermined the slim control she'd had over her seesawing emotions—and over her attraction to Linc.

She wanted to know him better…to explore that interest. Now—today—she felt this. She hadn't shaken off that old interest in him at all. It had lain in waiting, ready to ambush her for a second time. It was a shock to admit that to herself, and as she searched his eyes, she wondered if those thoughts were reflected in hers.

'Cecilia…' Grey eyes searched her face, and his head dipped closer.

Her lips parted and her breath sighed out in a soft exhalation. She leaned towards him, just a little…

In the next moment, shocked at her own lack of control, she pulled back. How *could* she have ended up standing there with her emotions churning, so in need of his kiss?

Would he truly have kissed her? Had that been his intention?

A peek at his face revealed a mixture of surprise and…guilt?

Then his dark brows drew down, and she couldn't see into his eyes any more.

'Today—today will be manic.' She felt rather frenzied herself. Worked up. Freaked out.

You simply touched hands with him. Pull it together, Cecilia!

And he'd wanted to talk. About her sister phoning? About Stacey being in a women's prison?

Cecilia did *not* want to talk about that.

And now they'd almost kissed, and she needed to think about that—to figure out how she felt about that and why, if she'd interpreted it correctly, he should feel guilt over that.

'Delivery trucks will be arriving, and it won't stop after that.'

No sooner had she uttered the words than a truck could be heard, backing up to the loading bay.

The driver leaned on the horn.

The office phone began to jangle.

Linc frowned.

Cecilia raised her hands, palms up, towards him. 'It's Valentine's Day. The customers deserve their happiness. I can't deliver on that if I have to—'

'You're right. Now isn't the time.'

Linc conceded to Cecilia's declaration. He shouldn't have tried to bring up yesterday's shock revelation now, anyway.

But that moment in the doorway, when their hands had touched. He'd wanted to kiss her. He almost *had* kissed her.

Linc operated with a lot more self-control than that in life. He didn't get affected by *hand touching*.

So what was going on with him?

'I'll help out today, if it's going to be frantic. The review work can wait.'

'Th-thank you. I hope that won't be necessary, but I appreciate the offer.'

Her relief was heartfelt. Not because he'd offered to help out, Linc imagined, for he knew she could manage just fine without him and had done so for years. Her relief was patently because he'd backed off on his desire for an in-depth conversation. Who could blame her? If the roles were reversed, would *he* want to talk about it?

Or was her relief because that awkward moment in the doorway had ended?

He waved his hand in the direction of the truck. 'You get that. I'll take care of the phone.'

Apparently, the moment had been saved by the ring of the telephone and a truck full of red roses. For now, at least.

'So how's my brother enjoying this business review?' Brent MacKay asked the question cheerfully while well-ordered chaos reigned all around. 'I have to admit I was surprised when you told me you're thinking of giving Cecilia a share in the business. You've only ever taken on business partnerships with family up to this point.'

'It wouldn't be a gift. She's more than earned it in hard work over the past six years.'

It was later that day. The brothers stood in the busy nursery courtyard.

Linc watched Cecilia stride across the other side of it with a customer at her side and several more trailing at her heels like lovelorn ducklings.

'The review is progressing nicely.'

Except perhaps for today, when all he'd done was watch Cecilia rush to and fro while he'd fielded phone calls and observed the madness and the mayhem.

He'd taken care of some customers as well, to help share the load.

'And Cecilia's different. I'd be comfortable having a shared holding with her.'

Brent's eyebrows lifted. 'Oh, yes? Any reason in particular for that?'

Conversely, Linc's brows lowered. 'Because she's a trustworthy manager, and owning a share of the business would only make her more so.'

Linc started towards the nursery exit, where Brent had his utility truck parked out front.

'You *could* sound happier about that.' A corner of Brent's mouth turned up. He'd drawn level with Linc as they passed through the nursery exit. 'Anyway, I thought you'd be happy to see all this profit occurring right before your eyes—today at least?'

'I am.'

Of course Linc was. Any business owner would be pleased to see money coming in. Unless that owner didn't care just at the moment, because all he wanted to do was take the manager of the business aside and slow her down long enough to—

To do what? Talk to her about yesterday's startling revelation of her sister's situation, when he'd already had to concede that it wasn't the time to have that conversation?

Cecilia had made it pretty clear she didn't want any such discussion at *all* and that no time would be the right time for her.

Is that what you feel miffed about, MacKay? Or is it because she recoiled from that moment your hands touched at the door as though her fingernails were on fire?

It wasn't, either.

Fine—it was both.

Blast it. He didn't know!

'Is there anything else you need while you're here, Brent?' He slung the final bird's-nest fern into the back of his brother's utility truck and turned.

'Another one of those that *hasn't* just had half its foliage knocked off would be a start. I'm quite particular about the standard of plants that go into my landscape garden designs.' Brent said the words in a dry tone.

'Ah, sorry.' Linc glanced at the thing. 'I can replace that.'

'Don't worry. I've got enough to do without it if I have to.' Brent clapped him on the back.

'Did you know Cecilia has a twin sister? Or a sister at all, for that matter?' The words passed through Linc's lips before he could stop them.

Brent was halfway into the driver's seat of his truck. He settled fully and turned a quizzical gaze Linc's way. 'No. Why?'

'I didn't, either.'

How could he have known Cecilia for so long and not know the first thing about her personal life? He'd let her into *his* life. She knew his brothers. She'd been to their warehouse home a couple of times on business matters back when they had all lived there. She'd met Brent's and Alex's wives here at the plant nursery when they'd come shopping for things.

That was a lot of 'letting in' for a man who held his personal matters as close to his chest as Linc did.

He ignored the knowledge of all the things he *hadn't* let Cecilia in about—such as his entire personal life aside from her interactions with his family, most of which had been instigated by those family members rather than Linc himself, if he were honest about it.

Not the point. He hadn't deliberately shut Cecilia out of any of it.

She wasn't trying to shut you out, either, MacKay.

Linc didn't wait for Brent to respond. What could his brother say other than to ask him if he was feeling okay or had received a blow to the back of the head or something? Linc didn't know what to make of his own thoughts, anyway.

He saw Brent off and went back to helping out around the nursery. Sooner or later this romantic day would end. Maybe then he'd finally be able to focus on getting the review done, and then getting out of here and on with his life again.

The thought should have cheered him, but instead it made him feel unsettled and restless.

At the end of the day Linc found Cecilia in one of the auxiliary sheds, sweeping up rose petals. Although the room was empty now, except for those remnants, the scent of roses still filled the air.

'I thought I might find you here. The rest of the staff have gone home.' He'd come to find her and encourage her to leave. 'You should stop. You've pushed yourself hard today.'

His gaze tracked over her, registering the exhaustion stiffening her shoulders, the faint bruises beneath her eyes. A single deep red petal had caught in her hair.

'I wanted to get everything tidied up before I left.' The broom stilled in her hands as she looked up at him. Her face softened, and a weary pleasure lifted the corners of her mouth. 'We sent a lot of people home happy today, at least.'

In this moment she seemed to have found a true and deep contentment that came purely from wearing herself to the bone in order to *give*. Linc couldn't have admired her more.

'*You* did.' He took the remaining steps to her side and gently retrieved the broom from her hold. He placed it against a pillar.

'You contributed, Linc.' Her words were unguarded. 'I saw you helping out that little old lady who wanted roses for all her children and grandchildren.'

He *had* done that and, in amongst the antsy feelings he hadn't understood, Linc had found pleasure in giving that assistance.

But so much more had he admired Cecilia's generosity in doing the same, regardless of her personal circumstances. And now, in her presence, some of his restlessness today distilled into what it had really been. The need for her company, her attention, to focus on her and be with her. He couldn't explain the feelings. He already knew he had to stay away from her. And yet here he was.

Maybe if he tested this interest in her he would

prove to himself that the feelings were no different from those he'd felt towards any other woman who'd passed through his life. Then he could move on.

It was either sound reasoning or the flimsiest excuse of all time. Linc didn't try to discern which.

'There's just one petal remaining.' He reached up, drew the soft velvety petal from Cecilia's golden hair and placed it into her palm.

'Oh.' Her fingers closed over the petal. Her gaze lifted and searched his.

That was all. Just a touch and a glance and he was lost.

'I've wanted—' He searched *her* face, her eyes, and when he found curiosity, consciousness, he kissed her.

The moment their lips met, hers softened.

Oh, so sweetly.

Linc drew their joined hands to his chest and held them there. He wanted to keep kissing her and never stop. He wanted this one moment to last forever so he didn't have to think about it, or about what it meant, why it felt different from any kiss that had gone before it. Why his arms seemed to need so very much to envelop her. Instead, his fingers tightened around hers.

Cecilia had waited for Linc's kiss. She didn't want to admit that to herself, but it was true. She had wanted and needed to know how this would make her feel, and now she was experiencing it.

Against their joined hands she could feel the warmth of Linc's chest through his shirt, the hard wall of muscle. Yet his lips were soft as they caressed hers. She felt cherished and as if she was the absolute focus of his attention in this moment. She felt...*dif-*

ferent inside. As though this was changing her even as it happened.

Oh, she didn't want this kiss to end.

Cecilia curved her other hand against the column of his neck and acknowledged that this was not like it had been with Hugh. This was not like anything or anyone before.

Uncertainty rose then—because how could this touch her emotions so immediately? With this man who dated but didn't seem to look for the same kind of relationship as Cecilia did? The long-term, permanent kind?

'Cecilia…' Linc murmured her name against the side of her face as his lips left hers. He enveloped her in a hug.

She felt again the magnitude of the barriers within herself, wanting so very much to let them topple and fall, to open her heart to at least the hope of him.

Oh, Cecilia. That would be such foolishness. A kiss is a kiss is a kiss. With a man like Linc, how can you believe it means anything beyond the moment?

Hugs weren't kisses, though, and she hugged back and then quickly freed herself, searched his face. Because if there was even a hint of pity for her circumstances…

But all she could read in Linc's expression was bemusement, before he blinked and blinked again.

What had happened to her emotions just now?

They'd kissed, and that had been wonderful and amazing for her, but she needed to find some reality here. Linc's bemused expression might be for a hundred reasons. Hopefully, not because he knew she'd reacted as though her whole world had tilted on its axis when they kissed!

Pride surfaced as she confronted that absolutely untenable possibility. It was Valentine's Day. He'd kissed her. It could easily have been nothing more than a spontaneous act of the moment. Indeed, he could be regretting it even now, because of their business relationship. Remember? What would happen to that now?

It would be reinstated immediately—that was what! And for the sake of her pride Cecilia wanted to be the one to initiate that.

'I—I believe I'll do as you've suggested and head home. There'll be work again, bright and early in the morning, and it's been a long and busy day.'

Maybe Linc would put their kiss—or at least any vulnerability he might have detected in her as a result of it—down to the physical drain of the day.

She didn't wait to find out. Instead, Cecilia turned quickly and left him there to lock up, to secure everything.

'Goodnight.'

For the second time Cecilia abandoned her duty because her heart was in the way.

Not her heart! Her emotions. There was a difference—a really big difference. She had been overwhelmed by the power of the day and her exhaustion and missing her sister.

Oh, yes? And somehow that had made her trip and fall onto Linc's lips and kiss him and feel things she had never felt before? Even now she wanted to turn around, to go back, to extend her time in his company. Because...

Because of hope that shouldn't exist and that needed to be extinguished *now*—before it was allowed to grow any further. How could she feel this way? Be so drawn to him and in some part of herself so willing to leap in and believe he had some kind of emotional investment in her when no evidence whatsoever existed to prove that?

Linc wasn't offering her anything! One stolen kiss that might have happened without forethought or reason did not add up to...*anything*.

He was probably thinking already that it shouldn't have happened. And Cecilia would think exactly the same—just as soon as she could get her emotions unjumbled and back into some kind of reasoning, sensible order.

Maybe she and her sister were doomed to pick out the wrong men in their lives. Well, at least in Cecilia's case Linc would walk away from this moment, and it would fade to oblivion and be forgotten.

The same way Cecilia had 'forgotten' a six-year-old crush?

Fine. *He* would bury it and forget it. She might take a little longer to get to that point, but in the end she would.

She would!

CHAPTER FIVE

'YOU'RE LOOKING AT a classic nineteen-forties pram, luv.' The man selling the item turned the frame this way and that so Cecilia could get a better view of it. 'A bit of paint and you've got yourself—'

'A refurbished carcass missing all its interior parts?' Cecilia softened her words with a smile. 'I *do* concede that the frame is still in decent order. There's not too much rust.'

She named her final offer.

'It's that or no sale, I'm afraid. I have my buying limits, just as you have your selling ones.'

Cecilia was at a used-items fair in an outer suburb of Sydney. Hundreds of sellers had taken stalls both inside the pavilion and outdoors on the grassed area, and there were plenty of browsers and buyers there to enjoy the day.

She was doing her best to focus on her surroundings, but she was struggling. All she could think about was those moments with Linc at the nursery. What was *he* thinking? Had he thought about it at all? Or forgotten it the moment it happened?

Why had it happened, in any case? Had it been a moment of forgetfulness on his part? Had he seen the rose petal in her hair and that had led to an automatic response that might have happened anywhere, with any person? Maybe he'd intended a quick brush of lips or something and she'd prolonged that?

No. They'd both been equally involved. Hadn't they…?

This was what happened when a girl spent too much time revisiting a few special moments. She lost any shred of objectivity she might have had.

'All right, then.' The seller gave a brief nod. A twinkle of approval for her bargaining prowess flitted through his eyes. 'You can have it for that.'

'Thank you.' Cecilia finalised the transaction and told herself to draw a line under her thoughts about that kiss with Linc at the same time.

She had just handed over the money and turned to begin the task of taking the pram frame away when a deep voice spoke.

'I thought I saw a familiar face. Grabbing more items for refurbishment?'

It was Linc. A rush of warmth flooded into her cheeks. Oh, she hoped he wouldn't be able to see that in the dim lighting!

'Linc! I was just think—'

She had just been remembering a kiss that had left her confused and fighting herself, and now Linc was right here. She needed to step past that memory and not embarrass herself or let him see in any way how much those moments had affected her.

'How—how are you? What are you doing here?'

He'd seemed to materialise beside her as though from thin air. In fact, the air *did* seem thin around Cecilia in that moment. She could barely breathe.

Linc, in casual Saturday gear, was—well, he was *Linc*. The man she had kissed with such shattering impact on her equilibrium. And then she'd left him and told herself to forget all about it. But she hadn't managed very well. She hadn't managed at all.

Had it affected Linc in that way or not at all? And what was he doing here right now? *Oh, my*. What if he wanted to talk about it? To make sure she understood it had been a momentary slip in good judgment on his part or something?

Yet there'd been that bemusement in him, so maybe he had been affected by it, too?

And he couldn't have known he'd find her here today.

'I plan to fill the pram with snapdragons and baby's breath and mint.' She prattled the words with a breathless edge.

Get a grip, Cecilia!

She forced herself to slow down and to ask as casually as possible, 'What's brought you to the fair?'

Unfortunately, as she asked the question she allowed herself to *really* look at him. He looked amazing, in a polo shirt that emphasised the breadth of his shoulders and faded jeans.

He'd kissed her, and she'd seen stars and flowers and all manner of romantic things.

Well, wasn't she better off admitting that to herself? At least then she could start fighting the foolish feelings.

'My sisters-in-law plan regular outings for the family.'

His gaze roved her face as he spoke. And in that

moment of examination Cecilia was certain that the memory of their kiss was in his eyes.

'Do—do they?'

'Yes.' He took a half step closer to her. 'They wanted to visit the fair because it has a number of vintage train sets and other vintage toys listed, and Fiona and Jayne know that Brent is mad about those. They…ah…they already have a restorer lined up to work on anything we find today.'

Oh, Linc. What's happening here? Do you feel this?

Cecilia realised in that moment that the hurt of Hugh was over. It had given way to more immediate things.

The thought brought panic with it. Was she allowing those barriers to disappear because of Linc? Surely that would do nothing more than open her up to far greater hurt?

'It's sweet that Fiona and Jayne are doing that for your brother.' And Linc was sweet too—for participating, for caring about his family.

There goes one corner of a barrier.

Fine. So maybe Cecilia *was* changed as a result of their kiss. She would just have to make sure it didn't show in any way that Linc could discern.

'Have you found anything?'

Enlightenment? A desire for us to be together or to find out more about these shared feelings that are so amazing to me?

And that probably didn't even exist for him!

'I've got a few items.' He pointed to the bag in his hand and gave a short laugh, but his gaze still searched hers.

Oh, how she wished she could simply read his thoughts.

'The girls went off together when we arrived, and Brent and Alex and I decided to split up and buy everything any of us came across and sort it out later. I'm not sure whether I've got junk or buried treasure, but at least I haven't come up empty-handed.'

Cecilia laughed. She just couldn't help it. This was a different side of Linc—a family-activities side— and it was adorable.

He smiled, and his gaze seemed to soften as he did so. That softening reminded her of when he'd kissed her.

So now she thought he was adorable, and she couldn't forget their kiss.

Bye-bye second corner of a barrier.

Don't you dare hope, Cecilia.

It was only as she warned herself against hope that Cecilia realised just how much she had allowed it to rise, despite all her warnings to herself.

Yet Linc was here, and she was here. Why couldn't she enjoy a chance encounter without getting bogged down in all kinds of worries and concerns and thoughts about who felt what? Linc wasn't making reference to their kiss, so why should she let it stop her from enjoying seeing him in this simple, everyday sort of way?

There. You see?

This didn't have to be a problem. She had let her thoughts run away with her, but she realised that now and would be able to bring them back into line. She and Linc had shared a kiss—it was over. He didn't seem to be about to mention it. She didn't have to, ei-

ther. They could just act as though it had never happened.

The completely illogical nature of this decision-
making process she simply ignored.

'What about you?' He glanced at the pram frame.
'Are you still looking around, or did you come just
for that?'

'I've been here all morning, and I've got more
searching to do.' She gestured towards the exit. 'But
for now I need to get this pram back to my car and
do something about lunch.'

That was fairly normal, wasn't it? She drew a deep
breath and caught the scent of his aftershave…not
blunted this time from a day's wear, as it had been
when they—

'It's later than I thought.' He glanced at his watch.
'I must have got caught up in my browsing. Let me
help you.'

As though he dealt with nineteen-forties baby carriages on a daily basis, he lifted the pram frame.

'Would you like to lead the way?'

*Yes. Yes, I would. I'd like to lead you all the way
to revisiting that kiss to see if I made up my reactions
or if they happen again.*

No sooner had the recalcitrant thought passed
through her mind than Linc shifted his grip on the
pram frame. The muscles in his arms flexed.

Had it just got really warm in there?

Not helpful, Cecilia.

'My car is beside the park.'

They left the building, crossed the road and Cecilia led the way to her car, where it stood at the edge
of a public park. The vehicle was an old model, red

because she hadn't been able to help herself and most importantly a hatchback, with seats that would lie down to make more storage space. She still felt completely flustered.

Linc tucked the elderly pram into her car. As he did so, he glanced at the items she'd bought earlier in the day. 'That's a nice load of junk—I mean *refurbishing items* you've got there.'

'Thanks.' She laughed and pointed to his bag. 'That looks quite bulky, and by the sounds of it you got quite involved in your shopping if you lost track of time. It seems I'm not the only one who has been engrossed in collecting junk—I mean *vintage items* today.'

Seeing shared amusement crinkle the lines around his eyes while his lips kicked up made her smile even more. She tried not to acknowledge that it also made her breathless.

Cecilia pressed the lock to her car and turned her back on it. 'Buying used items is a lot of fun. Maybe you'll want to keep doing it now that you've started?'

'Perhaps I will.' He gestured towards the park. 'My family are gathering for a picnic lunch. Join us. You said you were due for a break, and you can lend your expert opinion on the vintage items we've found.'

The invitation was casual, and yet her heart leapt stupidly and so easily.

Cecilia warned herself to thank him and say no. 'I guess I could take a look—but only if you're sure I wouldn't be imposing.'

'You won't be. They'll love it.' He started moving into the park, clearly expecting her to keep pace with him.

Cecilia did.

Fine. So she'd accepted his invitation? That didn't have to mean anything in particular. Lunch with his family didn't have to be a big deal unless she thought of it in that way. She'd obviously overthought the kiss they had shared, but if Linc could go on acting as though it hadn't happened, then so could she.

They made their way down a beautiful tree-lined avenue, past plane trees and palm trees and boab trees and a children's playground, and strolled up the curved path that skirted a classic fountain. Two soft grey pigeons rested right at the top, their heads close together.

Cecilia's glance remained fixed on them for too long, and she almost lost her footing on an uneven segment of the path.

'Careful.' Linc tucked her hand through his arm as though it were the most natural thing to do. 'It's tranquil here, isn't it?' He turned his head and glanced into her eyes.

'Yes.' She returned his glance before she looked away again. 'There's a sense of peace.'

They walked on in silence until finally she looked ahead and there, seated on a massive picnic blanket beneath the shade of a eucalypt tree, were Linc's family members. Two men. Two women. Each familiar to her.

She'd met them all before, at various times, but never in this kind of idyllic setting. Never while arm in arm with Linc and trying so hard not to make too much of that.

Cecilia dropped her hold of Linc's arm. 'Maybe I shouldn't—'

She thought he murmured, 'Maybe I shouldn't, either...' before he cleared his throat and said, 'I think it might be too late. They've seen you.' He gave his family a wave that on the surface at least appeared casual.

Cecilia forced her attention to the group. She glanced at the scattered bags the family had accumulated, particularly the pile beside Linc's sisters-in-law. 'It will be fun to look at the vintage items.'

'I thought you'd like doing that.' He gave a nod of his head. 'And I can guarantee the food will be amazing and there'll be plenty of it. Our family's housekeeper, Rosa, is an excellent cook.'

His family called greetings and, in the middle of it all, Cecilia found herself swept up into the heart of this gathering where she might have felt like an intruder and yet they made her so welcome that she simply couldn't.

Cecilia wanted to stay on her guard, but instead she relaxed as the family made her welcome. It *was* wonderful to be here, and if Linc's presence at her side contributed to that more than it should—well, she would simply have to worry about that later. She had no answers right now, anyway!

'Isn't it nice to enjoy the sounds of nature and this feeling of open space?' Brent's wife, Fiona, asked the question of the group. She glanced around. 'What a *great* way to relax.'

They all did exactly that. Cecilia examined the vintage train sets and toys they'd found and felt all of them had potential. 'I'm sure that some attention from a restorer would bring them right back to life.'

'That's what I thought.' Fiona returned a set of carriages to their faded box.

Conversation flowed across a range of topics after that and ended up rather randomly in a discussion about pet adoption before Cecilia began to notice the passage of time.

Linc had repeatedly drawn her into the conversation, as though he truly valued her thoughts and opinions. Somehow that made her feel safe.

Great.

That was all she needed—to start feeling *safe* around him. Self-delusion alert! She found the man attractive and interesting, but he was the owner of the business she managed—a millionaire, totally out of her reach. Did she even need to go on? What was safe about any of that?

Yes, but he'd also kissed her.

I don't believe he's not interested, said one side of her thoughts.

She pushed that side down, with the other side called *common sense,* and said in a bright tone as she forced her gaze around the group to encompass everyone there, 'This picnic food is delicious.'

'It is, isn't it?' Alex's wife, Jayne, encouraged Cecilia to take another lettuce cup, deliciously filled with seafood and a spicy dressing.

'It's nice to see you outside of a working environment, Cecilia,' Fiona said. 'We're so glad you could join us.'

'I was certainly surprised to see Linc when we bumped into each other at the fair.' Cecilia glanced at the man in question, where he half reclined in a very unmillionaire-like sprawl beside her.

How could one person look so alluring just by existing?

As she was about to turn her glance away again, Linc's mouth lifted at the corners. Just that and Cecilia's heart lifted right along with the turn of his lips.

She might have made her excuses and left then, but instead she became embroiled in a conversation about her refurbishing. Initially, it was with the whole group, but one by one they dropped out of the conversation to talk among themselves until it was only Linc and Cecilia left discussing the topic and she lost herself completely in it.

'If you outsourced the refurbishment work, that aspect of the nursery might increase its financial viability.' Linc made the statement laconically.

'At the moment it wouldn't,' Cecilia hedged, not really wanting to explain just why that would be the case.

'You're doing some of the work at home, aren't you?' Linc shook his head. 'I might have guessed you wouldn't stop at simply buying items on your own unpaid time.'

'It's a manager's privilege to donate time to the business.' She jumped in quickly to justify this. 'Besides, it's soothing work. I benefit from it as much as I give to it.'

'As much as I want to, I can't really argue with that.' His expression sobered as he went on. 'But I *can* encourage you not to let the work be a burden to you.'

'I enjoy it too much for that to happen.' Cecilia pursed her lips. 'You could be right about the outsourcing, though. Even if one of the lower paid staff took care of some of the basic work.'

'I was only teasing you.' Linc's gaze followed the movement of her lips. 'It's profitable enough as it stands now, and I'm sure part of the charm for customers is your ability to sell the items on as the person who breathed life back into them in the first place.'

'That does help.'

She realised then how close they were to each other, that at some point each of them had leaned towards the other, and her heartbeat skipped. Her breath caught in her throat. She had the sense that maybe he wasn't as impervious as he was making out, and it made her want to test that theory.

But they were here with all his family. This was not the time for her to indulge in a state of superawareness of Linc yet again.

She glanced guiltily around them, to discover that she and Linc were now alone!

'Did we cause them all to leave with our—?'

'Our long-winded work-related discussion?' A spark of devilment danced in his eyes, and this time he *didn't* bank it down or try to stop her from seeing his thoughts. 'Trust me, they're all just as bad—and, no, we didn't drive them off.'

Cecilia fell into those eyes then and there. She simply softened to Linc and that was that.

Something had got into her that she couldn't seem to control. It felt rather too much like anticipation, happiness or maybe even hope.

'I find our discussions very enjoyable.' His words seemed to emerge in a very deep tone.

Before Cecilia could fully register the pleasure in his voice, he went on. 'My family have wandered off to try to find an ice cream parlour somewhere, and then head for their homes. There was some sign language about all that just before they went, but you had your back turned at the time.'

'Going on about my refurbishing without noticing anything around me.'

She still felt a little mortified, but more than that she felt their shared consciousness of each other. She had to be sensing *that* correctly, surely?

'I should get back to the fair, too.' She forced herself to put more distance between them on the blanket and began to gather together the remnants of the family meal. 'Please thank the others for including me when you see them again.'

A part of her wished she hadn't made that belated decision towards self-preservation, but she had courted enough danger around Linc for one day. She didn't know how he felt, and until she could understand her own emotions better, she should keep her distance. The exact opposite of what she'd done today up until now.

Linc watched Cecilia gather plates and napkins and replace them tidily into the wicker picnic basket. With each movement she seemed to gather her barriers more closely about her.

Conversely, Linc's seemed to be slipping further away from him. Even as he watched her, he noted that she had beautiful hands, with slender fingers that were stronger than they looked—somewhat like Cecilia herself.

He'd gained great pleasure in drawing her out today. Knowing that she'd relaxed enough to forget her surroundings pleased him, too.

In all of it he'd told himself he *wasn't* thinking about their shared kiss, that his thoughts *hadn't* turned again and again to those moments and the emotions they had made him feel. Tenderness for her, and interest, a strong desire to know more of her—who she was and what made her tick and everything about her.

Those reactions didn't fall under the category of passing interest. He shouldn't have allowed any interest at all.

In truth, he shouldn't have invited her to this lunch. He'd told himself it would be a way to get them back on to a comfortable footing with each other, to leave that Valentine's Day kiss behind them, but that had been quite delusional—for him, at least.

He wanted even more to kiss her again.

Great going, MacKay.

And then, as though he had no control whatsoever over his own behaviour, he opened his mouth and added to the temptation.

'I'd hoped you might let me tag along this afternoon while you look over the rest of the stalls. There may be more train sets that I can pick up.'

Linc loved his brother. He totally did. And he'd cheerfully continue to buy Brent train sets if Brent continued to enjoy collecting them.

But why would Linc stay all day here, browsing for them, when the rest of the family had already left?

'You'd be more than welcome to join me.' Cecilia said it and bit her lip, but her eyes were luminous.

Immediately, Linc felt ridiculously pleased by that fact.

Fine. So he'd extended the time they would spend in each other's company today. So what?

He did what any good man would do in such circumstances, when he couldn't figure out which way was up or down in his life since a kiss had completely altered his perspective.

He pretended not to notice any of it.

The afternoon proved wonderful for Cecilia. She and Linc wandered the remaining stalls. Linc very quickly worked out the kinds of items that attracted her eye and pointed out several things to her that she would have otherwise missed. In turn she found two more vintage train sets that he purchased for his brother.

They laughed and made silly comments, and Cecilia remained constantly aware of him. Each time they bumped shoulders or had their heads close together over some item, her breath would catch.

Yet still she told herself that this was okay, that things were under control. That her attraction to him and interest in him *weren't* running full steam ahead.

Right or wrong, Cecilia felt happy for the first time in a long, long while, and she let herself relax fully into the feeling.

Maybe that was why at the end of the day, as they stowed the final item into her car and Linc turned to her, she remembered her sister in a sudden guilty rush and words poured out before she could stop them.

'I've had such fun today I forgot about Stacey completely.' Her words were low, almost inaudible and filled with guilt.

How *could* she have forgotten her sister so thoroughly? Especially now, when she should be waiting every moment for the call that would let her know when she could go to visit her?

Linc heard Cecilia's confession and she didn't need to say anything else, because those few words showed it all. The deep love, and the guilt that she had lived her own life for a few hours while her sister was shut away, only half living hers.

But there was a difference between a woman forgetting her sister for a few brief hours, when she couldn't do anything further to help her than she already was, and a man who'd completely neglected his brother's welfare for weeks at a stretch when he'd been charged with looking out for that brother.

While Linc acknowledged that he couldn't change his own past, he could offer comfort to Cecilia now. He opened his arms and pulled Cecilia inside them. 'It's okay. You haven't done anything wrong.'

His lips were in her hair, and for a brief moment her arms stole about his middle before she drew back. 'Thank you.'

Again, he watched her put herself back together, shore herself up and square her shoulders.

A feeling of pride in her welled. It may not be his place to feel it, but he did.

'Linc…'

In her beautiful eyes, and on her face, her appreciation for these moments showed. She seemed to be struggling to find words.

Linc struggled, too—against wanting to draw her close again. He knew he had to fight this awareness of her, that he should have fought it and won before they'd shared that Valentine's Day kiss.

Today he hadn't even controlled his urge to gain as much time with her as possible once their paths had crossed. In no reality could he justify that, when he knew there could be no future in pursuing that interest.

Linc needed to get his own boundaries back in place. That meant sticking to their working relationship. He shouldn't ever have allowed himself to waver from it.

'If there's anything I can do in terms of workload or freeing up your time to help with the situation with your sister, please tell me.'

Cecilia heard Linc's words and tried not to let them hurt her feelings. They came from the perspective of a business owner to one of his managers. She and Linc *were* those things, but even so…

She forced her chin up.

'Thank you. If there is anything I need in that respect I will let you know.' She gestured to her car. 'I must be going. It's been a nice day. I'll see you at work tomorrow.'

She couldn't be any more businesslike than that.

Cecilia congratulated herself all the way home. And if she also felt miserable and confused and unhappy in the middle of that congratulating, she buried those feelings in a flurry of repurposing work from the moment she stepped inside her front door.

It was good that she'd spent the day with Linc, because now she really did know that somehow she had to stop her thoughts and, yes, some of her feelings from running away with her any further when it came to her millionaire boss.

CHAPTER SIX

'HELLO, CECILIA? I'm just calling to seek your response to our invitation to attend the opening gala this evening.'

The words came from the president of the Silver Bells flower show organising committee.

'We don't seem to have heard anything back from you.'

The woman had called Cecilia at the plant-nursery office, and now Cecilia frowned with complete mystification as she registered the request. 'I'm sorry. I haven't received any invitation for the gala opening. I assumed it was for VIPs and organisers only when nothing came through.'

Cecilia *had* wondered but had put the thought from her mind as time had passed and the gala night had drawn nearer and still no invitation had been received.

'Oh, dear. I suspected that might be the case.' The woman's disappointment rang in her words. 'The invitation was to you and the business's owner. I'm afraid we outsourced the sending of our official invitations and a number of them appear to have been overlooked. That's a process that will definitely be changed for

next year, but in the meantime we really *did* want to
see you and Linc MacKay there tonight.'

'At such short notice I'm not sure—'

'It's *so* important to us, my dear.' The president
sounded determined.

Well, the committee hadn't got such an amazing
event into its inaugural year by hanging back, Cecilia supposed.

Cunningly, the woman went on. 'The masked ball
will be one of our premiere events this year, and as its
hosts we'd like to honour you. Surely there's a chance
you could both make it?'

'I'll be delighted to be there.'

Cecilia would. This was an opportunity for her to
promote the nursery and perhaps to gain some useful insights into the hopes the committee held for the
rest of the month-long event.

Would Linc want to attend, though?

Cecilia's glance lifted and sought him out, where
he sat at the other desk. As she glanced his way, Linc
straightened from his computer, stretched his arms
over his head and gave his shoulders a good roll. His
head was turned, his gaze focused out of the window,
so he wouldn't be aware of her eyes on him.

She was taking in the strong lines of his upper
torso before she realised what she was doing.

'I…um…let me check and I'll get back to you.
What exactly are the details?'

She scribbled down the return phone number, the
start time, all the other information she needed, ended
the call and turned to Linc, who was now working at
his computer again.

'Linc?'

He looked up. 'Mmm?'

'An invitation that should have gone out asking both of us to attend the opening gala for the Silver Bells flower show was somehow overlooked. That was the president of the organising committee on the phone just now.'

A ridiculous flutter started up in her tummy as she went on.

'They are hoping we can both be there. There's just one problem. It's tonight.'

Cecilia refused to dwell on the prospect of spending an evening in Linc's company, if indeed he decided to attend. This was work related. He would either go or not go, depending on his level of interest and his schedule, and Cecilia wouldn't care one way or another. She had her feelings about Linc completely under control now.

Maybe he had a date with some beautiful woman tonight, anyway.

Worse, maybe he would bring one as his date to the gala!

Cecilia shouldn't care but, oh, she did. She cared about that possibility far too much. Suddenly, she wasn't at all certain that she *did* want Linc there.

'It's short notice. I understand if you have other plans.'

'There's nothing on my schedule that can't be changed.' His gaze showed only businesslike interest. 'If it will be helpful to your cause then I'm happy to make an appearance with you.'

With her.

Okay, so that was good.

In a purely business way.

Right.

So it was agreed that they would attend the event together. As colleagues.

Which was how it came about that just hours later Cecilia stood waiting inside her modest cottage home for Linc to arrive and collect her.

She didn't feel businesslike at all, no matter how much she tried to talk herself into feeling that way.

She wore a rose-pink evening gown with a soft cowl neck and fitted bodice. The gown fell from a high waist in gentle folds. Pearl drop earrings and her hair piled high on her head completed the look, and she had classic white high heels on her feet. Maybe the evening clothes were the problem...causing the flutter of excitement in her tummy right now.

Cecilia glanced again in her hall mirror and couldn't help but note that the person looking back was a far cry from the one who went off to work in casual clothes and sturdy boots most days.

What would Linc make of the transformation?

Not that she cared one way or another.

Indeed, she'd spent hours fussing over her make-up and hair just to please herself.

Outside, a car door closed. Inside her small home, Cecilia held her breath.

Moments later footsteps sounded on the short pathway to her front door.

Breathe, Cecilia.

Somehow the hopes and expectations for this evening's outing had got into her blood before the evening itself had even begun. The lift of anticipation only increased as the doorbell chimed.

She collected her purse, made the short journey to the door and pulled it open.

'Hi, Linc. Thanks for stopping by to collect me.'

She got the words out before she looked at him properly. It was just as well, because when she did, she couldn't drag her gaze away again.

He had on a sleek evening suit in a dark pinstripe grey, a crisp white shirt and a thin powder blue tie. Polished black dress shoes completed the outfit, and as he moved his arm slightly, she caught a glimpse of a gold cufflink.

Oh.

My.

Gosh.

Could *any* man look more handsome than Linc did tonight?

'Good evening, Cecilia.'

Linc spoke the words in slow response to Cecilia's greeting.

His first glimpse of her in a gown of deep pink shimmery fabric had stopped him in his tracks. All he could seem to see was bare sun-kissed shoulders, hair piled high on her head, showing off the lovely lines of her neck, and her beautiful face: eyes made up subtly to draw out their perfect blue depths, lips accented in a soft shimmery pink to match her dress.

'You look…' *Stunning. Gorgeous. Kissable.* 'Lovely.'

Even in saying that he felt like a master of understatement. What she looked was indescribably beautiful.

His intention to behave in a highly businesslike manner this evening seemed to have flown away as he stood there, his gaze caught in the bright blue depths of her eyes.

Linc tried to call that business mood back, but how could he as Cecilia's eyelashes swept down and she thanked him for the compliment?

When she glanced back up again, her gaze moved quickly over him and returned to meet his. A hint of pink tinged her cheeks.

'You look nice, too.'

The words were simple; the appreciation veiled at the backs of her eyes was complication bathed in blue.

'Shall we?'

He held out his hand for her to grasp before he managed a sensible thought. Led her to the car before he registered anything more than the subtle scent of her perfume—not floral this time, but something more complex and very alluring.

Only when he'd closed the door after helping her into the car did Linc take a moment to draw a breath and wonder what had just happened there.

This was not the first time he'd called for a beautiful woman to take her out somewhere. There *had* been women in his life. A number of them up until about a year ago, when it had all started to feel pointless and his dates had become further and further apart.

But seeing Cecilia tonight had literally taken his breath away. How could he deny his attraction?

Yet how could he do anything else?

In this moment he had no answers to any of it.

Linc strode to the driver's side of the car, opened the door and got in.

As Linc started the car, Cecilia stole another glance at him. Tonight he looked every bit the powerful and wealthy man about town. She might have always known it, but seeing him this way really brought it home to her that Linc was indeed a man who'd left his mark on life and would continue to do so.

She felt a little Cinderella-ish at the thought.

This is no fairytale, Cecilia.

In an effort to distract herself, she spoke. 'Did I tell you that tonight will start with a tour of the Gantry-Bell estate gardens?'

At least she'd said something, and furthermore something that didn't relate at all to how attractive she found Linc.

'Apparently, this will be the first time ever that the estate has been opened to the public. Given the name of the charity, and the fact that for a whole month people will be allowed to visit and tour the gardens, the committee must have cut a deal with the owners.'

They entered into a discussion about the flower show. Before she knew it, they'd arrived at the venue. Acres of beautiful gardens surrounded them on all sides, and in the midst of those gardens stood a mansion Cecilia would have expected to see in a fairytale.

'Oh, it's beautiful! Look at the ivy growing all the way up that south wall. There are turrets, too—just like on a castle,' she murmured, and then felt more than a little foolish for showing her awe so obviously.

'And a tower.' Linc stopped the car and handed the keys to a waiting valet, but he opened Cecilia's door himself and extended his hand to help her out. 'Isn't there a fairy story about a woman being trapped in a tower?'

'There's more than one story like that among the classic fairytales.'

In that moment *she* felt rather like a princess in a modern-day fairytale herself. A princess waiting to be swept away by a millionaire prince, perhaps?

Except Linc wasn't royalty, and nor was she and Cecilia was certainly not a damsel waiting to be swept away by a fantasy love in any way at all.

Would that be so bad, Cee?

She must not allow such thoughts even the tiniest space in her mind—and yet hadn't she already started to believe that she and Linc…

So unbelieve it right now—or you might find a pumpkin dropping out of the sky at midnight and giving you a concussion or bringing you a prince who could be a shoe salesman!

Yet they were here, and this *was* rather magical and Cecilia was tired of being practical all the time.

For the second time tonight, she placed her hand into Linc's outstretched one, and she *did* feel just a teensy bit regal as she alighted from his car.

At least until her gaze moved around them and she saw the other couples making their way to the front of the mansion. Couples dressed in similarly glamorous clothing and all looking completely at home in these surroundings.

Couples…

'Look…' She whispered the word to Linc. 'Up ahead. Is that that famous Australian gardening celebrity?'

The tall celebrity with his distinctive features turned and shared a laugh with the woman at his side. Cecilia knew for sure then.

'It *is*. I can remember watching his show when I was just a child.'

Cecilia felt even more out of her depth. A millionaire at her side, famous people all around her... Well, all right. She'd only seen one. But who knew who else might be there?

She on the other hand was just a girl who ran a plant nursery. A girl who happened to be at the side of that very same handsome millionaire just now.

'I can do this.'

She muttered the words beneath her breath, but Linc heard them, anyway.

'Don't tell me you're intimidated by your surroundings, Cecilia?' He asked it with a teasing grin, as though he didn't have a care in the world.

Money would pave the way for that, she supposed.

Actually, Linc would pave the way for himself, whether he had money or not. Instinctively, Cecilia knew this.

So why should she be worried?

'I was a little awed by all this,' she admitted, 'but only for a moment.'

They made their way to the mansion's entrance, where they were met by the president, who'd called Cecilia earlier in the day.

'I'm so glad you're here.' The woman, a tall powerhouse in her late sixties, greeted Cecilia with an air kiss and clasped one of Linc's hands in both of hers. 'The committee are so happy you could both make it. We particularly want to catch up tonight.'

She gestured to a distinguished gentleman at her side.

'This is our host, Mr Gordon Gantry-Bell.'

'It's a pleasure to meet you.'

After a moment's small talk, their host gestured inside.

'Please make your way to the drawing room for light refreshments.'

As they strolled away, Cecilia turned her head to catch Linc's eye. 'I wonder what the committee want to talk to us about. Maybe it's just last-minute questions regarding the masked ball.'

The drawing room turned out to be a huge room, easily capable of holding three hundred people. A curved alcove made up of long sparkling windows looked out onto one aspect of the gardens. A grand piano filled the space in the alcove, and a man sat playing, his tall, thin frame concentrated utterly on producing the lilting melody.

Overhead, a long oval inlay graced the ceiling, and at its centre what must be a family crest in the form of an eagle was featured. Chandeliers hung at intervals along the ceiling. The room was stripped of furniture other than the piano and numerous oval tables spaced about. The pristine tablecloths bore the same eagle family-crest design, embossed into the cloth, while luxurious velvet-covered chairs surrounded each table.

'I really do feel as though I've stepped into another world.' Cecilia whispered the words even as she tried to ensure she had her most confident expression on as heads turned at their entrance into the room.

Immediately, another committee member separated herself from a small group of people near the entry, greeted them and introduced them to a number of other guests.

During a break in the flow of conversation, Cecilia leaned her head close to Linc's and murmured that she supposed they should do as others were doing and divide and conquer. After all, a room full of flower enthusiasts, sponsors and other interested parties allowed endless possibilities for networking. She shouldn't come across as though she wanted to cling to Linc's side.

'Don't even *think* about leaving me.' His low words sounded close to her ear, and her hand was lifted and tucked firmly into the crook of his elbow. 'The only conversation I have to offer about flowers is how to make money out of them.'

This was patently untrue, and Linc would be just fine on his own—Cecilia didn't doubt that for a moment. Still, if he wanted her company…well, that felt good. It shouldn't, but it did.

Minutes later the tour of the gardens was announced. Curtains were drawn back from a sweeping set of doors at the end of the room. These were thrown open with a flourish, revealing a vista of glorious colour and splendour so eye-catching on the other side that it was almost too much to take in.

'I've seen photos.' Cecilia almost whispered the words. She felt spellbound as they entered the gardens. 'But it's so much more when you're here. The perfect symmetry, the arches and blend of colours and shades, the different forms… I think these gardens may have taken some of their inspiration from the Butchart Gardens in Canada. This is so much more beautiful and complex than I realised when we first drove into the grounds.'

She understood now why the event would have

attracted celebrity interest—especially from a renowned gardening identity.

'It is.' Linc glanced into her eyes, and his seemed to shine with pleasure at her happiness. 'Brent and Fiona would love to see all this. Their landscaping and Fiona's artwork would both be inspired by it, I suspect.'

'You *must* encourage them to come during the month the gardens are open to the public, Linc.'

Cecilia herself felt inspired. Without even realising she was doing it, she clasped Linc's hand. His fingers curled around hers and her heart expanded, taking in the beauty and the pleasure of sharing it with him.

They wandered at their own pace. Cecilia barely noticed they had dropped behind the group at first, but after a time she became intensely conscious of the man at her side.

Would he think she had lagged behind deliberately? She hadn't.

But she couldn't deny that she wanted to be with him right now and couldn't be sorry that the rest of the group had moved ahead.

She forced herself to concentrate on this experience, and a thought occurred to her. 'The committee have achieved something quite amazing in getting these gardens opened up. They must be very determined.'

'And connected to the right people.' Linc added this thought as they paused to admire an ancient sundial.

Cecilia gave a contented sigh. 'This makes my efforts at Fleurmazing seem small-scale, doesn't it?'

'Not one bit. Don't downplay your success just because you're seeing something larger.' Linc held her gaze for a moment. 'Let it inspire you.'

'To even greater things?' She liked his philosophy.

'If you like.' Linc sounded relaxed.

Cecilia thought the gardens had worked their magic on him, too.

'My dears, we're about to make our way in. Will you join us at our dinner table?'

The question broke through Cecilia's reverie. The committee president had found them again. Indeed, it appeared the tour was over, because the entire group had dispersed and were making their way back to the welcome of the drawing room.

The president introduced another member of the committee. 'Do call us by our first names. I'm Susan, and this is Agneta. It would be such an honour to spend some quality time with you both.'

'Thank you,' Linc murmured.

'We'd be delighted,' Cecilia added and felt way too much like half of a couple.

She supposed she was—but they were a *business* couple!

They made their way to the table Susan indicated and took their seats. Shallow bowls filled with tea roses graced the centre and filled the air with their lovely scent.

At the urging of their hosts, Cecilia accepted a glass of white wine. The bottle looked French, and she suspected it would have cost her a week's salary. As she took a first sip she glanced at Linc.

His gaze was on her lips, and for just a moment in time their gazes met and held. Even her heart seemed to skip a beat, and then make up for it by beating fast.

'Madam…sir. Your entree.' A waiter discreetly placed fragrant plates before them.

'How long have you been in the plant-nursery business, Linc?' Agneta asked the question and gave a smile that was both coy and a little cheeky all at once. 'If you don't mind me asking, dear?'

Linc responded with the kind of smile and easy response that Cecilia would have expected if he'd been talking to an elderly aunty.

'I got into the business at nineteen after working two jobs and renovating houses until I had enough money to buy my first small nursery.'

Cecilia loved hearing this explanation. She'd never asked him these questions herself and took the opportunity to sit back and allow the older two women to grill him gently for all the information they wanted.

'And you, Cecilia? How long have you worked for Linc as a nursery manager?'

'Oh…' Guilty heat crept into her cheeks, because she knew she'd allowed the conversation to drift over her while she just enjoyed sitting beside Linc and hearing him share information about himself. 'It's been six years.'

They chatted easily with the committee members, getting to know others in the group as the evening wore on.

Cecilia was never unaware of Linc—whether he was talking to the committee member on his right or engaging in conversation with others around the table. She just couldn't seem to distance herself from a sharp consciousness of him.

She tried to focus her attention on the meal and on playing her part in the conversation. As the courses progressed from roasted fennel with blackberries to ocean trout and finally to a tangy lemon sorbet that was made with fruit from the lemon trees in the vast gardens, Cecilia felt tension building in the president and in some of the other committee members.

Tension was building within herself as well, but for different reasons. Sitting so close by Linc had her senses humming. Maybe it was the setting, the glamour or perhaps it was just that in other circumstances this might have been any girl's idea of a dream date. Whatever the reason, those two tensions—the one inside her and the one now being manifested by the committee—shortened her breath.

'No doubt you've both been wondering why we so specifically wanted to speak with you tonight.'

Susan's words brought Cecilia back to earth.

'We have a proposal that we feel will excite you. As you can see from tonight's gathering and our surroundings, the Silver Bells flower show will be prestigious from beginning to end. Now that we've inspected your maze and gained a clear insight into your plans for the masked ball itself, we know that yours will be a wonderful feature event, too.'

Here the woman paused and gave Cecilia an approving glance.

'Cecilia, we were pleased and impressed by your initiative when you approached us to make a masked ball at Fleurmazing one of our feature events this year. We believe it will complement the core activity of the flower show very nicely. Indeed—' here she glanced apologetically at Linc for a moment before turning back '—if the opportunity arose, we'd steal you to work exclusively on helping us with our arrangements for next year. A maze of the kind that you've produced at Fleurmazing, if undertaken here on these grounds, for example, could create a crowning glory for the event.'

Although it was said with a tongue-in-cheek smile, Cecilia didn't miss the keen look that accompanied it.

An opportunity to add to these beautiful gardens? To leave a creation of hers as a legacy to be enjoyed into the future?

'I'm stunned. Thank you. It's very kind of you to say such a thing.'

She glanced quickly at Linc and caught the shocked expression on his face before his brows came down and he quickly masked his thoughts.

'I'm certainly delighted to be holding the masked ball at the nursery this year.' Cecilia wasn't sure what else to say.

The group couldn't have asked her here simply to comment on her maze-making skills. There must be more.

'Regardless of any other possibilities, we'd like to offer Fleurmazing the chance to sign on now with us for future years.' The president drew a document from a satchel on the floor beside her chair. 'This outlines our offer in writing, but if I may elaborate now…?'

Her glance shifted to encompass both of them.

Linc was the one to respond. 'Please do.'

The president straightened in her chair. 'We'd like to bring our relationship with Fleurmazing onto a stronger footing for at least the next five years. We're in the throes of negotiating a contract with our hosts for the same time period, and we feel the two agreements would complement each other.'

She went on.

'Planning has already commenced for our second year of the flower show, of course. Imagine how great it would be to know at this stage that you'd be holding a masked ball for us again this time next year.'

'I'm flattered,' Cecilia said. 'It's wonderful that you'd like to continue the relationship into the future.' Her words were positive. She turned to Linc. 'I think you'd agree we should review the contract with a view to signing?'

'Definitely.'

Linc's response held just the right tone of business interest. Yet did he seem a little disconcerted, as well? Perhaps he hadn't liked it that the committee had all but offered Cecilia an alternative job right under his nose.

Cecilia smiled at the president, and then allowed that smile to encompass all those seated at the table. 'I would very much like to continue a working relationship with your committee, provided it can be done in a way that's workable for all concerned. If you'll allow us to examine the documentation, we will get back to you as quickly as we can.'

Later, as Linc drove her towards her home, she thought again about the committee's offer of an ongoing contract with Fleurmazing.

'That was an interesting way for the committee to handle their approach to us.' Cecilia made the observation quietly. 'I'm not complaining. It was a delightful night.'

As Cecilia spoke, she didn't seem to notice that she had slipped into using *us* rather than *the business* or even referring to herself as its manager. But Linc noticed.

He noticed it and he liked it. In fact, he had liked almost everything about this evening from the moment Cecilia had opened the door of her home and he'd seen how beautiful she looked.

To be so aware of her as a woman and to believe that she was equally aware of him had made it difficult to maintain distance in what had needed to be treated as business. Even in a setting of elegant glamour.

This shift in his interest in Cecilia should scare him. It *did* scare him.

'I guess the committee are looking to really cement their relationship with the Silver Bells owners.'

It also bothered Linc that the committee had all but offered Cecilia a job. He could see now that it had been naive of him, but he had never imagined Cecilia leaving his employ. The thought of it now made him uncomfortable.

Face it, Linc. The dividing line between a business and personal relationship when it comes to Cecilia is now irrevocably blurred. Just what do you plan to do about that?

'I don't blame the committee for wanting to consolidate. It's what I'd do in their shoes.' She nodded her agreement just as he drew the car to a halt outside her home.

Just so long as they don't take you from me in this 'consolidation'.

The thought came without Linc being able to

control it. Suddenly, the tie he'd been wearing all night felt constricting. With a tug he removed it and tossed it onto the console between them. 'At least that's gone.'

'Was it bothering you? You looked quite at home in all your finery.' Cecilia blurted the words, and then fell abruptly silent.

And everything changed, just like that.

No, it didn't change. Linc made himself acknowledge it fully. This need to pursue and build on what they had already shared, to take it further, to know Cecilia more wasn't a change. It was a truth.

'I—I should review that agreement tonight, before I go to— Before I turn in.' Cecilia said it as they alighted from the car. 'Did—did you want to come in, Linc, and look at it with me?'

'I'm happy to trust your judgment on it.'

They were some of the most difficult words he'd ever said. But they had reached her front door, and if he hadn't said those words, he'd have invited himself in and…

Silently, he held his hand out for her key. When she gave it to him, he opened her door and drew the contract from his breast pocket. He handed both to her together.

'You can tell me what you want to do tomorrow.'

Cecilia took her house key and the contract from Linc. Her fingers curled around both, and she felt the contract still warm from the heat of his body. It took will power for her not to hug that warmth to her.

'Thank you for attending the gala with me tonight.' It had been a night she would remember for a very long time. 'It was— I'm sure the committee must have been pleased that you were there. Good—goodnight.'

'Goodnight, Cecilia.' His words were deep.

She didn't know who moved, but somehow they were close, and he bent his head, and she lifted hers and all her good intentions, wobbly as they had been, disappeared.

Their lips met.

Cecilia's resolve, whatever it might have been in the first place, melted away. When his hands held her waist, her free arm wrapped around his neck and their kiss deepened naturally.

There simply was no hesitation—on Linc's part or on hers. Cecilia gave herself to this closeness and this man.

He tasted of lemon sorbet. She probably did, too. But more than that he tasted of Linc. Appealing and sensual and wonderful.

She said his name against his lips. 'Linc—'

'Cecilia.'

He spoke at the same time. His tone was low, and it let her know that he had been equally moved by their kiss.

One tiny shred of self-preservation surfaced within her. 'I have to go in—'

'I have to go—'

Again, he spoke at the same time, and she was glad then that she'd not asked him to come inside with her again, because he would have rejected her, and she'd been there before and it wasn't nice.

He stepped back and away from her, and she pushed her door open and stepped over the threshold.

'Goodnight, Linc. I'll see you at the nursery.'

She went inside and closed the door behind her, listened as Linc's steps faded away and his car door opened and closed. She heard the soft start of his car's engine.

He was gone.

CHAPTER SEVEN

'I'VE EARNED THIS TIME. Just fifteen minutes before I leave for the day.' Cecilia said it aloud, though there was no one there to hear her.

She was in the repurposing shed. She opened a can of paint, stirred it and carried it to an unfinished project.

Linc hadn't come in to the nursery today. He'd called to say he had to deal with the fallout from an overnight crash in the commodities market, and she'd been both relieved and disappointed by the news.

She'd prepared herself to see him, to acknowledge the kiss they'd shared last night and to say that it would be best if they focused on their professional relationship and didn't go there again. That was the sensible choice, and she needed to protect herself… to make sure she didn't get hurt again.

Couldn't you trust that this might be different from the disappointment you experienced with Hugh?

Actually, she was over Hugh. What she was really worried about was that she might allow herself to start to care deeply for Linc. It was her own developing feelings that scared her.

It would be for the best when Linc completed the

review and they could both just get on with their normal lives again—as they had done before this started.

Good. Fantastic. That was exactly what she wanted, and she 100 per cent believed they could go back to exactly the way they'd been before.

'Sure. Why *wouldn't* we be able to do that?'

She slapped the paintbrush against the side of an old crate with a little too much vigour. Spots of paint spattered onto her shirt and shorts.

When her cell phone rang moments later, she answered without even looking at the caller ID.

It was her sister.

'I know this is short notice, but is there any way at all that you can come in to see me tomorrow?' Stacey asked the question in a rush of words. A hint of excitement crept through into her tone. 'I've got approval for the visit, and I've made a booking for you in the morning group in the hope that you can make it. I understand if you can't come. I can book it for the following week. I just thought I'd ask.'

'Yes. I'll be there.' Cecilia didn't hesitate for a second. Emotion tightened her throat. A chance to see Stacey after so long… She would make it work! 'Oh, I can't wait to see you.'

'I'm so glad you're coming.' Stacey gave an audible sigh of relief.

They talked for a few minutes more before Stacey reluctantly ended the call.

Cecilia turned back to her painting, but her thoughts were filled with the upcoming visit to her sister.

She was deep in thought when she heard a footfall behind her. She swung around and there was Linc— and he looked so dear.

'Linc.' Here was her chance to talk about what had happened last night. 'You…ah…you gave me quite a start.'

'Is something wrong?' He stepped forward. Concern laced his voice. 'If it's about—?'

'No, no. Nothing's wrong at all.'

Instead of bringing up the matter of *them*, as she should have, Cecilia shied away from even mentioning it. Well, she had a major family matter on her mind right now!

'I just had a call from my sister, asking if I'd visit her tomorrow. I'll have to check that Jemmie can cover for me. I—I can't wait to go.'

The last sentence surprised her by being tougher to say than it should have been. Cecilia *did* want to see her sister. *So* much! It was just that it would challenge her emotions. The place itself and all that it represented… Her having to leave her sister there when she left… Having such distance from the reality of what Stacey was going through…

'That's great news.' His expression softened with happiness for her but also with a more sober emotion. 'Although I can't help feeling concerned about you going into that environment,' he said carefully. 'Even though I know you have no other choice if you want to see your sister.'

He had spoken the very concern that she felt deeply herself. But she couldn't speak of it, because it might make her sound selfish or unwilling.

Oh, Linc. You don't make it easier for me to stop caring for you when you show this caring side yourself.

The thought crept in, unannounced, and then it was

too late. She couldn't deny it. She *did* care for Linc. Her feelings had developed without her even wanting to allow it to happen.

What if those feelings continued to develop? What if she couldn't control them and…?

Why didn't you take the chance to say something just now, when it was right there in front of you? You should have drawn that firm line and given yourself the chance to get those emotions under control.

'It—the visit—will be fine.'

She would cope with how challenging it felt to pass through all those self-locking doors, the checkpoints, to feel hidden gazes upon her and not know who was looking or what they were thinking, because it meant a chance to see and be supportive to her sister.

Cecilia had visited Stacey just one time, and that had been such a disaster of a visit that she hadn't let herself think too much of how confrontational it had been in and of itself.

Well, Cecilia *had* to be fine.

'There are plenty of staff on duty in the visiting room. I'm sure if anything…worrying happened, they would know what to do.'

'Right. That's good.' He paused, and then couldn't seem to hold back his questions. 'What time is the… uh…the appointment? Fordham, isn't it? What amount of contact do you…ah…do you have with the other prisoners there when you visit?'

His questions about all the practical aspects of the visit were…well, they were adorable, actually.

Oh, Cecilia, you are in so much trouble with your feelings.

Perhaps, but it wasn't as though she loved him or anything. That would be beyond foolish.

She explained the details he had asked about. 'There will be other prisoners in the visiting room, where I'll see Stacey, but people keep very much to themselves. Fraternising with other groups is not allowed.'

Linc listened as Cecilia explained about her upcoming visit to her sister. With every fibre of his being he wanted to insist that Cecilia did not step foot into that place.

Surely there was some risk involved in being exposed to other prisoners and their visitors? What if someone decided to start a riot?

What if you let your mind run away with you a bit more, MacKay?

Yet at the same time he wanted Cecilia to go. This was her family, so of course she had to go. In the same circumstances—

In the same circumstances he had failed, in a way that had left his brother Alex paying the price. Linc had sworn an oath to himself that he would never let anything like that happen again.

He watched now as Cecilia turned and quickly closed up the paint can, tidied the area.

They'd kissed last night, and Linc had not been able to get those moments out of his mind. When he thought about her, his chest squeezed and he had an overwhelming need to…to be wherever she was—just so he could look up and she'd be there. What did *that* mean?

'I'd better call Jemmie and ask if she's happy to step in tomorrow and continue with the preparations for the masked ball.'

Cecilia's words broke through Linc's reverie.

She went on. 'I have an action list she can follow, but it's a really busy time.'

Linc welcomed this distraction from his thoughts, even though it brought him back to Cecilia's trip to visit her sister tomorrow. 'Everything is well in order, because you're such a good operator, so it will be fine. I'll come back to the office with you now.' He fell into step at her side. 'It's late to be starting, but I want to put some work in on the review.'

I stayed away from here all day but gave in and came looking for you, anyway.

He just hadn't anticipated that seeing her would fill him with warmth and something that felt rather like happiness.

'I hope that commodities crash didn't impact too badly on your businesses?' Cecilia made the statement to Linc and knew she should have done it earlier.

Did Linc want to work late like this because he couldn't wait for the review to be finished? Cecilia tried not to feel hurt at the thought.

He thanked her for her concern. 'It wasn't great, but these ups and downs happen.'

As they stepped inside the office, Cecilia brought up the flower-show committee's proposal. 'They're offering next year as a fairly solid proposition for Fleurmazing to host the masked ball again, with the proviso that the Silver Bells charity would still need to sign off on the overall plans for it all to go ahead.'

'That sounds reasonable.'

Linc took his seat at the second computer. He looked at home there now…as though he belonged.

The thought crept up on Cecilia and she frowned.

Linc didn't belong here. He belonged in his high-flying corporate world, running all his business interests and never giving her a thought.

She'd pushed for a review, and he'd rewarded her dedication by conducting it himself. Once it was done, that would be it.

But would it? Or had things changed for him, as well? Maybe he'd want to keep seeing her?

'The flower show committee want exclusive rights to the Fleurmazing masked ball for the next five years. I'm willing to give them that, but I'll want the contract updated first to spell out that Fleurmazing *can* conduct other celebrations and activities utilising the maze.'

'Well done.' His gaze met hers over the tops of their computer screens. 'It's clear you've considered this from all angles.'

She felt so proud in the face of his praise that it was difficult to keep a pleased smile from her face.

Tell him now that you want to be careful there's no repeat of what happened last night. Tell him. Because you can see for yourself that you're all but hanging off every word he speaks. You need to do something about your out-of-control and ever-developing feelings towards him before they truly get you into trouble.

'Thanks. I'd…um…I'd better make that call to Jemmie and then do my tidying up here for the night so I can get going.'

'Good idea. You'll need to get some rest tonight, too.'

Linc wanted to say more, to say that he enjoyed her company and didn't want it to end, but he stopped himself. An attraction that should have been easy for him to control seemed to be getting the better of him. Linc wasn't accustomed to that, and he didn't know how to address it.

Get his work here finished and remove himself from her life as much as possible, he supposed.

He ignored the knowledge that it wasn't only a physical awareness of her beauty and appeal that had him in its thrall and tried to focus on his review work.

Linc succeeded, somewhat, but his thoughts kept returning to Cecilia's upcoming visit to her sister at the correctional centre the following morning. To the kisses that he and Cecilia had shared. To this whole situation and how it was making him feel.

He needed to start working out just exactly *why* Cecilia was impacting on him the way she was and put a stop to it.

Yes, sure—he would work all that out and get it under control in no more than a blink of an eye and with a few minutes of careful thought and concentration.

He'd probably find the answer to world peace while he was at it…

CHAPTER EIGHT

'I'M READY. It's okay to leave early. There's nothing else I need to check or make sure about. It's time. I'm going to see Stacey.'

Cecilia said the words aloud as a means of stopping herself from fussing any longer, checking and rechecking that she was prepared for her visit to her sister.

It was 7:50 a.m. She had a lengthy drive to get to the facility, so leaving sooner rather than later made sense.

And if she was struggling to breathe through an onslaught of anxiety, if her heart was thumping—well, it was with hope and excitement, too. Stacey had realised she'd made mistakes, and she was choosing to set a better path for her life for the future. One that included her sister in it.

Cecilia pushed back the sudden surge of emotion—relief and hope for Stacey, and worry and pain for where her sister had landed herself already. She couldn't indulge such things right now.

She stepped outside, closed and locked the door behind her, and made her way along the short path.

Out on the street a man leaned against the back of

her car—a very familiar man, who removed his sunglasses and straightened as she approached.

Oh, how her emotions leapt in that moment of recognising him.

'Linc! What are you doing here?'

She didn't know what to think. In fact, her mind seemed reluctant to process more than how the sight of him made her heart ache a great deal less, and more, all at the same time.

'I know you won't have been expecting me.' His words were roughened, as though pushed past emotion. 'There might not be anything else I can do that'll take some of the strain off you, but I want to drive you there and back today. If that's okay with you?'

It wasn't pity. She knew that immediately. But had this come simply from an employer's sense of duty towards his employee?

She searched his face and saw the way his jaw clenched. As their glances locked and held, the deep steel grey of his eyes softened.

No. This wasn't about work. This was personal—a man wanting to help a woman he cared about. Cecilia was certain. That *had* to be what she was seeing!

Her emotions wanted to take hold of this and run with it. But she cautioned herself that any measure of affection that Linc now felt could be *any* measure. She did not need to set herself up to expect more and then be hurt.

So don't go hoping too much about Linc's feelings towards you. In fact, why are you even pondering that when your focus needs to be on your sister?

It was easy for Cecilia to use that thought to push aside any need to trust Linc beyond that. She didn't make any correlation to the impact of Hugh deserting her, and the blow that had given to her self-worth as a partner, but it was there in the back of her mind.

'Thank you, Linc, for coming here for this.'

His offer to drive her to the facility did mean a lot. She would thank him and say she would go on her own.

But Cecilia knew that she wouldn't do that. His company today, his willingness to be there for her... She simply couldn't turn her back on that, caution and past history or not.

'I would be grateful for your company, to tell the truth.'

As though to confirm her earlier hope about his feelings for her, he took an involuntary half step towards her and lifted one hand.

Oh, Cecilia, are you sure you want to believe that he really cares about you in an emotional sense?

Because that was what she was trying to do right now—to imbue Linc with a deep and personal caring feeling towards her when he could just as easily be feeling concern for a colleague he happened to have kissed a couple of times.

But sometimes people denied that they were emotionally entangled when in fact they really were, so could he be?

Was she saying that *she* was emotionally entangled in Linc?

No.

Maybe a little.

Can't you just accept his help today, just this once, because it will make the trip there and back easier for you, and not think about the rest of it? Focus on Stacey. That's more than enough to worry about.

'So if you really do have the time, Linc, I'd love the company.'

'I do, and I'm glad to hear it. I need—'

He cut himself off, but his shoulders eased.

Instead of finishing his previous thought, Linc simply said, 'Do you prefer that we go in your car or mine?'

'I'd rather it be my car. The parking area is underground, so you'll be able to wait there if you want, or you could come with me to the reception area and stay there while I—while I go in. You can't bring a cell phone with you, though, not even in the car.'

'That won't be a problem. My phone is in my car, and it can stay there until we get back.'

Linc took the driver's seat of Cecilia's hatchback car. He had to push the seat right back to fit his legs in comfortably. In truth, he'd deal with any amount of discomfort to ensure Cecilia didn't have to face this day on her own.

He'd known yesterday, when she'd first told him she was going to the correctional centre today, that he would want to go with her.

Linc hadn't understood the fierceness of that need at the time, and he had fought it because he hadn't known what she would make of it if he *did* ask to go with her. He had fought right up until he'd woken at five this morning, and then he had stopped fighting it.

He still didn't completely understand the strength of his feelings for Cecilia, but he could no longer go on pretending they didn't exist. Linc needed to know.

Somehow, yesterday, when Cecilia had told him she would be coming to visit her sister, something inside him had changed. He hadn't been able to let her face this on her own. That hadn't simply been about wanting to protect another person. If it had, he'd have been able to explain it away. He couldn't bear not to be a part of this with her. Linc needed this for himself.

All he could do right now was accept the need and be grateful she was allowing him to act on it—hope that a greater understanding of what was going on inside him would come.

'I'll give you the directions.'

She proceeded to do exactly that as they began their journey.

'Tell me about Stacey.'

I would love to know more about your family, your past, all the things that matter the most to you.

'What was your favourite thing to do together when you were little?'

He hoped, too, that talking would help take her mind off the more confrontational aspects of the day ahead.

Cecilia shared some memories from her childhood. Playing games with her sister…finishing each other's sentences.

'Our mother wasn't very loving towards us, but having each other helped. We look significantly alike even now, but we aren't identical, so we couldn't get away with switching places with each other. We used to daydream about it, though.'

Sharing those childhood memories now had brought a smile to Cecilia's strained features, but when she had first stepped out through her front door that morning, anxiety had radiated from her.

Linc felt it himself—on her behalf. He also felt the disappointment of knowing that she hadn't been surrounded by a loving family all her life. Every person deserved that, in his opinion. And now she had another hurdle to get over.

'I wish I could go in with you this morning.'

'Stacey would raise her eyebrows a bit if you did that!'

Cecilia managed the quip and even a laugh to go with it. Linc had done her a world of good by coming along this morning. Oh, how her heart had lifted when she'd seen him—but she couldn't tell him that!

'Unfortunately, you have to be booked in advance to visit, so it wouldn't be an option today, anyway.'

'And you'll want your sister all to yourself.' He said it in a matter-of-fact tone. 'I wouldn't expect anything else.'

They covered the rest of the trip speaking intermittently of matters of no importance. It helped her fight off the nerves until they drove into the underground parking area.

Rather than dwell on her unease at the upcoming visit, Cecilia got straight out of the car when Linc stopped it. He alighted, too, and she had to confess—silently, at least—that she was rather glad he would be with her for as long as possible before she went in.

After that it was identification, registration, the wait while names were called, until finally it was her turn and she got up. Linc quickly pulled her tight against his chest and released her again.

Cecilia made her way through all the security processing. She was electronically scanned and had to pass a drug-detecting dog's assessment. A band with a number on it was affixed around her wrist. The officers were professional, but she couldn't help a feeling of being just that number to them.

Did her sister feel that way? Of course she would.

An officer checked her wristband. 'You're at table twenty-three.' The woman pointed towards a separate building and gave some other instructions.

Cecilia drew a deep breath. 'Thanks.'

Once seated inside, Cecilia fixed her gaze on the inmates' entry point and waited. She wished Linc were there with her and was comforted to know he was waiting for her outside.

After what felt like hours but was probably only minutes, her sister stepped into the room.

'Stacey. Oh, I've missed you so much.'

Cecilia stood and hugged her sister and felt relief rush through her as Stacey hugged back just as hard. When they drew apart and took their seats, Cecilia looked carefully at her sister.

Stacey wore a dark green T-shirt and matching pants, with trainers on her feet. Around her neck was a chain with a tag on it. Had she lost weight? Or was it stress giving her that lean look?

Cecilia pasted a big smile on her face. 'I brought coins for the vending machine. Would you like something?'

'Maybe in a little bit.' Stacey's hands fidgeted together on the tabletop until she stopped herself.

'Would you rather just talk first, Stace?' Cecilia wanted to take her sister's hands but had to settle for hoping her love for her sister shone from her eyes.

'I made such a stupid mistake.' Stacey said the words quietly before looking up to meet Cecilia's gaze. 'Running around being an idiot with Joe and not getting out of the situation when I realised I'd got myself into something I didn't like and wanted nothing to do with. I wish I'd never met him. I'm not saying this is all his fault. I made the choice to be with him. But I don't want anything to do with him now. Not ever again!'

Cecilia drew a deep breath. 'I'm glad you've decided not to have any part of him now.'

Stacey glanced around them briefly, and then returned her gaze to Cecilia. When she spoke, it was in a quiet tone. 'He put me in a scary position—led me to believe that whole situation was very different to what it turned out to be. And when it all went wrong, he left me there to face the consequences while he disappeared.'

'It's not always easy to see what people truly are, Stacey.' Cecilia knew that from the time she'd spent with Hugh. 'Sometimes it's not until they let you down that you can see it. Anyway, I'm glad you've left him behind you. That's good.'

'It is.' Stacey gave a wan smile. 'And now I can find my way back from how I've messed up my life. I'm going to have to.'

Before Cecilia could respond, Stacey went on.

'I got in the habit of being rebellious years ago, because it helped me to feel better about the way Mum gave up on us.'

'That wasn't our fault. The problem was with *her*.' Cecilia had carried her own anger and hurt over it. To some degree she probably always would. 'It's up to us to choose how we let that influence us now.'

'I'm choosing to do what I can to get out of here on good terms and follow a better path once I do.'

They talked about Stacey's future then and about Cecilia's life too—the plant nursery and the upcoming masked ball, but not about Linc. The time disappeared so quickly. Before Cecilia knew, it they were being told that the visit was over and Cecilia had to leave.

Reluctantly, Cecilia got to her feet and hugged her sister goodbye. 'I love you so much, Stacey.'

'I love you too, Cee.' Stacey used her pet name for Cecilia, and for a moment her eyes shone with the sheen of tears before she resolutely blinked them back. 'I—I'll see you at your next visit, but I'll call you. I'll stay in contact now—that is, if you'd like—?'

'Yes!' Cecilia smiled past her own emotion, and then she was on her way back through all the checkpoints until she arrived in the waiting room.

She couldn't help but feel happier. She would come back and visit again soon. They could talk again. Stacey would call, so they could stay in contact. Cecilia felt as if a missing piece had finally been replaced back in her life.

Linc wasn't in the waiting room, and the clerk informed Cecilia that he'd been sent to wait in the car. 'We don't allow people to remain in the waiting room if they have no reason to be here.'

Cecilia was on the pathway outside, still some distance from the parking lot, with her thoughts on the future, when Stacey could live her life again outside of this place, when a man suddenly came up beside her.

He grabbed her wrist in a punishing grip and lowered his face close to her ear. It all happened so fast she wasn't sure what was going on.

'What did you say to your sister to turn her against me? What did you say to her in there just now? Tell me!'

Fear and adrenalin shot through Cecilia. Who *was* this? What was going on? Her head whipped around. She caught a glimpse of largeness, tallness, of a face tightened by anger and hair the colour of wheat, cropped close to the man's skull.

This had to be Joe. It couldn't be anyone else.

'Let me go.' Cecilia said it in a low tone as she tried to pull free.

His grip around her wrist tightened. 'I know where you live, Cecilia. I know lots about you.' His voice was harsh. 'Trust me, you don't want a visit from me. So stay away from Stacey. Stop putting ideas in her head about getting out early and anything else you might have in your mind. She's better off doing the full term. When she gets out that way, she's free. No one will be watching her, checking her every move. She can go back to supporting—' He broke off.

'She shouldn't have ended up in there in the first place.' Cecilia forgot to be afraid as protectiveness for her sister drove the words from her. 'What kind of man leaves a woman to pay for his crime?'

'I make my own rules—and you've just pushed me too far.'

He started to pull her forward, and Cecilia wasn't strong enough to hold back. Fear ripped through her as she stumbled and fell into him.

And then Linc was there, breathing hard. 'Get your hands off her!'

For a moment Cecilia didn't know if Joe would obey, but then he uttered a curse, let go of her and ran off. He leapt into a car at the end of the parking lot, and the car roared away.

'I'm driving.' Linc spoke the words as he pulled open the driver's side door of her car.

Cecilia hadn't even been aware of them making their way back there. Her ears were buzzing and she felt light headed.

Don't you dare hyperventilate or faint.

'What just happened?' Linc rapped out the question. 'What did that guy say to you before I got there?'

Cecilia climbed into the passenger seat and noted that her hands were shaking so much she had to try twice to fasten her seat belt.

'That was Joe—the man who was with my sister when she got caught committing a robbery. Stacey's told me that Joe was the mastermind, and I've no reason to doubt that. Aside from some teenage rebellion, my sister never did anything criminal before she became involved with that man. He's been sneaking messages in to her. But she's seen his true colours and wants nothing more to do with him, and he…he isn't happy about that.'

'Why would he be here this morning? He can't visit her. He'd be picked up as soon as they recognised who he was.' Leashed power echoed in each word Linc spoke as he drove the car through the parking lot. 'We have to report this to the police. There's a station not far from here. We'll go straight there.'

'Yes, I think we'd better.' Cecilia laced her fingers together tightly so their trembling wouldn't show. 'I don't know how he knew that I'd be visiting this morning, but I believe he was waiting specifically for me. He basically implied just then that he would harm me if I didn't stay out of Stacey's life.'

'Is that what your sister wants? For you to stay out of her life?'

'No!' Cecilia said it with vehemence. 'We may look at life differently at times, but we love each other. We…well, we really did mend our issues just now. I promised I'd keep coming to see her, and she promised she'll call me when she can.' Cecilia drew a deep breath.

'I'm glad to hear that.' His tone of voice underlined the truth of this before he went on, 'You could have been really harmed just now.'

'You could have been hurt too, Linc.' Her words were low as remorse began to fill her chest. 'I shouldn't have asked you to come with me today.'

'I asked if you'd let me. There's a difference. And this is not your fault.' Linc's jaw clamped into a tight line. 'If I hadn't got there when I did—'

'He would have dragged me into his car, and I dread to think what would have happened to me.' Cecilia suppressed a shudder. 'Thank you for being there and for acting so quickly to scare him off.'

They made their way to the police station, spoke to the police, looked at images, and found out in the process that Stacey's Joe was operating under an alias. He was wanted not only for the armed robbery in Australia, but for a string of other crimes in his home country of New Zealand—some of them very serious.

The police over there had been trying to catch him for two years.

'I don't think Stacey knows any of that.' Cecilia spoke as Linc drove towards her home after the interview with the police. They would meet officers there to ensure her house was safe.

Linc shook his head. 'The police said he can lay the charm on when he tries. He must have hidden a lot of the truth about himself from her.'

'He must have. It makes me scared for her, as well as for myself.' She pushed the words past a lump in her throat.

There was a long pause while Linc's hands maintained a death grip on the car's steering wheel. The street was quiet. Then he pulled over into a parking space, unclipped his seat belt and hers and pulled her into his arms.

The strength of Linc's hold let Cecilia know how concerned he had been for her safety.

Barriers Cecilia had tried to keep propped up fell away. Her arms tightened around him.

He didn't say a word. Neither did she. But, oh, it felt good to be held and to hold him.

'That situation ranked right up there with some of the worst moments I've experienced in my life.' The words were almost wrenched from Linc as he held Cecilia close. 'If he'd harmed you—'

He drew back, and his gaze searched her face, travelled over her. He lifted the wrist the man had gripped. Red marks showed on the delicate skin. Everything inside Linc cried out for justice, for the man who had done this to her to pay for it. In those few moments in time, he let his eyelashes sweep down, because he didn't want Cecilia to see his roiling emotions.

'There will be a bruise, but that's all.' Her words were soft, hushed almost and edged with a need for reassurance that she probably didn't realise was there.

Linc lifted her hand and pressed it against his chest, laying his own over it. His need to give to Cecilia won out over his memories and the guilt from the past. The emotions he felt, this need for connection, just couldn't feel wrong to him in this moment.

The knowledge sent a warning signal through him. But with so many other emotions churning, that signal quickly faded and disappeared. He gently kissed her, and then there was no thinking at all—just experiencing.

Cecilia's lips parted beneath Linc's as she gave herself to kissing him. Her lips softened, yielded to him and received from him at one and the same time. Her defences were down and she needed this.

They kissed softly and gently, exploring each other and healing the fear of those earlier moments.

And then a thought came to Cecilia.

She'd reconciled with her sister.

Surely that meant that anything could be possible.

She and Linc could be possible...

Once that last thought surfaced, there was no taking it back. It changed her. It infused her with hope. And while the common sense side of her warned that such hope was not wise, she couldn't heed it.

When they finally broke apart, Linc seemed to let her go reluctantly.

He sighed and restarted the car. 'We'd better get moving. Now, talk me through the layout of your home.' He cast a quick, apologetic glance her way. 'I'd like to know before we get there. I remember from this morning that there's no place in the front that a person could hide. I could see all of it while I was waiting for you. What about the sides and the back? Would it be easy to break in from any of those points?'

'I've never thought deeply about any vulnerabilities there in that way.' Cecilia forced herself to think about it now. She'd forgotten the threat of Joe during those moments in Linc's arms.

Oh, how easily she had forgotten.

'The back door is deadlocked, and all the windows have locks, but the house isn't alarmed. It backs onto a neighbouring property, but I guess that wouldn't really stop anyone. A person could also enter from the front yard and walk down the left side. The bathroom window is halfway down on that side.'

When they were several blocks away from her home, Linc spoke again. 'The police suggested you don't stay there for the time being. I'm holding you to your agreement to that advice.'

'I know I might not be safe.'

In a way she'd been waiting for this—and also dreading him bringing it up, because it forced her to think about the implications. The thought of being forced out of her home and looking over her shoulder until this situation could be resolved was hard to take.

'There's work, too. That will have to be managed so no one is placed in any danger. Oh, goodness! The masked ball. What am I going to do?'

'That isn't upon us yet, so let's worry about one thing at a time. We'll sort this out, Cecilia. I promise you.'

His calm words helped.

'For now I want you to wait in the locked car while I let the police in so they can check your place. Once I'm sure it's safe, you can gather some things together.

The police said they'll have a car there watching until further notice, in the hope that Joe *does* follow through and turn up.'

Linc stopped the car two doors down from her home.

She identified her front door key for him.

He reiterated that she was not to get out until he came back and gave the okay.

'How do I know you'll be safe?' The question burst from her at the last moment.

The smile he gave had an uncompromising edge to it. 'I'll be careful. You don't need to worry about my safety.'

She worried anyway, and it seemed he was gone for endless minutes before he returned to the car and told her he was satisfied she could safely enter her home.

Cecilia entered, retrieved her phone and started packing an overnight bag. It was reassuring to have Linc with her and to know that the police were watching from across the road in their unmarked car.

'Pack for several days.' Linc made the suggestion from the living room. It was the one place where he could see both her and the front and back doors. 'Since we don't know yet exactly what will be happening, I think that would be best.'

She packed. They left quickly.

Cecilia let herself think then about where she should go, and realised Linc seemed already to have a plan in his mind, if his confident driving gave any indication.

Rather belatedly, she asked, 'Where exactly are you taking me?'

CHAPTER NINE

'YOU'VE LEFT YOUR car at my house.'

Cecilia not only didn't know where Linc intended to take her—she didn't know what might happen to his vehicle if he left it outside her home.

'I made a couple of calls when I retrieved my phone out of it. Alex and Brent are on their way to collect my car.'

Linc's words were matter-of-fact, as though he called in his family to sort out other people's problems on a daily basis. As though he didn't find it strange at all to be helping Cecilia deal with this entire issue.

'The police will be watching, so I've let them know Alex and Brent will be doing that.'

'Okay. That's good to know.'

She couldn't deny that it was reassuring to have Linc's level-headed input just now. Was this what people experienced when they entered into a truly meaningful partnership? This alignment of emotion to the needs of each other?

Not that she and Linc had entered into such a thing.

She, however, *had* entered into believing it could be possible.

Not a smart way to start thinking, Cee.

Yet she couldn't undo the thoughts. They were a part of her now, and they did not want to be denied. She needed time to consider them, to think it through rationally and ask herself whether there really might be a chance and what that might entail.

Could she see Linc for a period of time, enjoy wherever it might lead them and then let it end with no regrets? Because wouldn't that be all Linc would offer?

'It's good of Alex and Brent to help.' She knew she was dodging her own question. 'Please thank them for me when you can.'

'Not needed, but I will.' He drew a deep breath before he spoke again. 'I want you to stay with me tonight, Cecilia.'

For a moment she felt as though he'd read right inside her mind just now, and her heart fluttered, but then she realised there must be a different motivation for his statement.

'It's good of you to want to keep me safe.'

If you'd asked me to stay for other reasons, I'd have agreed instantly.

Maybe it was just as well that he hadn't!

She cleared her throat. 'But I'd planned on going to a hotel.'

'I don't feel that would be safe enough.' His response was immediate and firm. He went on, 'We're heading for my place in the city. The building has excellent security. I realise I didn't ask you first. I should have. That scene back there left me more shaken than I care to admit, I guess, but I know I do need your agreement. I'll take you to a hotel if you insist, but please don't.'

Any problem she might have had over him not seeking her agreement first evaporated in the light of that final request.

Oh, Linc, you become more lov—likeable by the minute.

'I've only ever seen your warehouse building.'

That near slip-up in her thoughts shocked Cecilia so much she struggled to maintain an even tone of voice. It was one thing to contemplate seeing where a relationship might go with Linc in the short term, but to almost think the L-word about him was a whole other matter!

'I maintain both. The family all get together at the warehouse regularly. Rosa keeps everything ready for us.'

He shrugged his shoulders—a wealthy business-man with a busy lifestyle and the financial capacity to make that lifestyle as workable as possible for him-self and for those around him.

'I guess that would make sense for someone in your position.'

She'd known he had other properties and that both brothers had moved out of the warehouse to other homes. But knowing she was about to enter another one of Linc's properties did remind her of the dispar-ity in their circumstances.

Well, from Linc's perspective it would be the height of practicality to have a place in the city. If Cecilia wanted to think about anything, it should be how she was going to manage the rest of her commit-ments while this was all going on.

Yes, Cecilia. Maybe you should be thinking about

the actual circumstances that have brought about this temporary change in your place of residence.

And she should also be thinking about what she could do, if anything, to try and help get that man caught, so she could get back to her normal life and be totally sure Joe was out of Stacey's life for good.

'I appreciate your offer, and I'm grateful to accept the security measures that will go with it.' She forced her voice to remain as steady and even as his had been. 'I need to figure out how to manage things at work. I have to get back there. There's so much to be done, and I also need to make sure the staff are safe. What if this guy knows where I work, as well?'

'There are certainly measures that need to be taken, and the police don't have infinite resources.' He said it carefully, as though feeling his way.

When he went on, Cecilia understood why.

'I've asked Alex and Brent to arrange a security firm to provide around-the-clock surveillance at the plant nursery until further notice.'

Rather than contesting or questioning this, Cecilia simply expressed her gratitude.

'Thank you.' She would worry about what that would do to the business's bottom line later. For now the important thing was that everyone would be safe. 'That will help when I return there, as well.'

With a suppressed sigh she changed the subject.

'I need to make that phone call to the centre now. I know the police were going to alert the staff to what happened in the parking lot, but I need to put a request in for Stacey to call me. I haven't even had the chance to tell you that we had a genuinely wonderful reconciliation this morning.' Cecilia fell silent for a moment. 'I hope this happening won't undo that progress.'

'I'm glad you got that result with your sister, and I'm sure she will want to continue being closer to you.' Linc drew the car off the street, and his words rang with sincerity. 'We've arrived.'

'I didn't notice we'd come so far.'

They were on an affluent street in one of the city's most sought-after suburbs. A beautiful multistorey building loomed before them. It had secure underground parking. Other cars must also park there. Yet Cecilia saw only Linc's private parking area as they drove in.

At least by focusing on those details she could distract herself away from her softening emotions towards Linc.

Yes, Cecilia, but those emotions are still there. What are you going to do about that?

Fine. Maybe there *were* emotions. But it had been an emotional day. She didn't need to do anything about…anything.

So she stated the obvious instead. 'You're the owner of the whole building, aren't you?'

'Yes, it's one of my investment properties.' He said it without any particular inflection. 'Holding an apartment here works well for when I need to meet with my business broker or take care of other business without the trouble of going in to the office.'

Yet he and his brothers had created their own return-to-the-family oasis out at the warehouse building after the other two had moved out. Cecilia liked that concept, too. It spoke of a close-knit family who, while they went about their individual lives, still needed to reconnect on a regular basis.

That was what she'd had with her sister when they were younger, and now she believed she would have again. She *did* believe it and felt better for giving herself that reminder.

Minutes later they were safely ensconced in Linc's apartment on the top floor. The harbour views were magnificent, and the apartment was furnished in elegant yet comfortable style. A squashy black leather sofa and matching chairs dominated the lounge area. The kitchen shone in chrome, with a white marble workstation in the middle.

'This is—'

Opulent. And yet it was still Linc. A demonstration of his vast wealth, and yet it felt welcoming. Maybe that came from the clutter of kicked-off male shoes and boots inside the door, or the scatter of financial magazines tossed down beside one of the armchairs.

'It's a great place, Linc.'

Linc might wear jeans and work boots and look like a regular working man much of the time, but he *was* a millionaire—a self-made success story. This apartment certainly testified to that fact.

'I'm glad you like it.' He shifted her bag in his grip. He'd insisted on carrying it in for her from his car. 'There's a guest room through here.'

They passed a room that must be his, and an office, and came to the guest room. With her bag stowed inside the door, and Cecilia determinedly refusing to think about Linc's bedroom just an office space away, she followed him back into the living area.

'I don't know what to do.' She'd murmured the words before she realised she had spoken aloud.

About my feelings, about that threat, about anything at all right now!

'It will be okay, Cecilia.' Linc spoke the words from the open-plan kitchen.

He was boiling the kettle and had mugs, coffee granules and a teabag at the ready. Right there, in that chrome and marble masterpiece, Linc MacKay was preparing a fortifying cup of tea for her and making coffee for himself while he was at it.

Who was he, really? Which man was the real Linc? The one dressed in work boots and casual clothes who would drive a woman to a correctional facility first thing in the morning so she could see her sister? Or was he the man in this apartment, entertaining high-brow corporate colleagues? Was he the business magnate, or the loving, protective brother? Was he Cecilia's boss, or the man who would have fought today to ensure her safety?

He was the same Linc and yet not the same—because the Linc of six years ago had rejected her interest in him. *This* Linc had kissed her, held her and he was letting himself care about her. He *was*!

Cecilia told herself he must be all of those people, all of those things. His complexity had caught her attention from the first day they'd met, and it intrigued her more and more now as she came to know each new layer of him in a more personal way.

Cecilia made her call to the correctional centre then, and they surprised her by allowing her to speak to Stacey.

'Cecilia? What's going on? Are you okay?' Panic

rang in Stacey's tone when she came on the line. 'People don't get called to the phone here unless it's bad news, and on top of that they moved me into the strict protection section here today!'

'I'm afraid it *is* troubling news, Stacey.' Cecilia drew a breath and explained what had happened. 'I've been to the police, and obviously the staff there at the centre know about it as well now. I'm glad they've moved you. I was trying not to worry about whether harm could come to you. '

'It won't. Not in that way, now that I've been shifted. But this is still my worst nightmare.' Stacey's words were low. 'And I've brought it down not only on myself but on you. I'm so sorry, Cecilia.'

'We're going to be okay, Stacey. We can get through this together.' She had to tell her sister what she'd discovered about this man. 'There's more you need to know. Joe has warrants out in New Zealand for offences the police described as "both violent and serious", as well as for the robbery here.'

'Are you completely sure about this?' Stacey's voice shook as she asked the question.

Cecilia's heart ached for her sister so much in that moment. 'I'm quite sure.'

'He needs to be caught.' There was a pause and then Stacey spoke again. 'There are things I can tell the authorities that might help them to track him down. Cee, I know you may not believe me, but I thought he and I were going to have a life together. That sounds ludicrous now, but I thought he was someone different.'

'I understand, Stacey. Please don't give up on yourself because this has happened.'

'I won't.' Determination fuelled Stacey's words. 'If I do that, then I'll be letting him get away with how he used me.'

Cecilia was grateful to hear the words but knew her sister would need to hold on to her determination as hard as she could. 'I love you, Stacey.'

They talked for a minute or two more, until Cecilia was finally able to put the phone down.

She turned to Linc, and all the pent-up emotion surfaced. 'She's going to work with the police to try and help them catch him.'

'That's good.'

He handed her the cup of tea and settled beside her on the sofa with his coffee. His calmness helped her to centre herself again.

'She's not a criminal.' It was a relief to say it and to let it sink into her own heart. 'Stacey has a great deal of passion for life, but deep down she has a good heart.'

'Something tells me that with you to help her, she'll find her way back to the best of herself in time.'

'Thank you, Linc—for helping me with these issues.' She went on, 'Most people wouldn't even want to try to understand what it's like to have to deal with a person you care about being incarcerated, let alone today's problems.'

'I understand more than you know.' His words were low.

'What do you mean?'

How could he understand more? For a moment she wasn't sure if he would answer, but then he spoke.

'My brothers and I had a great deal of our freedom taken from us when we were growing up.' His gaze fell to his hands for a moment. 'Being stuck in an orphanage, with no option to get away until we were old enough to leave under our own steam. Scant meals, and all of them identical. I know it's not the same as your sister's situation, but it had a strong impact on each of us.'

'How did that happen to you—to them?' She knew Linc and the other two weren't blood brothers, yet their love for each other was as strong as hers for Stacey. His brothers even carried his last name now.

'Brent's father thought he was a disappointment.' Linc's words were low, edged with harshness, as though even to say it, let alone reveal that it had happened to Brent, infuriated him. 'In my case my mother had died and my father was an alcoholic. He didn't want the responsibility of raising a child so he dumped me at the orphanage.'

'Like our mother leaving Stacey and me…' There was an oddly comforting affinity in knowing that she and Linc held this common bond. 'In our case she waited until we finished school, but even that much was a strain for her—and she didn't hold back in letting us know that.'

'Regardless of their age, no person deserves to be treated that way.'

Linc said this with finality, just as his brother Alex buzzed to come up, and Linc got up and punched a code into a number pad on the wall to allow Alex access.

Minutes later Linc's youngest brother stepped into Linc's apartment, clapped his brother on the back and turned his attention to Cecilia. 'You're all right? Linc said there was a bit of a shake-up with some guy threatening you.'

'I'm fine. Thank you, Alex.'

In that moment Cecilia knew that Linc hadn't exposed any more of her story than had been necessary. She valued Linc for that but couldn't help wondering why he'd left Alex out of his explanation about the orphanage.

Cecilia forced her attention back to Linc's brother. 'It was good of you and Brent to go to my home and collect Linc's car.'

The brothers might have grown up in difficult circumstances, but it appeared to have brought out the best in all of them.

Cecilia's glance shifted to the man holding her thoughts, and her heart softened despite herself.

Linc's gaze locked with hers, and for a moment she thought she saw deep emotion churning in his eyes.

Seconds later he'd looked away, and Alex's calm words filled what Cecilia hadn't noticed yet was a silence.

'So you're okay, big brother?' The younger man glanced from one to the other of them. His gaze finally settled on Linc. 'There's nothing else I can do for you? I could ask Jayne to come over for a while to visit with Cecilia. Brent's waiting in the parking area, but I can get him up here now, too, if needed.'

'I've got it covered.' Linc's face softened. 'But thanks.'

'You'll both be safe here for as long as necessary. I know nothing will happen. It's just—' Alex headed for the door. 'Aw, well, you know… Anyway, if you need anything, you know I'll come in an instant.

As will Brent. Keep us informed of developments, please.'

Linc stopped him before he got through the door and clasped his shoulder for a long moment. 'I know, and I will. Say hi to Jayne.'

Alex's glance drifted to Cecilia for a moment and then back to his brother. 'See you later.'

The day passed. There were further conversations with the police, and then Cecilia and Linc prepared an early evening meal together. Linc proved a dab hand with pasta and confided that he'd worked for a time in a restaurant when he'd been trying to amass enough resources to get his brothers out of the orphanage and make his business empire strong enough that he could afford to support them.

He seemed sad as he spoke.

'You never mentioned how Alex ended up in the orphanage.' Cecilia carried her plate to the outdoor dining seating on Linc's balcony.

'We never knew.' Linc pushed his food around on his plate.

Cecilia tried to give her attention to the meal. The food was delicious, the wine Linc had poured to go with it beautifully refreshing. Yet she really couldn't do the food justice. Linc seemed to be struggling, too.

'Not hungry?' Linc asked of Cecilia and wished he could take the strain from her slender shoulders.

She shook her head. 'It's delicious, Linc, but I keep thinking about all that's happened today and about families and the difficulties they face. I hate thinking how hard it must have been for you and your brothers.'

'For you and your sister, too, by the sounds of it.'

He set down his fork and, by silent mutual consent, they moved back inside. This time when she settled on the sofa, he sat right beside her.

He went on. 'It sounds as though both of you needed your mother's support and missed out on it.'

'Yes.' That was certainly true. 'I ended up trying to be a mother to Stacey, and that hasn't always worked out well for our relationship with each other. You know, this has been a rough day, and I'm worried about what's ahead. I *have* to go back to work tomorrow. There's just too much to be done.'

'You would have managed on your own today if you'd had to, but I'm glad to have been able to help. And we'll see how things are going tomorrow when tomorrow arrives.'

His fingers threaded through hers. It was just that—such a simple thing—but Cecilia sighed and closed her eyes and he drew her head onto his shoulder as they sat there side by side.

She needed this comfort more than she ever would have wanted to admit. So she took it and let herself absorb the healing it brought.

That it would shift from comfort to something more than that was inevitable. Cecilia knew it, and when Linc turned his head, she met him halfway— wanting this, wanting *him*.

Outside, night was falling over the city, and there was a man on the loose somewhere who'd threatened her and who had to be caught.

But here in Linc's apartment Cecilia was safe, and she lost herself in Linc's kiss. That kiss became another. And another.

As their lips meshed, tenderness for him swept

through her and she received tenderness from him. That tenderness brought healing from the most overwhelming aspects of the day they had both shared. Fears receded to a more manageable level. Gratitude was registered and remembered, and then placed aside to allow her to focus wholly on these precious shared kisses with a man who was perhaps also becoming precious to her.

She'd asked herself where a relationship between them might go. Tonight there was desire and need and tender emotion, and she wanted all of those things with Linc. She wanted that beginning. Cecilia didn't let herself think of where such a beginning might lead.

'I have longed for this more than you can know.' Linc's words were low.

His fingers sifted through her hair, and his hand came to rest on the nape of her neck. A shiver of pleasure followed his touch.

She cupped his cheek and, when the kiss deepened, gripped his strong upper arm and allowed delight and need to blend in the giving and returning of each breathless moment. Cecilia could have continued like that forever, and yet she wanted more. So much more.

'Cecilia...'

Oh, so much was expressed in that simple speaking of her name, in a voice that had deepened and mellowed with all they had shared.

Yet there was a question there—a silent seeking of agreement.

Yes, Linc. Yes, with all that I have and all that I am. Yes.

The response was deep within her soul, surpassing any conscious thought of warning to herself that she might have formulated. She couldn't have denied that 'yes' if she'd tried.

And there were no thoughts of warning or caution or 'what ifs' or concerns. There was this and only this, and her heart was engaged.

She acknowledged that in this moment she should gently extract herself, end this here, cherish these shared kisses and seek nothing more. But Cecilia could only focus on the desire for her that glowed in the depths of Linc's eyes, on all the emotions she felt within herself, both named and unnamed, and on the soft and gentle expression on his face. On the touch of his hands that now cupped her shoulders and stroked her face.

'Take me to your room, Linc.'

Linc heard Cecilia's words, saw the need and longing reflected in her eyes, and faced a watershed moment deep within himself.

He had turned his back six years ago, for her sake, because he'd known he would never truly commit. Now Linc knew that his emotions *were* invested in Cecilia, that his feelings were real and only for her.

Linc wanted to give her those things, but would she be able to receive them and let it end there without being hurt? For that matter, could he give in that way and end it without hurt to his own emotions?

Too late, Linc. You're already there.

Deep down he knew that, and he hoped for this chance to just this once do all that he could to show her those feelings.

'I need you, Cecilia, and I need this night. But I can't… In terms of the future…' His chest hurt and he struggled to go on.

'I don't care, Linc. I need—' She broke off, and her gaze was clear and determined as it held his.

Thank you. With all my heart and soul, thank you.

Linc took Cecilia's hand and drew her from the sofa. It felt like the most natural and right thing to lead her to the door of his room.

He drew Cecilia inside with him, turned her into his arms and lowered his mouth to hers once again, knowing that now there would be more. There would be the fulfilment of all the desire that hummed in the air surrounding them, the opportunity to cherish and give and revere.

He gave himself to making it the most special experience for her that he possibly could. Valuing her with all he could invest in that valuing. Expressing without words the emotions running through the fabric of his soul.

If you don't say it, it's not real.

The childhood words were silly, because these emotions were entirely real, whether they were verbalised or not. Yet they couldn't be spoken because he couldn't look for a future.

Linc didn't ask himself in that moment just what those deep emotions meant. He wasn't sure he could afford to know. Instead, he breathed deeply and inhaled Cecilia's closeness and let it fill him.

Linc gave himself to these shared and treasured pleasures, this precious giving and receiving. He was all of himself and yet more within himself than he had ever been. That was all Linc knew—that and the deep, resonating need to demonstrate to Cecilia how much sharing this with her meant to him.

His breath caught as she melted wholly into his

embrace. His arms trembled with how deeply he valued holding her. Chest to chest, warmth shared, soft lips against caressing lips, they explored as people who knew each other but didn't really, and now they needed so much more.

Today had acted as a catalyst for him. He felt as though layers had been peeled from his soul and that he could finally acknowledge that he *did* long for Cecilia. That he did not simply *want* but *needed* to carry their closeness to this inevitable conclusion.

Linc needed this with everything within him. Just once…and only with her…

'Linc…' She whispered his name against his lips.

He swept her closer and gave all his being to the *sense* of her—the soft loveliness of her arms about his neck and the delicate arch of her spine where his hands held her. She pressed closer still. She seemed unable to be near enough.

Something inside Linc, in some place that he hadn't known before, felt *right* for the first time in his life. *This was right*—holding her, sharing these precious moments.

His chest rose and fell on a deep breath. He pushed away the thought that there could never be this again—pushed it far, far away, where it couldn't tighten its grip until he could no longer breathe, where he might not feel it even existed any more.

'Cecilia…' He murmured her name against her lips and grounded his emotions in this giving.

'Oh, Linc…'

My heart is so full of emotion for you right now.

Cecilia couldn't speak the words, but they rose in her mind as she embraced Linc and he embraced her.

Everything about these moments imbued her with thoughts and emotions so deep she couldn't fathom how she could feel so much.

Impossible to try to stop herself, to protect those emotions. So she told herself not to label them, not to give them names—because while they were nebulous and unnamed she could have this and not think about tomorrow...

Linc's hand rose to stroke her hair. 'Your hair is beautiful. It's so soft.'

He murmured the words before his lips touched hers again.

'I want this.'

Conviction echoed in her quiet words. Her hand rose to his chest, felt its strong rise and fall as he registered her words.

She went on. 'I want to share this—with you. Everything there is to share...' Everything that could be shared from her emotions to his.

He'd made no promises, had been careful that she understood there would be no tomorrow. And Cecilia did understand, and it made this easier. One chance to give and receive and close a chapter. She would feel happy because of that.

Surely she would...

His hands stroked her arms reverently, with the lightest touch against her skin, and she let go of the uneasy thought.

As clothing fell away she felt only a sense of rightness so strong and so comforting that it was infinitely beautiful finally to become one with him. Every barrier was removed and only this existed.

He held her tenderly and his gaze locked with hers.

Each touch seemed to value her deeply, each moment of delight seemed to bring them closer.

Time ceased to exist. Nothing existed but the two of them. His touch. Their shared kisses. And more…

A crescendo built—until finally she looked deep into his eyes and felt that their souls must have merged as they yielded together.

Held in his arms in the afterglow, Cecilia asked herself how she could feel as though her world had stopped still and as if Linc held the key to all that she was and would ever be. This didn't feel like 'closure' from her six-year-old feelings.

Inside her was a burgeoning emotion. It spread through her heart until she felt overtaken by it. She realised in that moment that she had fallen deeply and irrevocably in love with Linc. Rather than having closed the chapter, she had unleashed this.

The knowledge was so large, so all-encompassing, that she thought he must surely sense it. She tensed, and her breath stopped. Because he mustn't know. Not now. Not until she could come to terms with this and know how to deal with it.

She *loved* him! Loved him in a way that would dictate her wanting to be with him and be part of his life forever. No, not just part. She would want to be right there in the centre of his world, and him in hers, living out life *together*.

Linc gave a deep sigh and drew her gently closer, encouraging her to curl into his arms. He seemed close to sleep as he placed a soft kiss in her hair.

'Your hair is beautiful. It's so soft.'

The echo of his earlier words reverberated.

She thought he'd also whispered that she humbled him, that he didn't know himself right then.

She realised that Hugh was the chapter that had been closed completely. That had been a weak shadow of real emotion in the first place, and it was now so completely gone. She had wanted true love, but Hugh had not been that.

Cecilia understood this now because of the man who held her and the love she held for him.

How would she face tomorrow?

She closed her eyes and willed the thought away.

Exhaustion won out at long last.

She slept.

CHAPTER TEN

'I SHOULD BE at the nursery, making sure my staff are safe and continuing with preparations for the masked ball.'

Cecilia spoke with emphasis as she addressed her words to the small group gathered in the rooftop garden area at Linc's family's warehouse building the next morning.

'How can I hide myself away and leave them vulnerable?'

It was still early. Linc had called this family meeting to put the situation to his brothers and sisters-in-law and seek their collective input.

Cecilia had agreed to the meeting. In truth, it had seemed easier than trying to deal with her new-found emotions alone with Linc at his city apartment. But those emotions were still there, and so were the demands of the rest of her life.

It was clear Linc wanted to gain his family's support in convincing her to stay out of the limelight. Linc had said as much when he'd woken that morning and joined her in his kitchen, where she'd been already showered, dressed and waiting to tell him she *had* to go to work.

All the shock and uncertainty she had been too exhausted to process late last night, in those incredulous moments when she had realised she'd fallen in love with Linc, had awoken her before dawn, determined to make themselves well and truly known again and demand that she work out what to do about them.

As she'd showered and dressed, a need to be by herself and process this new knowledge had overwhelmed her to such a degree that she hadn't known how she could even face Linc.

She loved him.

There could be no future for them.

Her heart was breaking.

All her heart and emotions, everything she had inside her, had fallen in love with one amazing man. That was the beautiful part...the wonderful, incredible part.

But Linc hadn't expressed those emotions—had not at any point in time led her to believe that he had fallen for her. On the contrary, he had tried not to yield to the deepening attraction and interest between them, and last night he had warned her...

She had to acknowledge that if they'd not been through such an emotionally charged day yesterday, in all likelihood he would have continued to avoid taking things further between them.

And his succumbing to temptation did not mean that his emotions had changed whatsoever. That part shattered her heart all over again.

Cecilia caught his gaze. Oh, it was so hard now to look into the grey eyes that had looked into hers in the very moments before she'd realised she loved him!

The only thing Cecilia could think of to do was

hiding herself in her work and finding distance from him so she could shore up her defences.

'Linc, you said yourself that you've assigned a security team to the nursery, so there shouldn't be any problems with me going back to work today.'

You have to let me go. I can't be in your company—especially not just the two of us, shut away from the world. Not yet. Not now. Not ever. And I can't think of that right now, either!

She needed to gather her strength and figure out how to go forward from here.

'I should be safe enough at the nursery with a security detail in place. And if I'm not, then my staff aren't, either!'

This was a genuine concern, and it made complete sense to her.

Until Jayne spoke.

'I have to agree with Linc.' Concern for Cecilia shone in Jayne's eyes. 'At least for today allow the security team at the nursery to monitor things and give some feedback as to whether anything odd or unusual occurs. It would be better if you didn't go back to your workplace, Cecilia. You'd be distracting them from being able to watch the others as well as they would without you there.'

Cecilia's hopes fell. 'I hadn't considered that…'

She *should* have considered that. It should have been completely obvious to her.

Linc heard Cecilia respond to Jayne's comment and silently thanked his sister-in-law for voicing the concerns that he shared. But Cecilia looked so crestfallen as she acknowledged Jayne's point, and—as they had done since he'd first woken that morning—

Linc's emotions churned. He'd thought that he could give himself last night. That if he made sure Cecilia understood there would be no tomorrow it would be okay. He'd convinced himself he could do it without causing hurt, provided he was honest about it at the start.

If all that was true, then why did he feel so empty inside right now? Why did he feel that he'd lost something wonderful? And Cecilia... She didn't look happy and fulfilled—as though she'd been able to answer a question that had been in her mind and now could happily move on. She looked as though she wanted to run as far and as fast as she could.

What if she did? What if she took up the offer from the Silver Bells committee and left him?

You mean if she left working for you.

Either would have the same result. She would disappear out of his life, and he wouldn't see her any more.

Panic tightened Linc's chest. He couldn't let that happen!

So help her sort out these issues and, the first chance you get, talk to her about last night. Tell her how it made you feel. Tell her you want more.

But Linc couldn't *have* more. He glanced across the room at his brothers. He could *not* have more.

'It's still early.' Linc offered the words quietly.

There was still the situation of a dangerous man who had threatened harm to Cecilia, and that situation had to be managed, whether Linc had other things preying on his mind or not.

So he waited until Cecilia finally raised her gaze to his, and then he said, 'We have time to contact Jem-

mie, to let her know the basics of the situation and ask
her if she'll be comfortable taking charge for today
while the security team do their thing. I am confident she and the others will be protected if anything
does transpire.'

'I have to work.' Cecilia's words held an agitated
edge. 'It's not that I believe the nursery can't get
along without me—certainly for one day, anyway—
although the timing isn't great. I just can't spend the
day in idleness with nothing to do but think.'

The others would believe she wanted to avoid
thinking about the man on the loose, her sister's plight
and of course those things *would* be causing her worry
and stress. And she *would* think about them if left to
her own devices.

Somehow Linc had lost sight of that for a bit—
had failed to remember all the pressure that would
be weighing on Cecilia's shoulders today.

He felt selfish in that moment, to have believed all
her thoughts would be of what they had shared. Last
night he could have controlled that situation—not allowed it to reach the conclusion it had.

Yet even as he thought this, Linc knew it wasn't
true. For the first time in his life he had *not* been able
to fight his way out of core emotions that had been
so strong.

Cecilia sought his gaze and held it. 'You know I
need to be at work. I can't possibly— I need—'

'Whatever you need, you will have. I will make
this work for you, Cecilia.'

He simply made that commitment to her. Linc was
a man who'd struggled, triumphed, lost, loved, given
and been blessed beyond anything he'd imagined his

life could be. The family he, Alex and Brent had built out of the ashes of abandonment had saved Linc.

If Cecilia needed space, he could give her that and still keep her secure. He could help her, even while he tried to sort out his own emotions.

Linc felt a degree of calmness return as he realised he could do this.

Cecilia heard Linc's words and felt the kindness and care in them. Oh, she wanted so much to believe that those words came out of a deeply held love for her, but she knew Linc would do this even if they had never shared so much as a kiss.

Don't think about it. Not yet.

She glanced about at the gathered group. 'I'm grateful to all of you. None of you needed to weigh in on this but you did so without hesitating, and that means the world to me. I just—' For one panicky moment she thought she might choke into tears in front of them all. 'I need—'

'Not to have everything taken away at once?' Brent broke in.

'Not to feel overwhelmed with pressure?' Fiona added. She turned her gaze towards Linc. 'You're quite certain everyone at the nursery will be safe?'

'I don't believe anyone could get past the teams that are in place.' Linc's words were resolute. 'But I still have to take every precaution, and because the guy threatened Cecilia directly, made it clear his grudge is towards her specifically, I can't make that same guarantee for her.'

When he went on, it was as though he had focused inwardly.

'I've made the mistake in the past of letting a bully

harm someone—' He broke off and his gaze rested on Alex. 'That was unforgivable, and I will not ever allow it to happen again.'

'That was a long time ago, and it wasn't even your—' Alex got halfway to his feet.

'Worry about it later, Alex.' Brent cut him off almost sharply. 'We need to focus on the current issue.'

What had Linc meant? And why had his words caused Alex to respond in that way, and Brent to cut the conversation off completely?

Brent spoke again before Cecilia could think any further. 'We've established that the security team should be able to cope and that they'll need at least today to observe without the bulk of their attention being on keeping Cecilia safe.'

'Yeah. We have.' Linc turned his gaze to Cecilia. 'I'm sorry, but that's where I stand on it. I'd shut the place down rather than have you there today.'

She knew that he would, and she paused to consider and then reject that option. 'I'd rather avoid that, if possible. It would only draw more attention to the fact that there's a problem.'

'I have what I hope will be a tolerable second option for you.'

As Linc spoke the words he could only be grateful for his family and for the support they'd given by rallying around this morning. Last night had thrown him so far off balance he'd been concerned that he might miss something or make a poor decision.

Linc didn't feel worried about that any more, but he was still thankful.

'I'll bring some of your repurposing items here. You can work on them today and stay for as long as is needed. You'll have access to the phone and internet, so you'll be able to give support to Jemmie remotely, as well.'

This apartment was large. They could work all day and barely see each other if they chose.

'Great idea.' Brent nodded his approval.

'We can take turns coming here if you need to go away anywhere, Linc.' Alex added his thoughts.

'I'll agree to that plan—for today at least.' Cecilia didn't love it, but if she could busy herself that would help. She caught each person's gaze in turn. 'Thank you all for—for caring.'

At least by accepting this today, she would ensure that Linc's relatives didn't do dangerous things such as turning up at the plant nursery, where protection would be more difficult, wanting to express their support for her. Given their care and concern this morning, she wouldn't put it past them!

'Being able to do my repurposing here would be ideal—just while we're waiting to see how the security team are feeling about things.' She filled her tone with determination.

'Thanks, everyone. Why don't we make a start on breakfast?' It was Linc who made the suggestion. 'I'll head to the nursery to collect some of Cecilia's items. I've got the truck downstairs. I haven't had it out for a while. It will be a good chance to give it a run and for me to check in with the security team at the same time.'

'You'll keep safe?'

Cecilia wanted to go with him but knew that he wasn't inviting her and that he wouldn't do so. She had to stay out of the limelight, whether she wanted to or not.

'I'll phone Jemmie and bring her up to speed.'

'Remember that you don't have to tell her about anything more than the threat itself if you don't want to.' Linc turned the grey-eyed gaze on her that was now so familiar and dear. His words were protective, but perhaps only she could hear that? Or was she making it up because she wanted to believe it?

A moment later Linc had gone, and Cecilia was left with his loving, amazing family, all examining her with interested gazes.

'Will you excuse me if I step away to make the call to my assistant manager?' She grasped at this plan a little desperately and hoped her emotions—the ones that related to Linc, at least—weren't all over her face.

Hopefully, Linc wouldn't be gone too long.

Hopefully, Cecilia would soon get control over these new feelings for Linc that had thrown her so profoundly off balance. Maybe she only *thought* she felt this way due to the stress of the current circumstances?

Dream on, Cecilia.

Fine—then she would focus on what had to be done today, one step and one moment at a time, until sooner or later she would get some time to herself and figure out how to deal with these feelings, protecting herself from heartbreak in the process. There had to be a way.

Cecilia stepped away and phoned Jemmie.

CHAPTER ELEVEN

'THEY NEED TO catch this guy.'

Cecilia spoke the words after jumping when the fridge in Linc's kitchen gave a shuddering sound at the end of its auto-defrost cycle.

She went on. 'Either that or I'm going to turn into a complete, neurotic mess.'

It was the following evening. They'd agreed that they would go in to the plant nursery for the day that morning.

Doing so hadn't been as easy as Cecilia had thought it would be. She'd spent all day looking over her shoulder and worrying. Was everyone safe? Could the security team really cope, no matter what happened? Was Stacey truly safe in the correctional facility? What if Linc was holding off talking about the night they'd shared because he didn't want to let her down when she was relying on staying at his home until she could be safe elsewhere?

And so it had gone—all of yesterday and even more today—until finally they'd returned to his apartment to a dinner prepared and left for them by Linc's housekeeper, Rosa.

Cecilia was once again only picking at her food.

There seemed to be a permanent lump lodged in her throat.

Linc watched Cecilia push food around her plate and couldn't deny the relief of having her back here, where it was a whole lot easier to keep an eye on her. All except for the fact that they were now alone, and he'd had all day today and all of yesterday to think about what they'd shared, and all he'd been able to think was what if he'd made such a mess of things that he couldn't turn that around?

'You've got every right to be jumpy.' He stood, cleared their plates and they made their way to the living room.

'I had a call from Stacey today.' She settled into an armchair as he took his place on the sofa. 'It came through while you were doing a check with the security team.'

'How was she?'

'She's okay. She's had several conversations with the police.' Cecilia paused and worried at her lip with her teeth. 'It's been done discreetly, and she's really hoping what she's told them will help them catch the guy.'

'You never stop thinking about her, do you?' It was an observation as well as a question.

'Only when—' Cecilia stopped and shook her head. 'Stacey's very important to me,' she said instead. 'That will never change. I know it's the same for you with Brent and Alex. You love them deeply.'

Her voice held a hint of wistful longing, but all Linc heard was praise for his caring nature. He didn't want to tell her the truth, and yet he couldn't withhold it.

You'll lose her. She won't want you if you tell her what happened. It will be one more rejection in your life, and this time you'll deserve it.

'I *do* love Brent and Alex.' At least he could say that much with absolute assurance. He forced himself to go on. 'But there was a time when I abandoned Alex. He suffered because of my self-interest—because I put what I wanted before making sure he was okay.'

'I can't imagine that, Linc.' Surprise tinged her words.

Linc felt ill. He'd been asking himself how he could hold on to Cecilia, but he knew he didn't have the right to that kind of wonderful relationship. He shouldn't have allowed himself to ignore that fact. Not for a moment.

'I ignored him for weeks on end when he was at his most vulnerable and needed me to be there for him.'

'What—what happened?' Concern filled her expression.

'I was the oldest, and as a result the first to leave the orphanage—though I was able to get Brent out soon after. I got Brent a job. Alex, because he was younger...'

'He had to wait before he could join you?' Her expression showed empathy. 'It must have been tough, having to leave him there?'

'It wasn't as tough for me as it should have been.'

Linc had never discussed this. Not even with Brent, back when it had all unfolded. Not his emotions about it. He hadn't needed to say anything. He'd done something profoundly selfish and wrong, and he'd shoved that acknowledgment deep down inside himself where it would never leave him. Where it belonged.

'I was so focused on making money as fast as I could. Instead of paying attention to what was happening to Alex, I let weeks go by without checking on him.'

He'd allowed the old adage of 'out of sight, out of mind' to take hold in him.

Cecilia's expression sobered. 'Go on.'

'Brent had been keeping closer contact with Alex, but he got some work that took him away for a month.' Here Linc's eyes clouded over, as though in remembered pain. 'He came and saw me one night and asked me to make sure I visited Alex often. Brent was worried about a new employee the orphanage had taken on. He thought the man could be violent. With him going away, he knew he couldn't keep an eye on him.'

'Oh, Linc...' Cecilia wasn't sure that she *did* want to know the rest.

'I checked on Alex just once—asked if he was doing okay.' Linc shook his head. 'I asked him if he'd mind if I didn't come in much because I was so busy. He didn't want me to worry or feel I had to leave my work because of him, so he told me everything was fine.'

'But it wasn't?' Cecilia almost whispered the words.

Linc forced the rest out. 'When I finally visited Alex again, he was trying to hide that his ribs were bruised.' Linc closed his eyes for a moment. 'That man had beaten Alex where he knew no person would be able to see it. He'd done it because he was mean and because he could—and I'd allowed it to happen.

I didn't listen when Brent expressed his concerns, and I put it on Alex to tell me whether something was wrong or not. And he didn't want to stop me being able to work.'

The self-condemnation and the agony of what had occurred while Linc should have been on watch were rife in his tone as well as in his words.

'Oh, Linc. You must have been devastated.' She offered the words carefully, and she had to add, 'But surely you know that might have happened even if you *were* visiting? Unfortunately, there are people in this world who do such things any chance they get.'

'I took Alex straight out of there, of course.' Linc said it as though there couldn't possibly have been any other option. 'I walked him out on the spot and consequences be damned. Brent and I kept him hidden until he was old enough that the authorities couldn't take him from us. It was only a few months. Why didn't I do that in the first place?'

'Because you didn't know.'

Cecilia could only imagine how he must have felt—how hard it must have been for Linc to face Brent as well, knowing that he'd failed to give the situation the attention he should have at the time.

'You removed Alex from the threat as soon as you could. That was a *good* thing.'

'Yeah, but way too late.' Linc shook his head, as though that just hadn't been enough. 'He'd been beaten for trying to protect one of the smaller kids.'

'You know, none of us are infallible—'

'Not like this.' His tone was harsh and filled with self-directed censure. 'I left my brother there to be harmed—and I did it even though Brent had brought his concerns to my attention. Thanks to me, Alex ended up being preyed on by that guy. And it wasn't just about the physical beating. There are emotional scars from things like that, which last much longer.'

Had Linc and Alex talked about this? Did Alex blame Linc? Cecilia couldn't imagine that. In fact, she was convinced that Alex not only would have forgiven him long ago, but that he would never have blamed Linc in the first place.

'It sounds to me as though Alex had the bravery to step in where a lot of other young boys wouldn't have to protect the other children.'

'I guess that's the irony.' Linc glanced at his hands before his gaze met hers again. 'Brent and me, we raised him well in there. His ethics were rock solid.'

Yet Linc couldn't let himself experience anything that resembled forgiveness for his own actions. Cecilia could see that very clearly now.

His words as he went on confirmed it. 'It was way too easy for me to forget about him. I've had to conclude it's a character flaw in myself.' He drew a breath. 'There's something wrong—wrong in me— to make me able to do that. They chose to become my brothers, and I let them down. I don't deserve the kind of happiness they've found.'

Cecilia realised in that moment that this was Linc's morning-after talk. He'd gone away and thought about what they'd shared, and he'd ruled out the possibility of any kind of a future for them because this part of his history was insurmountable for him. He couldn't forgive himself. He believed there was a flaw in his make-up that made him unworthy.

Oh, Linc. How could you believe that about your-self when you're such a good person?

Yes, he'd made a mistake—but people did that. He'd been young! He'd also been breaking himself, trying to secure things so they could all be safe, so he could make a life for all of them outside of their horrid upbringing.

Had Linc thought about and longed for a future with Cecilia as she had with him? Was that why he was saying all this now?

Cecilia couldn't let herself think that he was say-ing it because he'd realised how she felt about him.

As she hesitated, trying to formulate words, trying to know what to say, to understand where she stood and try to figure out what to do, Linc got to his feet.

'I had to tell you.' He seemed to be experienc-ing a deep pain but also to be resolute. He drew a breath. 'The time we shared together was the most precious I've experienced in my life, but I shouldn't have allowed it to happen and…and I can't let it hap-pen again. You understand why now. You deserve more. I hope you'll forgive me.'

Linc left the room.

'We may still have no news on our wanted man, but I *can* give you some good news about the nursery.' Linc spoke the words the following day as he sat back from his computer.

They were in Cecilia's small office at the plant nursery. Cecilia wasn't as jumpy as she'd been the day before. Maybe she should have been, but she'd had very little sleep…and her heart hurt. She suspected that if she let herself feel everything to the depths that she could at the moment, she might break down.

She'd made her decision. There was no other choice that she could see. Her love for Linc would never be returned. She was trying to accept it, to be grateful that he didn't know how she felt. But mostly she was just trying to hold a great wall of pain at bay.

What news could Linc have? They were going ahead with the masked ball. They hadn't told anyone other than their staff about the issues going on. If need be, they would bring in the biggest contingent of undercover security any place had ever seen, but they *would* go ahead.

Cecilia couldn't actually think of any other good news to do with the nursery. She had news for Linc that would affect the nursery, but she doubted he would want to hear that. Then again, maybe it would be an answer to his prayers.

She forced her gaze up and away from her inspection of the catering lists spread across the desk in front of her. It wasn't easy to look at Linc, but she did it.

'What is it?'

'I've finished the review, and it should be no surprise to you that everything's fine.' He drew a breath. 'I'm more than happy to agree to the percentage share in the nursery that you proposed when you initially approached me about doing this review.'

For a moment she simply didn't comprehend his words—and then they sank in.

'I'm grateful for that, Linc, truly I am…'

She fought to say the rest of the words that needed to be said and to keep her chin up while she did it. Now was the perfect time. So she went on.

'But I won't be taking the offer up after all.'

She couldn't stay here—be here while Linc reverted to stopping in periodically, expecting her update calls as he'd done before this review had started. It wouldn't matter whether those visits took place weekly or were months apart. Or that those phone calls would be all about business. She would hurt a little more each time she saw him. Because loving someone who didn't share those feelings would do that to her.

Cecilia understood his self-blame over his brother, his belief that he wasn't deserving of love. But she *did* love him. And it hurt her every single moment to know that in the end he simply didn't share those feelings.

If he did, he would fight for her, whether he regretted his past or not.

'I thought you were just keeping a presence here today because of the safety issues—though I am pleased about the review results.' She met his gaze. 'It's just that I've decided to take up the offer from the Silver Bells flower show committee. I'm going to work for them. Actually, I'm planning to leave here as soon as the masked ball is over. In the end…it's best. I'm— It's an exciting new opportunity for me, really.'

She felt like two people. The one sitting there, saying those words and trying to appear calm, as though this was what she wanted to do, and the one who loved Linc and was being torn apart by that love.

'If this is because—' Linc's words were strained.

'I've just realised I'm ready for a change.' She pushed the lie past her teeth. This was harder than she had thought it would be, and she prayed that she wouldn't break down.

Linc got to his feet. 'I—I wish you well. Would you excuse me, Cecilia? I need—'

He didn't say what it was that he needed. Linc simply left the room.

CHAPTER TWELVE

'IT LOOKS GOOD, LINC.'

Alex made the comment as he and Linc stood back from the area in the centre of Fleurmazing's signature maze, which now held a fully constructed and functional raised and canopied dais, in readiness for the masked ball that would commence three hours from now.

'People are going to love it. And you can relax now, knowing that guy has been caught.'

When Alex had learned that Linc was planning to assist with the construction of the dais, he'd put his hand up to come along and help. Linc hadn't really wanted the company, yet Alex's presence had done him good.

Now the construction was finished, and it was just the two of them admiring the result of their handiwork.

Linc glanced at Alex. 'He was picked up in New Zealand. He'll face charges and do jail time over there. It's looking like at least a decade of accumulated charges.'

'He won't be allowed back into Australia after that.' Alex said it with certainty. 'How's Cecilia taking all of this?' His gaze focused on the maze beyond the dais as he went on. 'She must feel as though she's been put through a wringer, one way and another.'

'What do you mean by that?' Linc asked the question too quickly before he realised Alex probably meant nothing at all beyond the comment itself. 'Sorry. It's been a tense time. Cecilia is visiting her sister this afternoon at the correctional centre. I'm sure she's relieved the guy's been caught.'

'You don't sound real convinced about her state of happiness, brother.'

Those words drew Linc's gaze to Alex, and he saw his younger brother was looking right at him now.

Alex searched his face. 'Yet seeing the two of you together just days ago, I would have thought maybe both of you were on the brink of something special.'

Linc didn't even ask himself how Alex had discerned that. 'I'm not enough for her. She's better off without me.'

'That's the most foolish rubbish I've heard in all the time I've known you.' Alex's words were sharp. 'Give me one good reason for that belief.'

'When the chips are down, I just think about myself.' Linc fired the volley straight back.

He wanted to tell Alex to keep out of this and mind his own business. His heart hurt, and Alex prodding around in his emotions wasn't helping. Instead, he flayed himself with their shared past.

'You of all people ought to know that—considering you were the one who suffered thanks to my self-interest.'

Instead of backing off, Alex took a step closer to Linc to emphasise his response. 'It wasn't until recently that I even realised you blamed yourself for what happened way back when I was still in the orphanage. Brent and I always believed you were so locked down about it at the time because you were rightly angry—infuriated that such a piece of scum existed and had got into that place to smack around little kids. Just as we were.'

'He preyed on you because I failed to keep watch. I failed to protect you—'

'You're not to blame. *You* weren't the person who bullied me, who had been bullying other kids, as well.'

'I should have made time to visit you. You and Brent let me into your lives.' Linc said it with all the pain he'd carried for so long. 'You chose to accept me as a brother. I was the oldest. I had a responsibility to look after both of you, and in your case I failed.'

'You mean while you were working yourself into the ground so you'd be able to provide for me once I was old enough to leave?'

Ah, don't make me out to be a hero, Alex.

'I don't think you and Brent realise,' Linc said slowly. 'You saved me. I don't believe I could have handled that place without you both.'

He'd have died from lack of love without them. Maybe not immediately, maybe not for all his lifetime, but inside he'd have died.

Alex's gaze held his as he responded, 'We all saved each other. Do you think I shouldn't have married Jayne because I wasn't good enough for my parents to want to keep me? Or that Brent shouldn't have found happiness with Fiona because his father shoved him into that place just as yours did you? Do you think we're not good enough? Because it seems if you think that way about yourself, that's how you think about us.'

'It's not like that. You're twisting the situation.'

And yet...

'This can't just be about me punishing myself.' Linc said it slowly. 'If it is, then I've been using it as an excuse—'

To avoid something?

To avoid letting himself love in case he wasn't loved in return?

'I love her.' He uttered it with complete knowledge. 'I love Cecilia.'

And he'd pushed her away. Shoved her away hard in case—God forbid—she might love him in return. She'd handed in her resignation. After tonight she would be cut off from him.

Alex gripped his arm for a moment, and then let go. 'Brent and I both love you, Linc. We want you to be happy. Neither of us blame you for the past. You held the three of us together and you should be damn proud of that fact. Just know that the past is the past. If we can both let go of it, so should you.'

As Alex started to leave the area, he turned and a satisfied smile came over his face. 'Remember how we all went back to the orphanage the night after you got me out? It was probably wrong of us, but we were going to dish out a bit of justice of our own to that guy?'

'Yeah.' Linc remembered. 'The police were there. One of the little kids you'd protected had sneaked into the office and made the call before we could— had told them the guy was there, beating everyone.'

'The orphanage was shut down and the kids got

shifted into better situations. Most of them got placed into loving families.' Alex raised his brows. 'Do you think that would have happened if I hadn't been beaten that one time? For me, personally, I reckon that was worth it.'

Alex left then.

Linc felt humbled. And he had to ask himself: *had* he been hiding behind the guilt from his past in order to refuse to let himself look ahead and hope for the future? Had he been afraid to love because he hadn't been loved by his father?

If that was the case, had he left it too late to do something about it? Had he lost Cecilia forever?

Because in his heart of hearts he knew that he loved Cecilia with everything in him. That the idea of a life without her in it filled him with pain. That he wanted happiness with her if he could find it, and if she would be willing to take him on and try.

The masked ball was hours away.

Linc needed a plan.

He strode from the nursery.

CHAPTER THIRTEEN

'THANKS, JEMMIE, for all your help.'

Cecilia couldn't believe the evening of the masked ball was here at last. But everything was in place. Jemmie had stayed after hours to give Cecilia time to go home and change in readiness for the ball itself, but now Cecilia was back, the guests would arrive within the hour and Cecilia's heart was so torn she didn't know where to start.

Jemmie said her goodbyes and left the office. At the entrance of the nursery, members of the Silver Bells flower show committee had started to gather. They would greet the guests and send them into the maze to begin what Cecilia hoped would prove to be a magical adventure for each of them.

All Cecilia had to do was get through this night, hold it together and then…

Leave.

Make a complete new start somewhere she'd have some hope of forgetting Linc.

The pressure for tonight to be perfect was even greater because she knew she would be leaving. She wanted to give Linc this one last thing and do it really well. Not that he would see it. With the way things had gone, there was no way he would be here.

But he would hear about tonight and know she'd done a good job.

With a sigh, Cecilia stepped out into the courtyard area, locked the office door after her and made her way into the maze. It was time to go to where the dais had been raised, to check everything one last time and then, as the guests finally began to arrive, to smile and make sure each of them had a night to remember.

Cecilia lifted the delicate mask she held in one hand and placed it over her face.

Maybe it would hide her heartache.

Linc shifted from foot to foot where he stood at the edge of the dais area. He straightened his bow tie and hoped he would be able to carry this off when Cecilia arrived. It was difficult not to feel foolish wearing a mask that the woman in the shop had said made him look like—what was it?—*some swashbuckling hero*?

He just wanted to see Cecilia and to let her know that he loved her. He hoped with all his heart that she might be able to return those feelings, that he hadn't messed things up so badly he couldn't come back from it. But this night meant a lot to Cecilia, so he wanted to be sure that he looked the part.

Linc had told Cecilia about Alex. The guilt Linc had felt had been very real, but Alex had shown Linc that he'd been holding on to that past experience and blaming himself for being human. That he needed to let go of it and reach out for his own happiness. That he had to trust that he could be loved and accepted— just as Brent and Alex loved and accepted him and were themselves loved and accepted.

Behind Linc the string quartet finished tuning up

and began to play a soft, haunting melody. He had asked them to come earlier, to be ready to start playing and keep playing once Cecilia arrived.

Rosa had given him a crash course in waltzing. She'd patted his face and hadn't asked why. She was the closest thing to a mother that Linc could remember.

The rows upon rows of lights in the canopied cover above the dais came on, lending a soft glow to the fading twilight.

In that moment Cecilia stepped out of the maze and he saw her—and, oh, she looked so beautiful. A shimmering deep gold gown made her seem as one with her surroundings. Gold sandals covered her feet, and her hair was piled high on her head. Her mask of gold and blue highlighted her beautiful eyes.

She also looked fragile, as though the weight of this world sat on her shoulders.

Could she love him?

Linc's chest expanded with all the love he felt for her.

She spotted him standing there and, for just a moment, her step faltered and surprise made her eyes round.

Linc stepped down from the dais and quickly walked to greet her.

Don't leave. Don't walk away before I've had a chance to tell you—

'Cecilia. You look beautiful.'

She did. He wanted to see her in all her stages of beauty, all throughout their lives.

Her gaze searched his face. 'Thank you. I didn't think you'd be here.'

Along with the strain, did her gaze show pleasure that he was there? Or did Linc just long to see that?

'I had to come.'

As he looked at her, he knew he wanted—no, he *needed* to wake up beside her every day, forever. He needed that as much as breathing. And he hoped with all his might that she would give him that chance.

'Will you dance with me, Cecilia? Now? Before the guests start arriving?'

He held out his hand.

The string ensemble began the strains of a waltz.

Cecilia searched his face. He thought she would say no, but after a long moment she silently put her hand in his.

Linc released the breath he'd been holding and led her onto the dais. He drew Cecilia into his arms, and they circled the floor together. His arms had hurt from the lack of holding her, and now there was this symmetry, this beauty of touch and music and movement. She matched his steps perfectly, and it was effortless and so right.

He looked down into her upturned face, into the dark blue pools of her eyes, and knew that he could trust his heart in her care just as much as he wanted to care for her heart forever.

Cecilia gazed into Linc's eyes as they moved around the dance floor. She heard the quartet playing, but she saw nothing but Linc, felt nothing but the touch of his hand holding hers, his other hand against her back.

The scent of flowers kissed by the cooling night air surrounded them. Everything was perfect. She wanted to cry and never stop crying, and still she hadn't been able to deny herself this.

Oh, she had not expected to be held in Linc's arms, to be whisked about the dais as though she and no one else meant the world to him.

Please don't break my heart all over again, Linc. I don't know why you're doing this.

Why had Linc come here, asked her for this dance? She wanted to hope—and that was the most dangerous and heartbreaking thing she could do!

She'd prepared herself to leave him, to try and mend her heart away from him and, when this dance was over, that was still exactly what she had to do.

Eventually, the dance came to an end. Linc led her off the floor. 'Will you walk with me in the maze for a minute? I need to talk to you.'

'All—all right.' His serious tone made her heart thump.

'This is where I found you that first day of the review.' Linc spoke the words quietly.

She looked around her and realised they were in front of the statue of the sun goddess. Her favourite part of the maze. All of a sudden the affinity she felt with this place, with the work she'd put in, her vision and seeing her dreams come true here all welled up, and that sorrow added itself to the sorrow of unrequited love.

She started to speak before she could stop herself. 'I'll miss—'

'You remind me of her tonight.'

He spoke at the same time, and his gaze briefly rested on the statue before it returned to Cecilia.

'It's not just the colour of your dress.' He seemed

to search for words to express his thoughts. 'It's how you are inside yourself. You spread light. You warm people.'

The words weren't flattery. They were far deeper than that.

She searched his gaze. 'That's a lovely thing for you to say.'

Linc had his chance now, and he didn't want to blow it. He pulled the mask from his face and gently removed hers, dropping them both at the foot of the statue. There were some things that just couldn't be said with barriers in place.

'We've known each other for a long time...'

He started there, because that had been the start of their journey.

'Back then, when we first met...' She'd shown an interest in him and he'd rebuffed her. 'I was convinced I didn't deserve love and a happy-ever-after. I didn't know it at the time, but I was using it as an excuse.'

Linc paused for a moment. He took her hand in his and cherished the connection, the simple sense of rightness the touch gave him.

'I've realised that I *wanted* to blame myself.'

Her fingers tightened on his for an instant, and she frowned. 'Why?'

'Because it let me hold back from people other than my brothers.' He'd been afraid of being hurt. The big, strong millionaire Linc MacKay hadn't known how to protect his emotions, so he'd used that as an excuse to hold them at bay from the world. 'I didn't want to risk being given up on again, as my father gave up on me.'

'How others behave towards us can have a pro-found impact.' Cecilia's words were open and honest, and she knew she had to go on. 'Our mother telling us repeatedly that we were a burden on her not only harmed Stacey and helped her along the path of self-destruction that led her to where she is today, it also harmed me.'

It had. More than Cecilia had ever wanted to admit.

'I had very little faith that a loving relationship could be built and could last. When I tried to form one with…with Hugh, and he disappeared out of my life the moment things got challenging, it not only damaged my faith in others but my belief in myself that I was worth sticking around for.'

'And I added to that—both six years ago and re-cently.'

Linc's words were low, filled with remorse. Yet as he spoke, his expression became determined and his grip on her hands firmed.

'I'm in love with you, Cecilia. I'm worried sick that I've left it too late to tell you, but I love you with all my heart and I want us to be together.'

Cecilia stared at Linc mutely. All her breath seemed to have escaped from her lungs. She dragged in air. 'Wh-what did you say?'

'I love you.' The truth of it shone from his eyes. 'I'm *in love* with you. Is there any chance, Cecilia? Any chance at all that you might come to return those feelings? I want to spend the rest of my life with you. When you said you were leaving, I felt as though my world was ending.'

'Six years ago I was attracted to you…' Cecilia said it slowly, remembering that time, the immaturity of her emotions. 'But it took coming to know you closely for me to…to totally fall in love with you.'

Linc's gaze searched her face. 'I want to marry you—have children, God willing—and grow old together. I want to love you for the rest of our lives. Please tell me there's hope for that.'

Cecilia might have hesitated on the brink of Linc's proposal but, oh, she wouldn't. She simply would not—because this was worth the risk. This was worth reaching out for.

Linc was worth it.

'Yes.' She broke into a smile that was full of love and relief and happiness. 'Oh, yes, Linc. That is what I'm saying. I want all of those things, too. With *you*. It's what I want more than anything.'

'You've made me the happiest man in the world.'

The relief and acceptance in his voice showed his belief in those words. And the kiss they shared was filled with all the hope and relief and joy they both felt. Cecilia finally believed then—and, oh, it felt good to do so!

As they finally drew apart, Linc asked her, 'Will you still go to work for the Silver Bells committee?'

She searched his gaze and thought for a moment. 'Do you know, I think I will? But if you don't mind too much, I might like to take that on part-time and work on my refurbishment projects the rest of the time.'

'From our home?'

As she nodded, a smile spread over his face.

'I already do a lot of my work from home.' He looked a little sheepish. 'I'm not all that keen on the idea of working out of an office full of staff. We could work from home together...take coffee breaks and do what we liked. The warehouse—'

'Would make a perfect home for us.'

Happiness welled up inside Cecilia, and she couldn't contain it. She reached out for him, and they hugged each other for long moments before they once more drew apart.

Linc reached into his pocket and brought out a small velvet box. He dropped to one knee. His fingers shook as he opened the box and held it out to her.

'Will you marry me and accept this ring as a token of my love for you?'

Cecilia understood his vulnerability then. Knew that they could walk through life together and strengthen each other, that they truly could be stronger and greater together than either of them could ever have been on their own. Her heart opened up to all they could have and be, and she gently received the box from him.

Inside nestled a solitaire engagement ring. The band was white gold, its design cut low, to give all the attention to the glittering jewel it held.

'Oh, Linc, it's lovely.'

His quiet exhalation held both satisfaction and a hint of relief.

He got to his feet and clasped her left hand in his own. 'I'm glad you like it. I bought it today. When I saw it, I thought it was the right one for you. I had to plan, to hope you'd say yes, that it wasn't all too late. I had to put my faith on the line.'

She closed her eyes. 'Oh, Linc. I love you so. I thought I would never have the chance to tell you, let alone to think about a future together.'

'And I thought I'd lost any chance with you by being buried in fears from the past.' He blew out a breath that seemed to let the last of his tension go.

And then he slipped the ring from the box and onto her finger, and she realised it was possible that she could adore him even more.

'It fits perfectly, Linc. Like it was meant to be there. I will be proud to wear this, and every time I look at it I will remember this night and this moment.'

'The start of our future together.' Linc liked the thought a great deal.

Beyond them, they heard the murmur of the first guests entering into the beginning of the maze and knew that the masked ball was truly about to begin.

'Shall we give everyone—and ourselves—a night to remember?'

Linc retrieved their masks from where they rested at the foot of the statue.

Cecilia donned her mask and smiled a little to herself as Linc donned his and immediately took on the persona of a man of mystery.

He was *her* man now, not at all a mystery to her any more, and she liked that fact just fine.

'Yes, Linc. Let's make this a night to remember.'

They made their way back to the dance floor and, as other people arrived, one after another, the first thing they saw was a couple obviously deeply in love with each other, circling the floor in each other's arms to the strains of a beautiful waltz.

It was indeed a night to remember.

EPILOGUE

'DO YOU, LINC MACKAY, take this woman, Cecilia Anna Tomson, to be your lawfully wedded wife?'

The celebrant's words rang out in the beautiful country chapel. She went on, adding words of love and fidelity, commitment and forever.

Cecilia stood before Linc in her wedding gown and knew that her love for him was written all over her, and she didn't care one bit that it was!

Linc's words were low and heartfelt as he responded, 'I do.'

It was Cecilia's turn then, and she saw her sister's hands shake where she stood to her left, holding Cecilia's bouquet of perfect creamy roses and baby's breath along with her own bouquet of deep red blooms. To have Stacey here, so happy herself, added to Cecilia's joy.

When the celebrant had finished her words, Cecilia smiled and saw her love reflected back in Linc's eyes, and she said, with all the conviction in her heart, 'I do. I *do* take this man to my heart, and I will keep him there forever.'

They kissed, and the strains of the 'Wedding March' rose through the church and filled it.

The party made its procession outside onto the steps, facing a field of spring flowers. Linc and Cecilia, and behind them Brent and Fiona, Alex and Jayne, and then Stacey and a man by the name of Brendan Carroll, who seemed to have some special history with Alex. And, of course, Rosa—the family's wonderful housekeeper, who was so much more.

There were other guests—friends and colleagues from the plant nursery and from elsewhere. The family sent them on to the wedding reception, but instead of staying at the church for hours of wedding photos, they took just a handful in front of the chapel and in that field of spring flowers.

At the end of it, Cecilia glanced about the group. 'I couldn't be happier—and especially to be sharing this day with all of you.' She reached out her hand and clasped her sister's in hers for a long moment. 'I'm so glad you're here, Stacey.'

It wasn't just about the day, and they both knew that. It was about the fact that Stacey had stuck to her word and turned her life around. She'd even managed to be civil about their mother making an excuse for not being there when Cecilia had got her courage together and invited her. It really didn't matter. Cecilia *had* her family, and deep in her heart she knew it.

Linc. Stacey. The others. And...

'Oooh!' Jayne rested her hand over her abdomen and a look of surprise came over her face. She turned to Alex. 'The baby just moved. It was like butterfly wings! That's the first time I've felt it.'

Cecilia's love and happiness expanded even further as she observed the quiet joy shared by the couple.

She saw Fiona glance into Brent's eyes, and they both looked sheepish as they broke into smiles.

Cecilia gave a soft laugh. 'Do you two have something you want to share?'

'We're pregnant, too.' Fiona's smile burst right across her face. 'We weren't going to say anything until after the wedding.'

At this, it wasn't Cecilia who laughed but Linc, who unexpectedly threw his head back. But he quickly sobered and clasped Cecilia's hand, and all his hope and love were in his eyes, too.

'We were waiting for Stacey to be here for the wedding…' he began.

'To tell you all that we also may have pre-empted the baby part,' Cecilia finished for him.

'Oh, my God!'

'That's wonderful!'

'That's the best news!'

'I'm going to be an uncle once more than I thought.'

Everyone broke into happy speech at once, and then Stacey spoke quietly into the midst of it.

'I will guarantee you're having twins.'

She said it with such conviction that Cecilia's eyes widened.

'So it's just as well I'm around now, because you're going to need me once they come along.'

Brendan Carroll, the man at Stacey's side, gave a low laugh. 'Double the trouble? I like the sound of that.'

Stacey looked startled and a little intrigued. 'Are you planning to be in Sydney for a while?'

'Actually, I just opened a gallery in the city.'

Cecilia looked at her sister's glowing face, at all

the happiness around her, and suspected that Stacey was going to be just fine.

And her sister was probably right about the possibility of twins, too. Cecilia had a feeling about that herself.

Whether one baby or two, Cecilia would indeed want her sister to be a big part of her life from now on.

'Shall we go to this reception?' Linc whispered the words into her ear. 'The sooner we arrive, the sooner I can sneak you away so I can have you to myself. I want to discuss the possibility of twins…' Love and warmth and desire mingled in his gaze. 'Among other things.'

And so Mr and Mrs Linc MacKay led the family—*their family*—towards the cars that would take them to the reception.

As Linc settled beside Cecilia in the back seat of their chauffer-driven car, he couldn't believe how happy she had made him and went on making him in every single moment.

'I can't imagine life without you now, and I'm longing for this child or these children to join us. Do you think your sister is right?'

Cecilia's contentment flooded over, and she blinked to dispel the sudden rise of emotional tears to her eyes.

She glanced down. 'It would explain why I've had to have this dress let out three times in the last month, even though I'm so early along in the pregnancy.'

Linc gave a delighted laugh. 'Cecilia MacKay, I love you with all my heart and I always will. Did you know that?'

And, actually, Cecilia did!

* * * * *

Braden leaned toward her.

The very moment he touched her skin, her breath caught and her heart fluttered to a stop.

As her pulse scrambled to make up for the lost beat, Elena couldn't take her eyes off him. Why was that? You'd think she didn't trust him, but the truth was, right this very minute, she didn't trust herself.

She ran her tongue around her lips, hoping to lick off whatever sweet, sticky mess she'd left there. Yet, as she did, their gazes zeroed in on each other once again, and her hormones spiked. A jillion silent words seemed to swirl around them, yet neither of them uttered a single one out loud.

This was so not good. Not good at all.

Could she last the three weeks?

* * *

Brighton Valley Cowboys:
This Texas family is looking for love
in all the right places!

THE COWBOY'S
DOUBLE TROUBLE

BY
JUDY DUARTE

First Published in Great Britain 2016
By Mills & Boon, an imprint of HarperCollins*Publishers*
1 London Bridge Street, London, SE1 9GF

© 2016 Judy Duarte

ISBN: 978-0-263-91978-3

23-0416

Our policy is to use papers that are natural, renewable and recyclable products and made from wood grown in sustainable forests. The logging and manufacturing processes conform to the legal environmental regulations of the country of origin.

Printed and bound in Spain
by CPI, Barcelona

Since 2002, *USA TODAY* bestselling author **Judy Duarte** has written over forty books for Mills & Boon Cherish, earned two RITA® Award nominations, won two Maggie® Awards and received a National Readers' Choice Award. When she's not cooped up in her writing cave, she enjoys traveling with her husband and spending quality time with her grandchildren. You can learn more about Judy and her books at her website, www.judyduarte.com, or at Facebook.com/judyduartenovelist.

To my critique partners, Crystal Green
and Sheri WhiteFeather. Can you believe we're
celebrating our twentieth anniversary this year?

I have no idea where I'd be without you, your story
skills—or, more importantly, your friendship.
I love you, guys!

Chapter One

A snarl, a hiss and a cat's frantic "meeee-owww" shattered the silence in the barn.

Braden Rayburn turned away from the stall of the broodmare that was ready to foal and spotted six-year-old Alberto climbing up the wooden ladder to the hayloft while juggling a squirming orange tabby in his arms. The boy had found the small stray earlier this morning, but clearly, the cat wasn't up for an adventure.

"No!" Braden called out, hoping to stop an accident ready to happen before any blood could be spilled. "Alberto! Put it down."

The small boy turned at the sound of his name and froze on the third rung, but he continued to hold the cat. He undoubtedly understood the word *no*, but that was it.

Alberto—or "Beto," as his twin sister called him—didn't speak English. And Braden's Spanish was limited to a few words, mostly isolated nouns.

"Put the…" Braden blew out a ragged sigh and tried to remember how to say *cat* in Spanish. "Put the *gato* down. It's going to scratch the living daylights out of you." From the tone of his voice, his frustration was coming through loud and clear.

Fortunately, Beto seemed to finally understand and climbed down. Still he held the poor critter that didn't appear to be the least bit relieved by their descent, so a bite or a scratch was imminent.

"Let the *gato* go." Braden used his hands in his own form of sign language and motioned as he added, "Down."

Reluctantly, the boy released the cat. But the frown on his face indicated he wasn't happy about doing so.

"Where's your sister?" Braden asked. Then, attempting to bridge the language barrier, he added, "Bela? *Dónde?*"

The boy pointed to the corner of the barn, where his twin sat, holding a black cat, undoubtedly the tabby's littermate.

What was wrong with people who dropped off their unwanted animals near a ranch, assuming the owner would be grateful to take in another critter to feed?

Having grown up on this horse ranch near Brighton Valley, Braden was all too familiar with what ranchers like him and his late grandpa had to put up with.

Ironically, he thought about the twins and how they'd ended up with him, and he slowly shook his head. Not that he couldn't afford them or didn't care about their emotional well-being, but he was completely out of his league when it came to dealing with young children, especially when there was a serious communication problem. But then again, the twins had been raised in Mexico, so the language barrier was to be expected.

He glanced at the boy and girl, who were now sitting together with the stray cats and jabbering a mile a minute, although Braden had no idea what they were saying. He wished he did, though. And that he could talk to them, explain how sorry he was that their parents had died.

Three months ago, Braden hadn't known they'd been living in a Mexican orphanage—or that they'd even existed. But once he and his half siblings had found them, the older Rayburns had decided to bring them back to the States and provide them with a home.

Now, two weeks later, here they were in Texas. They'd been staying in Houston with Jason, Braden's older half brother. But Jason and his wife were now on a business trip in Europe, while sister Carly was on a cruise with her new husband's family. So the only one left to look after them was Braden.

He'd like to reassure them that they were with family now, but he was limited to pointing, miming and, when his memory of high school flashcards came through for him, uttering a Spanish word or two.

Yet in spite of the struggle to communicate and more than a twenty-year age difference, the kids running around his barn and chasing a couple of cats had something in common with him and his half siblings.

They all had the same father.

Wasn't that just like their old man to have a second family in another country? Charles Rayburn may have been a successful businessman with a net worth of nearly a billion dollars, but he'd been a real failure when it came to making any kind of lasting commitment to a woman.

When Jason headed to the airport with his wife, he left Braden in charge of the six-year-olds. And then he'd driven off like the guy who'd dropped off the two stray cats.

Okay, so it wasn't the same thing. Beto and Bela were *family*. And there was no way Braden would want them to be taken in by strangers, although that's what they were. And if the twins didn't pick up English quickly, they'd never really get to know each other.

Still, even though Braden had agreed to keep the kids until Jason returned, he'd panicked at the thought of being left in charge of his newfound little brother and sister. What if he failed them—like his… Well, his father hadn't exactly deserted him. He'd come through with the child support and money for braces, swim lessons or summer camp. But Charles Rayburn had been so caught up with his business ventures that he'd never attended a school play, a football game or even a graduation.

To make matters worse, Braden had never been close with the two half siblings he'd known about for practically all of his twenty-eight years. So he'd always felt like the odd man out, especially since his dad hadn't even married his mom.

And now there were two more Rayburns to get to know, and Braden didn't have any idea where he should start.

Heck, even if he and the kids spoke the same language, having Beto and Bela with him for the next three weeks was going to be a real challenge.

But he had a plan. Once Jason and his new bride returned from that business trip, Braden was going to suggest that the twins live permanently with them. After all, kids their age would be better off with a married couple. And the fact that Juliana would be having a baby soon made it all the better.

And if that didn't work out, his half sister, Carly, had just gotten married, too, and would return about the same time Jason did. She was also pregnant, so there was another opportunity for the twins to join a real family.

In the meantime, the poor kids were stuck with him. Only trouble was, he needed to focus on running the ranch he'd just inherited from his grandpa Miller. Unlike his wealthy and womanizing father, Braden took his family responsibilities seriously.

But how in the hell was he going to get any work done while they were here? Babysitting was turning out to be a full-time job—and one he hadn't been prepared for. He'd been raised on the Bar M as an only child, so he didn't have any experience with kids. He'd do his best to do right by them, of course. But these two, as cute as they were, would be much happier with someone else—preferably someone who could communicate with them.

If they were in school, it would be easier. But it was still summer.

Maybe he should hire a nanny to look after them so he could get some work done.

The more he thought about that idea, the better it sounded. Unfortunately, he didn't know where to begin to find someone qualified. And that was crucial. The woman who'd looked after the twins in Mexico had proven to be cold and rigid. As willing as he was to pass their care on to someone else, he had to be careful.

The poor little orphans had been through enough already, and he was dead set on making sure they were well cared for—and loved. They definitely deserved someone more qualified than a bachelor who was more comfortable around horses and barbed wire than around people, especially those who bore the Rayburn name.

"No!" Beto called out. *"Vengan gatitos!"*

Braden turned toward the child's voice, just as the two cats dashed out of the barn, the little boy and girl in hot pursuit. He didn't blame the animals for running off.

Hell, he'd only had the kids for three days and he had half a notion to run away himself.

Elena Ramirez unlocked the front door of Lone Star Hay and Grain, then set about to welcome the first customers of the day.

She'd already checked on the baby ducks and chicks that were for sale, as well as the rabbits. Her dad was running a special on the small animals this week, so she wanted to make sure the coops and pens, which she'd put on display near the front door and by the register, were clean and that the food and water had been replenished.

Elena had shopkeeping in her blood, and she knew all the best sales strategies. But recently, the merchandise she sold was the kind to grace the covers of fashion magazines instead of agricultural catalogs.

Now, as she studied her father's store, she realized not much had changed in the years since he'd bought it, something she intended to remedy while she was here.

She'd been a senior in high school at the time her father purchased the store and moved the family to Brighton Valley. She hadn't been happy about leaving all her old friends and making new ones, but she was glad her dad finally had the opportunity to be in business for himself. He'd been one of eight children and the first to no longer have to work for someone else.

Taking over a floundering feed store had been tough for him in the beginning. There hadn't been enough money coming in to hire an assistant, so Elena had worked with him after class each day and on the weekends. By the time she'd gone off to college in Austin that next fall, he'd finally been able to afford to pay an hourly employee.

On the upside, Elena's retail experience had enabled her to get a job at a dress shop near the university, where she usually had the highest commission of all the other sales associates.

In fact, when she'd graduated in May, she'd continued working in Austin, but between her student loan payments and the cost of rent and utilities, life had eaten into her earnings. Since she had plans to open a store of her own one day soon, one that specialized in trendy fashions and quirky, unusual items, she'd moved back to Brighton Valley until she could sock away some money.

Working at the feed store felt like a step backward, but Papa was so happy to have her home again that she didn't mind.

"I missed my little girl," he'd said when he helped her carry her suitcases into the house.

She knew her absence bothered him, but since she was the oldest of his children by seven years, and with six younger siblings, there were still plenty of little ones in the house.

She stopped by the small display pen that held baby ducks, picked up the smallest one and rubbed its soft down against her cheek. Then, after she set it loose again, she brushed off her hands on her oldest pair of jeans.

All of her good clothes—the ones she wore for her old job—were still in a suitcase under the bunk bed she was sharing with her twelve-year-old half sister. She arched her back, thinking of the small twin-size mattress that was much firmer than the one she'd been used to.

While she didn't mind coming home to help out her family and save money, she definitely missed living on her own in the city.

The first twelve years of her life, she'd been raised by her mother as an only child, so it was only natural for her to enjoy her solitude.

When her mom died, she moved in with her dad and stepmom full-time. She'd tried to help whenever she was needed, and before long, she was babysitting, cleaning up spills and wiping tears.

These days, she often had to referee fights. She loved her siblings, she truly did. But she'd enjoyed getting away from them, too.

A truck engine sounded outside, announcing that their first customer of the day had arrived. She secured the hair clip that held the thick, dark mass of curls away from her face, neck and shoulders while she worked.

Moments later, a man and two children entered the store. The kids both appeared to be Hispanic and didn't resemble the blond-haired cowboy in the least. So her interest was immediately piqued.

When the little boy noticed the rabbits on display, he immediately brightened. *"Conejitos! Bela, mira!"*

The girl—his sister, Elena guessed—hurried to his side, and they each found a bunny to pet.

Elena turned to the fair-haired cowboy, who stood about six foot one. When he noticed her, a pair of dazzling green eyes locked on to hers and sent her heart rate on a mad scamper to find a normal pace.

Too handsome for a local cowboy was the first thought that came to her mind.

"Can I help you?" she asked.

"Not unless you run a day care center out back."

Elena laughed. "Only when my mom brings my younger brothers and sisters by the store. Why do you ask?"

He shrugged a single shoulder. "Just my attempt to find humor in a sticky situation."

She lifted a brow, and he slid her an easy grin.

"I'm looking after these kids for my brother," he said, "and they don't speak English. So I'm in a real fix when it comes to communicating with them. I'm doing my best, but I have to find a bilingual nanny—like yesterday."

Elena felt a tug on her sleeve. When she glanced down, the little girl with large brown eyes and lopsided pigtails pointed to the rear of the store, where the boy had wandered over to a display of straw cowboy hats. He'd apparently knocked several to the floor.

"Sorry about that," the handsome cowboy said. "I'll get those picked up."

"Don't give it a second thought." Elena strolled to the table display and smiled at the boy. *"No es problema, mijo."* She helped him restack the hats, then took one and placed it on his head. In Spanish, she asked if he wanted to be a cowboy.

He smiled, revealing a missing front tooth, and nodded, the oversize hat flopping forward and back. *"Si, yo quiero ser un vaquero como Señor Braden."*

So he admired "Senor Braden" and wanted a hat like his. She glanced at the fair-haired cowboy, then back at the boy, who was pointing to the man. Then it clicked.

"Now I know why you looked familiar," she said. "You're Braden Rayburn. Your great-grandmother owned a ranch near here."

"Yes, and my maternal grandpa owned... Well, I now own the Bar M."

"I was sorry to hear about your grandfather's passing," she said. "My dad told me that he attended his celebration of life. I'm afraid I was still in Austin at the time."

"Forgive me, but I don't recognize you. But then again, my grandpa was the one who always picked up supplies or had them delivered. After my rodeo days, I spent most of my time on the ranch."

She reached out her arm in greeting. "I'm Elena Ramirez, Paco's daughter."

He took her hand in his, enveloping her in a warm, calloused grip that sent her senses reeling. "No kidding? I knew Paco had a lot of kids, but I had no idea that he..." His voice trailed off, but she knew what he'd been about to say. He hadn't realized Elena was one of them. Well, that's not a surprise. She found it difficult to believe at times, too.

"I've been away at college," she said. "And for the past four years I haven't been back to Brighton Valley as often as I should have."

Before either of them could speak, the boy walked up carrying a black and white bunny. *"Perdona me, señorita. Quanto dinero por el conejito?"*

She smiled at the little guy and said, *"Cinco dolares."*

"Did he want to know how much the rabbits cost?" Braden asked.

Elena nodded. "I told him five dollars. But you're in luck. We're running a sale this week. They're two for eight."

Braden put up the hand that had once gripped hers to motion a halt. "Sorry, but no way. I have two children more than I can handle as it is—not to mention a couple of stray cats they found this morning."

She glanced at the kids, who'd returned to the rabbit cage, clearly enamored. "Are you sure you won't reconsider? Look at them."

"I'm tempted—but only because Beto has managed to stay out of trouble for five minutes."

She smiled. "Actually, my brothers and sisters have pets. It teaches them responsibility."

"What did you major in at college?" Braden asked. "Child psychology?"

She laughed. "Business, actually, with a minor in art."

His grin deepened, creating a pair of dimples in his cheeks, and his green eyes sparked. "You've got a talent for sales. I'd say it might be wasted at a small-town feed store."

She felt the same way, although she'd never come out and tell her father that. He hoped she'd stay at home forever, but she had plans to make her mark in the world—and in a big city.

"I only plan to be here until the first of the year," she said. "I've been saving money to eventually open up my own dress shop in Houston."

His gaze swept over her, from her red Lone Star Hay and Grain T-shirt, to the faded blue jeans with a frayed hem, down to the old boots she wore, then back up again.

She tossed him a smile. "Believe it or not, when I'm not working here, I do have a bit of fashion sense."

"I'm sure you do." A boyish grin suggested he might have found her attractive in spite of her well-worn clothing.

Her heart fluttered at the thought, but she tamped it down. She wasn't looking for a cowboy, especially one who was local. "As I was saying, the sale on small animals we're running is actually advertised in the newspaper. It was my idea because those little critters can sure multiply if you aren't careful."

Braden chuckled. "It would serve my brother right if, when he returned, I gave him the kids as well as two rabbits."

"I like the way you think." Elena studied the handsome cowboy, who was tall and lean—broad shouldered, too.

From what she'd heard through the rumor mill, Braden Rayburn was one of the most eligible bachelors in town, and quite a few of the local ladies had him in their sights.

But looking at Braden in that Stetson and those

Wranglers certainly could make a woman—well, maybe *another* woman—rethink her career path.

The boy reached into his pocket and pulled out a twenty dollar bill. *"Quiero dos conejos, por favor."*

Elena laughed. "It looks like Beto can afford to purchase rabbits for himself and his sister."

"Where did he get the money?" Braden asked.

Elena turned to the child, first taking time to speak to him long enough for him to introduce his sister, Maribel, whom he called Bela.

She laughed at Beto's animated explanation about how he received the cash, then interpreted for Braden. "He said he earned it—fair and square."

"Is that a direct quote?"

"Not exactly. But it's close enough. It seems that Beto here is quite the negotiator. He bartered a horned toad for the cash."

"With whom?"

"Apparently, the nice man who brought him to the United States paid him to give up his new pet."

"That would be my brother," Braden said. "But Jason is a suit-and-tie sort of guy. What would he want with a horned toad?"

"My guess is that Jason paid Beto so he could take custody of it, then turn it loose, although that's just an assumption. But from what I gathered, it seems that Beto's horned toad nearly scared the bejeezus out of Jason's wife. I have a feeling she may not have wanted to sleep in the same house with it."

Elena glanced at the smiling six-year-old. When she returned her focus to their temporary guardian, Braden's meadow-green gaze had already zeroed in on hers, the intensity making it difficult to breathe.

"I'd like to offer you a job," he said.

"I already have one."

"Whatever your father is paying you, I'll double it if you can start today."

She stiffened, not quite following his line of reasoning, but sensing where he was going with the offer. "Excuse me?"

"I need someone to help with child care for the next three weeks. And not just anyone. I need someone trustworthy who's also bilingual."

Elena stood up straight. "Are you out of your mind?"

Okay, so that came across a little harsher than she'd meant it to, but surely he wasn't expecting her to be a…a babysitter. It already seemed like a huge move backward from big girl on campus and star sales associate to a feed-store clerk. But now this guy was suggesting she be a child-care provider?

"I'm sorry if I offended you," he said.

She threw her shoulders back. "I didn't graduate from college with a business degree so I could become a nanny. Besides, you don't even know me. I could be an ax murderer."

He swept a long gaze over her, and a smile tugged at his lips. "Nah. I'm a good judge of character. Besides, I know your parents. And they raise Girl Scouts, honor students and high school football stars."

The guy had a down-home charm about him that could cause any determined woman to weaken, but Elena wouldn't. She couldn't.

"Let me sweeten the pot," he said. "I'll triple whatever you're earning here."

Was he dangling a carrot with no intention of following through? Who could afford to pay that kind of money for a sitter?

Of course, she hadn't been home in years but she'd heard tales about the Rayburns. Rumor had it that all three of the half siblings had a sizable trust fund from their late father.

"I need someone with experience," he added.

Elena crossed her arms. "Doing what? Wiping noses? Mopping up spilled milk? With six younger brothers and sisters, I can assure you that I've had more than enough experience doing that. Sorry, I'm not interested. There are other women I know, empty nesters who are also bilingual, who could help you."

"But I want *you*." A spark electrified the air around them as the possibilities of his statement arced between them. But she brushed aside any attraction she might feel for him.

"Sorry, nope." He wasn't going to turn her into a nanny. Nor could he put her in the uncomfortable position of telling her father she couldn't help him any longer.

"Wait," he said. "I've also been trying to digitize my grandfather's old-fashioned accounting system on the Bar M. In the evenings, I could put you to work on the books and the filing system, and that way, you could help me modernize the ranch office."

"I realize that I'm wearing cowboy boots and jeans, but don't let the clothes fool you. I'm not looking for a position as a ranch accountant."

"I just need you for three weeks, and I'll make it well worth your time."

"What happens in three weeks?"

"Both my brother and sister should be back in Texas by then, and since they're both married now, one of them will be able to provide the kids with a loving, stable home." His gaze met hers, and his expression was...pleading, desperate.

They both knew that she had him over the proverbial barrel. But she'd had her fill of babysitting. She glanced down at the kids in question. Not that they weren't sweet or in need of someone who could speak their language.

"I'll pay you four times whatever you're earning now, plus a bonus for saying yes."

Talk about dangling carrots. She was afraid he'd keep making offers, thinking he would eventually come up with one she couldn't refuse. So she breezily said, "I'll tell you what. Pay off my student loans, and I'll do it." That ought to get her point across and shut down the conversation quickly.

He hesitated only for a moment. "Deal." Then he held out his hand for a shake.

"Really?" With what he was offering her, she'd be able to open that dress shop in time for the Christmas rush.

"Absolutely. I'd need you to live in, but you'd have a private room and bath. And it's only for a couple of weeks." He tilted his head and arched a brow, his arm still extended to her.

She slipped her hand in his and gave it a shake, just as a couple of quacks sounded and a duckling scurried between them, followed by another.

"When do you want me to start?" she asked.

He glanced at the runaway ducklings, then tossed her a crooked grin. "Is now too soon?"

Chapter Two

While the kids sat in the back of his crew-cab truck, cuddling their new rabbits and chattering to them in Spanish, Braden loaded the ranch supplies into the back. He'd just locked the tailgate when Paco Ramirez, the owner of the feed store, drove up in his white Chevy Tahoe.

Braden could say hello to the man and then take off and let Elena tell her father about the deal they'd just struck, but that hardly seemed fair. Besides, he wasn't one to avoid conflict or to be rude to someone he normally did business with. So he headed over to Paco, who was just climbing out of his SUV, and extended his hand in greeting. "Hey, there. I hoped I'd see you this morning."

"How's that sprinkler system working out?" the older man asked.

"Great. That south pasture is looking pretty good now. Valley Ag Supply had it installed sooner than I expected."

"Did you tell them I sent you?"

"I sure did. And they gave me a great deal. So thanks for the recommendation."

"No problem," Paco said. "When you're ready to purchase those calves, I know a rancher about twenty miles north of Wexler who's looking to sell."

The older man might only be a small-town business owner, but he was a great source for referrals.

"Thanks," Braden said. "I'll keep that in mind." Grandpa Miller had raised rodeo horses until his passing, and while Braden would continue to do so, now that the ranch was his, he wanted to expand and run some cattle, too.

He'd never expected to become a rancher. In fact, he hadn't had plans to do anything other than to ride rodeo, like his grandpa Miller had. But when his grandfather first became sick last year, Braden had come home to help his mother with the ranch. And now that the ranch had become his… Well, he'd sort of fallen into the lifestyle. Not that he minded. He'd been raised for it, he supposed. And while he had the money to do whatever he wanted in life, he didn't flaunt it.

Paco glanced into the truck bed. "What have you got there?"

"Cages for the two rabbits I just purchased."

The feed store owner chuckled. "I take it that you met my daughter Elena. She suggested we run a special on the small animals. Ever since she was seventeen and we had our grand opening, she's been a great saleswoman."

"Yeah, well, I have two kids staying with me for the time being, and when they saw the bunnies on display, Elena didn't have to do much hard selling. Although, come to think of it, I hadn't realized a sale on rabbits would turn out to be nearly a hundred-dollar investment in cages and food and whatnot."

"That's my girl." Paco lifted his John Deere cap off his head and ran a hand through his thinning dark hair. "I'll have to give her a raise."

Here was the opening Braden needed. But how did he go about telling Paco that he'd stolen his best employee away from him? Braden might not have his older brother's business acumen, but he prided himself on being a straight shooter and an honest negotiator.

He supposed there was no other way than to just come out and say it.

"I hate to tell you this," Braden said, "but I just convinced your daughter to jump ship. I offered her a better position."

Instead of showing disappointment or raising his hackles, a slow grin slid across the store owner's face. "As much as I hate to lose her, she's a bright girl. I'm sure she'll be an asset to your family's corporation."

Braden had never had anything to do with Rayburn Enterprises, his father's business. And he'd never even wanted to. It was Jason who ran the business now.

"Actually," Braden said, "I asked her to come and stay at the Bar M and be a temporary nanny for the kids."

Elena's father stiffened, and his grin morphed into that frown Braden had been expecting to see a moment earlier.

Paco was a good man, a family man with strict, cultural values. He probably had qualms about his daughter moving in with a single man at the Bar M, even if everything was aboveboard.

"She'll have her own room," Braden added. "And it's just a temporary position."

"Not that she isn't good with kids, but my girl has her head and her heart focused on her future and she's not easily swayed by smooth talkers or macho cowboys. How'd you manage to talk her into that?"

He'd bribed her, that's how. He'd tempted her with more money than she could earn from her father in three months and then agreed to pay off her student loans—without even asking how much they were. Yet while his method might have made Charles Rayburn proud, something told Braden it wasn't going to sit well with Paco Ramirez.

"I'm in a real bind," he admitted. "And it's just for three weeks. The kids staying with me don't speak English. And with my Spanish being practically non-existent, I'd be hard-pressed to order a beer with my dinner in Laredo on a Saturday night. So I need someone to help me look after them until my brother gets back to Texas."

Paco took a look into the truck. Hadn't he noticed the kids before? Had he thought Braden was pulling his leg?

"What's Jason going to do with the kids?" the older man asked.

"Become their legal guardian, I suspect. We... uh..." He glanced in the cab, noting that the windows were up. While he knew the twins wouldn't understand him anyway, Jason hadn't talked about their situation in front of them—and Braden wouldn't, either.

"Apparently, my father had a secret family in Mexico. Beto and Maribel are my little brother and sister. Jason brought them to Brighton Valley, and I'm looking after them until he and Juliana get home from their business trip in Europe."

Paco merely looked at Braden in awkward silence, as if this new twist in his paternal family's notorious dysfunction was somewhat expected. Braden himself was a Rayburn bastard. He was used to the pitying looks the good people of Brighton Valley passed along to the unorthodox and ever-expanding brood of Charles Rayburn's offspring by multiple women. Really, it should be no surprise that Elena's father was too polite to voice his disapproval at the scandal.

So then why did he clench his fist like he used to when he was back in grade school and the kids used to ask him why his daddy lived with another family?

Elena was an adult and could make her own decisions, but Braden didn't feel quite right about the way he'd orchestrated the whole thing. Trouble was, he was so desperate, he'd be damned if he'd put too much thought to it. Otherwise, he might try to backpedal on that job offer. And then where would he be?

"Looking after the kids won't be her only duty," he added. "I've also asked her to modernize my grandfather's old accounting system. If I'm going to run the ranch right, I'll need to have everything digitalized. And she'll be a big help with that."

Paco seemed to think on that for a moment, then said, "Elena is a good girl."

Braden wasn't sure where he was going with that. Or why his expression had sobered. "Yes, sir. I'm sure that she is."

"Just so you know, I had a good relationship with your grandmother, Rosabelle Rayburn. And I knew your father."

Damn. Did he think that Braden was a chip off the old block? It was true that he might resemble Charles Rayburn, but that didn't mean he'd inherited his father's character flaws.

He just hoped Paco didn't think this was a ploy for Braden to get his single daughter alone and seduce her. Maybe he feared that the fertile apple didn't fall too far from the scandalous Rayburn tree.

"All I ask is that you be good to my daughter and treat her with respect," the man said.

"You have my word." Braden reached out and offered a handshake to seal the deal. He didn't have any qualms about making a promise like that to Paco. Trouble was, the older man's words had struck him to the quick.

The truth of the matter was, as hard as Braden had tried to emulate his grandpa Miller, he wasn't entirely sure how much of Charles Rayburn's genes he'd inherited.

By the time Elena arrived at the ranch, Braden had practically paced a furrow in the front yard deep enough to plant corn.

Okay, so he'd just kicked up a little trail dust. Still, she was a sight for sore eyes—and in more ways than one.

She drove a small blue Honda Civic—nothing out of the ordinary. But when he saw her climb out from behind the wheel, his pulse rate shot up as though she'd just blown in on the Texas wind, holding a magical umbrella and a black carpetbag containing a spoon-ful of sugar.

Thank goodness she was finally here.

But damn. She'd changed out of the snug jeans that had molded her shapely hips and now she wore a color-ful gypsy-style skirt and bright red tank top. Her dark hair had been swept into a twist of some kind back at the feed store, but it now hung loose along her shoul-ders in a soft tumble of glossy curls.

What do you know? His Spanish-speaking Mary Poppins had morphed into a sexy Latina beauty.

How could a lovely woman become even more beau-tiful in a matter of hours? She'd said that she couldn't come out to the ranch until afternoon, when her fa-ther finished making deliveries and could finally re-lieve her at the store, but it looked as if she'd spent the entire time fussing with her hair, makeup and outfit.

Not that he was complaining. She'd mentioned that she had fashion sense, but he'd had no idea just how true that statement was.

"Where are the kids?" she asked, as she reached into the trunk and pulled out a suitcase.

"They're on the back porch, playing with their rab-bits." He probably should offer to carry in her things, but for the life of him, all he could do was stand in the middle of the yard and gape at her like a moonstruck teenager.

Get with it, man.

As she proceeded to the front porch, she asked, "Are you having buyer's remorse?"

"No, I want you here."

She laughed. "I didn't mean me. I was referring to those bunnies."

Of course she was. If he hadn't been having a testosterone moment, he would have picked up on that immediately.

"No," he said, "I'm not at all sorry about buying them." He reached the screen door before she did and pulled it open for her. "In fact, I'm not even sorry that I let you talk me into buying two cages, watering receptacles and food dishes, not to mention five pounds of rabbit pellets and the shaved wood bedding you insisted they needed."

She blessed him with a bright-eyed smile. "You could have gotten by with one large pen."

"Yes, I could have," he said, as she brushed by him into the living room, taunting him with a whiff of her exotic floral scent. "But it's a known fact that rabbits multiply like crazy. And since neither of us knew how to tell the males from the females, purchasing two meant I could end up with more rabbits than horses on the Bar M."

Her laugh had a magical lilt, making him again think of Mary Poppins until he took another look at her. There was no way anyone would confuse Elena Ramirez with a nanny. But that was okay with him. Just as long as she was bilingual and experienced with kids, she was going to work out fine.

"Is there someplace you'd like me to put my things?" she asked.

Yes, his bedroom. But he vanquished the inappropriate thought as quickly as it came to mind. He'd been gifted with an abundance of common sense, as well as self-control. And as long as Elena and the kids were staying on the ranch, he was going to need to exercise every bit of both.

He led her upstairs and down the hall to the guest room, which was across from the room he'd given Bela and Beto—and the farthest from his own.

"The kids have been happy and chattering up a storm ever since we got home," he said, "although I really can't make out what they're saying."

"I told you that pets were good for them. If they've been shuffled around a lot, the bunnies might give them a better sense of permanence—or at least security."

"Yes, you did say that, and I'm sure there's some truth to it, but I still think you were trying to sell some rabbits and all the paraphernalia that went with them."

"You do realize," she said, her caramel-colored eyes sparkling, "that my father has a return policy."

He laughed. "And don't think I'm not tempted to take advantage of it. But I don't want to disappoint those kids. Besides, I need my peace and quiet. I've also been putting off chores since they arrived on Sunday, so I have a ton of work to do. And now that you're here, I plan to get after it."

She smiled. "Go right ahead. I'll settle in; then I'll find the kids. What do you have planned for their dinner tonight?"

"I…uh…" He shrugged. "Nothing in particular. But don't worry. There's plenty to choose from. I stocked up on a bunch of easy-to-fix, kid-friendly stuff at the market yesterday. So you have the option of hot dogs, mac and cheese, chicken tenders, pizza or frozen burritos."

"That's not very healthy."

"Okay, I admit I like junk food. My mom usually did all the cooking when she was living at home, so I got my share of healthy stuff. Now that I do it myself, I make the things I like to eat. Don't get me wrong. I like home cooking, but I can get that at Caroline's Diner or when my mom invites me over."

"Where is your mom?"

"She married her old high school boyfriend a couple of weeks ago and moved in with him. Erik—or rather, Dr. Chandler—has a medical office in town, and she's going to be his receptionist." It had all happened so fast, but Erik had been such a kind and loving support to her during her father's illness that it seemed like the most natural thing in the world for them to have gotten back together. Braden just wished she would have invited him to Vegas when they'd tied the knot during a weekend trip. But then again, they'd apologized and said it had been a spontaneous decision.

He glanced at Elena, whose brow was furrowed. He got the feeling that she was probably a health nut, and he didn't want to concern her or scare her off the very first day. "I actually like cooking, but I'd be willing to share kitchen duties—if you want them."

"I like cooking, too. So I'll trade off with you."

"Sounds good to me. Feel free to take charge of the household—that is, if you want to. You can even go to the market and purchase anything you think the kids might need." He reached into his front pocket, pulled out a wad of cash and peeled off a couple of hundred-dollar bills, handing them to her. "I had a feeling their visit was going to cost me. But that doesn't matter."

"I suppose it doesn't. A Rayburn can pretty much pay for anything he wants and hire anyone he needs."

Braden felt a trickle of heat steal up his neck. It was an easy assumption that all the negative Rayburn traits were passed down to him, yet he spent his whole life striving to live up to the more admirable qualities of the Miller side of his family.

Yet hadn't he done just that today—paid for what he wanted?

He wouldn't fault himself for it, though. He'd only gotten what he needed. Elena not only spoke Spanish, but she was experienced with kids. She was also a business major who could prove to be helpful in the home office—if she ever found any free time.

Bad thing was, she was gorgeous, which meant he'd have to keep his mind and his eyes to himself.

Still, she was the perfect solution to at least one of his more recent problems. And before he knew it, Jason would be back to take the kids off his hands.

It was going to cost him plenty, but he had a slew of money tucked away in that trust fund he rarely had need of. Besides, whatever it cost to get by as peacefully as possible for the next three weeks would be well worth it.

As Braden led Elena to the guest room, he couldn't help but smile. The good old Rayburn business ingenuity had saved the day once again. Braden's father would be proud of him.

Yet that realization raked over him like fingernails on a blackboard, causing his gut to twist and his conscience to rumble. Very early on, Braden had learned a simple truth that his father apparently never had. Money could buy just about anything but love.

Elena stood beside the guest bed and watched Braden head out the door and turn down the hall. It was difficult to imagine him as one of three heirs to a billion-dollar corporation, especially when he was clearly a rancher and dressed as a cowboy.

He was handsome, to be sure. Intriguing, too. A man to be studied, especially if she wanted to know what made him and his family tick. Not that she really needed to know anything about him or his siblings. Yet there seemed to be something vulnerable about him. She wasn't quite sure where that suspicion had come from. Still, it niggled at her just the same.

As she unpacked her clothes, a task that wouldn't take long, she thought about what her father had told her before she'd driven out to the Bar M.

Braden had grown up on his maternal grandfather's ranch. Gerald Miller, a former rodeo cowboy who raised horses on the Bar M, had been well thought of in the community, just as Granny Rayburn, Braden's paternal great-grandmother, had been.

On the other hand, his father hadn't been able to escape country life soon enough and had rarely returned, even for a visit. From what Papa had said, Charles had gone to a private college in California and had quickly adapted to the lifestyles of the rich and famous.

Elena couldn't help wondering about the family dynamics, especially since Papa had claimed Charles Rayburn had been a world-class womanizer—and had only been married to two of the four women who'd born his children. But she wasn't being paid to figure out their dysfunction. She had a job to do, and she'd better get started.

After putting away the last of her lingerie in the top bureau drawer, she closed her suitcase and placed it in the closet. Then she made her way to the kitchen and out the mudroom to the back porch, where Bela and Beto were playing with their new pets.

Braden had been right. The kiddos appeared to be happy with their bunnies.

"Como se llaman los conejos?" she asked the kids.

Maribel grinned proudly and held up her brown bunny. *"Oso."*

Elena smiled. Bear seemed like a funny name for a sweet, gentle rabbit. But the little girl obviously didn't think so.

"El blanco es de mío," Beto said, *"se llama* Cowboy.*"*

Hmm. He'd named his white bunny Cowboy, not *Vaquero*? Apparently, Braden had been teaching them English. She'd have to work on that, too. It would make things easier for the kids, especially if they were going to start school in the fall. What was the plan with these children anyway? Where would they go when their three-week stay was over?

But that was a question for their guardian, not the poor kids.

After they chatted for a while, she left them on the porch to take inventory in the kitchen. She checked the items Braden had stocked in the pantry, as well as the refrigerator and freezer.

In spite of nearly a case of macaroni and cheese, she found brown rice, pasta and canned vegetables. She even spotted spaghetti sauce.

There were two gallons of milk in the fridge, which she'd feared Braden might have neglected to stock up on. She saw juice, too. There were even a few fresh veggies in the crisper, although the green pepper and tomatoes looked as though they'd been there for a while.

Next, she swung open the freezer door and gasped when she saw all he'd crammed in there—personal size pizzas, frozen burritos, ice cream, Popsicles…

As she shuffled the boxes around, she found some ground beef. She might be able to pull off fixing a spaghetti dinner tonight, rather than a feast of junk food.

For a moment, a wave of rebellion washed over her. She hadn't studied her butt off in both high school and college to become a babysitter or a short-order cook.

But then again, she'd accepted the nanny job. And if there was one thing to be said about her, when she made a commitment, she followed through with it.

She blew out a sigh. She wasn't about to go shopping this late in the day, so it looked as though she'd have to make do with what she could find. And fortunately there was a well-stocked spice rack and quite a few canned goods.

Braden had said he didn't know anything about kids, but by the stuff in his pantry, she suspected that, deep down, he might still be a kid at heart. That was good because it meant that he'd soon adapt to the change in his life and get used to having his little brother and sister around.

But it would be bad if he turned out to be some spoiled rich boy who thought he could boss her around or slack off on his duties thinking the poor help would gladly pull his weight. She didn't care how good the cowboy looked in his Wranglers.

She returned to the back porch and explained to the children that they only had thirty minutes to play with their pets before it was time to put the bunnies back in the cages. Then they'd need to wash up for dinner.

Unlike her own brothers and sisters, at least one of whom surely would have had some kind of objection, Bela and Beto readily agreed.

With the start of a game plan in place, Elena returned to the kitchen and made a list for her trip to the market, including plenty of fresh fruits and veggies. She'd never wanted to be a chief cook and bottle washer, but if that was on her job description, she intended to be the very best one Braden Rayburn ever had.

By the time Braden finished up in the barn and headed for the house, dusk had settled over Brighton Valley. He was bone tired and hungry enough to eat a horse—not Chester, of course, who was practically family at the ripe old age of twenty-two. But his gut was grinding and growling to the point that he'd wolf down just about anything else.

He had no idea what Elena had planned for dinner— whether she'd cooked or if she wanted him to take them all to Caroline's Diner. They hadn't really talked about what her duties would be at the house. Maybe he should've laid out a better job description before hightailing it out to repair a corral this afternoon. Only trouble was, after lifting lumber and hammering nails for the past three hours, he didn't feel like driving anywhere, especially with a truckload of kids.

Maybe he ought to suggest pizza. The frozen ones weren't nearly as good as the ones he could have delivered, although neither could hold a candle to the ones made at Maestro's. Either way, the kids probably wouldn't complain.

As he made his way into the kitchen, he found Bela and Beto seated at the table, eating spaghetti with meat sauce that had chunks of tomato, zucchini, peppers and onion. They were so busy slurping up the noodles that they hardly looked up or even spoke to each other. But he couldn't blame them. If the food tasted as good as it smelled and looked, he'd be in heaven before he swallowed the first bite.

His gaze lit on Elena. In a sunflower yellow half apron his mother had left behind, she looked like a beautiful domestic goddess.

She'd pulled those abundant brunette curls up into a twist—no doubt to keep them out of her face while she cooked.

What a shame. He preferred to see her hair hanging loose, the way she'd worn it when she arrived earlier.

She leaned against the kitchen counter—taking a well-earned break, he supposed—and eyed him as closely as he was studying her.

"Are you hungry?" she asked.

Yes, but no longer for food. However, there was no need to open that hot topic of conversation. So he said, "Dinner smells amazing." *She* was amazing. "Where'd you learn to—" he swept his hand across the kitchen "—to do all of this?"

"Not in college." She smiled, then pushed away from the counter, turned back to the overhead cupboard and removed a plate.

Okay, so she'd given him a clear reminder that she hadn't studied to be a nanny, wife or mother. And in spite of what appeared to be a delicious meal and a tidy kitchen, her message came through loud and clear.

In fact, so did her sexy, don't-call-me-matronly appearance. Had she done that on purpose? Had she planned to make sure that she dressed in a way that kept him from having any domestic thoughts about her?

It would seem so. That gauzy skirt and red tank top that molded to her body set his hormones pumping— even though they were slightly hidden by his mom's apron.

Elena turned around, and in spite of holding a heaping plate of pasta loaded with sauce that must be for him, he couldn't help but gaze at her eyes, at her face. He swallowed—hard.

Whether she realized what was going on in his testosterone-loaded bloodstream or not, she swept past him. Her light, exotic fragrance taunted him as she placed his plate on the table. "Here you go."

"Aren't you going to join me?" he asked.

"I don't eat red meat. In fact, I'm practically a vegetarian."

Seriously? It didn't make sense that she would cook beef tonight. Most women—well, the vegetarians he'd dated in the past—would have made some kind of tofu-quinoa crap and tried to convince him and the kids how tasty it was. Although, he suspected that an old cowboy boot would have been lip-smacking good if it had simmered in that sauce long enough.

"You didn't have to make something you weren't going to eat," he said. "The kids and I would have been okay with the bean burritos."

She shrugged. "I'm not a big fan of processed food, either, so I figured you'd rather have beef."

Sure, he liked it but he usually opted for fish or chicken when he had a choice. "The meal looks great, but what made you think I'd prefer red meat?"

"Because this is Texas. And my father told me that the Bar M will be raising cattle soon."

"So what are you going to eat?" he asked.

"I just finished a small bowl of pasta, along with some of the veggies and sauce before I added the beef. So go ahead and have a seat. As soon as the kids are finished, I'll take them upstairs and supervise their baths."

Braden ate alone all the time, but for some reason, it felt awkward for him to do so tonight. Was this some passive-aggressive attempt to remind him that she was the hired help and they were not to socialize in any way?

But he was too hungry to ponder the thought, so he shook it off and said, "Sounds like a plan." It also sounded as though she had everything under control.

Yet as she herded the kids out of the kitchen, leaving him to eat in peace and quiet, he couldn't help watching her go—and wishing she hadn't sworn off Texas beef and possibly even the small-town cowboys who raised them.

Chapter Three

Thirty minutes later, Braden had not only finished the plate Elena had fixed for him, but also the second helping he'd served himself. Then he washed the few dishes that were left in the kitchen.

On his way to his bedroom, he heard chatter in the bathroom down the hall, as well as splashing in the tub. Elena sure had the kids talking and laughing a lot. The twins deserved a little fun. Lord knows, Braden hadn't been capable of providing them with any, which was another reason they'd be better off when his brother or sister arrived and could step in.

For a moment, his gut twisted. What if neither Jason nor Carly wanted to take on a commitment like that? He couldn't imagine that they'd both refuse to take the kids. After all, the twins were family—blood relatives. And there was no way he'd want to see them shuffled off to foster care or...

A rustle of insecurity slid over him. If there was no other choice, he'd have to keep Beto and Bela—a scary thought.

But surely Jason or Carly would see the benefit of those children growing up with a married couple.

No, this was only a temporary gig. Braden would help out when he could, and the kids needed him now. So here he was.

Thank God he'd found Elena.

Fighting the urge to step in and see what was going on in the bathroom, he ignored the commotion and ducked into the privacy of his master suite and closed the door. Then he took a long, hot shower.

He could have remained in his steam-filled private bathroom or stretched out on his king-size bed, locked away from the hubbub, since Elena was far more competent with the children than he was. But he couldn't help thinking that the kids could be running amok and that she might need him.

So after drying off, he slipped on a pair of faded jeans and a black T-shirt. Things had gotten quiet, so he suspected she had it all under control. But he wasn't going to hang out in his bedroom all evening. While he was growing up, it had been the hour right before bedtime that he'd enjoyed the most. That was the time when his mom would let him snuggle in next to her on the old plaid sofa while she read to him. Or when he'd sit next to Grammy and Grandpa and watch *Wheel of Fortune*.

But he wasn't the only adult in the house tonight, and he had no idea what the protocol was for the first night for strangers who had become new roommates.

Either way, it seemed as if he should at least thank Elena for a job well done and a mighty fine meal.

When he stepped out into the hall, she was leaving the kids' room. A water mark darkened the red fabric of her tank shirt, right across her left breast.

"The kids are bathed and tucked in bed," she said.

Keep your eyes off that damned water spot. And look at her face. She's got beautiful eyes—big, brown, expressive...

And she's an employee, for cripes' sake. A child-care worker. Domesticity at its finest.

But she wasn't giving him any reason to think about kids or home and hearth at the moment.

Again, he shook off the sexual distraction and asked, "How about a cup of coffee?"

"Caffeine would keep me awake. But I might have a Popsicle instead."

He laughed. "That sounds good to me, too."

"I'm going to pick up the mess the kids left in the family room first. I would have asked them to do it themselves, but by the time I got them settled down and in bed, I didn't want to rile them up again."

"Good idea. Isn't there an old saying about letting sleeping children lie?"

She lobbed him a bright-eyed grin. "I think you mean 'dogs,' but it's pretty much the same thing."

He stepped aside and swept his arm in front of him. "I'll help. After you."

As she passed by him, he caught another whiff of her floral scent and watched as the hem of her skirt swept across her shapely calves.

Damn, she was lovely. What in the hell had made

him think his problems were finally solved now that she was here?

As they headed to the family room, where coloring pages, crayons and workbooks were spread about, Braden said, "I really enjoyed dinner."

"Thanks. When I moved in with my dad, one of my first chores was to help Laura in the kitchen."

Laura? Not Mom? Then it dawned on him. "I hadn't realized that Laura wasn't your..." His words drifted off. He hadn't meant to probe into her personal life. But he'd seen Paco and Laura Ramirez together with their other children in town and at the feed store on many occasions and had assumed the happy couple had always been together.

Then again, Elena had to be seven or eight years older than their first born son, who was a star quarterback on the Brighton Valley High football team.

"My mom died when I was twelve," Elena added.

"I'm sorry." Braden rarely talked about his past, but for some crazy reason, he found himself saying, "But you're lucky to have a father like Paco. My dad was never really involved in my life."

He wasn't sure why he'd opened up about that. He never hinted at any chinks in his armor and, while Elena's disclosure had caused him to lower his guard, he wasn't about to say any more than he already had.

But the truth of the matter was, from what he'd observed of the man, he would have given up his share of the Rayburn riches to have had a father like hers.

"Actually," Elena said, as she placed the last crayon in the box, "my early years weren't sunshine and roses."

Her comment took him aback. "Your dad seems

like he has it all together. Your mom—well, I mean Laura—does, too."

"My dad's awesome. And Laura is the best, but I didn't spend much time with them until I was older. And when I did visit them as a little girl, it was always pretty stressful. My real mom made life rough for all of us."

Braden wanted to ask, "How so?" But he never liked people prying into his business—or the awkward relationship between his mom and dad. From the first week of kindergarten, Braden had learned that his family situation wasn't the norm and he'd always been interested in what happened inside other kids' families and what he was missing out on. So he kept quiet, hoping she'd continue.

After a long, thought-filled moment, she said, "My parents got married right out of high school, and I was born six months later. But they fought all the time and separated right after my third birthday."

"It sounds like splitting up was for the best."

"That's true. Unfortunately, my mom was one of those people who thrived on drama and conflict. And she always wanted to have the last word. Believe it or not, their divorce proceedings lasted longer than the marriage."

"That's too bad. I know some people can remain friends during a split like that, but from what I've heard, my father's first divorce was pretty sticky, too."

"I can understand that."

Could she? Apparently the Brighton Valley rumor mill made sure town newcomers got the scoop, especially on the neighbors who'd moved on to greener pastures, leaving a few locals behind to deal with the embarrassment of dalliances and indiscretions. But then again, Shannon Miller's situation had been juicy. When Braden had been conceived, Shannon was only seventeen. And at the time, his father was still married to Jason's mother.

Elena reached for a couple of puzzle pieces that had fallen on the floor. After replacing them into their box, she stretched and arched her back, her hands splayed on her hips, her breasts begging to be noticed.

And he'd noticed, all right, but he'd be damned if he wanted her to catch him at it.

"My dad tried to be fair with my mom so they could put it all behind them," she added. "But she fought him on every possible issue, using me as a pawn and making my life miserable until I was in the sixth grade. In fact, even though I was only a kid, I felt sorry for him—and a bit guilty, although I know it hadn't been my fault."

Braden had struggled with guilt as a kid, too. And he'd been as much of a victim as anyone in his parents' affair.

"You said it lasted until you were in the sixth grade," he said. "Is that when she finally quit fighting him?"

"Only because she died." Elena crossed her arms. "I swear she used to lie awake thinking of ways to create problems for him. And then she'd have to medicate herself to finally go to sleep. But one night, she took too many of her pills."

"Suicide?" he asked.

"I'm not sure. That might have been her plan because she'd driven to the liquor store for a bottle of vodka. But on the way home, she lost control of her car and ran into a tree. She was probably just strung out on the meds, but who knows what she was thinking at the time. The police ruled it an accident."

"I'm sorry," he said.

"Thanks. It was tough, but to be honest, I was torn between grief at losing her and relief that the fighting and misery were finally over."

Braden's parents hadn't really fought, at least, not that he knew of. But their relationship had always been strained and tense, something he'd often thought was all because of him. If he hadn't been conceived, they would have each gone their own way.

His mom wouldn't have had to face the guilt she sometimes carried for being a "home wrecker," either.

He suspected that was one reason she'd never gotten married—or really even dated before she recently ran into her old high school boyfriend at the hospital. Braden had asked her about it once, why she'd kept to herself and remained single, but she'd refused to discuss it.

Was it any wonder he wasn't able to see romance as an end-all answer to life's problems? That's why he kept his relationships temporary and unencumbered. Well, for that reason and for a rather hurtful snub he'd received in high school by one of the cheerleaders.

But he wasn't going to stew on any of that. Sometimes people got a raw deal in life, although he counted himself lucky in every other way.

"Now that the mess is cleaned up," Elena said, "how about that Popsicle?"

"You bet."

As they entered the kitchen, he said, "I realize things haven't always been easy for you, but it sounds as if you've made the best of it."

"I've been fortunate," Elena admitted. "But it was still hard moving in with my dad and Laura. I'm so much older than the other kids. In fact, I still don't feel as though I really fit in."

Braden could certainly understand why she wouldn't. He and his siblings had never been close, mostly because they'd had different mothers and had always lived apart, other than holidays and shared visits with Granny Rayburn on the Leaning R Ranch.

"It's not fun being a half sibling. If you're like me, you never felt as if you belonged in the same family." Once the words rolled out, he wished he could reel them back. He didn't like revealing any emotional vulnerability, although her raw self-disclosure had triggered him to lower his guard.

"Actually," Elena said, "no one ever made that distinction about me. I'm always introduced as their daughter or as the other kids' sister. And vice versa. So I don't know why I feel that way." She opened the freezer, removed the brightly colored box and opened it. Then she handed him a red Popsicle.

"Thanks."

"I guess there's another reason I never quite fit in…" She paused and bit down on her lower lip.

"What's that?" he prodded.

She let out a soft sigh. "My mom was an artist, although as far as I know, she never did much with it. She was too busy feeling sorry for herself. But while I can't really draw or paint, I inherited her creativity and eye for color and style."

Braden tore open the wrapping, then tossed the paper in the trash. "That makes you different?"

"Yes, but…it's complicated." She opened up her

Popsicle, too, and tossed the wrapping. Then she licked the orange treat.

Damn. The woman couldn't even eat a kid's snack without looking as sexy as hell and setting his hormones pumping.

As if not having a clue what she was doing to him, she continued. "Laura is a good cook and a great mom, but she's not very artistic or creative. So her decorating skill leaves something to be desired. A couple of times, I rearranged things to make the house more appealing or the artwork better balanced. And I think it bothered her."

"Did she say something about it?"

"Not the first time, which is why I didn't think anything about doing it again. But this last time she got very quiet afterward. When I returned last week, I saw that she'd put things back the way they were." Elena's brow furrowed, and she worried her bottom lip. Then she said, "Maybe it offended her. Or it could remind her of my mother and all the grief she put them through. I don't know. Maybe I'm just being sensitive." She shrugged. "Boy, listen to me going on and on about myself."

As curious as Braden continued to be, he was a little relieved that she was done talking about her personal life. He'd never been comfortable with anyone expressing their emotions, or expecting him to talk about his own.

He took a seat at the kitchen table, and she followed suit. They sat quietly for a while, lost in their thoughts, but he couldn't ignore the beautiful woman sitting across from him.

"So tell me your plans for the dress shop you intend to open," he said.

"I'm going to call it The Attic. But it'll be more than just a dress shop. I'm going to have a lot of other things for sale."

Something told him she'd be a real success at whatever she chose to do. "What kind of other things?"

"Shoes; fun, quirky gifts; decorator items and things like that. Have you ever shopped at Anthropologie?"

He shook his head. It sounded like a college course to him.

She gave a little shrug. "Well, if you're not familiar with that store, then it wasn't a useful example. Not that I'm going to copy them by any means. The Attic will be unique. I'm going to place my own mark on it." She began to brighten, those honey-brown eyes glimmering with building excitement. "I have big plans for it and have already done a lot of the footwork. I've found suppliers for the exact kind of merchandise I want to offer for sale. I'll also be able to sell used treasures I purchase at estate sales. And best of all, when this all comes together for me, I can finally leave Brighton Valley behind."

Brighton Valley?

Or her dad and stepmom?

He supposed it didn't matter. "So why Houston and not Austin?"

"The store where I used to work is a little similar to what I plan for The Attic. Besides, Houston is only two hours away, so my dad and Laura won't think I abandoned them completely."

"I didn't realize you were so eager to move away," he said.

She flashed him a pretty smile and pointed at him with her half-eaten orange Popsicle. "Don't get me wrong. I'll come home to visit, especially on holidays, but I'm really looking forward to finally establishing my life and career in the city."

Braden didn't want to think about her leaving right now. Not when he was just barely getting to know her and had the urge to learn even more. He stole a glance her way and caught her studying him intently.

"Tell me more about the twins," she said. "I've only spent a few hours with them, but they're cool kids. They're not only cute, they're bright and funny, too."

"The language difference makes it tough for me to get a handle on their personalities, although I've figured out that Bela is sweet and motherly, while Beto is inquisitive and loves animals."

"I'll work on teaching them English, and before you know it, you'll be able to communicate with them." She took another bite of her frozen treat. "What do you know about their life before coming here?"

"Not much." Braden finished off his Popsicle, then tossed the stick in the trash. "Did they say anything to you about their background?"

"I didn't quiz them. Do you want me to?"

"Yes, if you'd be sensitive and do it gently. My brother and sister don't speak Spanish, either—at least not well enough to broach a difficult subject with two kids who lost both their mom and their dad within two years. We're pretty sure about what's gone on in their lives in the past six months, but the whole Camilla mystery has all three of us curious."

"Who's Camilla?"

"Their mother. Camilla Cruz was an artist who died of breast cancer two years ago."

"What do you mean by her 'mystery'?"

"Camilla's father, Reuben, used to be a foreman on the Leaning R Ranch, but he quit and returned to Mexico about four years ago, telling Granny Rayburn that he had a family emergency to tend to." Braden raked a hand through his hair. "Camilla had visited the Leaning R, and she and my dad became lovers. But she left Texas without telling him where she was going."

"Was she pregnant with the twins when she left?"

"Apparently. I'm not sure he knew it, though. I suspect that he only learned about their existence in the past year or so because, six months ago, he hired a private investigative firm to find the kids in Mexico. Then he went with the PI to bring them back to the States, but he and the investigator were both killed in a car accident. So I'm afraid any other details about Beto and Bela died with them, as well as the reason he had placed various pieces of Camilla's artwork in storage in San Antonio."

Elena leaned forward and placed her elbows on the table. "How do you know the twins are his?"

"They were born in San Diego, and Charles Rayburn is listed as their father on their birth certificates. Their passports reflect the same thing, and we have reason to believe that once he learned of their existence, he never doubted that they were his."

"So you don't think he knew about them until recently?"

"My dad was always financially generous with his kids, and there was no record of him having paid any child support payments for Beto and Bela. So it's pretty obvious that he'd only recently found out about them and meant to bring them home."

"How *did* they get here?" she asked.

"When it was learned that my dad had been working with a private investigator, I wondered what he'd been looking for."

"He didn't tell anyone?"

"*My* dad?" Braden slowly shook his head. "He never shared his personal life with me—or with anyone. Jason worked for Rayburn Enterprises, and even he didn't know why our old man had left the country or hired a bilingual PI firm."

"How did you find out about the twins? Did you go through the investigator's company records?"

"There weren't many notes that could help. I'd just gotten home from my first and last go round on the rodeo circuit and didn't have anything else going on at the time. So, to appease my curiosity and to get my mind off the fact that my body was in no shape to pursue a career in bull riding, I took a little trip south of the border to see what I could find out. A week later, I learned that my dad had been looking for twins who'd been placed in an orphanage. Come to find out, they were Camilla's children, and she'd passed away a couple years earlier."

"So you were able to bring them back to the States?"

"I would have, but when my grandpa took a turn for the worse, I rushed home to be with him and my mom. So Jason took up the search and found them living with a woman our old man had hired just before the accident."

Elena seemed to consider everything he'd told her. And he couldn't blame her. It had been a lot for him—

for any of them—to wrap their minds around. But she was a good listener, at least better than the buckle bunnies he'd gotten involved with on the pro rodeo circuit.

"I can see where you'd be curious about their early years," she said. "I'll ask a few questions to see what they have to say."

"Thanks. Jason and his wife made it a point not to discuss the situation in front of them, even though they don't speak English. So it would be nice if we could get a better understanding of what went down with their mother and our father before we tell them anything."

"You mean, they don't know what's going to become of them?" she asked, her pretty brow furrowed. "Do they know they're related to you? It could be very unsettling not to know where you're going to live or who will be taking care of you."

"Either Jason or Carly will probably become their legal guardian, although we haven't decided who's going to do it yet. We're still trying to deal with the news and to determine what's best for them."

"Who took care of them while they were living in Mexico?" she asked.

"For the past six months, it was the woman my dad hired, but she didn't offer much information."

"Because of the language barrier?"

Braden blew out a sigh. "That was only part of it. She wasn't very warm or loving."

"Did she treat them badly?"

"You might ask them, but they didn't appear to have been neglected or abused. Apparently, when my dad didn't return when he said he would, she assumed that he'd abandoned them and cheated her out of the money he owed her. She was just about to return them to the orphanage where they'd been living before my dad found them."

"That's so sad."

"We thought so, too." Braden tore his gaze away and studied the pattern on the tile floor. His heart went out to the poor kids, and he was determined to be a good big brother. He just wished he would have had one he could emulate. Jason had often avoided him or ignored him while they'd grown up. Not that he'd been eager to make friends, either.

But that was just one more thing he could blame on his father, one more handicap he hoped he'd overcome.

Fortunately, things were better between the half siblings now, which only made him regret the years they could have had. But that was all water under the bridge.

Yet, in spite of his resolve not to stew about the past—or his lovely companion—his thoughts and his gaze drifted off anyway.

Elena hadn't meant to stare at the handsome cowboy, but he was so deep in thought that his expression was hard to read, even though a slew of emotions filled his meadow-green eyes like a soft summer rain.

Besides, he intrigued her. His family did, too, especially when she considered the great effort they'd gone to in order to bring the kids to Texas and their determination to provide them a home.

Even the late Charles Rayburn, with his obvious faults, had gone to retrieve his son and daughter when he'd learned of their situation—and maybe even their existence.

It would seem that finding the twins and claiming them as equals would cost the older Rayburn siblings when it came to dividing their inheritance. She'd heard their father had been worth jillions, so maybe the money didn't matter that much. Either way, she suspected there was some kind of honor between them, which was nice.

While she didn't know much about the Rayburn side of the family, she did know something about Braden's maternal grandfather.

Gerald Miller had ranched in Brighton Valley for years. He'd even spent time on the town council for a while. And Shannon Miller, Braden's mom, was involved in the women's auxiliary at the Wexler Community Church. They were what Elena's father called *buena gente*—good people.

When Braden looked up and caught Elena studying him, her cheeks warmed and she quickly turned away.

Okay, so maybe there was another reason she'd flushed with embarrassment when he caught her gaze just seconds ago. She hadn't been just noting his furrowed brow.

She'd also been checking out his profile, his chiseled cheekbones and his square-cut jaw.

He stood, drawing her attention, and returned to the freezer with a long, lean cowboy swagger.

"You want another Popsicle?" he asked, as he turned to face her, a dimpled smile on his handsome face.

"No, thank you. One is enough." She'd already spent enough time with him and had opened up in an unexpected way. All she needed was to lower her guard to the point of doing or saying something she'd regret in the morning.

Braden was the kind of man who could turn a woman's head, but Elena wouldn't let her attraction get out of hand. Of course, that was easier said than done when her hormones were triggering romantic thoughts that were totally inappropriate.

She blamed it on the stillness of the house in the evening and the admiration she felt for him because he was trying so hard to do right by Beto and Bela. But she couldn't continue to chat with him tonight. It could only lead to trouble—or, at the very least, temptation. She had a job to do. And while it was far removed from anything she'd created on her vision board back in January, she would see her commitment through. She hadn't been lying when she'd said she loved her stepmom, but Elena had made a vow to herself that she would never settle down as some country house-wife and pop out a bunch of babies, especially with a former rodeo cowboy.

"Well," she said, as she got to her feet and tossed the stick into the trash can. "I think I'll turn in."

He looked at her as if she'd announced that he was going to need to find another nanny, which probably wasn't a bad idea, either. But she'd never suggest that when she could really use the money he'd promised her.

"Is something wrong?" she asked.

"No, not at all." He smiled. "I'll just sit here for a while longer."

"All right, then, good night. I'll see you in the morn-ing." She felt a little guilty, leaving him alone in the kitchen while she headed for the guest room he'd as-signed her when she arrived. She would think that he would relish the peace and quiet in the house after the hectic day. So then why did his eyes provoke her sym-pathy, much like those of Max, the basset hound her dad had once found abandoned behind the feed store and she'd insisted they take home?

Stop it. Braden Rayburn and his look of loneliness was not her problem. The guy probably had an entourage of rodeo queens lined up to take on his illustrious family name and help him spend his inheritance.

Once inside her room, she gathered up her sleepwear and her toiletry bag, then she carried them into her private bathroom, where she took a long, peaceful soak in the tub.

When she finished, she dried off and dressed for the night. After brushing her teeth, she climbed between the sheets and found a comfortable spot.

She thought it might take a while to fall asleep in a strange bed, but she'd been wrong. She'd dozed off immediately—only to be awakened by a child's scream.

Elena's heart slammed in her chest, and she shot up in bed, tossing off the covers as she came to her senses.

Was that Bela?

She rolled out of bed and hurried down the dimly lit hall to the little girl's room without giving a thought to anything other than the frightened child.

Bela thrashed from side to side and cried, *"No! Quiero mi mamá! Dónde está mi mamá?"*

Elena's heart wrenched as the girl called out for her mother. She considered flipping on the switch on the wall, but she feared that the sudden light might be too much of a jolt to the frightened child. Besides, the light from the hallway enabled her to see. So she took a seat on the edge of the bed, placed her hand on the girl's shoulder and tried to reassure her in Spanish. "It's all right. I'm here."

The little girl stopped struggling for a moment and her eyes opened, clearly confused and frightened from the nightmare.

Elena continued to speak softly, to comfort her. To tell her it was okay, that she was safe. And that Elena would make sure no one would hurt her, even if that meant staying up all night and keeping watch.

Chapter Four

When a cry rang out down the hall, Braden had been seated at his desk in the home office, concentrating on an accounting problem he'd been dealing with off and on for the past couple of days.

He hadn't been able to sleep, so just before ten o'clock, he'd decided to use the time wisely and productively. As a result, he'd spent the past couple of hours poring over the files and the spreadsheets he'd made to help him figure out where his late grandpa had made the math error.

He was so focused on why the numbers didn't add up that it took a moment for the cry to actually register. It jolted him from the computer screen.

Was that Bela? Was she having a nightmare? Had she gotten sick again from sneaking into the cookie jar and eating more than her fill of Oreos?

He pushed back the desk chair and was about to rise when he heard footsteps padding down the hall. Oh, good. Elena had gone to check on her. Some kind and gentle words should help.

His first thought was to let Elena handle the child's outburst, but a niggle of guilt objected. Maybe she'd been right about the kids being unsettled and confused by their recent move. If so, he'd have to tell them something to set their minds at ease—using Elena as an interpreter, of course. But it would be best if he could tell them exactly where they'd be living and with whom. So he wasn't sure what to say.

Nevertheless, he got up from the desk and started down the long illuminated hallway. Apparently, Elena had flipped on the light switch.

When he reached the twins' bedroom, he glanced into the open doorway. Beto, who apparently was a heavy sleeper, continued to doze undisturbed in one of the twin beds, while Elena sat on the edge of Bela's mattress, speaking softly, comforting the fretful little girl.

Thank goodness she'd gotten there first. Not that he wouldn't have attempted to do the same thing, but Elena was much better at it—and she spoke the children's language.

He folded his arms across his chest and leaned against the doorjamb, listening as Elena continued to console the girl, to caress her arm and hold her hand.

As Bela settled down and her eyes fluttered shut, Braden's focus didn't stray from Elena. It wasn't as though her tank top and pajama shorts were inappropriate, but it… Well, it was just the fact that she was in nightwear, he supposed, and tousled from sleep, that he found incredibly arousing.

Her long glossy dark hair hung loose over her shoulders in a mass of curls. The look was so damn sexy that he couldn't seem to tear his eyes away from her. It was enough to make him wish he'd been the one who'd had a nightmare and was in need of her gentle touch.

No doubt sensing that he'd been ogling her, Elena glanced over her shoulder to the doorway where he stood, charmed by the sight of her. As their eyes met, their gazes locked, binding them together by something he hadn't expected.

She was the first to break the spell and turn away, looking down at the hands clasped in her lap. Braden followed her gaze, noting the boxer-style shorts she wore, her bared thighs, the bend of her knees and the petite feet that boasted pink nail polish.

Was she concerned about the way she was dressed because of their new living situation and her employee status?

But then again, it wasn't as though she was working for him at a nine-to-five office job. She had a live-in position and had been awakened from a sound sleep. Neither of them had expected to be caught unaware like this. Besides, they were both adults with healthy hormones. And he wasn't thinking of himself as her employer right now.

Okay, so he'd talked himself out of a sexual harassment situation. But was his concern for Bela a good enough explanation for him to hang out in the doorway and continue to gawk at the beautiful nanny?

Probably not.

He should turn around, head back to the office and pretend that their eyes had never met, that neither of them had revealed a heated need, that he'd never even noticed her sexy sleepwear or considered how tempting it was going to be to have her living with him for the next three weeks.

His first impulse was to disregard his common sense and make the best of their time together. But nothing lasting could possibly come of it. Besides, allowing his thoughts to take a romantic turn wasn't a risk he should take. Not when he needed his nanny too much.

But for some crazy reason, he found himself lowering his voice and asking, "Are you up for a midnight snack?"

The question caught Elena off guard. Braden was hungry? For food?

There'd been no mistaking the way he'd been watching her and it was… Well, it was flattering, to say the least. It also unbalanced her and made her want to rush back to her room and slip into something more suitable.

Surely he realized that she'd been so concerned about the troubled little girl that she hadn't taken time to give any thought to what she was wearing.

Still, she found herself agreeing to have a snack with him and returned to her room to get her robe.

Moments later, she wandered into the kitchen, where Braden had pulled out a gallon of ice cream from the freezer and was filling two bowls.

Upon hearing her approach, he glanced over his shoulder and smiled. "I hope you like chocolate."

"I love it." The moment the word rolled off her tongue, her cheeks warmed, and she wished she could take them back. She'd always been reluctant to use the *L* word lightly, especially when she was talking about her fondness for a certain flavor, TV show or clothing style. In fact, she rarely let it slip out even when talking about her fondness for her family.

Not that she didn't love them. She did. But it had never been easy for her to come out and admit it.

That probably had a lot to do with her not feeling as though she completely fit in with her father's new family when she'd been a child. Then again, maybe it had something to do with her own mother not being very affectionate or demonstrative toward her—or anyone.

Either way, Elena would have to work on expressing her feelings, especially if she ended up getting married and having kids someday. She, more than most people, knew how important it was for a child to feel loved and accepted. Adults needed that, too, she supposed.

"Here you go." Braden handed her a full bowl of ice cream and a spoon. Then he reached for the one he'd fixed himself. "Let's eat this in the other room."

They left the kitchen, entered the living room and took a seat on the worn brown leather sofa. It was scarred from years of daily use, but it made for a comfortable seat.

Elena placed a spoonful of ice cream in her mouth, relishing the cold, sweet treat.

"When I headed for Bela's room," she said, "I saw the light on in the den, but I hadn't expected you to be awake. I thought you might have forgotten to turn it off when you went to bed."

"I wasn't able to sleep, so I decided to use the time wisely and get some work done."

"Did you?" she asked. "I mean, get any work done?"

"Some." He drew his empty spoon from his mouth and smiled. "But don't worry, there's still plenty for you to help me with—once you settle in. I think I've finally found the error in my grandpa's addition. So there won't be anything holding us up in getting a new accounting system up and running."

They continued to eat in silence, the rich chocolate ice cream hitting the spot and making a perfect midnight snack.

On the other hand, sitting beside Braden in a quiet house stirred her attraction, leaving her feeling a bit uneasy from the strength of it.

The more she got to know the rugged rancher, the longer she spent with him, the more intriguing she found him. If she wasn't careful, he might catch her gawking at him and get the wrong idea.

Yet as tempted as she might be, especially on a night like this, she wasn't interested in a fling, especially with a man in this small town. So it was best if she remained focused on the future instead of the hormone-laden present. Still, she stole another peek at Braden, and when she did, he caught her looking at him once again.

He smiled, then pointed to her mouth. "You have ice cream on your face."

"Oops." She swiped at her lips with her fingertips. "Did I get it?"

"No. You missed." He leaned toward her and used his thumb to stroke the spot at the corner of her mouth. The very moment he touched her skin, sending a spiral of heat to her core, her breath caught and her heart fluttered.

She should excuse herself and go into the bathroom, where she could look in the mirror and clean her face, but she couldn't seem to move. All she could do was gaze at Braden, who'd scooted over and was now sitting a little too close to her.

Or was he just close enough?

As her pulse scrambled to make up for the lost beat, she couldn't take her eyes off him. Why was that? You'd think she didn't trust him, but the truth was, right this very minute, she didn't trust herself.

He had a small smudge of chocolate on his lips, too, but she didn't dare point it out or—God forbid—place her fingers on it, as he'd done to her.

She ran her tongue around her lips, hoping to lick off whatever sweet, sticky mess she'd left there. Yet, as she did, their gazes zeroed in on each other once again, and her hormones spiked. A jillion silent words seemed to swirl around them, yet neither of them uttered a single one out loud.

This was *so* not good. Not good at all.

Could she last the three weeks?

She'd have to—or at least, she'd have to give it her best try. But starting tomorrow, she'd begin to teach English to the kids and Spanish to Braden. That way, she wouldn't feel guilty about ditching them the minute the agreed-upon time was up.

Thank goodness she'd finally finished her ice cream and could excuse herself before she said or did something she'd regret.

"It's time for me to go back to bed," she said with a smile. "I'm clearly too drowsy to eat without making a mess."

He took her empty bowl. "Don't worry about the dishes. I'll take care of them."

She could argue, but she thought it best to get away from him, to retreat to the privacy of her room.

Nevertheless, as she headed for the stairs, she couldn't help glancing over her shoulder at the handsome cowboy seated on the sofa, his long legs stretched out in front of him.

And dang, he caught her looking at him again. But she shrugged off any embarrassment and continued upstairs.

By the time she entered her room, she no longer feared feeling guilty about quitting before her commitment was up. Instead, she just hoped that, if she had to leave, she could do so without any lasting, heart-stirring regrets.

Braden snaked a hand out from beneath the covers and walked his fingers across the night stand till they reached the jangling alarm. He hit the snooze button.

It had taken a long time to fall asleep last night, and while he could blame his insomnia on the accounting error he'd finally found in the bookwork, there was another reason that had caused him to lie awake.

Elena.

Not only had she grown prettier and more attractive with each hour they spent together, but he'd found himself wanting to know more about her, about her hopes and dreams. And while he'd meant for their chocolate-ice-cream nightcap to douse the sparks he'd been feeling earlier, to put them back on steady ground, it had only increased her appeal—even when she'd covered her sexy sleepwear with a robe.

But falling for the twins' nanny would really mess up his life right now. He needed to shake the attraction and maintain an air of professionalism for the next few weeks.

And afterward? Her plan was to move on with her life in the big city, while he was firmly planted in the rich, Brighton Valley soil.

It had been nearly three o'clock when he finally nodded off, providing him with a couple hours of much needed sleep till the alarm had gone off just before dawn, as was his usual routine.

Now as it rang again, Braden was sorely tempted to shut the fool thing off and steal another hour or two of shut-eye, but he couldn't do that. It wasn't his style. So he lumbered into the bathroom and took an invigorating shower before beginning his day.

Once he'd shaved and dressed, he headed to the kitchen, where he chugged a cold glass of orange juice. The label said "fresh squeezed," but he wasn't buying it. Nothing tasted as good as when his mom used to actually take a bag of oranges and squeeze the juice herself. Drinking bottled juice was the least he could do, especially since his mom was so darn happy these days. Not that she'd never smiled or laughed while he'd been growing up, but her happiness was so apparent now that she could practically light up any room she entered, especially if she was holding her new husband's hand.

Braden rinsed his glass in the sink, then entered the mudroom, picked up his hat from the peg near the back door and headed outside. The sun was coming up, and he was burning daylight.

Two hours later, after he'd fed the horses and completed the morning chores, he returned to the house to make a pot of coffee and fix a bowl of cereal for breakfast. As he entered the mudroom, he caught the sounds and the hearty aroma of bacon sizzling in the skillet.

His belly let out a growl and a rumble, reminding him just how hungry he was and how tired he was getting of cold cereal each morning.

He returned his worn Stetson to its peg, then headed into the kitchen, where Elena stood in front of the stove in her bare feet. She wore a pair of blue jeans that rode low on her waist and hugged her hips, as well as a white button-down blouse.

Her hair was still damp—no doubt from a morning shower—and she'd swept it up in a topknot. The woman was an amazing contradiction in style, and it seemed that he could never be sure how she'd be dressed. Or how the very sight of her could stop him dead in his tracks.

"Boy," he said, shaking off his attraction, "something sure smells good."

She turned and flashed a pretty smile. "While the kids are cleaning their rooms, brushing their teeth and washing up, I thought I'd better get started on their breakfast. Are you hungry? I'm making scrambled eggs. I also defrosted a pound of bacon I found in the freezer."

"Sounds great." And a hell of a lot more filling than that granola stuff he'd eaten nearly every day this week. "I'll put on a pot of coffee."

Once the brew was dribbling into the carafe, Braden turned to the stove, where Elena continued to cook, and moved next to her. He leaned his hip against the counter. "Maybe we should talk to the kids this morning about their memories of their mother and the life they led in Mexico."

"Sure. That would probably be a good idea. And you should let them know that they'll be living with you."

"*Me?*"

Elena cocked her head slightly to the right. "Well, with *one* of you. Isn't that what you told me?"

It was. And that's what he'd meant.

During the last Rayburn family meeting with Carly and Jason, their first plan had been to find the kids a new home in the States, but once they learned that Beto and Bela were actually their younger brother and sister, they'd regrouped, realizing they'd have to come up with a plan B. And while Braden would do his absolute best to be a role model, to spend time with them, to let them ride horses and go out to the old swimming hole, he couldn't actually have them live with him permanently.

"Yes," he said, "that's what I said. But let's be careful how we word that to them. I'm not sure whether they'll move in with Jason and Juliana or with Carly and Ian. We'll have to make that decision as soon as they both get back."

She nodded, then returned to her work. A moment later, she glanced over her shoulder and said, "Would you mind setting the table, please?"

"Sure." It was the least he could do.

Before he could place the spoons and forks next to the plates and glasses, the twins bounded into the kitchen, babbling something to Elena. When she responded, they pulled out chairs and took a seat at the table.

Braden had an urge to greet them, to ruffle Beto's glossy but unkempt hair, to cup Bela's chin, but the damned language barrier made it difficult to know whether they'd appreciate it or not. So he finished laying out the flatware, then tucked his thumbs into the front pockets of his jeans and watched Elena serve the kids.

They dug in immediately, and before long, they'd cleaned their plates and drunk their milk. Elena served Braden and herself, while he poured the coffee.

Moments later, before the kids could dash off again, Elena launched into a gentle interrogation. At least, Braden hoped that's how she handled her questioning.

It must have worked because both children responded to everything she asked them. He listened intently, even though he only picked up a word here or there, like *mamá* and *abuelito*, which he knew was an affectionate term for grandfather.

He lifted his mug and took a sip of the rich morning brew, wishing he could join in the exchange.

When the chatter died down, Elena excused the children to go outside and play on the back porch with their pets. Then she refilled her coffee, added a splash of milk and took a seat.

"So, what did you find out?" he asked.

"They lived with their mother for the first four years, but they never met their father. They only learned his name recently."

That made sense. As far as Braden knew, Charles Rayburn had never ended a romantic relationship well. He lifted his own mug and took a sip. "So that validates what we were thinking. My dad probably didn't know of their existence until six months ago."

"They speak fondly of their mother. She was fun to be around, and when she worked in her studio, she allowed them to have their own easels and paint. She may have actually owned an art store or gallery. I'm not sure."

"That makes sense. She was very talented and painted an amazing likeness of Granny. We have several more of her pieces. One is a portrait of the twins that Jason and Juliana found in my dad's storage unit in San Antonio." He paused, an idea bursting in his brain. "Maybe I should check into some art classes for kids and enroll them."

"Good idea. I'm sure they'd enjoy it."

While the kids were with him and Elena was there to help out, she would be able to take them back and forth to class. But what about after? Maybe he ought to wait and suggest that Jason or Carly look into those classes once it was decided where the kids would be living.

"Did they say where their mother's store was located?" he asked.

"No, I didn't think to ask." Elena stood and began to clear the table. "When their mom got sick, she left them with their *abuelito*, who had come to live with them. Then she went 'far away' for medical care."

To California, Braden assumed. Camilla had been born in the States and had died in San Diego, so that seemed likely. From what he and his brother had gathered, their maternal grandfather had passed away about nine months ago, which was when the twins had been sent to the orphanage.

"Did they say anything about their grandfather?" he asked.

A smile stretched across Elena's face. "According to Beto, he was the best cowboy in the whole world, possibly better than *you*."

Braden placed a hand over his heart, as if he'd been wounded, then laughed. Reuben Montoya had been one hell of a foreman when he'd run things for Granny at the Leaning R, but he'd never competed in the rodeo or won the buckles to prove it.

Elena laughed along with him. "On the other hand, Bela lowered her head and got very still during that bit of the conversation. I assumed that she'd been especially close to the man. But Beto provided me with an explanation, one you should be aware of."

Braden pushed his coffee mug aside. "What was that?"

"Bela was the one who found her grandfather collapsed on the floor of the living room, near a stone fireplace. And apparently, it wasn't a pretty sight. Beto ran to get a neighbor, but it was too late. The neighbor told them his heart had given out and that he'd hit his head when he fell."

"That's awful." Braden wondered if the trauma had left Bela with nightmares, like the one she'd had last night. It probably had, and his heart went out to the little girl.

"The neighbor kept them until the funeral," Elena said, "then she took them to a place where there were lots of kids."

"That must be the orphanage."

"That's what I thought," Elena said. "I'm not sure how long they were there, but one day the director told them that their father had been found and would be coming for them. Two days later, a man showed up and brought money to the orphanage—a gift for taking care of them until their father could get them himself."

That man must have been the private investigator Charles had hired. And wasn't it just like the busy exec to offer money in lieu of himself?

Then again, at least he'd gone after the kids with the intention of bringing them home.

"What happened after that?" Braden asked.

"The twins were taken to the home of Olivia Morales, who was to keep them until their father came to take them to the United States. They were told they had to wait there for him to come for them, but he never did."

That was only because their father had died on his way to get them. Braden would have to explain it all to them, but not now. He didn't have the heart to tell them there was another loss to be added to the two they'd told Elena about.

"Let them know that they're with family now," Braden said. "And that they won't have to be shuffled off anywhere again." Well, other than to Jason's house or to Carly's.

"Is that all you want them to know?" she asked.

"For the time being, yes."

He pondered the decision for a moment, then asked Elena, "Who told them about their father's existence?"

"Apparently, they never even knew they had a father until they learned about him at the orphanage. But from what I gathered, their grandfather may have realized he wasn't well and probably contacted your father right before he passed. At least, that's my best guess."

It seemed like a good one to Braden. "I'm sorry they didn't get a chance to meet him."

"According to Beto, they waited and waited for their father to come and get them. As time passed, Senora Morales became more and more irritated by the delay. She would threaten to take them back to the orphanage each time one of them forgot to do a chore or didn't do it correctly. Beto said the only reason her threats frightened them was because they feared their father might never find them if they went away."

Poor kids. Charles had obviously been delayed—by business, no doubt—and hadn't gone to get them the minute he'd learned of their existence, which wasn't a surprise, knowing Charles Rayburn as he did. If there was anything he, Jason and Carly had learned early on, it was that they would always be provided for financially, but they would always come second to Rayburn Enterprises.

Nevertheless, Braden was going to have to level with them about their heritage, their relatives and the fact that they had a home now.

At this point, it was the best he could offer. He just wished he could tell them where they'd be living.

Staying with him on the Bar M wasn't an option.

Chapter Five

Elena hated to be the one to tell the twins that they'd not only lost their mother and grandfather, but that their long-awaited father had passed away, too. However, with the language barrier, that job would fall on her.

The blow would be softened if she could let them know where they would live and who would be looking out for them, but since Braden didn't know for sure, she couldn't offer them much in that respect.

So she'd have to wait on any explanations for the time being. In the meantime, she had work to do and English lessons to start. So why not do her chores and work with the kids at the same time?

At a quarter after ten that morning, she found the twins coloring in the living room. Sometimes her younger siblings would balk at running errands when they had other things they'd rather do, so she told Bela and Beto they would be going with her to the grocery store and that she'd buy them a treat if they were good.

At that news, their faces brightened, and before she could grab her purse, they'd set aside the crayons and coloring books and hurried out the door.

Braden had placed the booster seats his brother Jason had dropped off when he'd brought the twins on the porch. So she had them each grab one and then climb into the backseat of her car.

After making sure they were both buckled in, Elena slid behind the wheel and started the ignition. Then she turned the vehicle around and headed down the long graveled driveway that led to the county road.

When they arrived at the Valley View Market, a small mom-and-pop store owned by Jim and Cindy Calhoun, she found a parking spot near the front and reached for her purse. Beto and Bela waited for her to exit the car, but once she did, they sprinted for the entrance before she could lock the vehicle.

"Esperen me," she called out.

They both turned and waited for her to join them. Once she had, she followed the happy kids into the store.

Jim, who wore a green apron and pushed a broom, was just inside the door, next to the newspaper stand. He greeted her with a warm smile, then he headed to the cash register, which his wife, Cindy, manned. He reached into a lower shelf for a couple of suckers the older couple kept on hand for kids who shopped with their parents.

Beto and Bela quickly glanced at Elena, waiting for her to give them permission to accept them.

"Of course," she said, nodding her approval.

They retrieved the candy and thanked him in Spanish.

The Calhouns were an older couple who'd come to town nearly twenty years ago and had built quite a business with the locals. But from what Elena had heard, now that the new supermarket had gone in at the north end of town, they were struggling to make ends meet.

That's why she'd decided to shop here. She believed in supporting people who owned small businesses, like her dad.

"What darling children," Cindy said. "Are they twins?"

"Yes, they are." Elena placed her hand on Beto's shoulder. "This is Alberto and his sister, Maribel."

Jim and Cindy made no secret of their love of children, although they didn't have any of their own. Elena wondered if they'd been on Braden's list of potential local couples who might want to adopt Beto and Bela. If so, they would have been perfect.

Of course, the Rayburns wouldn't be looking for another home for the kids now. Still, it didn't sit well with Elena that neither of the siblings had stepped up to the plate and offered to take them. But then again, she supposed there was plenty of time for that. They'd just learned of their existence a couple weeks ago.

Cindy gazed at the twins, blessing them with a warm smile.

"Who are these beautiful children?" she asked. "Are they your cousins?"

"No, they're staying on the Miller ranch with Braden." Elena didn't offer any more information than that. She didn't want to be accused of stirring up local chatter that might only lead to gossip.

When Cindy brought up Elena's family, Jim quickly chimed in about high school football and how he looked forward to watching Jesse, Elena's oldest brother, as the starting quarterback this fall.

"Heard he banged up his hand working on the Leaning R this summer," Jim said. "I hope that won't slow him down."

"Not much slows that boy down," Elena said, proud of the young man Jesse was growing up to be. "His wrist is healing nicely, so the doctor said he should be able to play the opening game against Wexler High."

"I'm glad to hear that." Jim, who was tall and slender, grinned. "I was a basketball player myself, but I know how injuries can set a college-bound kid back."

That was true. Jesse had been worried at first, but he was doing everything the doctor told him to do.

"We don't want to keep you," Cindy said. "You must be busy. I know I would be if I were watching those two."

Elena scanned the small market, only to find that Beto had wandered off to a display of sweet rolls and donuts. "Well, I'd better get my cart filled with the necessities before I get too much help with the junk food."

Both Jim and Cindy chuckled.

Elena snatched a cart, encouraged Beto to stick beside her and then began to move up and down the small aisles. When she reached the bread, she lifted a loaf from the shelf and pointed to it. "*Pan*. Bread." Then she asked the kids to repeat the English word, which they did easily.

Interestingly, they didn't have much of an accent, which was good. Maybe they'd learn quickly and become bilingual in no time at all.

When she reached the dairy case, she did the same. "*Leche.* Milk." Again, she asked them to say the word, which they did.

She'd heard that children picked up a new language much faster than adults, which was nice to know.

She placed the half-gallon jug in the cart, then proceeded to the produce section, which was smaller than what she was used to having in the city, and continued to point out various fruits and veggies, offering the English words for oranges, apples, bananas, green beans and corn.

The kids giggled at times, but they repeated each of the words. Hopefully, they'd remember some of what they'd learned today.

After stocking up on the fresh produce, she led the children to the freezer section, where she would let them pick out a treat. They appeared delighted to look over the selection of ice cream, so she asked what flavor they wanted.

"Chocolate," said Beto.

"No, *vainilla,*" his sister said.

Elena's eyes lit upon the Rocky Road, and she wondered if she should pick up a gallon of that, too. Braden had said that he liked choc—

She glanced down at the small boy. What had Beto said just moments ago? She could have sworn the boy had asked for chocolate, instead of *chocolaté.*

No, she had to be mistaken.

Bela tugged on her arm, begging her to get the flavor she requested.

Elena smiled and placed all three cartons into the cart. After she checked out, the kids helped her carry the bags to the car. She didn't have much time before the ice cream melted, so she'd have to get home quickly. But there was one more stop on her agenda, a store that sold DVDs. There, the twins helped her pick out several Disney cartoon movies, which she hoped would help them learn English a little faster.

As she herded them out the store to the car, Beto bolted to the right and ducked down behind an old green trash can.

"Wait," she called out. "Where are you going? Come back here." When she realized that, in her haste, she'd spoken the wrong language, she translated her instruction in Spanish. The boy uttered something in protest, then dropped to his knees on the other side of the battered green container.

Elena meant to scold him, but when Bela gasped and hurried to his side, she followed to see what had snagged their attention.

There, huddled in a corner, was the dirtiest, scruffiest little dog she'd ever seen—a mutt who must have been on his own for some while. She guessed he might have had light brown fur—once upon a time. It was so matted and so grungy from grit and motor oil that it was hard to tell.

It seemed to be favoring its front paw, which had left a small smear of blood on the sidewalk.

Elena's first impulse was to tell the boy and girl to get away from it, that they'd get their clean clothes dirty, that the poor little critter might even be sick, but it was too late. Beto had already lifted up the dog and held it close to his chest, oblivious to its unkempt appearance or to the dirty smudge and small blood stain on his shirt.

Elena sighed, then told them to leave the dog alone,

adding, *"Vamanos, niños."* But she hadn't been prepared for their objections, their pleas to take the dog
back to the ranch and feed it.

"No," she said, explaining why they couldn't adopt
a dog without Braden's permission. Yet the kids only
seemed to be worried about what would happen to
"Pepe" if they left him behind to fend for himself.

Seriously? They'd named it already?

Nevertheless, there was no way she could let them
take the dirty little critter—especially in her car. But
when she glanced at the twins, who were orphaned
themselves, and saw the compassion on their faces,
she gave in.

Maybe she'd drop off the groceries at home, making sure the frozen goods got into the freezer. Then she
could swing by the veterinarian's office so Dr. Martinez could examine "Pepe" and treat its injured paw.

Elena was on a limited budget and knew darn well
she couldn't expect Braden to pick up the tab. But
Dr. Martinez also ran an animal rescue in back of his
Brighton Valley clinic. It was doubtful, under the circumstances, that he'd charge anything at all.

But something told her they would all end up in the
doghouse once Braden got home.

Braden had spent a long, satisfying day on the ranch
and was pleased at how much work he'd finally gotten done. Hiring Elena as a nanny had been the perfect
solution to his dilemma, and his life seemed to have
settled back into a normal pace.

He was tired—a good tired—and dirty and ready
for dinner. He wasn't sure if she'd cooked anything,
but if not, he'd call out for a couple of pizzas.

Her car was home, so he figured the shopping trip had gone without a hitch and that all was well on the home front. But when he scraped off his boots and entered the mudroom, he wasn't prepared for what greeted him.

Beto and Bela sat on the kitchen floor, playing with what appeared to be the end of a dust mop. No, it was a mutt.

Had someone dropped off another stray at the ranch? Apparently so. Maybe he ought to put up a sign warning people not to leave their unwanted pets at his place.

He opened his mouth to speak, to tell the kids they'd have to take the dog to the pound tomorrow, when he caught a whiff of…pot roast?

Damn, it sure smelled good. And while he knew he ought to compliment Elena and acknowledge the work she'd put in today, he couldn't help glancing back at the mutt and asking, "What in the hell is that?"

"It's Pepita," Elena said, with a lilt in her voice. "We called it Pepe until we stopped by the vet's office this afternoon and found out he's a she. Actually, before that, she was so dirty I hated to even look. But the vet tech gave her a bath. And now we know."

Braden blinked, then studied the scraggly-furred critter again. "You took it to the vet? Why?"

"She had an injured paw—but not to worry. It was only a piece of glass. Dr. Ramirez removed it, cleaned it out and gave us an antibiotic."

"Whoa. Slow down. You found a stray, took it to the vet and now you expect it to stay *here*?"

Elena turned away from the counter, where she'd been making a green salad. "The kids found her. She was starving and neglected. How was I supposed to tell them that I didn't have any sympathy for a lost, homeless pup?"

Braden merely stared at her, dumfounded. What did she think this was, a zoo? Or an animal shelter? He'd just acquired the twins, albeit temporarily. But their entourage now included two stray cats, a couple of adopted rabbits and now this…stray mutt.

"Besides," Elena added, crossing her arms as if taking a stand and pressing her point, "every ranch needs a dog."

Braden and his family used to have one, a Queensland Heeler named Blue who'd been amazing at herding and working on the ranch. He'd been a part of the family until he died last year. Braden and his grandpa had both taken the loss hard. They'd buried him in a field of wildflowers about a hundred yards from the house. Ol' Blue had been one in a million. He'd also been irreplaceable.

"If I wanted a dog," he said, "I would have purchased one of the Australian Shepherd pups your dad had on sale last month."

Her stance didn't soften, but she lifted a brow, her eyes bright. "You probably should have gotten one. Still, this sweet little girl is in desperate need of a home."

"I don't doubt that, but she's too small to amount to any help. Besides, she looks like she's three parts poodle, one part dust mop."

"What's wrong with poodles?"

"They're prissy little things that strut around at dog shows and go to the groomers. She'd never be able to pull her own weight around here."

"Let's talk more about this after we eat," Elena said, reminding him just how hungry he'd been. And how good that beef smelled. Then she spoke to the kids in Spanish.

Apparently, she was sending them to clean up for dinner because they scooped up the furry little mutt and carried it off.

Still, he had every intention of continuing this argument and putting his foot down once he finished eating.

Like the children, the dog, rabbits and cats were only here temporarily. He'd send the critters, along with the kids, to either Carly or Jason when they returned home.

Since Jason had been the one to find them in Mexico and bring them to the States, the twins knew him better. Maybe that would be the best place for them.

A grin tugged at Braden's lips as he thought about dumping the whole kit and caboodle on straight-laced Jason, who lived in the city and wore fancy suits to work most of the time. His older brother may have softened up a lot since falling in love, but there was still no way he'd find room for the kids' menagerie.

Giving in to his hunger, Braden said, "I'm going to take a shower. And we'll definitely talk later." Then, lowering his voice, he added, "But for the record, Pepita is only passing through. I'm not going to keep her here permanently."

Poor ol' Blue would probably roll over at the thought of that little thing taking his place. And Braden couldn't blame him. He'd experienced so many life changes himself in the past couple of months that he wasn't sure what to expect next.

As he climbed the stairs to his bedroom and its private bath, he heard Bela shriek, "No!"

What now?

He'd just reached the open door to the kids' room,

when he spotted them kneeling on the floor with the dog—if you could even call it that. The little mutt was chomping the strap of one of Bela's shoes, which it must have had in its mouth for quite a while, since it was only hanging by a thread.

"No, Pepita," Beto said, as he took the battered shoe from the little mutt's mouth. "Don't."

Don't?

Had Braden heard correctly? Or had the boy uttered something in Spanish that had a similar sound?

"What's going on in here?" he asked, hoping for an answer he could understand.

Neither child said a word, but Beto tucked the chomped-on shoe under his leg as if hiding it from sight. Protecting his new friend, huh?

If Braden could be sure the boy understood English, he'd deal with it now. But for all he knew, he'd be talking to the walls—or the pesky little pooch, who wouldn't understand, either.

Shrugging it off—and planning to let Elena talk to them at dinner—he continued on his way. He needed to escape into the shower in the worst way.

And not just because he was dirty and dusty.

After dinner, which had been surprisingly quiet and free of the children's usual chatter, Elena began to clear the table.

"Let me do that," Braden said.

"All right. Thanks."

"Once the kids have bathed and gotten ready for bed," he added, "I'd like to talk to you."

"About what?"

"A suspicion I have."

Elena had no idea what he had on his mind, but she herded the kids and Pepita to the bathroom. Thirty minutes later, she'd tucked them in, told them goodnight and went looking for Braden.

She found him in the kitchen, putting away the last of the clean dishes. Pausing in the doorway, she drank in the sight of the rugged rancher doing household chores, especially dressed in faded jeans.

Sure, her dad helped out a lot at home. But that was different. This was… She wasn't entirely sure how to describe it, other than breathtaking and mind swirling.

He turned and caught her gaping at him. Thank goodness he couldn't hear the sound of her heart banging in her chest.

Her voice came out a little wispy and breathless when she asked, "What's up?"

Instead of answering, he nodded toward the open cupboard. "Can I pour you a glass of wine? Or maybe fix a pot of coffee? I have decaf."

Apparently, he didn't just have a question to ask or a comment to make. He had more on his mind. But that didn't matter. It had been a long day, and she looked forward to unwinding. "Wine sounds good."

He reached for two glasses and handed her one. Then he removed a bottle from the small wine rack on the counter. After uncorking it, he said, "Let's take this out on the front porch."

Surely he wasn't making a romantic gesture. Or was he?

Would it bother her if he was? It probably should…

Shaking off the crazy thought, she followed him outside, her curiosity growing. A waning new moon shone overhead, amidst a twinkling, star-studded sky. In the distance, a horse whinnied.

"Is this where you want to sit?" she asked, nodding toward two rocking chairs on the porch.

"Yeah. I hope it's okay with you."

Again, she wondered what he had on his mind, but she bit her tongue and took a seat instead. He filled their glasses to the midway point, then set the bottle on the small table between them.

As she waited for him to open up, she took a sip of the red wine. Did he want to talk about the kids? Or had he found fault with her in some way? She supposed she'd find out soon enough.

"It's peaceful out here," she said.

"Yeah, it's nice. Are the kids asleep?"

"I think so."

Eager to move past the chitchat, she set the rocker in motion and asked, "What did you want to talk to me about?"

"Beto." He waited a beat before continuing. "I think he might be able to speak English, but for some reason, he doesn't want anyone to know."

She stopped the chair and sat up straight. "It's funny you should say that. I've suspected the same thing."

"Really?"

"I don't know for sure. It's not like I overheard anything in particular, but…" She paused, gathering her thoughts. "I guess it's really just a hunch."

"Same here. But if we both sensed it, maybe it's true. Maybe he's been holding out on us."

"If he is, it doesn't make any sense. Why would he keep it a secret?" She searched Braden's stoic expression as if she'd find an answer there.

But he slowly shook his head. "I have no idea why he wouldn't admit it. You'd think speaking English would make things a lot easier for them. Hell, it would certainly make things easier for me."

As they pondered the possibility, silence stretched between them until only the sound of creaking rockers and the faint scent of night-blooming jasmine filled the air.

"Do you think we should put him to a test?" Braden asked.

"Sure, but how would we do that?"

He shrugged a single shoulder. "I'll have to think about it, but don't worry. I'll come up with something before morning."

When she finished her glass of wine, he reached for the bottle to replenish it.

"Just a little," she said. "I've had a long day and I need to turn in." She also needed to stay on her toes, especially this evening, when the moon seemed to be shining a little brighter than usual and their conversation about the children had stalled.

He set his rocker in motion, and she caught a whiff of the masculine soap from his evening shower, as well as the musky cowboy scent that seemed to be his own.

She could get used to sitting on the porch with him in the evenings, although even the passing thought about doing so was a bad idea. She didn't date cowboys, and this one was her boss—albeit only for the next couple of weeks. She had to get away from this romantic setting and get back inside. It was far too tempting.

She gulped down the last of her merlot and brought her chair to an abrupt stop. "Thanks for the wine."

"I should be thanking you. I was able to get a lot of work done today."

"That's nice to know." She stood with her empty glass in hand. "Do you want me to take the bottle inside?"

"I'm going to sit outside for a little longer and might want more."

She offered him a smile, then walked around his outstretched feet and opened the screen door. Before she could take more than a half step forward, a furry blur darted outside, knocking her completely off balance.

What in blazes…?

Braden must have darn good reflexes, because he was up in a flash, grabbed her arm and braced her before she took a tumble. They were at an awkward angle, not quite standing upright. His fingers dug into her flesh, but not in a painful way. It was far more pleasant—and alluring.

"Are you okay?" he asked.

The heat of his touch, as well as the warmth of his breath at her neck, sent warm shivers through her, playing havoc with her ability to stand on her own. Her breath stalled, while her pulse went topsy-turvy.

She wasn't sure if she'd ever recover from this unexpected and embarrassing moment, but she managed to say—or squeak out, "Yes. I'm fine."

He helped her straighten, then released her and took a step back. Yet the distance he'd placed between them left her even more unbalanced than she'd been when the dog had dashed outside and caused her to stumble.

"Looks like that shaggy mutt you guys brought home decided those kids weren't going to give it a moment's peace," he said. "And so it decided that, in the long run, it wasn't all that bad being homeless."

"That's not likely," she said, realizing she'd neglected to remind the kids to let the dog out for a potty break, especially before bedtime. "But on the upside, I think it's safe to say she's housebroken."

About that time, Pepita trotted back to the porch and into the house, proving Elena right.

"See what I mean?" she asked, turning to Braden.

But he wasn't looking at the dog. He'd been gazing at her with an intensity that shook her to the core. He'd been looking at her lips before zeroing in on her eyes.

Had he been thinking about kissing her?

Surely not. But on the outside chance that had been the case, she excused herself and headed inside before that highly unlikely and definitely irrational thought took on a life of its own. And she did something that she'd surely regret in the morning.

Chapter Six

The screen door snapped shut behind Elena as she entered the house, leaving Braden standing outside on the porch, stunned by what he'd almost done.

When the dog had tripped her, he'd only tried to hold her steady and keep her from falling. He'd done a good job of it, too, until she'd leaned into him. The faint orange blossom scent of her shampoo had snaked around him, charming him in a way he hadn't expected. And for a moment, the unanticipated embrace had knocked him senseless.

His hormones had shot through the roof, and he'd been sorely tempted to wrap her in his arms and kiss her thoroughly. Fortunately, his better judgment had kicked in.

What if she'd balked? Or worse, what if she'd decided to pack up and go, leaving him alone with the kids?

He'd fought the temptation and hadn't acted on the

wild impulse, but not before she'd caught him gaping at her like a lovestruck adolescent.

Had she known what he'd considered doing? Was that why she'd hurried inside?

No, she'd been going into the house anyway. Still, he hoped he hadn't scared her off. He needed her help until either Jason or Carly arrived and could take the kids. Then she could leave town, and his life in Brighton Valley would go back to normal.

He strode to the edge of the porch, placed his hands on the railing and looked out into the night. The Bar M was his life, his legacy, his inheritance. And he was determined to continue his grandpa's horse breeding program. In fact, Eddie Hollis, one of his grandfather's old buddies, had called last week and said that he was looking for more horses. He'd also mentioned the rodeo that was going to be held at the Wexler Fairgrounds later this year.

A yearning to compete once more stirred in Braden's soul. He missed the rodeo, but he couldn't very well go out on the circuit again. The Bar M was where he belonged. And he'd known that from the time he'd been old enough to toddle after his grandpa, mimicking his every move.

Unlike him, his brother Jason thrived in the city. He'd also been groomed to take over Rayburn Enterprises, a game plan their father had put in motion years ago.

Rather than being envious, Braden had actually sympathized with Jason, who'd had to work with their old man each day, constantly under his thumb. On top of that, Braden would hate to spend his life in an office, rather than outdoors.

What kind of life would that be for a cowboy?

Besides, Charles Rayburn had left each of his children a healthy trust fund, which had been set up for them from the time they were babies, and the estate was set to be divided equally among the three.

Of course, Jason, as executor, would now have to set up two more trust funds and divide the inheritance five ways, but that didn't matter. Braden had never had a greedy streak. And thanks to Charles Rayburn's golden touch and insatiable drive for financial success, there would be plenty of money and property to go around.

A horse whinnied, and he glanced at the corral, where Gracie, one of the prize broodmares, was housed with her yearling, a filly he'd named Starlight. Near the herb garden his mother had planted, a cricket chirped.

Braden loved the sounds of the ranch at night. So no, he'd never move to the city. He wasn't at all like Jason, who loved to travel and seemed to thrive in busy, traffic-congested places like Los Angeles or Manhattan. That was just one of the many reasons the two brothers had never been close.

However, their relationship seemed to be changing—and improving. After their father's funeral, they'd begun to talk regularly and seemed to be on the same page most of the time.

Their first family meeting had been intense and somewhat strained, but each time they'd come together since then, things had gotten progressively better, and their time spent more productively.

They'd have to schedule another meeting as soon as both Carly and Jason got back to Texas. Once the two of them decided who was going to take permanent legal custody of the kids, they could all get on with their lives.

A lonely coyote howled in the distance. Braden used to feel sorry for the pesky wild critters when he'd been a kid, although Grandpa had called them a nuisance. Maybe, as a fatherless boy, he'd identified with them somehow. After all, he'd always been a loner. Maybe that was in his genes. But more likely, it was because his mother had never married his dad.

Either way, up until he'd taken off to be a bull rider, he'd always felt a bit out of sync whenever he'd been in town. Not that anyone had ever said anything about it, but he'd sensed the looks, the whispers. As he'd grown older, he'd gotten over it and moved on. That is, until Cathy Thomas had dumped him in high school because her father hadn't approved of him. But he'd picked himself up after that and quit thinking about ever settling down with one girl, one woman.

Hell, it was better that way.

And now, all that mattered was getting through the next couple of weeks. He just hoped he hadn't done anything to send Elena packing this evening. He needed her to stick around until he, Jason and Carly got everything settled at their next family meeting.

The thought that he might want Elena to stay for more reasons than child care crossed his mind. And so did that kiss they'd almost shared. But he'd better shake those thoughts completely loose.

He pushed away from the railing, determined to avoid Elena as much as possible from here on out.

The last thing he needed to do was to complicate his life any more than it already was. Even if he was interested in pursuing something with her, she was the kind of woman who'd expect a long-term relationship.

She also had a father who might not approve of her dating a man like him.

As soon as Braden woke up, he slipped quietly into the kitchen, made a pot of coffee and ate a quick bowl of cereal. Then he headed out to do the morning chores. He'd have to return after the breakfast hour, though. During the night, he'd come up with the perfect plan to test Beto.

At a few minutes before nine, he reentered the house through the back door and found Elena and Bela making cookies.

"Where's Beto?" he asked.

Elena, who wore a pink apron and a smile aimed at the little girl, looked up from the chocolate chip–dotted dough she'd been spooning onto a baking pan. "He wanted to help us, but since he'd been playing with Pepita, I sent him to the bathroom to wash his hands."

"If you don't mind, I could use his help with the broodmares for a while. Would you mind sending him out to the stables when he's finished?"

She nodded in silence, but her caramel-colored gaze asked a slew of questions he wasn't ready to answer yet.

He thanked her, then headed to the barn, eager to learn whether their suspicion was right.

Minutes later, Beto joined him, his big brown eyes bright. *"Señor? Me necesita?"*

Braden motioned him over to the sealed container that held oats and molasses. Then he opened the lid and put several scoops into a bucket.

"Here you go," he said, handing it over to the boy who loved animals.

Beto took it, then glanced up with a questioning gaze.

"It's time to feed the horses. And I'd like you to help me."

A smile tugged at the boy's lips as if he knew what Braden had said, which was one more reason to suspect he'd been holding out on them.

Braden nodded toward the line of stalls. "Come on."

Beto struggled to match his stride, the bucket slowing him down.

"This is Miss Posey," Braden said, introducing him to the old bay mare he'd brought into the barn earlier that morning.

Beto didn't respond, but he didn't have to. His luminous big eyes were soaking in every detail.

Braden bit back a smile at his mesmerized expression. "Miss Posey is getting up there in years, but she's a great horse for kids. If I was going to give you riding lessons, this mare would be perfect for you."

The boy's mouth dropped open, and his gaze sparked with excitement.

"Aw, never mind," Braden said. "I have no idea why I even said that. It's not like you can understand me anyway."

"Que dice?" Beto asked, as if wanting Braden to repeat what he'd just said. Then he stood on his tiptoes and peered into Miss Posey's stall, his excitement apparent.

The six-year-old was doing his best to keep his cards close to his vest, which was typical of a Rayburn. But Braden was determined to get a confession out of him.

"I said this would be a good horse for you to ride."
Braden pantomimed a gallop. "I'd give you lessons, if
you spoke English."

Beto almost jumped out of his sneakers. "I do
speak—a little."

Now they were getting somewhere.

"I don't know, Beto." Braden furrowed his brow as
though he wasn't sure "a little" was enough. But realizing the boy didn't have a noticeable accent, he doubted
Beto was having any trouble at all understanding.

He needed to push this little charade a bit more.
"You'd have to speak a lot of English if you want to
learn how to ride like a real cowboy. It's too dangerous for me to give you lessons if you can't understand
my instructions."

"I speak a lot of English. Like a ton. I even taught
Senora Olivares at the orphanage how to say some of
the words so she could read my *Horton Hatches the
Egg* book to us."

Apparently, these little fakers were not only bilingual, they were educated, too. "You've read *Horton
Hatches the Egg*?"

Beto nodded. "My *abuelito*, my grandfather, gave
me and Bela our own copy of the book when we were
little. He said that it was Senora Rayburn's favorite
story. She told him to give it to us."

Granny had known about the twins? Apparently so,
if she'd given the book to her former foreman when
he left for Mexico. But had she known the kids were
her great-grandchildren? Or had she merely sent the
book as a gift since she'd known both Camilla and
her father?

The sweet old woman had given Braden a copy of

the book when he was a boy, too. And whenever his father came by, she'd ask him to read it out loud to Braden—and to Carly, if she also happened to be at her house that day.

It was the story of a faithful elephant that had been tricked into sitting on a lazy bird's egg. And in spite of all the trials and tribulations poor ol' Horton went through, he'd given his word and remained on the egg until it hatched. But instead of favoring its tricky and absent mother, the hatchling was an elephant bird resembling the elephant who'd nurtured it.

"So will you teach me how to ride a horse?" Beto asked, his excitement impossible to deny.

Braden was so caught up in the memory and in the meaning behind that particular story, he'd forgotten to gloat in the fact that he'd just succeeded in getting Beto to admit to speaking English.

But why had he kept that a secret?

"I don't understand," Braden said. "Why didn't you tell me you spoke English?"

The boy glanced down and used the toe of his shoe to push some straw back under the gate of Miss Posey's stall.

Braden knew what it was like to struggle with trust issues, especially those involving Rayburn men. Yet here he was, asking this kid who'd just lost both parents and a grandfather, been transported to a new country and had his world turned upside down to trust someone he probably still thought of as a stranger.

"I'm sorry," Beto said. "We used to live in San Diego. Everyone spoke English there. Well, not everyone. But most people. And when my mom took us to Mexico, we had to learn Spanish."

The boy dodged his question, but Braden would give him time. For the moment, he was satisfied that he'd learned the children's secret. That would make things easier—as long as the kid didn't have any other surprises in store for him.

"Will you promise not to keep any more secrets from me?" Braden asked.

The boy looked up, relief splashed across his face, and nodded. Apparently, Braden had reached some level of trust with the child.

"You know what, Beto? Come with me. I want to show you something."

His little brother glanced up questioningly, but quickly followed him out of the stables and across the driveway toward the house. They entered the kitchen through the mudroom.

Elena was removing a cookie sheet from the oven, while Bela stood on a chair beside her.

As they passed through, Bela asked her brother, *"A dónde vas?"*

"Senor Braden wants to show me something. And then he's going to give me a riding lesson."

"Beto!" his twin scolded. Using her eyes, she gestured toward Braden, apparently chastising her brother for speaking English and giving away their secret.

"He already knows," Beto said. "I couldn't help it."

Elena raised her eyebrows at him, but Braden waved the girl to him. "Come on, Bela. I want to show you this, too."

Both kids and their nanny followed him upstairs and into his bedroom. When he reached the nightstand, he sat on the edge of his mattress, leaned forward and opened the bottom drawer. Buried deep in the back, behind rodeo flyers and various first and second place ribbons from his high school days, was a children's book, worn from use.

Braden pulled it out and, since Bela was standing closest to him, he handed it to her. The girl's eyes grew big and she showed it to her brother.

"My great-grandmother gave me that book," Braden said.

As they studied his old copy of *Horton Hatches the Egg*, he added, "She used to ask my dad to read it to me whenever he came to visit me at her ranch. I think that's the same reason she asked your *abuelito* to give it to you."

Did they realize what he was implying? Did he have to explain?

"So now that you know that we can speak English," Bela said, her sweet voice bearing only a hint of an accent, "are you going to tell the adoption people?"

Braden cocked his head slightly, not sure he was following her logic. Couldn't they see that he was telling them that they were family? He looked at Elena, who was leaning against the doorframe, and silently asked her to help him.

Elena moved forward. "Why are you worried about the adoption people?"

Braden was getting used to her coming to his rescue and could easily grow to depend upon it. As she sat beside him on the edge of the bed to be at eye level with the twins, he tried not to think about how close her hip was to his, how easy it would be to reach for her hand.

The twins looked at each other, probably conveying that they might as well come clean now.

Bela spoke first. "One of the big boys at the orphanage asked us to teach him English because he said the kids who were bilingual had a better chance to be adopted."

"But we didn't want to be adopted," Beto added. "We already have a father, Senor Rayburn. And he promised to come back for us."

"Okay," Braden said, although he was only more confused. "But once you left the orphanage and came here, why didn't you tell me you spoke English? It sure would have helped if you had."

"Yes, but we didn't want you to keep us forever," Bela said. "We thought you would send us back to the orphanage. And then Senor Rayburn would be able to find us there. But don't be mad at Beto. It was my idea."

Braden felt like a bucking bronc had just delivered a kick to his gut.

"Nobody has explained anything to them," Elena whispered. But her eyes spoke volumes. They were fiery mad and hinted at a deeper passion that she kept well hidden.

He looked at the little faces staring at him expectantly and then glanced back at the beautiful woman sitting beside him. Her expression all but said, "You're on your own with this one, cowboy."

He lowered his head so that he met the children's gazes. "Listen, kids. I have some bad news. Senor Rayburn, your dad, isn't able to come for you."

Beto tilted his head as if to process what he'd just heard, and Bela's eyes filled with tears.

"What I'm trying to say," Braden added, "is that he meant to come for you, but he died in a car accident."

Beto's eyes grew watery, too, and his bottom lip

trembled. "But will you still teach me to ride a horse before you send us back to the orphanage?"

"No," Braden said. "I mean, yes, I'll still teach you to ride a horse. But no, I'm not sending you to the orphanage."

"Why aren't you sending us back?" Bela wanted to know.

"Because we're family. And families stick together."

"How can we be family?" Beto asked. "You don't look like us. Your hair is a different color, and you don't even speak Spanish."

Elena finally swooped in for the save. "Braden is your brother and he's going to take care of you until Jason, your other brother, comes home."

"But how can they be our brothers?" Bela asked. "They're old, and we're not."

Braden was used to explaining concepts like that to people. He'd grown up understanding exactly how he fit into the Rayburn family—and how he hadn't. "We have different mothers, but we all have the same father. That makes me your half brother."

"Senor Rayburn is your dad, too?" Bela had finally lost some of her sadness and replaced it with an expression of hope.

"Yes, he was my dad. That's why I showed you my copy of *Horton Hatches the Egg*. We have the same granny, who loved the same book."

"Does Senor Jason have that book, too?" Bela asked.

How the heck should Braden know? He didn't even know the guy's food preferences let alone what his childhood reading habits were.

"I'm not sure," Braden admitted, realizing it wouldn't hurt to ask him. "He might have one."

"Jason's dad was Senor Rayburn," Elena said. "And Carly's dad was Senor Rayburn, too. So you have two half brothers and one half sister. Does that make sense?"

"Kind of," Beto said.

"So are we going to live with you?" Bela scooted closer to Elena, who placed her arm around the little girl. "At first, we didn't want to stay. But we like it here now."

"You're going to live with Braden until Jason and Carly get back," Elena explained. "And I'm going to stay here with you and help him until then."

That was a relief. He'd hired her because she was bilingual, and while there was no longer a language barrier, Braden still didn't feel competent enough to look after the twins on his own.

"After that," Elena continued, "Jason, Braden, and Carly are going to decide who gets to be the lucky one and have you live at their house permanently."

"Do they have horses, too?" Beto asked.

"Senor Jason doesn't," Bela said. "Remember? We stayed with him, and his house doesn't even have a yard."

That would, of course, present a problem when it came to sending the kids' menagerie along with them, but Braden wasn't going to worry about that now.

"Carly has a ranch," he said. "But no matter what we decide, you will always be able to visit all of us. And you can still ride horses."

"So our father isn't ever coming back?" Bela asked. "We'll never get to even meet him?"

Braden shook his head, knowing that he needed to allow the kids time to let the grief soak in and to sort through all the new changes in their lives. "But I'll try to make up for that. And I promise that you won't ever have to go back to the orphanage."

After a few moments of silence, nobody quite knowing what to say, Elena finally spoke. "I know that this will take some getting used to. So if you guys want to hang out by yourselves and talk things over, you can. I'll be in the kitchen putting away the cookies, and Braden will be…" She lifted her brow.

"In the barn," he said, "cleaning out the stables."

"So whenever you're ready to talk, you can come find us. And if you don't feel like talking about it, that's okay, too. We're both here for whatever you need."

The twins nodded solemnly then turned together and walked out of the bedroom.

Braden reached over and squeezed Elena's hand with gratitude. How had he made such a mess of that explanation?

When she squeezed back, he felt buoyed, strengthened. Thank goodness he had her to help him muddle through this.

"I can't believe no one told them until now," she said, her voice soft, low.

"How could I when I didn't think they spoke English?"

"You're right. I'm not blaming you. It's just sad that they had to find out about their father this way."

"Is there any good way to find out that your parent died?"

"No, I guess not. I was called into the principal's office during PE. Mrs. Cornwell, the school guidance counselor, was the one who told me about my mom. I was sad to hear it, but at the time, I was more confused about the changes that were bound to take place. My mind was racing and spinning."

"I can imagine how difficult that must have been."

Elena slowly shook her head. "It was right after lunch and Mrs. Cornwell had a bit of tuna fish stuck in her teeth. I remember worrying that if I started to cry, she might try and hug me, and then I'd have to smell her fishy breath. Emotions and memories are crazy things. Sometimes there's no rhyme or reason to them."

A few seconds passed, yet Braden kept her warm palm firmly inside his own. He'd never been good with words or with revealing the "inner man," whatever the hell that actually meant. The last woman he'd dated accused him of being emotionally mute, which had led to their breakup. He hadn't been upset by the split, but then again, he really hadn't been invested in the relationship, either.

Still, while he might not talk about what was going on inside him, he was definitely filled with emotions. He just didn't like sharing those feelings with others.

"Thanks again," he told Elena. "Not only for everything you've done this week, but for being here when I told them about Dad and for helping me find the right words."

"You're welcome." She squeezed his hand then released it. "The kids probably need some time to process everything. And nothing helps comfort kids like warm cookies. I better go back to the kitchen."

Braden watched her leave, his palm still warm and tingling from the intimate contact with hers. He should be relieved he'd just made it through one potential crisis.

So why did he feel as if he had even bigger problems coming his way?

* * *

The kids never did seek out Elena to discuss the revelation Braden had laid on them, but they seemed to have taken the news well. At least, Elena assumed they had.

Later that afternoon, she went in search of Braden and found him in the barn, where he was leading a mare from her stall.

At the sight of the cowboy and the sexy swagger she'd come to appreciate, her heart leaped. But she quickly downplayed the unwelcome reaction and said, "I thought I'd find you here."

He slowed to a stop. "Oh, yeah? What's up? Are the kids doing okay?"

"Yes, I think so. I haven't seen any sign of tears or sadness. In fact, they're in the backyard, building a pretend zoo."

Braden slowly shook his head. "What's to imagine? I have no idea what I'm going to do if they keep adding to their stray animal collection."

"At least the dog, cats and bunnies are keeping them entertained." Elena eased closer to the mare and stroked her neck. "What a pretty horse. What's her name?"

"Miss Posey. I'm going to take her to the corral closest to the house. I promised to teach Beto to ride, so I'll be saddling her regularly. It'll make things easier on me if she isn't out grazing on the range, where she was up until this morning."

"That boy sure loves animals," she said.

"Tell me about it." A slow smile stretched across his face, putting a spark in his eyes. "I'll have to admit, though, he's a kid after my own heart. I used to be enamored with my pets, too. In fact, at one time, I thought about being a vet."

"Really? Why didn't you pursue it?"

He shrugged. "I decided to ride rodeo instead."

Braden was an interesting man, and an intriguing one. He might appear to be a simple cowboy on the outside, but there was so much more to him than she'd realized.

"By the way," he said, "I thought it might be a good idea to order pizza tonight. We can call it a celebratory dinner and make the kids feel as though we're glad they're part of the family."

"That's a great idea. All children need to feel as though they're loved and that they fit in."

"That's true. I ought to know." A pensive expression settled over him, but he seemed to shake it off as quickly as it came. Then he tossed her a grin. "I'll drive into town later and get the pizza from Maestro's. It's my favorite. And I'll get salad and breadsticks to go with it."

"That sounds good to me. I spotted a tree full of peaches in the backyard. If they're as ripe as they look, I'll slice them and put them on top of vanilla ice cream for dessert."

"Perfect."

They continued to stand there, neither speaking further, neither moving. Elena didn't have anything else to say, so it was only natural to excuse herself and head back to the house. She was about to do just that when Braden reached out for her. His hand touched her hair. At the unexpected intimacy, her breath stopped, and her pulse raced.

"You have straw caught in here," he said, removing a small piece. "It must have fluttered down from the rafters."

She feigned a smile and tried to compose herself for making way more out of his touch than he'd meant it to be. "Thanks."

Again, neither made any attempt to move, something she'd better rectify if she knew what was good for her.

"I guess I'd better go back to the house," she said. "Who knows what else will flutter down on me." Or flutter through her.

"Just a hazard of ranch living," he said, reminding her that her time here on the Bar M was only temporary.

"One of them, anyway." Another would be to let any romantic thoughts take root. So she offered him one last smile, then turned and walked away.

The horse's hooves plodded along behind her, as Braden and Miss Posey followed her out of the barn and into the yard.

"I don't suppose you want riding lessons, too," he said to her back.

She paused and turned. *"Me?"*

He gave a half shrug. "Beto is going to hold me to my promise, and Bela will probably want them, too. Unless you'd rather watch or hang out in the house, I could teach you all at the same time."

After moving to Brighton Valley, she'd gone riding a few times with a friend she'd met at school. But she'd never considered herself a horsewoman by any means. Nor had she ever thought about taking riding lessons. She'd never felt the need to learn. After all, she and her parents had lived in town. Their house was large, but the yard was small.

She was about to tell him it wasn't necessary to give her any pointers, but standing in the yard with the handsome cowboy blessing her with a boyish grin, the whole idea suddenly had merit. "I have no idea when I'd ever ride again, but sure. It sounds like fun."

She actually liked the thought of it. Still, a little voice deep inside warned her about lowering her guard and having too much fun with Braden and the kids. After all, this was a job—and one that would end before she knew it.

So why did she have the sudden urge to enjoy it while it lasted?

Chapter Seven

After Braden and Beto left for town to pick up the pizza, Elena took Bela out in the backyard to pick peaches, as Pepita tagged along after them.

Quite a few of the plump fruit were already ripe, so they picked the ones they could reach and took them inside. Next, with the small shaggy dog seated on her haunches and watching them work, they washed and peeled the peaches. Since there were too many to eat over the next couple of days, they froze what they wouldn't use tonight.

While Elena wiped down the countertop with a warm soapy dishcloth, Bela turned her focus on the little dog, who'd been waiting patiently for a playmate.

"I think Pepita needs a haircut," Bela said. "Her bangs are way too long for her to see."

"Or maybe you can use a barrette to pull them out of her face."

Bela's eyes widened. "Yes, and she'll look pretty that way."

Elena had no idea what Beto was going to say about that, but she smiled and watched the child dash off, the shaggy mutt on her heels.

Before Elena could find something else to keep her busy, the guys arrived with dinner.

Braden laid several pizza boxes on the table and opened the first lid, releasing a whiff of Italian sausage, spices and rich tomato sauce. "I know you're not big on meat, so I also ordered a small vegetarian one."

"Mmm," Elena said. "It sure looks and smells good."

"Wait until you taste it." Braden smiled and turned to Beto. "Let's open that bag and get the salad and breadsticks out."

Beto did as he was told, but stopped the moment Bela returned with Pepita, who now sported a red barrette on her head.

"Cool," the boy said. "Look at her big eyes."

"I know." Bela crossed her arms and grinned. "She's happier now that she can see us."

Elena sent the kids to wash their hands. "We'll eat as soon as you're finished." Then she went to the pantry, retrieved the paper plates and napkins and set them next to the pizzas.

She glanced at Braden, who was removing glasses from the cupboard. "We probably won't be able to finish all of this. You bought enough for an army."

"No, I didn't. In fact, we probably won't end up with any leftovers. You have no idea how much I love eating anything from Maestro's."

Minutes after the kids raced back into the kitchen,

everyone was seated at the kitchen table with full plates.

After taking the first delicious bite, Elena told Braden he was right. "This is the best pizza I've ever had. Thanks for suggesting it—and for taking the time to drive into town to get it."

"Believe me," he said, as he dabbed his napkin to his mouth, "it was my pleasure."

As Elena reached for her own napkin, she couldn't help but smile, locking that bit of information away. Not that she'd need to remember his preferences...

"Senor Braden," Beto said, "when do I get to ride Miss Posey?"

Braden looked up from his plate, a slice of half-eaten pizza in his hand. "I'm your brother, Beto. Don't call me *Senor*. You don't have to be so polite."

"Okay." The boy brightened, his eyes hopeful. "But when are you going to teach me to ride?"

"Maybe tomorrow. I have some chores to get done in the morning, but I should have some free time after lunch."

"Can you teach me, too?" Bela asked her big brother.

"You bet. Beto won't have as much fun riding by himself."

The kids shot a glance at each other, then giggled in delight.

When they finished eating nearly all the pizza, as well as a bowl of vanilla ice cream and sweet peaches, Elena suggested a card game. Much to her surprise, Braden agreed to play. And for the first time, the Rayburn siblings experienced a family night.

After a second "last" game of Go Fish, Braden sent

the kids to watch television in the family room, while Elena set about cleaning up the kitchen.

"Is there anything I can do to help?" Braden asked.

"No, I'm just about finished." She turned to face him, her gaze locking on his dazzling green eyes. When he looked away, she continued to study his profile, as well as his broad chest and narrow hips. How could a cowboy be so handsome and so darn tempting?

"What about bath time?" he asked. "I can supervise so you can get some rest. I hadn't meant to work you from sunup to sundown."

She smiled. "Do you think you can handle their bedtime routine?"

He shrugged. "At least I can talk to them now."

That had to be a huge relief. Maybe he could finally begin to bond with them. And then he'd be able to handle them better when she left.

"Just make sure they don't flood the bathroom," she said. "And don't worry. They can dress themselves in their pj's."

"But then what? Do I just tuck them in and tell them good-night?"

"Why don't you read *Horton Hatches the Egg* to them," she suggested. "I'll bet they'll like that."

"They probably would, but I haven't read aloud since I was a kid."

"It's like riding a bike." She offered him an encouraging smile. "You won't have any problem."

"I guess you're right. Besides, it's the least I can do after leveling with them about Dad's death."

"I wouldn't worry too much about that, especially since they seem to have taken the news so well. Besides, they hadn't met him yet, so I think they're feeling disappointment rather than grief."

"I'm not so sure about that. They may have some fantasy built up about fathers, but my dad wasn't…"

She waited for him to continue in his own time, but when he didn't, she prodded him. "He wasn't what?"

"Involved. Demonstrative. Affectionate. Pick one." He shrugged, as if it didn't matter to him, as if it never had. But that surely wasn't the case.

Elena had a close, loving relationship with her father, so she felt badly for Braden, who hadn't experienced the same thing with his.

She placed her hand on his arm, felt his bicep flex at her touch. She'd meant the gesture to be sympathetic and compassionate—even supportive—yet it seemed to have stirred up something else. Something that was way out of line if they wanted to keep their relationship platonic and professional.

Doing her best to shake it off, she took a step back and said, "I'm sorry."

"Don't be. I turned out okay. My grandpa stepped up and became my male role model, which was for the best."

From what she'd heard about Charles Rayburn, that was probably true. Mr. Miller had been well-respected in the community and a good man for Braden to emulate. And now he'd taken over the Bar M, no doubt as his grandfather had expected him to.

Elena tucked a strand of hair behind her ear. "So you're breeding horses, just like he did?"

"Why not? He made a name for himself and the Bar M in the rodeo circles."

"I heard he once was a bronc buster—and a good one."

"Yes, he was." Braden moved toward the sink, closing the distance between them. "I rode a few broncs in my day, too. But I preferred riding bulls."

She turned and leaned against the kitchen counter. "Do you miss the rodeo?"

"Yes, but it's not feasible for me to compete anymore."

"Because of your responsibilities on the ranch?"

"For the most part. Someone has to run things around here." He nodded toward the ceramic cookie jar on the counter. "I saw you baking this morning. Did the kids eat them all?"

She laughed. "Nope. I managed to save plenty for you. I had no idea you had such a sweet tooth."

He tossed her a crooked grin. "What can I say? I'm just a kid at heart."

Maybe so, but he was a man through and through.

He reached into the jar and pulled out a couple of chocolate chip cookies. "I'll down these, then tell the twins it's time to get ready for bed. After they're both dozing, maybe you and I can watch a movie. I think my mom left behind a few chick flicks."

As appealing as that sounded, she didn't think it was a good idea. She didn't want to get into the habit of spending the evenings alone with him. Yet it was too early to turn in for the night, and she didn't feel like reading.

A movie with Braden was winning out, although she refused to wonder why.

She really ought to give her response more consideration, but she found herself saying, "Sure, a movie sounds great."

* * *

The bath-time ritual had gone off without a hitch, and so had the bedtime story. Braden hadn't been sure how to go about tucking in the kids, so he'd simply told them good-night and turned off the light.

Now, as he and Elena sat next to each other on the sofa, with a bowl of popcorn between them, he tried to focus on the movie. In spite of his best efforts, he couldn't seem to concentrate on the story.

He didn't know why he'd suggested a chick flick when his preference would have been a thriller or an action-adventure movie. Just trying to be a good host, he supposed.

But was that really it? Or had he actually been trying to ensure that Elena would agree to join him this evening?

He told himself that wasn't the case, but his libido argued otherwise.

Okay, so maybe there was some truth to his attempt to spend the evening with her. He was definitely attracted to her—and he sensed she was feeling the same way.

Would she be open to a romantic fling? In his experience, a lot of women would. But Elena wasn't like other women. She would want some kind of commitment, and he couldn't offer that. He'd had his share of temporary relationships, but he'd been avoiding anything serious since marriage was out of the question. What did he know about happy unions?

Of course, his mom and Erik were giving him a good idea about what "till death do us part" might be all about.

And even if he decided to settle down with someone like Elena, he doubted she'd be interested in living with a cowboy. She had definite ambitions that didn't include life on a ranch.

"Are you enjoying this?" Elena asked, the popcorn bowl now in her lap.

She meant the movie, of course, which wasn't bad. In fact, it was somewhat entertaining. The problem was his mind kept drifting to thoughts of creating a little romance in real life.

"Yeah, it's pretty good," he said.

While the onscreen lovers shared a lusty kiss, Braden stole a peek at Elena, saw her looking dreamily at the TV screen. So, he thought, she wasn't opposed to romance.

As if aware of his perusal, she turned and caught him watching her. Rather than look away, he continued to study her, letting things take a natural course—if she was game.

She bit down on her bottom lip, then asked, "Popcorn?"

Before he could respond, she thrust the bowl at him. As their fingers touched, a blast of heat shot along his nerve endings. She must have felt it, too, because her grip fumbled, and the bowl slipped from her hands, spilling popcorn and kernels onto the floor.

"Oh, shoot. I'm such a klutz." She dropped to her knees in a flash, attempting to clean up the mess.

He joined her on the floor, scooped up a handful of popcorn and placed it back in the bowl. "Don't worry about it," he said, chuckling at the result of her reaction to their touch. "We can always make more."

She glanced up, her gaze wounded or possibly…

Something powerful passed between them. Attraction? Arousal?

Without taking time to analyze exactly what it was—or what the results of his action might be—he cupped her cheek. "Relax. It's no big deal."

At least, the spilled popcorn wasn't. But the growing sexual awareness that had settled over them seemed like a huge deal.

She blinked, but didn't break eye contact. Then she ran her tongue along her bottom lip, which was his complete undoing.

He might be sorry about this later, but he lowered his mouth to hers. And the kiss was just as sweet, just as stirring as he'd hoped it would be.

Her lips parted, inviting him to take full advantage of the moment, to explore her mouth, to savor her taste. And while he'd kissed plenty of women in the past, this time was different. Elena was different.

As his tongue sought hers, the kiss damn near exploded in passion.

Braden wanted nothing but to continue to see it through, to take part in what was sure to unfold, but common sense demanded to be heard. *Don't risk losing her.*

He stifled the warning and deepened the kiss, and Elena responded in kind. She seemed to be every bit as invested in the heated moment as he was. That is, until she ended it and pulled away.

"That was a bad idea," she said, her eyes lighting on the sofa, the popcorn, anywhere but on his.

"Maybe so, but it was nice."

She bit down on her bottom lip, "Yes, it was. But now what?"

Making love came to mind, but he knew better than to suggest that. He struggled to come up with a response.

"I think," she said, her gaze finally meeting his, "under the circumstances, it would be best if you hired another nanny. I'll stay until you find someone competent, of course."

He wanted to object, but she was right. Still, he couldn't seem to find his voice, couldn't seem to admit it.

"It's for the best," she added.

Elena was the kind of woman a man married—not one with whom to have a brief sexual fling.

"You're probably right," he said. "And I'd definitely like your help in finding a replacement."

But if it was so right, why did his gut twist at the thought of her leaving the ranch and going off to find a new life in the city?

Three days later, Elena sat in the home office at the Bar M, studying the latest application that had been emailed and was displayed on the computer screen. She couldn't believe how many people responded to the ad Braden had placed in the online newspaper. He'd also set up a private email account for them and told Elena to feel free to look over the applications and voice her opinion.

Brighton Valley was a small town, and as a result, most of the applicants lived in the bigger city of Wexler. Several were high school age and would view the position as a glorified babysitting gig, so as far as Elena was concerned, they were out. Three of the women who expressed interest didn't speak Spanish, and while it was true that the children spoke English, Elena felt that they'd benefit from someone with a similar cultural background.

Voices sounded outside. She heard Bela squeal with delight, followed by a burst of Beto's laughter.

Elena glanced out the window at her charges, who were getting another riding lesson today. As Braden led Bela around the yard on Miss Posey, the little girl's pink sneakers wiggled as if she wanted to urge the mare to move faster.

Beto followed close behind, his lips moving a mile a minute as he chattered away, no doubt talking Braden's ear off. She couldn't help wondering what the precocious little boy was saying. She got a kick out of him— and sweet Bela, too.

She was going to miss them both when she left. Ten days ago, when she'd taken this job, it had seemed exactly that—a job. But this past week, she'd actually found that she enjoyed being around the kids. Every new discovery they encountered on the ranch excited them.

They weren't whiney like her younger siblings tended to be. They appreciated everything she did for them and never seemed to complain about much— even when she had to comb tangles out of Bela's hair or shoo Beto outside to scrape the mud off his shoes.

They also played well together, rarely finding anything to squabble about. Plus, even though this was Braden's house and he was supposed to be their principal caretaker, Elena never felt as if she had to play second fiddle, the way she often did when she was at home with her dad and stepmother.

She supposed that was because Braden tended to

defer to her on all matters related to the children and the house. And being her own boss made it seem like less of a chore. Of course, spending time with Braden wasn't much of a chore, either. Well, maybe she should rephrase that. It took a great deal of effort to tamp down a growing attraction to the man she'd begun to admire and respect.

Her gaze drifted from the children to the cowboy who'd once claimed he didn't know anything about kids. When he threw back his head in laughter at something Bela said, Elena's heart slammed against her rib-cage.

Kissing him the other night had been a mistake. Although it had been fun playing house with him the past week, a relationship with him couldn't possibly blossom into something special, something lasting. She needed to move to Houston and open her own shop. And he wanted to... Well, she had no idea what Braden wanted to do. Stay in Brighton Valley and raise rodeo horses, she supposed. He probably didn't have any dreams other than that.

No, cutting ties now was for the best—before either of them got too attached. So Elena returned her focus to the computer, liking what she was seeing in the re-sume of Francisca Flores.

After emailing directions to the ranch to the woman, who'd said she could come out for an interview tomor-row, Elena pulled up the website that had listings of storefront properties for rent in Houston. It took some searching, but she finally found a place that appeared to be the perfect location for the quirky little shop she envisioned. With the money Braden would be paying her, she'd have enough to cover the deposit on the lease and to purchase some fixtures.

She picked up her cell phone to call the listing Realtor, just as the back door opened.

When she heard Braden's voice tell the twins, "Make sure you guys wash your hands before getting a snack," she ended her attempted call and shoved the cell back into her pocket.

Elena's dream would have to wait—at least, temporarily.

She walked to the kitchen to see if Braden needed any help in fixing the afternoon snack and found him pulling a jug of apple juice from the fridge. His blond curls were matted down, thanks to the Stetson he'd been wearing that now hung on the hook by the back door.

She fought the urge to close the gap between them and comb her fingers through his hair.

Down, girl. A move like that was sure to get her into trouble.

"Hey," she said, "how did the lessons go?"

His broad smile lit the room and touched her heart. "Great."

Before he could continue, Beto entered the kitchen and responded for him, his excitement racing through his voice. "Braden said I was good enough to try mutton bustin' when the Brighton Valley Rodeo starts in October."

"What's mutton busting?" she asked. Her dad might be in the feed business, but she'd always been big city bound and never been too interested in livestock or rodeos or anything that seemed too country.

"We get to ride sheep," Bela said, as she joined her brother.

Elena tried not to appear as confused as she felt. "Why would you want to ride sheep when you can ride a horse?"

"It's really cool," Beto said, his accent all but non-existent, reminding her that the twins had been born in the States and might have lived here much longer than either Braden or his siblings realized. "It's like riding a wild bronco, but they make the kids do it on sheep so they don't get hurt."

"Yeah, they do it at all the rodeos," Bela added, sounding as if she'd grown up on the circuit.

"Don't worry," Braden said. "The kids wear helmets so it's completely safe. And it doesn't bother the sheep."

Why did Elena suddenly have the feeling that she'd become the odd man out? For the past week, everyone had turned to her for guidance, and now it seemed as if they no longer needed her.

She should feel satisfied and relieved, knowing that she'd completed her job successfully. Yet it was still a little unsettling to think they'd have no trouble getting along without her.

"Here," she said, handing each child one of the peach muffins she'd made earlier. "Grab a glass of juice and take these out on the porch."

"Mmm," Beto said as he bit into one, leaving a trail of crumbs on the floor.

Elena would have told him to clean up after himself if Pepita hadn't trailed after him, picking up the droppings.

"These muffins are even better than your cookies," Bela told her as she followed her brother outside.

Well, at least Elena was still useful in the kitchen.

"Did you hear back from anyone about the nanny job?" Braden asked, as he reached for a muffin.

"Yes, I did. We got two more potential candidates today, although I'm not sure if you want to interview one of them."

Braden took a bite of his muffin, then closed his eyes and grinned. "Bela was right. These *are* better than the cookies."

A surge of pride rushed through her, but she took a step back, unsure of how to react to being in the room alone with him.

"Thank you," she said, then added, "I've narrowed the field down to two women. One is Francisca Flores, who's coming tomorrow morning for an interview and to meet the twins. In her email, she said she has three children. Her youngest is going off to college, so she'd like a little extra money to help with school expenses. The other one hasn't gotten back to me about coming tomorrow, but it would be nice if we could make the interviews back-to-back so that you wouldn't have to take any more time away from your chores."

"Tomorrow works out great. I was talking to Miguel Garcia, a guy who used to be on the circuit with me. His sister is visiting from Juarez, but she'd like to stay in the States. She needs to get a work visa, but would be interested in the job, too. She's also willing to go to Houston with Jason or move onto the Leaning R with Carly. So I'll tell him to send her over tomorrow, as well. What time would be best?"

Elena didn't want to sound too dismissive of his friend's sister, but it nagged at her that the woman might only be interested in the nanny job so that she could stay in the country. Still, she said, "Ten o'clock would work—and it won't interfere with the other two interviews."

"I'll give him a call and line it up."

Before Elena could broach her concerns, Braden grabbed two more muffins, as well as his hat in the mudroom, then went outside.

She couldn't help finding fault with Ms. Garcia before she'd even met her. Beto and Bela weren't just some means to an end. They were also emotionally vulnerable and still adjusting to their new surroundings. They needed someone who cared about them, someone who could provide them with a sense of security.

Sure, Elena hadn't necessarily taken all of that into account when she'd taken on the job for purely financial reasons, but it was different with her.

As she placed the gallon jug of juice back into the fridge, she told herself she'd have to give Miguel's sister a chance. Besides, she had a feeling that Braden would lean toward hiring someone related to a friend. So she just hoped things were different for that woman, too.

But that didn't prevent her from wondering about the nanny who would take over her job and insisting that she have a say in the hiring decision.

Chapter Eight

At a quarter after ten the next morning, Elena and Braden prepared to meet the first potential nanny, who'd just driven into the yard. She'd arrived fifteen minutes late, but Elena wouldn't hold that against her. After all, things happened, cars didn't start, people took a wrong turn… Still, the directions to the ranch were pretty easy to follow.

When the bell rang, Braden answered the door, introduced himself and greeted the sister of his friend. "It's nice to finally meet you, Lola."

The attractive woman, who was in her mid to late twenties, took his hand in both of hers. *"Mucho gusto, Señor Rayburn."*

"Call me Braden," he said, as he led her into the living room. "Please have a seat."

Elena could only gape at the woman seeking a nanny position. Surely Braden had noticed her inappropriate outfit—the black spiked heels, the leopard-print miniskirt that revealed long, shapely thighs and the black Lycra tank top that barely contained a pair of breasts, the size of which would cause anyone to question whether they were natural or enhanced by surgery.

"Can I get you something to drink?" Braden asked. "Coffee, iced tea, water…?"

Lola must have been in awe of the man or undecided about what she wanted because she merely stared at him and failed to answer.

Elena could excuse herself to bring out a tray of drink selections, but she remained rooted to the living room floor, giving Lola another once-over and coming to an early judgment.

Did this woman think she was interviewing to be a cocktail waitress, rather than a nanny?

Elena was stunned, although Braden didn't appear the least bit unbalanced by her appearance. But then why would he be? He was a man, wasn't he?

"Well, then," Braden said, rubbing his hands together and looking a bit sheepish.

Okay, so he *had* been a little taken aback by the attractive woman.

He turned to Elena, as if handing off the baton to the interview. But even though she tried to come up with a couple of questions to ask, she couldn't help focusing on the double Ds that spilled out of Lola's scooped neckline.

Enough of that, she told herself. She shouldn't write off the woman too quickly. So she opted to give her another chance. That is, until she caught Braden smiling as if he'd just met Sofía Vergara—or rather, her sexy younger sister—on the red carpet in Hollywood.

"So, Lola," Elena asked, "have you ever worked with children before?"

The well-endowed Latina appeared to be stumped by the question, so Elena asked her again in Spanish.

Lola brightened and lifted up her right hand, spreading all five fingers and flashing long, bright red acrylic nails. *"Si. Mi mamá tiene cinco niños."*

Oh, wow. So she couldn't speak English? If Braden chose her, how the heck was that going to work out for him?

Interpreting, Elena said, "Her mother has five children."

"So you helped raise them?" he asked.

"Que dice?" Lola glanced at Elena quizzically.

Great. Braden was going to need an on-site interpreter if he wanted to communicate with her.

When Elena translated his question, Lola spoke in rapid-fire Spanish. But instead of directing her response to Elena, she spoke to Braden, who clearly couldn't understand a word she was saying.

After Lola finally stopped talking, ending with a comment about the night school course in conversational English she'd signed up for at the local junior college, Braden looked at Elena and lifted his brow.

"She said that she helped out with child care at home until she was fourteen, and then she got a job at the beauty salon down the street from where she grew up. She's been a beautician in Mexico and was hoping to find a job in a salon here in the States, but she found out that she needs a cosmetology license to work in Texas. She's also taking English classes at night." Elena fought the urge to roll her eyes and continued. "She'd be happy to watch the children during the day, but she can't commit to helping out indefinitely. She's waiting to learn whether she'll be accepted at the beauty school in Wexler this fall."

Braden nodded, then cast a gaze at his friend's sister, no doubt noting how attractive she was. That is, if a man liked a woman who had a sexy, flamboyant appearance.

Elena wanted to tell Lola that she wasn't quite what they had in mind for a nanny, but she needed to talk it over with Braden first. Surely, he'd agree with her. But before she could come up with another question or figure out a way to end the interview completely, the twins came downstairs, Pepita trotting along behind them.

"This is Beto and Bela," Braden said.

Lola stood and greeted the kids in Spanish. Unfortunately, Elena missed most of what they said because she was trying to snag her boss's attention so she could tell him, at least with her eyes, that there was no way he should hire that woman.

She wasn't sure if Braden had picked up on her body language or facial expression, but he must have sensed something because he told Beto and Bela to take Lola outside. "Show her the backyard, where you play, and introduce her to your pets. Then you can take her out to the stables. She might like seeing the horses."

"Que dice?" Lola asked again.

This time, Bela acted as the translator.

No, Lola wasn't going to work out. Not only would Braden have a major language issue, but it also would be too tempting for the kids to manipulate the situation to their benefit.

Elena glanced at Braden, who'd stood as Lola left the room. She hoped he'd come to the same conclusion, but his gaze followed the woman teetering on four-inch heels as she passed through the doorway that led to the kitchen and out the back door.

Elena hoped those stupid sling-backs sank into the grass and picked up dirt along the way.

Okay, so that wasn't true. They were actually very nice sling-backs, the kind that she hoped to sell in her shop one day. And wasn't her ambition reason enough for her to let Braden hire whomever he wanted to replace her?

But then why was she feeling so darned…? Well, she certainly wasn't jealous. Lola just annoyed her, that's all.

As Braden took his seat and settled back into the sofa cushions, he said, "The kids sure seem to like her."

Seriously? He was leaning toward hiring her?

Elena's annoyance level spiked. "Of course they like her. She's pretty and shiny like a brand-new toy." The moment she caught the envy in her voice, she wished she'd kept her thoughts to herself.

"I'm sure she only wanted to make a good impression," Braden said. "So that's why she dressed up for the interview."

Dressed up? Why, Lola was hardly dressed at all, at least when it came to hiding her attributes or merely hinting at them. Surely Braden saw through her.

Then again, his father had been a notorious womanizer. Maybe the apple didn't fall too far from the tree.

But did he have to be so blatant in his appreciation of feminine beauty? Especially when he'd kissed Elena senseless just four nights ago.

"So what do you think?" Braden asked.

Elena didn't trust herself to speak for fear she'd blurt out a string of criticism. So she said, "You go first."

Braden studied pretty Elena, who was clearly un-impressed with Miguel's sister. Apparently she wanted him to voice the same opinion.

To be honest, Lola was nice enough and would work out if he were in a pinch, but she really didn't seem to be nanny material. Elena probably had come to the same conclusion. But he'd also sensed a bit of jealousy on her part, and for some crazy reason, he couldn't help but egg it on.

"Lola needs the job," he said.

Elena's delicate brow shot up, and she folded her arms across her chest. "She might *want* the job, but I wouldn't say she *needs* it. There have to be other posi-tions she could take on. And as for the kids liking her, how could you tell in such a short amount of time?"

"They seemed eager to take her outside and show her around."

A spark blazed in Elena's brown eyes, setting off flecks of gold. "You told them to give her a tour of the ranch—and to introduce her to their pets. It's not as if they came up with the idea on their own. Besides, Beto and Bela are polite and obedient. They were just following your orders, so you can't possibly know how they really feel about her until you take them aside later and ask them."

Braden hadn't issued an order. It had been more of a suggestion to move things along—and to have some private time with Elena so they could talk. But he wasn't going to make an issue out of it. Besides, he enjoyed seeing Elena's spunk, which hinted at her pas-

sionate nature. Of course, the heated kiss they'd shared
had revealed plenty of that.

A smile tugged at the corner of his lips, but he did
his best to tamp it down so she wouldn't pick up on the
fact that he liked seeing her attempt to discredit Lola.

But before Elena could voice another objection, she
was cut off by the sound of an approaching vehicle.
Braden rose from his seat and peered out the bay window and into the front yard, where a white older model
Ford Taurus had just parked near the house.

"Looks like applicant number two is here," he said.

"She's early. That's a good sign." Elena stood and
headed for the door. When she reached for the knob,
she paused long enough to add, "And don't forget, I
told you I would stay until you found the right replacement. So you don't need to make any quick decisions."

That was true. And if he had his preference, he'd
stick with the nanny he already had, even if kissing
her led to something deeper and complicated, something that would screw up both their lives. So he'd have
to settle on hiring someone else until either Jason or
Carly returned.

Hopefully the woman would be willing to move
with the twins, which meant they wouldn't have to
make any more adjustments than necessary.

Elena would agree to that. She'd also clearly decided
that Lola was out of the running. And while he'd never
admit it out loud, she was right. He would just have to
figure out something to tell Miguel.

Maybe he'd suggest that Lola should apply for work
at The Stagecoach Inn, although she'd have to learn
English.

His grin deepened into a full-on smile. Either way, she'd definitely help them sell more drinks.

In the meantime, they had another interview to conduct. He watched as Elena invited a pleasant looking, middle-age Latina into the house.

"You must be Francisca Flores," Elena said, as she stepped away from the door to allow the woman inside. "Why don't you have a seat?"

"Thank you." Mrs. Flores, whose salt-and-pepper hair had been pulled up into a neat twist, chose one of the overstuffed chairs.

Again, Elena and Braden sat on the sofa. But this time, much to Braden's relief, the interview continued in English.

"I'm glad you could come to talk to us," Elena told the matronly woman. "Your application sounded very promising. And I really liked the fact that you've raised three children. The twins are sweet kids and need someone who's experienced, as well as kind and loving."

"I adore children," Mrs. Flores said. "I'm also a good cook, so I'd be happy to take on that responsibility, too."

Elena glanced at Braden, approval glowing in her eyes even though they'd barely started the interview. But he suspected she was even more determined to find a replacement now that she'd decided Lola wasn't going to work out.

During the course of their conversation, they learned that Francisca's oldest daughter had graduated from nursing school and now worked at the Brighton Valley Medical Center. Her oldest son was completing an internship at a law firm in Houston and her youngest was a freshman at the University of Texas in Austin.

"All I ever wanted to be was a mother," Francisca said. "My husband had a good job, so I was able to stay home with the kids. They were my life, and now that they're gone and my nest is empty, I thought I'd get a job. But in truth, even though I have some secretarial experience, I think I'm better off seeking a position where I can use my best skills—providing child care for others."

They took turns asking questions and Braden had to admit he liked Francisca's answers. He'd just opened his mouth to ask a follow-up when the back door opened, and the kids led Lola into the living room. The scruffy little dog they'd adopted padded along beside them, its bushy hair pulled out of its eyes with a little pink bow.

Braden snuck a glance at Francisca and saw her checking out the younger applicant, no doubt coming to the same conclusion Elena had, though her expression remained professional.

An awkward silence filled the room until Beto announced, "Lola wants to learn how to ride a horse like me and Bela. Can you give her lessons, too, Braden?"

He didn't dare glance at Elena, who undoubtedly would find fault with the idea. Yet he couldn't believe his rodeo buddy's sister didn't know how to ride. But then again, look at her. She appeared to be... Well, citified came to mind. And if he remembered correctly, Lola was Miguel's half sister. Unlike Miguel, she hadn't grown up on a ranch. Braden, better than anyone, knew how those family dynamics worked.

"Sure," he said, "I can teach her." Maybe that would

make up for choosing Mrs. Flores for the job instead of her.

He took a moment to introduce the two nanny candidates. To Francisca's credit, she smiled and shook Lola's hand. As soon as she realized the younger woman didn't speak English, she lapsed into their shared language.

Braden had no idea what they were saying, but Elena did. She was also wearing a smile. When she responded in Spanish, Braden picked up the word *gracias*, so he assumed she was thanking them for coming.

The women nodded, then addressed the children. Francisca extended a hand to them, greeting them with respect.

However, Lola stooped to their eye level, her miniskirt and tank top having one hell of a time keeping her feminine attributes modestly covered. Her movements also provided Braden with an eyeful. Then she gave each of the kids a kiss on the forehead.

As she straightened, she turned her back to the twins, unable to see Bela roll her eyes or Beto swipe at his forehead with the back of his hand.

Before they gave themselves away, Braden suggested that they take Pepita out for a potty break, and they quickly obeyed. He didn't dare look at Elena to gauge her reaction. It had to be the same as the kids'.

Instead, he walked to the front door and opened it for the women.

Mrs. Flores exited first, but Lola paused in the doorway. *"Mucho gusto, Braden."* Then she puckered up and gave him a kiss on his cheek, which took him by surprise. It must have also left a red splotch of lipstick, which he wanted to wipe away, just like Beto had done. Only he'd use a bit more discretion.

Once both Lola and Francisca were headed to their respective vehicles, Braden shut the door and turned to Elena, hoping they'd soon have something to laugh about. But she stood straight and solemn, her arms crossed, her lips pursed.

So much for finding anything comical about Miguel's sister and the impression she'd made on all of them.

"Is there a third nanny candidate?" he asked.

Elena softened her stance—ever so slightly. "There was one more woman who was interested, but she had car trouble and couldn't get a ride out here. We could probably talk to her tomorrow, but since we really don't have a lot of time to waste, maybe it would be best to make a decision based on the two we've met."

Braden didn't need Elena to remind him that she was leaving soon. He'd been trying not to think about it ever since they'd had that after-the-kiss talk the other night.

"So what did you think of the women we talked to today?" he asked, though he already knew what she'd decided.

Elena unfolded her arms and strode toward the sofa, where she'd been seated before. She ran her hand along the top of the backrest, then turned to face him. "Francisca is obviously a better fit and more experienced with children."

He agreed, but for some reason, he didn't say so. Instead he pointed out, "Mrs. Flores didn't seem to be as friendly or as affectionate as Lola. And kids, especially Bela and Beto, need a lot of love and reassurance."

Elena seemed to consider his comment as she sat

down on the sofa. "Yes, that's true, but most kids need time to warm up to a person. And Lola pushed herself on them too quickly."

She'd also warmed up to Braden too quickly, although maybe it was a cultural thing and she'd assumed he and her brother were closer than they actually were.

He was tempted to level with Elena, to tell her they were on the same page, but he couldn't help teasing her a bit more and letting her think he was leaning toward hiring Lola.

"Did you see Bela take a hold of Lola's hand?" he asked.

"No, when did that happen?"

"When the kids took her outside to give her a tour of the ranch."

Elena clicked her tongue. "Bela's a bright girl—and observant. She probably thought Lola was going to fall flat on her face if she wasn't careful going down the porch steps."

At that, Braden laughed. "I'll admit she wasn't dressed for being on a ranch."

Elena smiled, then added, "I don't think Lola is very sincere, either. She seemed shallow. And she was way too forceful."

"You didn't like the fact that she gave everyone but you a kiss goodbye?"

Elena scowled, and he realized he might be taking things too far.

"I'm just teasing you," he said.

"Come on, Braden. That was way over the top for an interview. Just because Mrs. Flores didn't do that kissy-face goodbye like sexy Lola did doesn't mean she isn't affectionate."

He'd decided to end his teasing—or was it more like flirting?—but he couldn't help asking, "You think Lola was sexy?"

"Don't tell me you *didn't*. I saw the way you were gawking at her."

Actually, Braden was staring at her because he'd been surprised to see someone show up for an interview dressed like that. And since he couldn't understand a word she'd been saying, he'd smiled and nodded in an effort to be polite. But if truth be told, Elena was far more appealing, more attractive and more…everything than Lola.

"I've been messing with you," he finally admitted. "Lola may be my friend's sister, but Mrs. Flores will make a better nanny for the twins."

"Good. I'm glad to hear that."

Silence stretched between them for a couple of beats. Then he added, "Lola knows how to get all dolled up because she went to beauty school. She was probably just trying to show off."

"No," Elena corrected. "She worked at a salon in Mexico, but she didn't have any formal training. She *wants* to go to beauty college and plans to get a job in a shop here. So the nanny position would only be temporary for her."

"This job was only temporary to you, too," he reminded her.

"Yes, but I'm different."

That was true. Braden could count off any number of reasons why that was the case. But he wondered what Elena thought made her so different from Lola. Or maybe he just hadn't wanted to quit teasing her completely.

"How so?" he asked.

She merely shook her head and got up from her seat.

Had he pushed her too far?

Elena strode to the sliding glass door that looked out into the backyard to check on Beto and Bela. She spotted the dog, but not the kids, so she remained there.

Had Braden uttered that silly question because he'd yet to learn anything about her? Or was he still "messing" with her?

She turned and faced him. "I'm different because I truly care about the twins."

"You may have grown to care, but you didn't know them very well when you first came to work here. And we all adjusted to the change."

You'd think he was ready to get rid of her. It might have been her idea to put some distance between them, but that didn't mean that she... Oh, heck. She didn't know what any of that meant. And she didn't dare stew on it any longer. She might read more into it than she should.

"You know," he said, "I hope we don't settle on a nanny too soon."

Her heart stalled, and she waited for him to explain. She knew better than to hope that his reason for making that statement had nothing to do with convenience and everything to do with her, with them, with what they could have together. So she rallied her senses. "Why is that?"

"Because there's one other candidate. We should probably talk to her. And besides, I haven't taken you horseback riding yet."

Seriously? That was his reason?

"You don't have to do that," she said. "Who knows when I'll have another chance to go riding. I'll probably be working 24/7 once I move."

"Maybe so," he said with a boyish grin. "But a promise is a promise."

He crossed the distance between them and placed his hand along her jaw. His thumb caressed her cheek, causing a bevy of butterflies to flutter through her.

"It's too bad we both have different futures mapped out for ourselves," he said.

True, but they'd also been damaged by their pasts, and while she'd thought that she'd moved on—and he probably thought he had, too—something told her they were still leery of getting romantically involved with anyone, especially if the relationship wasn't going to be lasting.

Yet right this minute, as Braden's gaze locked on hers and his thumb caressed her cheek, going for a ride with him—in bed or on horseback—sounded way too appealing.

Chapter Nine

The next afternoon, Braden made good on his offer to teach Elena how to ride a horse. And no one seemed happier than Beto and Bela.

The six-year-olds, who'd had several lessons already, stood beside the corral, leaning against the white wooden rails and grinning from ear to ear as they waited for Braden to teach Elena everything they'd learned.

"Now you can go with us," Beto called out.

Apparently he thought horseback riding would be a family activity—or one they could do together. But Elena wasn't a part of the Rayburn clan and wouldn't be staying here much longer. So she would have to set the twins straight and let them know she'd be leaving soon.

Braden had already saddled two of the older mares for the kids, although he hadn't let them mount yet. He also had a gelding he'd chosen for Elena. But shouldn't he be running out of gentle mounts for beginners to ride? After all, he bred and trained rodeo horses on the ranch. Most of his stock had to be young—and unbroken.

"I'd like you to meet Chester," he said, as he saddled the large black gelding. "Back in the day, he would have been better suited for an experienced rider. But he's pretty mellow now."

"So what's his purpose on a ranch like this?" she asked. "I mean, he's obviously beyond his prime."

Braden stroked the gelding's neck. "Chester was my grandpa's horse, and when it was time to retire him, Grandpa put him out to pasture. I probably should sell him to someone who'll ride him regularly and spend more time with him, but… Well, there's no way I can let him go."

Braden certainly had a soft spot for animals, some-thing she'd suspected when he'd purchased the rabbits for the kids and then when he hadn't insisted they take Pepita to the dog pound.

She moved forward and offered her hand for Chester to sniff, to let him know she was friendly. Then she stroked his nose. Maybe she was getting soft on ani-mals, too. A hazard of ranch living, she supposed. But she'd be moving to greener pastures soon.

"When can we get on our horses?" Beto asked Braden.

He chuckled. "Let me get Elena situated first. I don't want all of you mounting at the same time."

She turned to the eager children, who wore T-shirts, shorts and sneakers today. They really needed some clothing that was better suited to living on a ranch.

"Would you mind if I took them shopping tomorrow for some jeans and boots?" she asked Braden.

He glanced up from his work. "No, I don't mind a bit. Maybe you should pick up a couple of child-size hats, too." He shielded his eyes from the late morning sun with his hand, then tossed her a smile. "That is, if you don't mind adding one more thing to your list."

"I like to shop, even when I'm not going to spend any money. It allows me to check out various retail stores to see what they have to offer. And it also helps me plan the layout of my own place."

"You're still thinking about how you want to display the things you intend to sell?" he asked.

"No, I have that all figured out. But I'll be changing displays around often. That's what will keep things fresh. And keep bringing my customers back."

As he slipped the bridle on Chester, he said, "Sounds like you have a good game plan in mind."

Yes, she did. She'd even talked to the Realtor about the store she'd found online, but it had already been leased. So he was going to keep his eye open for something similar. She told him she was eager to find the perfect location and get started buying her inventory so she would be able to open for business before Christmas.

"Okay. Chester is ready to go." Braden bent and clasped his hands together, making a step for her to use. "Let me give you a boost up."

She gripped the pommel, slipped her own sneaker into his hands, wishing she'd packed her work boots when she left home, and swung up into the saddle as if she'd done it a hundred times before.

"Are you sure you need lessons?" Braden asked.

"I never said I hadn't ridden before. But I'm not an experienced rider."

He placed his hand on her knee and gave it a couple of pats. "We'll take care of that. I'll have you turned into a horsewoman before you leave for Houston."

Instead of removing his hand, he slid it down her calf, setting off a sensual barrage that shot to her core. Then, as he adjusted the stirrups, his proximity and his touch, while surely not meant to be sexual, continued to electrify her senses.

She'd never been attracted to cowboys before, so why this one?

She studied the way Braden wore his hat, the way his broad shoulders and muscular torso filled out his shirt, the way his jeans hugged his narrow hips.

Enough of that. There was so much more to life than sex. And that's all she was feeling for Braden. Desire and physical attraction. Yet in spite of herself, she'd also found other things about him that were alluring, too. His kindness to the children, for one thing. His sense of humor...

"Okay, kids," he said, oblivious to Elena's thoughts and her perusal. "Let's mount up."

He didn't have to ask the kids twice. They each led their horse to an old stump he'd taught them to use for ease in saddling up. He had them circle the corral several times, then he opened the gate.

As the children rode out into the yard, Braden swung up onto the saddle of his own mount, a spunky Appaloosa gelding he controlled with ease. Even his sure, steady movements drew Elena's attention.

He swept the hat from his head. Using it to gesture

toward the opening, he tossed a chivalrous grin her way. "After you."

Once upon a time, she'd considered cowboys to be slow-talking, tobacco-chewing rednecks. But she was going to have to reconsider that assumption, now that she'd gotten to know Braden. This cowboy could be sweet, polite and kindhearted when he wanted to be. A dangerous combination.

"Where are we going today?" Beto asked.

"To the swimming hole," he said. "You lead the way, and I'll take up the rear."

The boy nodded, eager to show off his new skill. They rode for about twenty minutes. All the while, Elena took in the sights and sounds of the Bar M.

Mares grazed in the pasture, while a couple of foals frolicked and kicked up their heels. Wildflowers grew on the hillside, and a soft summer breeze stirred the treetops.

Elena could get used to having pleasant outings like this. Not that she'd have much opportunity in the near future, when she was in the big city. But maybe she could come out here for a visit sometime. She'd grown fond of the kids and would miss them when she left. Besides, Houston was only two hours away.

She glanced over her shoulder at the rugged rancher who rode behind her. She would miss Braden, too. They'd become friends, as well as teammates. And if she stayed any longer, they might even become lovers. But no good would come of that. Long distance relationships rarely lasted, assuming he'd even want to continue what they'd started.

"There it is!" Bela pointed up ahead. "Do you see it, Elena?"

She was looking, shielding the sun from her eyes with her hand and craning her neck, but she hadn't spotted it yet.

After another ten yards, she glanced through the cottonwood trees and saw the pond, although it appeared to be larger than she'd expected, more like a small lake.

As Beto led the way, following a path to the water, she noted the bluebonnets growing wild, the butterflies flitting to and fro.

Should she suggest they have a picnic out here on Sunday? It might be fun. That is, if she was still here.

It was becoming a little too easy to imagine herself as part of a family—*this* family—rather than her own. And that wasn't emotionally wise or safe.

"I used to swim out here when I was a kid," Braden said.

"Cool!" Beto turned in his saddle, his eyes bright, his smile wide. "Can we go swimming? Me and Bela already know how, so you wouldn't have to teach us."

"Maybe some other day," the big brother said. "I have some things that need to be done back at the barn this afternoon, so I don't have that much time. Besides, you don't have swim suits with you."

"We don't have any at all," Bela said. "We used to when we lived in San Diego. That's where we had swim lessons."

"Then we'll make sure you get a bathing suit," Braden said.

Beto urged his mount forward, and Bela did the same, leaving the adults behind. Elena couldn't help but ask the man who'd grown up in the country, "Did not having a suit ever stop you from swimming when you were younger?"

Braden laughed and shot her a boyish grin. "It wouldn't stop me *now*."

Her cheeks warmed, and her pulse shot through the roof—or rather, the Texas sky.

"How about you?" he asked. "Did you ever go skinny dipping?"

She cleared her throat, hoping to clear her sexual thoughts, but it didn't seem to work. She swallowed, then ordered herself to speak. "No, I'm afraid not. I've always been pretty conservative."

"Come on." He chuckled. "The woman who plans to open what she calls a 'quirky' dress shop in the city is a straight arrow and hasn't ever had a stray or creative thought?"

"I'll admit that I'm very creative. And I do have a wild side, but not when it comes to…" She glanced at the secluded pond, then back at the handsome cowboy.

Did he know the thoughts that were raging through her mind?

"Well, I've never been naked in public." Then she gave Chester a kick with her heels, urging him on so she wouldn't have to explain herself further—or look into those playful green eyes any longer, wondering if Braden was imagining the two of them splashing in that cool, clear water in all their naked-as-a-jaybird glory.

Because, heaven help her, that's exactly where her thoughts had wandered.

Late that afternoon, while Elena chopped tomatoes and lettuce for the tacos she planned for dinner that night, she reminisced about the amazing horseback ride they'd taken earlier. She couldn't remember when she'd had a better day than this. Being outdoors with Braden and the kids had been invigorating and fun. The weather had been perfect, the children had been not only eager to explore, but happy to be together. Even Braden had smiled and laughed more than usual.

Only trouble was, with each memory of the time they'd spent together, her thoughts drifted to the swimming hole, where she imagined Braden swinging from the rope—as naked as the day he was born. As much as she appreciated the imagined sight, as often as it brought a smile to her lips, she didn't dare allow herself that kind of daydream.

She blew out a heated sigh. Braden had become way more tempting than she'd anticipated. She'd just have to find more ways to avoid him until she was free to move on. One way to do that would be that shopping trip she'd planned.

Of course, she could always leave that chore for her replacement to do, but she was looking forward to taking the kids into Wexler. Maybe they could stop for lunch or a frozen yogurt. And while in town, they could also take in a movie.

She'd have to talk it over with Braden, though. He'd be springing for the shopping, food and entertainment. But she doubted he would mind if she took the kids on a play day. And that's exactly what it sounded like to her—fun and games.

She glanced at the seasoned meat sizzling in the frying pan, as well as the beans and rice on the stove.

Dinner was nearly ready, so she'd better find the kids and tell them it was time to clean up. She'd no more than turned down the flames on the burners, when Bela entered the kitchen.

"Beto's in *big* trouble," she said.

It was the first time the girl had snitched on her brother, something Elena's siblings seemed to do all the time.

"What did he do?" she asked.

"We were playing Hide and Seek, but he went into the office, where you told us not to play, and made a big mess."

Uh-oh. Elena rarely had to discipline the children, but it sounded as if she'd have to this time. "Thanks, honey. Go wash your hands. We're going to eat in a few minutes."

Bela nodded, then dashed off to do as she was told. Elena followed her out of the kitchen.

As expected, she found Beto in the office. He was on his hands and knees, picking up large chunks of glass from a broken vase, which had fallen off the desk and onto the floor. Thankfully, it had been empty so there wasn't any water to worry about. But several of the files Braden had been working on had slipped off the desk, as well.

"Don't touch the glass," she warned Beto. "I'll pick it up. I don't want you to get cut."

He straightened, but continued to kneel. When he looked up at her, tears welled in his eyes. "I'm sorry, Elena. I wasn't supposed to come in this room. But I only did it because I knew Bela wouldn't look for me here. And then, when I heard her coming, I turned around in a hurry, and I knocked a bunch of stuff off the desk. Are you mad?"

She should be. But the boy already knew what he'd

done was wrong. And now he was paying the price for it. There was no need to make him feel any guiltier than he already did. But that didn't mean she wouldn't address the incident.

"This is an office," she said, "a room where adults work." She swept her arm toward the shattered glass and the files of paperwork that lay all over the floor. "And this is the reason you were told not to play in here."

"I'm sorry. I won't do it again. Is Braden going to be mad at me?"

If he spotted Beto's tears, if he saw how torn up the poor kid was by his mistake, he probably wouldn't be. Good grief, as it was, she wanted to wrap Beto in her arms and tell him it was no big deal. Then again, didn't he have to realize it was wrong to disregard the household rules?

"I'll take care of the cleanup from here," she said. "Go get ready for dinner. We can talk more about it later."

He nodded, then hurried to do as he was told.

Once he was gone, Elena picked up the pieces of glass and placed them in the trash can that sat near the desk. It looked as though she'd gotten all of it, but she'd have to run the vacuum cleaner to make sure. She supposed that could wait until after they ate. In the meantime, she set about picking up the loose papers and trying to determine which file they came out of.

One paper, a pink piece of stationery that had once been folded in thirds, stood out from the rest, and she couldn't help but peruse what turned out to be a letter written to Braden. She hadn't meant to read something that wasn't addressed to her, but she couldn't help noting it was signed by a woman named Christina.

She told herself to set it on the desk before studying it any further, but curiosity wouldn't let her. And she did something she'd never done before—she read a letter she had no right to.

Hey, baby!
It was great seeing you again at The Stagecoach Inn last night. I would have said something right then and there, but you were with that redhead, and I didn't want to make things awkward for you. Like I said, I just moved back to town.

But what I didn't have a chance to say was I've missed you and hope you'll give me a call. My cell number is the same. And even if it's just a one-night thing, I'm okay with that.

I would have sent an email, but the internet in my new place, one of the new houses by the park, isn't up and running yet. So I thought I'd send this the old-fashioned way.
XOXOXO
Christina

The woman clearly wanted them to hook up again. And it sounded as if all she wanted was sex.

Was Braden a womanizer like his father had been? It certainly seemed possible. After all, he'd been with a redhead when Christina spotted him at The Stagecoach. No telling who that woman was—or if he was still seeing her.

The fact that Braden had no shortage of lovers didn't

sit well with Elena. But what right did she have to be uneasy?

None.

She'd hardly set the letter aside when she heard footsteps in the hall. Heavy ones. Her tummy twisted into a rock-hard knot, and she quickly placed a file on top of the note she'd just read.

"What's going on?" Braden asked from the doorway.

Heat flooded her cheeks. *I'm snooping. Reading your mail. Making assumptions about your love life.*

She shook off the staggering guilt and managed a smile. "Beto accidentally knocked some files onto the floor. I was picking them up."

"You don't have to worry about the mess. I can take care of it."

Was he afraid Christina's pink letter was somewhere in the paperwork spread out on the floor? Did he want to make sure it stayed hidden?

"Okay." Elena got to her feet, replacing the files she'd gathered, the pink letter still hidden at the bottom of the stack. "You can probably figure out what goes where. While you do that, I'll get dinner on the table."

"It sure smells good. And I'm starved."

She offered him another smile, hoping her cheeks had cooled and that she'd shed all signs of a guilty expression. "Thanks. I'll have everything ready in five minutes." Then she headed for the kitchen, hoping he hadn't realized that she was such a green-eyed snoop.

Two hours later, Braden had yet to say anything about the mess on the office floor, so Elena assumed she'd made it through the night unscathed. Still, she would have deserved to be reprimanded. She'd never done anything like that before.

Why had she been so nosy? Did it matter who he dated? Who he slept with?

It shouldn't. And it really *didn't*. Yet she couldn't shake her curiosity. And even a twinge of jealousy.

While Braden handled the bedtime routine, she picked up a romance novel she'd found on a small bookshelf in her bedroom and carried it to the living room. She took a seat on the easy chair and opened the cover. It was the story of a handsome billionaire and a runaway bride. She'd only read a couple of pages when Braden approached.

"The kids are bathed and in bed for the night," he said, drawing her completely out of the story she was still trying to sink into.

She set the small paperback aside on the lamp table and smiled. "You're getting to be an old hand at the bedtime stuff."

"Yeah. They're great kids—and I actually like spending time with them." He returned her smile and winked. "But don't tell anyone. I have a reputation to uphold."

She'd grown fond of the motherless twins, too. And for that reason, she felt a bit guilty about leaving before the agreed upon time was up.

"Would you like a glass of wine?" he asked. "Or maybe a cup of decaf? There's also a little ice cream left."

She didn't want to get too relaxed or cozy around him tonight and said, "No, thanks. I'm fine."

A flash of disappointment crossed his face, but he seemed to shake it as quickly as it arose. "So what did you think about our ride today? Do you want to do it again before you go?"

Actually, yes. But did she dare admit that to him? She didn't want him to get the wrong idea about her staying. She might have once dreamed about falling in love and creating a family of her own, but her burning desire to open The Attic was too strong to set on the back burner.

"I had a lot of fun today," she admitted. "So maybe I can come back and ride again sometime. But that reminds me, what do you think about taking the twins to a picnic at the pond on Sunday?"

"Sure, why not?"

"That is," she added, tossing out a reminder, "if you haven't hired my replacement yet."

"I thought we should wait until we talk to the last applicant. Is there any word on when—or if—she can come for an interview?"

"Her name is Helen Schnebly. And she said she could come Tuesday, assuming the parts needed come in and her car is repaired by then. That is, if it's okay with you."

"That works. And just so you know, I'm not in that big of a hurry to replace you."

Her heart pounded at the thought, but she tamped down the sentiment. Instead, she rose from her seat and crossed the room to the stone fireplace and the array of photographs that lined the mantel. Opting for a change of topic in their conversation, she picked up the picture of a young Braden and his grandfather and studied it carefully. "You were a cute kid. And you look so happy in this picture."

"Thanks." He approached the fireplace. "Do you have a lot of family pictures?"

"Some, most of which are in albums. But there aren't any displayed. At least, not of me."

"Why not?" He was standing beside her now, close enough for her to breathe in his manly scent. Close enough to touch.

But she kept her hands to herself. "I never gave it much thought. We have an eight-by-ten framed picture of my brother Jesse in his football uniform on the living room wall. And there are several of my sister Monica in her dance outfits. I guess I never really did anything to stand out in the family."

She hadn't meant that to come across as a complaint, merely a fact that had eluded her until now.

Braden placed his hand on her cheek, drawing her eyes to his. "That's not true. I'm not sure why your parents never framed photos of you, but you stand out in ways you might never imagine."

The subtext of what he'd said set off sparks and a flurry of pheromones in the room. Their gazes locked, bonding them in an unexpected way. Then his hand slipped around to the back of her neck, and he drew her mouth to his.

She needed to step back, to make it more difficult for him to kiss her, but she was lost in a swirl of emotion she couldn't explain, facing a mind-numbing temptation she couldn't fight.

As their lips touched, she wrapped her arms around him and pulled him close. Her breasts pressed against his chest. His hands caressed her back and the slope of her hips, drawing her closer still, and the kiss exploded with a passion that nearly stole the breath right out of her.

She didn't know how long they remained there,

caught up in the heat of the moment, but it was long enough to know they'd have a choice to make about where this was heading.

With an almost overwhelming regret, she ended the kiss before they had to decide which bedroom to use.

"I'm sorry," she said, "but this isn't a good idea."

"What isn't?" His voice was soft, yet deep and husky. "Acting on our attraction?" His eyes never left hers as he added, "It feels like a pretty damn good idea to me."

"It's just our hormones talking."

"Is it?"

In all honesty, she wasn't sure. She probably shouldn't admit it, but she'd always been taught that honesty was the best policy. "Okay, Braden. I feel something for you, but I have plans. Remember?"

He nodded, then slowly released her.

Yet even if she were willing to set her dreams aside, she wasn't sure if Braden was a risk worth taking. Was he capable of making a lifelong commitment?

No, she had to leave the Bar M with her heart still intact.

"So, now what?" he asked.

"Maybe you'd better place a call to Mrs. Flores— assuming she's the nanny you plan to hire."

"She is, but—"

"If I don't leave soon…" Her voice faded along with her drifting thoughts.

Braden raked a hand through his hair. "I feel something for you, too. So, under the circumstances, you're probably right."

She nodded, glad that he agreed. Yet as she turned and headed for the stairway that led to her bedroom, the little girl who still lived deep inside her begged her to object. She wouldn't, though.

But as she climbed each step, she couldn't help wishing that Braden had been able to provide her with a reason to stay.

Braden remained in the living room after Elena went upstairs. With the way his head was spinning after that blood-stirring kiss, he doubted he'd be able to sleep.

On top of that, when Elena had announced her plan to leave, he'd tried to keep his panic under wraps. How was he ever going to handle the kids without her?

Sure, he could hire another nanny, but the kids had grown attached to Elena—and they needed her. He needed her, too. Not in a weak and vulnerable sense. He didn't let women get close enough for that. But he liked her—a lot. And he found himself wanting to spend more and more time with her.

A glance at the clock on the mantel told him it was close to ten. Maybe he'd better go to bed, even if he only tossed and turned. But before he could make a move, the old-style telephone rang, and he hurried to answer before the caller woke up everyone in the house. "Hello?"

"You're just the guy I wanted to talk to," his older brother said.

Braden grinned, wondering if Jason realized that he had a few things to discuss with him, too. Either way, he'd have to work up to it. "How's the honeymoon going?"

"Amazing. Juliana is everything I'd ever hoped a woman could be—and more. You ought to consider marriage someday."

"I'd have to find the right woman first." Braden glanced toward the stairway, where Elena had gone.

Had he found the right woman, only to have her leave before he got a chance to know for sure?

He shook off the possibility. He'd never been one to stew about a lost cause.

"How are the twins doing?" Jason asked. "Are they settling in? I know the language barrier is tough."

"They're doing great. And you'll be glad to know there isn't a communication problem anymore. They've been pulling the wool over our eyes for a while. Believe it or not, they speak English—fluently."

"You gotta be kidding me. Why didn't they tell us? Juliana and I had a real struggle communicating with them."

Braden filled him in on how the kids had been worried about being adopted before their father came for them.

"Wow," Jason said. "I guess the woman taking care of them never explained who I was or why I was taking them with me. But then again, she made it clear she wasn't happy about being left with them."

"I'm happy you got them away from her and brought them home," Braden said. "And speaking of home, when are you coming back?"

"We'll be stateside at the end of next week, although I have to stop by the office for a few days." Jason whispered something under his breath—to his wife, Braden supposed. "Sorry about that. Juliana asked if I wanted to join her for tea in the hotel lounge."

Braden glanced out the window, into the dark. He'd nearly forgotten the time difference in London. "You're going to go with her, aren't you?" He'd hate to think that his brother was as business minded as their father had been.

"Of course, I am. This is one Rayburn marriage that's going to be happy and lasting"

"So you're glad you got married?" Braden asked, his gaze drifting back toward the stairway that led to the guest room where Elena was staying.

"More than I'd even imagined."

"I'm glad to hear it." And he was. Jason deserved to have someone in his corner—and to be happy with her.

"So how are Beto and Bela?" Jason asked again. "Are they settling in?"

"Actually, they're awesome kids. Beto is a little on the mischievous side, but that's what keeps life interesting. He's also been adopting stray animals like you can't believe. And Bela is a real sweetheart. I'm not sure how she keeps up with him, but they're very close."

"How do you feel about letting them live on the Bar M with you?" Jason asked.

"With *me*? I wasn't planning on doing that. I figured they needed a mother figure. And now that you have Juliana…"

Jason took a deep breath, then slowly let it out. "I'm not opposed to taking them. Hell, they're family. We can't ship them off to strangers."

"Those are my thoughts, too. And they seem to love living on a ranch. Maybe Carly and Ian will want them to live with them."

"That's a possibility, but she's expecting her own baby soon. Maybe she'd rather you or I take them."

"That's true, but with a little girl on the way, they'll be family minded."

"Let's talk it over with her," Jason suggested. "But either way, I don't want the kids thinking that we're too busy or too wrapped up in our lives to take them."

Braden didn't want them to think that, either. That's the way his old man had made him feel when he'd been growing up. And Bela and Beto had been through enough already.

"We could also share custody," Braden suggested, surprising himself.

"That might work. Juliana and I could take them on school breaks, while you and Carly live close enough to share custody the rest of the time."

Braden thought of the days when the court had ordered him to visit his dad, only to have his father drop him off at Granny's house on the Leaning R instead. Not that Granny hadn't done her best to make sure his time spent with her was loving and special. But it had grated on him that his old man had always seemed too busy to spend any quality time with him.

"On second thought, I'm not sure about shared custody," Braden said. "I don't want to put them through the visitation schedules we had."

"It wouldn't be like that," Jason said. "We wouldn't let it be."

No, they wouldn't. And, now that he knew where Jason stood, Braden felt confident that Carly would agree.

Jason paused for a beat, then added, "By the way, I felt badly dumping the twins on you like I did, especially when we didn't think they spoke English. Did you ever find a nanny?"

"Yeah. Her name is Elena, and she's been great with

them. I'm going to lose her, though." His chest ached at the thought.

"Why?"

In the past, Braden would have kept the reason to himself. But things had changed between him and Jason. The guy seemed more approachable these days, more understanding. "I only hired her for three weeks, hoping you or Carly would be able to take the twins by then. But… Well, things got…complicated."

Jason chuckled. "Don't tell me. You've fallen for the nanny."

Had he? He was damn sure attracted to her. But fallen?

He glanced toward the stairs where Elena no doubt lay in bed, soft and warm, and much too tempting. His heart soared at the thought, and he had his answer.

"I guess you could say that," he admitted. He heard the wistfulness in his voice and cleared his throat, altering his tone when he added, "But she has big plans to move to Houston, so things would never work out."

"That's what Juliana and I once thought. But we've learned that love will find a way."

"I'm not sure about that," Braden said. He was happy everything had come together so nicely for Jason and Juliana, but that didn't necessarily mean it would for him. Based on how Elena had ended yet another of their heat-stirring kisses, he'd have to guess it wouldn't. No matter how much he now admitted he wished it would.

Meanwhile, he had more pressing issues to deal with.

"Anyway, about the nanny… I do have another woman I can call to help out. I'll deal with that tomorrow. But, Jason, we're going to have to schedule another family meeting to determine who's going to raise the kids."

"Do you want to consider keeping them?" Jason asked. "I will, but they seem to be doing well with you on the ranch."

Braden had certainly enjoyed having them around. But taking on a paternal role with them was a big responsibility. Huge. "Let's talk it over once you and Carly are back in town."

"Sounds like a plan to me."

After ending the call, Braden remained in the living room, thinking over the conversation he'd just had, the thoughts that were just now beginning to take place.

If Elena was going to stay in town and continue working for him, he might have told Jason they didn't need a family meeting. He'd take the kids.

But Elena had made her intentions known. And Braden wasn't sure he could handle the twins on his own.

Or if he even wanted to try.

Chapter Ten

Elena woke to the aroma of fresh-perked coffee and sizzling bacon. Obviously Braden was cooking. She glanced at the clock on the bureau. Six thirty-seven. He should be out doing his morning chores now, which was his habit.

Surely the kids weren't trying to surprise her by fixing breakfast. They knew better than to use the stove without adult supervision.

She quickly dressed and hurried to the kitchen, where she found Braden scrambling eggs in a small blue mixing bowl.

"Good morning," she said, as she tucked a strand of hair behind her ear. "Don't you have chores to do?"

He set the bowl aside and turned away from the counter, the fork still in his hand. "I did some of them already, but the rest can wait. I need to talk to you and I thought I'd keep busy while I waited for you to wake up."

He probably wanted to talk about what they'd done last night—or what they would have done, if she'd fallen into temptation. Then again, that kiss might not have affected him the same way it had her. Maybe he hadn't thought about it all night long.

There was only one way to find out, so she asked, "What's on your mind?"

Before he responded, he took a peek at the flame under the cast-iron skillet that held the bacon, then shut it off and returned his focus to her. "Last night, after you went to your room, I called Francisca Flores, but she didn't answer. She'd probably already gone to bed, so I left a message for her to get back to me at her earliest convenience."

Apparently he'd moved forward in finding a nanny to replace her. She should feel relieved, although for some reason, she wasn't nearly as eager to leave right now as she'd been last night. "That's what you wanted to tell me?"

"Yes, but there's also something else."

She had an idea that, whatever that "something" was, it might take him a while to explain, so she poured herself some coffee. She would have offered to pour a cup for him, too, but he'd already served himself.

After taking a seat at the table, she said, "The kids are still asleep, and they'll probably stay that way for a while. So now's a good time to talk."

"I know, but I'd rather discuss it over dinner."

Her curiosity, which had been growing steadily, shot through the roof. "You want to wait until this evening, when the kids are around?"

"No, that's not what I meant. We need to talk privately, so I asked my mom to come out and stay with the twins while I take you to dinner at Maestro's."

He'd made plans and put them into motion before he'd even asked if she wanted to go with him? She wasn't sure if she should be pleased or uneasy.

"My mom and Erik will be here around five thirty," he said.

Elena had yet to see his mother on the Bar M. "Has your mom even met Bela and Beto?"

Braden nodded and took a sip of his coffee as he leaned back against the stove. "Actually, she stayed here for the first couple of days and helped the kids settle in. But after she left, I knew I'd need to find someone else to help me, someone who spoke Spanish."

"So that's when you hired me."

He nodded. "But speaking Spanish is no longer going to be a prerequisite."

Elena hadn't wanted to leave Braden in a bind and, apparently, now she wouldn't. She ought to be happy about that—and relieved. But the fact that she could be easily replaced and was no longer needed rubbed salt on something raw inside of her, an unhealed wound she hadn't even known existed.

She didn't dare dwell on her discomfort, though. So she asked, "Are you sure your mother doesn't mind coming out here tonight?"

"She was glad that I asked her. She's been busy with work, especially since she's helping Erik reorganize his medical office, but she wants to spend some time with the kids."

Elena wasn't surprised. She'd heard a lot of nice things

about Shannon Miller—now Shannon Chandler—especially her volunteerism, not just at the church, but also in the community.

"Just for the record," Braden said, "when my mom heard that Jason had to drop off the kids with me to look after, she was glad. She thought having Beto and Bela around would be good for me."

Elena had to agree. They'd softened the rugged yet quiet cowboy and made him more approachable than before. More likable. More…lovable?

"Some people might not understand," Braden added, "given the situation she'd once been in because she hadn't married my dad, but she felt some kind of kinship with Jason and Carly. So she was quick to accept them, and she tried to be good to them whenever they were around. She feels the same way about the twins."

"That's admirable," Elena said, "but it's also surprising. A lot of women would find it difficult to be around the kids their ex had with other women."

"My mom adores children and probably should have had a houseful of her own."

But Shannon hadn't married until recently, and so she only had Braden.

"What do you say?" he asked.

Apparently, he'd thought of everything. He'd also convinced her that Bela and Beto would be in good hands. And since going out for pizza with him wasn't a real date, she agreed.

But when he turned to make the scrambled eggs, she caught a glimpse of his profile, noting his dimpled cheek and bright-eyed grin. He said he only wanted to talk. She just hoped there wasn't more to his invitation than he'd implied.

* * *

Braden's mom had not only been delighted when she'd been asked to babysit the twins, but now that she and her husband had arrived on the ranch, Erik seemed just as happy to be here as she was.

The newly married couple had come bearing gifts, including a box of fancy cupcakes they'd purchased at a bakery in town, two packages of nontoxic, washable markers, several coloring books and a children's board game.

Beto and Bela, who'd seemed a little shy at first, quickly warmed up to the couple. But Braden had expected them to. His mom was a rock star when it came to finding fun things for a kid to do, and he couldn't wait to introduce her to Elena, who was still upstairs getting dressed.

He didn't have to wait very long. A moment later, Elena entered the living room wearing a long flowing turquoise skirt and a black silky top. She'd swept her dark hair up into a messy topknot that was both stylish and attractive. Big hoop earrings and a pair of sandals rounded out the classy ensemble.

She'd added a splash of makeup, too. She looked great without it, but damn. She could put a photoshopped cover girl to shame.

His mom, who looked up from the attention she'd been giving the twins, noticed Elena's entry and glanced at Braden. She wore a smile, clearly expecting an introduction. But he was so caught up in the nanny's mesmerizing approach that he couldn't manage a response.

Finally, he said, "Mom, this is Elena Ramirez. Her

father, Paco, owns the feed store. She's been helping me with the kids."

His mother, who'd been seated on the sofa and bent forward to chat with Bela, stood and extended a hand to greet her. "It's nice to meet you."

"I've heard a lot about you," Elena said, the silver bangles on her wrist clinking as she shook Shannon's hand. "I'm glad I can finally put a face to your name."

His mom turned to Erik, who was now standing beside her. "This is my husband, Doctor Erik Chandler."

After they made the customary small talk, which resulted in smiles and chuckles all around, Braden said, "Well, we'd better take off. Call me if you have any trouble."

His mom gave him a pat on the shoulder, dismissing his concern, but the glimmer in her eyes spoke volumes.

"Have a good evening," Erik said. "And don't worry. We'll be just fine. You couldn't get a better babysitting team than your mother and me."

He had that right. Not only was Braden's mom a whiz in dealing with children, Erik could handle any medical issue, if one cropped up.

Braden shook his new stepfather's hand. "Thanks again." Then he turned to Elena. "Are you ready to go?"

She nodded, and they were off. When they reached his pickup, she asked, "I'm not overdressed, am I?"

Maybe for Caroline's Diner, but not for Maestro's. The new restaurant was a little fancy and high-priced for a lot of the Brighton Valley locals, but it seemed to be doing well. Besides, Braden had dressed up, too, in his best black jeans and a white button-down shirt.

"You look great," he said. "I won't be able to keep my eyes off you."

Her cheeks flushed, and she glanced down at her sandals, which revealed newly manicured toes with bright turquoise polish that matched her skirt.

Had he embarrassed her? He hadn't meant to. But hell, she looked amazing tonight. And while he'd suggested this dinner as a peace offering, he also hoped it would provide him with an opportunity to convince her to stay until the end of their agreement—or even longer, if she was willing. He'd hedged his bet with the decision to hire Francisca, but that didn't mean he didn't hope he wouldn't need to hire the new nanny after all.

Fifteen minutes later, they arrived on the tree-lined main drag of Brighton Valley, the quaint little town in which Braden had grown up and had come to love. Finding a parking place on a summer evening was never easy, but when he noticed a car pulling out near Ralph Nettles' Realty office, he snatched the prime spot.

As they climbed from his truck, he pointed out Maestro's, the Italian restaurant that had opened several months ago. "I'm not sure how this place will compete long-term with Caroline's down-home meals, but I've heard you need a reservation most nights, especially on the weekend, so I think they're here to stay."

As they approached the crosswalk, the hearty aroma of Italian sausage, tomatoes, basil and garlic filled the air.

"I had no idea this place was even here," Elena said.

"They even have outdoor dining." Braden pointed to several couples seated at the white linen-covered, wrought iron patio tables.

"It's much fancier than I expected," Elena said. "I thought we were going to a pizza joint."

He wouldn't have taken her to a cheap place. Not after all she'd done to help him. And not when he wanted to convince her that Brighton Valley might not be the big city, but it still had a certain appeal.

As they neared the restaurant, a woman walked out of The Mercantile. The local dress shop was practically a landmark around here, much like Caroline's Diner, which was located only a few doors down.

Knowing that Elena had an interest in stores, he asked, "Have you ever shopped at The Mercantile?"

"No, their clothing has always been a little too conservative for my taste. But my stepmom shops there sometimes, especially when she doesn't want to drive into Wexler."

"So I take it you don't expect The Attic to attract the same type of patrons as The Mercantile."

"I wouldn't say that." Her steps slowed, and she shot a glance his way. "Their regular customers might not be drawn to the clothing styles I'm going to offer, but there will be plenty of accessories for them to choose from, as well as funky odds and ends that they might find appealing. Maybe you can come to Houston and see it. After I open, that is."

"I'd like that." He took her arm and escorted her to the red front door of Maestro's, where the receptionist asked if he had reservations.

"Yes, we do. For Rayburn. At six."

"A party of two?" the young woman asked. When Braden nodded, she snatched a couple of black, leatherbound menus. "If you'll follow me, I'll show you to your table."

Moments later, Elena and Braden were seated outside, where they had a pleasant view of the tree-lined street.

A busboy delivered two glasses of water with lemon, as well as a basket of warm focaccia and a platter of olive oil and balsamic vinegar. "Your waiter will be right with you."

Braden thanked him as Elena took in the sights and sounds around her. A couple walked by with a Boston terrier on a red leash, followed by a teenager carrying his skateboard. Moments later, an elderly man wearing a veteran's cap and pushing his walker stopped to scan the menu that had been displayed outside.

Elena seemed caught up in all the activity, but Braden was only interested in her.

"So what do you think?" he asked.

She turned in her seat and blessed him with a breezy smile. "It's great so far, but it's not at all what I expected."

As she took in the crisp, white linen tablecloth, the candle burning in a glass votive and the three red roses in a budvase, he wondered if the romantic ambiance bothered her.

"I thought Maestro's only made good pizza," she said.

He smiled. "They actually specialize in a variety of Italian dishes, but they do make a great pizza."

She selected a slice of bread from the basket he held out to her. "It's still warm."

"Try it with olive oil and balsamic vinegar," he said.

She dipped it and took a bite, smiling as she chewed. "Delicious, you're right. Thanks for bringing me here, Braden. It's very impressive."

He hadn't been trying to impress her. He'd just wanted to get her alone and off the ranch so they could have time to talk—alone and uninterrupted. There had to be some way to convince her to stay for another week or two. Hell, he'd be happy with an extra couple of days.

She'd been right, though. The longer she remained on the ranch, the more tempting it would be to become intimately involved. And as much as he'd like to argue the point, he had to admit a romantic relationship with her would probably crash and burn.

So why did he find himself forgetting the reasons they shouldn't get sexually involved and considering all the reasons they should?

Elena had enjoyed her evening out with Braden more than she'd expected. The food had been amazingly delicious, the ambiance romantic and the company… Well, Braden had turned out to be the most charming dinner companion she'd ever had.

They'd laughed at some of the silly things the kids had said, and they'd reminisced about the various characters they both knew who lived in the community. They'd even shared a few childhood memories that were sad, yet sweet.

Finally, when Braden had paid the bill and pulled out her chair to leave, she remembered. "You never said… What did you want to talk to me about?"

"It wasn't that big of a deal, I suppose." He placed his hand on the small of her back as if claiming her as his date. "I just wanted you to know that I like you, and that I wouldn't be opposed to us becoming lovers."

His statement hit her like a charging bull, and she

actually stumbled as she took her first step away from the chair.

He reached for her, holding her steady. Had he realized it had been his comment that had unbalanced her, rather than a misstep?

He didn't say anything. How could she tell him the same thought had been running through her mind, chased closely by her conviction that whatever they shared wouldn't last?

Truthfully she wouldn't be opposed to becoming Braden's lover. She was just afraid to admit it. Besides, she didn't have flings. At least, she'd never had them in the past.

As much as she'd wanted to remind him that she would be leaving soon, she couldn't seem to do anything other than relish the here and now, the feel of his hands on her skin, the glimmer in his eyes. He must have felt the same way, because he didn't press her for a response. He merely ushered her to his truck, never breaking contact.

The ride home was awkward at best, strained at worst. Braden tried making small talk, but she couldn't forget his comment. It burned in her mind like hot embers just waiting for a breath to ignite them into flame. She was never so grateful to reach the ranch.

When they entered the house, Shannon and Erik had already put the kids to bed.

"I hope they weren't any trouble for you," Braden said, as he hung his black Stetson on the hook by the front door.

"Not at all. We had fun with them, didn't we, honey?" Shannon turned to her husband, who was seated next to her on the sofa, and placed her hand on his knee.

The doctor gave her a wink, then smiled at Braden. "We had a great time. We also told the kids that we'd like to have them over to our house one day soon. We have a guest room, so they can even have a sleepover. That is, if you don't mind."

Braden said, "That's fine with me. I know they'd enjoy spending the night with you."

"By the way," Erik said, as he got to his feet. "I'm not sure if their immunizations are up to date. With school starting soon, you'd better check into that. And neither of them can remember seeing a doctor in a long time, so physicals are in order. I'd be happy to do it for you and offer you the family rate."

Shannon laughed. "By family rate, he means free."

Braden thanked the doctor for the offer. "I'll call and make an appointment for them to see you. But I'm not entirely sure where they'll be attending school yet." He glanced at Elena, their gazes meeting momentarily.

It seemed as if she stood in the balance. But that couldn't be the case. He probably wasn't sure how to explain to his mom why he wasn't going to insist upon keeping the kids. So Elena helped him out. "Braden, Jason and Carly haven't decided who will take full custody yet."

"They're sweet kids," Shannon said. "I'm sure whoever takes them will be glad they stepped up." Then she slipped her arm through her husband's and they walked toward the door. Before they left, she cast her son a happy smile.

When Braden shut the door and turned the deadbolt, Elena's breath caught. She was alone with the cowboy, a thought that she found both exciting and unnerving.

Feeling suddenly self-conscious, she was eager to make conversation. "They seem very happy together."

"They are. Erik is a great guy. I'm glad they found each other again."

Even though her nerves were on end, she couldn't help but marvel at the sincerity in his voice. And she had to agree. "Seeing them together kind of renews my faith in love and marriage." She wished she could say the same thing about her own parents, who seemed to be happy. But her stepmom was so caught up with the kids and their activities that she didn't have that same spark Shannon had when she looked at her husband.

She supposed romance faded in relationships. If so, that was a shame.

Braden strode over to the entertainment center, flipped a switch and turned on the stereo. A couple of beats later, Taylor Swift began to sing a romantic ballad. He held out a hand. "You want to dance?"

This was just what she'd been worried about the minute that front door shut. Being alone with Braden and picking up where their conversation had left off at Maestro's.

She stood there a moment, wrestling with temptation and better judgment. She'd have to address his comment sooner or later, but for now she'd hold off. It had been a wonderful evening, and she wasn't ready for it to end. So she crossed the room and stepped into Braden's arms.

As they swayed to the beat, his musky cologne snaked around her, taunting her, tempting her. She closed her eyes, enjoying the feel of his embrace too much to fight it.

When the music ended, he continued to hold her

close. She could have pulled free, had she really wanted to. But as he stroked the slope of her back, she leaned into him, determined to take whatever he offered her this evening, whether it was a warm embrace, a heated kiss…or even more.

His hands slid to her derriere, lingering. Still, she remained in his arms, willing him not to stop.

A moment later, much to her regret, he loosened his arms and rested his forehead on hers. "You know, back at dinner I'd planned to ask you to stay on the ranch longer, but I never actually said as much."

Apparently the cowboy was determined to knock her off her feet tonight. His comments had her reeling. "Are you asking me now?"

"I—I'm not sure if I should. You made it clear where you stood."

What would she say if he did ask her not to go?

Yesterday, she might have refused. But tonight? She supposed it depended upon how long he needed her.

He raised his head and looked deep into her eyes. There was no mistaking what she saw in his gaze. Desire.

"We're both attracted to each other," he said. "And that seems to be growing stronger each minute we're together. I know you plan to leave, no matter what. But before you do, shouldn't we see where a relationship might go, even one that's long distance?"

Her skeptical nature insisted that was a bad idea, yet she couldn't say no. Not when she stood there in his arms, when her heart was pounding out yes, yes, yes.

"It's probably not wise," she said, although her conviction sounded halfhearted even to her own ears.

"You might be right about that. But it might be foolish to let the opportunity to make love slip away without knowing for sure."

"But the kids—"

He placed his index finger on her lips. "We won't wake them up. They're sound asleep. And my bedroom door has a good lock."

She couldn't seem to utter the refusal that echoed in her mind. Not when she longed to kiss him. Besides, what if he was right? Why not make love just once? Just tonight. What would it hurt?

As his eyes continued to search hers, looking for an answer to his question. She gave it to him by wrapping her arms around his neck and drawing his lips to hers.

The kiss deepened immediately, their tongues dipping and tasting, their breaths mingling, making all thought flee. Once he pressed his erection against her, she was lost in a swirl of heat and desire.

He stroked her back, her hips, her sides. When he reached her breast, his thumb skimmed across her nipple, sending her senses reeling and silencing any possible objection.

Her body ached for him and for more of his magical touch.

As if sensing her longing, Braden broke the kiss long enough to whisper, "Come with me." Then he took her by the hand and led her upstairs to his bedroom.

After they stepped inside, he locked the door.

"Wait," she said. But her objection didn't have anything to do with the decision she'd already made. "Do you have a condom?"

He smiled, then strode to his nightstand, opened the top drawer and pulled out a small packet. Should she be concerned that he'd been prepared? That she might not have been the one he'd originally purchased them for?

She shook off any apprehension and joined him beside the bed. He took a seat on the mattress and removed his boots and socks. She followed suit, sitting beside him, unbuckling her sandals and setting them aside.

Once their feet were bare, she kissed him again, long and deep. His caresses stoked a hunger and longing she'd never known before, and a surge of heat shot right through her.

This might be a crazy mistake, and she might be sorry in the morning, but right now she wanted Braden. She needed him.

The fact that she might even love him crossed her mind, although that would certainly complicate things.

Still, she'd come too far to back out now.

Braden felt instantly bereft as Elena backed away. Then his spirits buoyed when he watched her step out of her skirt and drop the flowing garment in a pool on the floor. She followed it with her blouse.

Her gaze never left his as she stood before him in a skimpy black lace bra and matching panties. Damn. She was lovelier and shapelier than he'd even imagined.

She'd mentioned that she wasn't conservative enough to shop at The Mercantile, and now he could see why. She had a unique style that set her a head above every other woman he knew.

He followed her lead and removed his clothes, too, with her help. Her eager fingers stumbled onto his and together they stripped him to his boxer briefs. Then he drew her to him.

She skimmed her nails across his chest, sending a shiver through his veins and a rush of heat through his blood.

"You're killing me," he said.

She smiled. "Good. Turnabout is fair play." Then she unhooked her bra and freed her breasts, full and round, the dusky pink tips peaked and ready to be touched.

More than willing to oblige, he laid her back on the bed, pressing a kiss at the base of her throat. When her breath caught, he dragged his lips lower, finding her breast, teasing one nipple and then the other.

She whimpered, clearly aroused, and he stretched out on top of her. He wanted nothing more than to be inside her, moving in rhythm, coming together. But not yet. He'd waited too long for this. He wouldn't rush it.

With his hands and tongue he explored her body, every inch of it, and from the whimpers he heard past his rushing blood, he knew she liked it. He wanted to make this a night she'd remember forever. Finally, when they were both delirious with need, he tore open the condom and slipped it on. Then he found the pleasure he was looking for when in one smooth motion he entered her.

Her body responded to his, arching up to meet each thrust. Their hearts pounded in unison, as did their breaths. Nothing else mattered tonight except pleasuring each other.

His thrusts went deeper, and as he pulled his head back and looked into her passion-glazed eyes she cried out. Seeing her gripped in the throes of pleasure, he couldn't hold back any longer, and they came together in a mind-spinning moment of pure ecstasy.

When their pulses slowed and their breaths evened

out, he remained there, inside her. He couldn't move. His body still trembled with the aftershocks of the most amazing sex he'd ever experienced. Making love with Elena had been all he'd hoped for and more.

But too quickly as they lay in the sweet afterglow, reality set in. And he asked himself the question he'd tried hard not to think about.

Now that he'd met Elena, now that they'd experienced sex the way it was meant to be, how was he ever going to let her go?

In spite of his better judgment, he was falling for her. But there was no way he could ever admit that. Opening himself up, revealing his thoughts and feelings would only leave him vulnerable. That's why he'd always kept his relationships simple, unencumbered.

Why throw his heart out there, only to have it stomped on? He'd experienced that once, back in high school, and it still stung. Cathy Thomas, the prettiest cheerleader on the squad, had dealt him quite a blow. After finally agreeing to date him, she'd canceled, because her dad hadn't wanted her to date "that Rayburn kid." He'd insisted that nothing good could ever come from a relationship with Braden, and she had agreed.

This was years ago, he told himself, and Elena certainly wasn't anything like Cathy. But she'd already told him she was walking away from him. It was just a matter of when. Even if he told her how he was feeling—and what he was thinking—she was leaving for a career in Houston. So why set himself up for disappointment?

Besides, how could he expect a career woman to accept a maternal role, especially with a couple of kids who weren't even her own? Assuming she cared for

Bela and Beto as much as it appeared, she might agree at first, but that would only stifle the Elena he'd come to—

Oh hell. As much as he'd fought it, as much as he hated to admit it, he'd come to love her. How was that for rotten luck?

At one time, he'd needed her because of the kids. But along the way, he'd grown to care for Bela and Beto. And now, the thought of being around them—or even raising them—no longer scared him.

But what if Elena didn't want a ready-made family? What if, when he told her what he was thinking, what he was planning, he lost her for good?

Maybe, if she realized that he wasn't going to hold her back, she'd come to love him, too. And if she came to him, if she admitted that she loved him first, then they had a chance.

What was that old saying? If you love something you set it free…?

Did he dare let her go?

Better yet, how could he not?

Chapter Eleven

As Elena lay in Braden's arms, her heart swelled with warmth and contentment. The reason for that wasn't just the result of great sex, either.

She'd never felt so cherished and special, and she hoped Braden felt the same way. She'd come to admire him and to trust him, especially with her heart. She wasn't entirely sure what to call the emotion that filled her chest to overflowing, but she suspected she'd fallen in love with him. And that she'd fallen hard.

Yet she didn't know how her newfound feeling was going to affect her plan to open The Attic, which she was still determined to do.

He'd mentioned a long-distance relationship, which she hadn't wanted to consider before. But could an arrangement like that work out for them? She wanted to believe that it could, but she'd be at the store seven days a week—and not just during the business hours. So when would she find time to spend with him and the kids?

Granted, he hadn't said he would keep Beto and Bela longer than the three weeks that Carly and Jason would be gone. But even if they went to live with one of his siblings, she would want to visit them. Beto, with his impish smile and love of animals, had burrowed into her heart. And so had bright-eyed Bela, who had an outlook on life that was as bright as the colors of her happy drawings, a child who only wanted to love and be loved.

Yet even if Elena wanted to remain a part of their lives, it was a two-hour commute to the Bar M from Houston. Just thinking about the logistics, about the difficulties she'd have in pulling off regular visits, drew her out of the sweet contentment.

Braden ran his hand along the slope of her hip, and she tilted her face up to look at him. In spite of her many concerns about the future, she smiled at the memory of what they'd just shared.

"That was amazing," he said.

She was glad he felt the same way she did, and her smile deepened. "I know. It was…perfect."

His fingers trailed along her outer thigh, and he broke eye contact as he said, "I'm not going to hold you back from leaving or try to convince you to stay."

Her heart cramped, releasing some of the warmth it had once held. They might have had an agreement, and she wanted to go, but a part of her wanted him to give it one last shot, to tell her he'd come to care for her more than he'd expected, that he wanted her, needed her…

"You don't have to wait until I find someone else to

look after the kids," he added. "I've already called and left a message with Mrs. Flores. I can handle things on my own until she starts work."

She supposed she should feel good about his offer, but was he trying to be thoughtful and kind? Or was he pushing her away?

What if she wasn't so sure she still wanted to go, at least right away?

"I don't understand," she said.

"I want you to be able to open your shop. I know how much it means to you. I'll even give you a bonus, an extra thousand dollars."

He'd agreed to pay off her student loans and was already paying her more than was reasonable. And now he was offering her even more? He was giving her mixed messages, and she wasn't sure if she should thank him or slap him.

"What about the kids?" she asked. They'd grown attached her, and she to them. They needed her. And she had a feeling Braden did, too. At least, she hoped he did.

"The kids and I will be fine. Once you get settled, I'll take them to visit you in the city. You can also come see them on the ranch whenever you want to."

But *when*? She had no idea how long it would take for the store to earn enough for her to hire a real employee, someone she could trust to handle things for her when she was gone.

No, it wouldn't work out. How could it?

Originally, she might have wanted to leave and not look back, but their lovemaking had changed things between them. Or rather, it had changed things for her.

That didn't mean that she'd given up the dream completely, but she wasn't opposed to postponing it for a while. After all, being with Braden and the kids on the Bar M hadn't been nearly as dull and stifling as she'd thought it would be. She'd actually enjoyed her time here. It had given her a real sense of purpose, at least it had while it lasted.

"What do you think?" he asked. "You can go to Houston to look for the perfect place to lease, even as early as tomorrow."

So soon? Was he eager to get rid of her?

"I can't go tomorrow," she said. "I promised the kids I'd take them shopping in Wexler."

"That's right. I wouldn't want to disappoint them. But you're free to leave after that." He paused for a moment, as if pondering his offer. Or maybe he was just choosing the right words to say when lying in bed with a lover and ending things before they'd even gotten started. "Why don't we have a special dinner tomorrow night? We can celebrate the opening of your soon-to-be store?"

Her thoughts were in such a turmoil she couldn't respond. Sure, she'd looked forward to moving to Houston, but... Well, she didn't need to go the day after tomorrow.

Still, The Attic wasn't just a dream, it was a huge part of her life plan. So she couldn't very well put off opening the store indefinitely.

She should thank Braden and move on, but that wasn't going to be easy to do. She'd come to feel something unexpected for him. And she adored the kids.

But why *him*? And why the twins?

Then again, what did it matter? Braden wasn't asking her to stay. In fact, it was just the opposite. He was telling her to go.

"I appreciate your offer," she said, as she rolled out of bed. "It's more than generous, and it will come in handy."

When she padded to the place she'd discarded her clothing and picked up her skirt, he propped himself up on the bed.

"What are you doing?" he asked.

"Getting dressed." She stepped into the skirt and put on her blouse. Then she scooped up her panties and bra.

"Where are you going?"

She tried to conjure an unaffected smile. "To my room."

His brow furrowed. "Why so soon?"

She offered the only plausible excuse she could come up with. "I don't want the kids to wake up and find us like this."

His brow furrowed, but he nodded, accepting it as a reasonable explanation.

She bent and picked up her sandals, then headed for the locked door, blinking back the tears welling in her eyes.

As she let herself out into the hall, she hoped he hadn't realized that her real reason for taking off in a rush was so he wouldn't see her cry.

As Elena walked out of his bedroom, shutting the door behind her, Braden swung his legs off the bed, sat on the edge of the mattress and raked his hand through his hair. What just happened?

The moment he'd offered her his support, as well as a hefty bonus, she'd hightailed it out of there. You'd think that all she cared about was the money. But that couldn't be right. Surely he hadn't misjudged her character.

Maybe she just needed to process what he'd said. And how she felt about it.

Either way, this hadn't gone as planned.

He went to the bathroom to dispose of the condom, pondering their conversation. But before he could come up with a solution to the problem, the telephone rang. He snatched the receiver from the cradle before the noise woke the twins. "Hello?"

"Mr. Rayburn?" a woman asked.

"Yes…?"

"It's Francisca Flores, returning your call. I'm sorry for not getting back to you sooner, but I was in Colorado, visiting my parents. They live in the mountains, and there's very poor cell reception."

"No problem." Braden got to his feet. "I'd like to offer you the nanny position. How soon can you start?"

He'd expected a happy response, but the woman didn't speak right away. Finally, she said, "I'm sorry, but I can't take the job. I just agreed to work for another family."

His heart sank. He should have known a woman as experienced as Francisca wouldn't have difficulty finding a position. Why hadn't he contacted her sooner?

"Congratulations," he said, his voice lacking any enthusiasm.

Now what was he going to do? He'd practically told Elena to go pack her bags, and he had no idea how he'd replace her.

Francisca apologized again. "I probably should have told you that I had several interviews last week."

If she had, he would have snatched her up while he had the chance. But there wasn't much he could do about it now. "I guess our loss is that other family's gain."

"Thank you for understanding."

Yeah, well, the way he saw it, he had no other choice. When the call ended, he stared at his discarded clothing and blew out a weary sigh. Who knew when Mrs. Schnebly's car would be fixed? At this point, there was only one possible solution. He'd have to call Lola and offer her the job by default.

But rather than talk to her directly, he would call Miguel and ask him to give her the message.

Right now, the only woman he wanted to talk to was Elena. And she'd made it clear she wasn't up for any further conversation.

He returned to the en suite bathroom, then took a long, hot shower. After drying off, he reentered the bedroom and his eyes lit on the sheets and comforter rumpled from their lovemaking. He tried to shake the memories from his mind—Elena, the feelings he'd come to have for her, the amazing sex. But in spite of his best efforts, it didn't work.

So instead of the peaceful, after-the-loving sleep he'd hoped for, he tossed and turned all night.

Finally, just before dawn, he got up and headed outside to do his morning chores. All the while, he thought about Elena, about what she meant to him. About how difficult it would be to let her go.

A part of him hoped her business endeavor would fail, and that she'd be forced to return home to Brighton Valley—and maybe to him. But that wasn't fair. If truth be told, he wanted to see her happy, even if her happiness meant they couldn't be together.

Just after eight o'clock, he returned to the house, hoping she was awake and that she'd put the coffee on to brew. As he entered the mudroom to wash up, he caught a whiff of the aroma.

Good. It was time to face her, and he'd like to send a little caffeine into his bloodstream while they talked.

"Breakfast is ready," she said, as she stood at the stove, her back to him.

She'd dressed in a pair of cropped white jeans and a colorful top. Her hair was swept up in that messy top-knot that appealed to him. Hell, Elena just plain appealed to him, no matter what she wore or how she'd fixed her hair.

"We're having hotcakes and sausage," she said.

"Sounds good. I've worked up an appetite."

She turned, and when he noticed that she was wearing lipstick, he asked, "Going somewhere?"

"I'm taking the kids shopping for boots and jeans. Remember?"

"Oh, that's right. And to buy swimsuits." Thank God she wasn't leaving yet. He still had some things he needed to say, an explanation to give. Or so it seemed.

He reached into his back pocket and pulled out his wallet. Then he peeled off a couple of hundred dollar bills. "Will this be enough?"

"I'm sure it'll be fine." She smiled, and although he tried his best to read into her expression, to sense her sentiment this morning, he couldn't spot a tell-tale thing.

"Have a good time," he said. "And don't worry about

dinner. I'll fix it tonight. And just so you know, I plan to make it special."

"Yes, the goodbye celebration. Got it. Thanks."

He watched as she folded the bills and tucked them into her front pocket. He was just about to bring up the subject of their lovemaking when the kids walked into the kitchen.

So much for that. He'd have to talk to Elena about it tonight. After the kids went to bed.

Trouble was, he wasn't exactly sure what to say. Part of the reason for that was because he hadn't come clean and told her what he was really feeling. But then, he'd always kept his emotions close to the vest—something he'd no doubt inherited from his old man.

He'd never experienced indecision with a woman before, but this was different. Elena was different. And he hated to think that everything about her, about them, had drifted out of his control.

Unable to help himself, he reached back into his pocket and pulled out two fifties.

"Here," he said. "Just to make sure you have enough money for lunch and whatever."

She studied the bills for a moment, then took them. But she didn't smile. Instead, her brow furrowed as though taking it wasn't sitting well.

Right this minute, offering up the extra cash wasn't sitting too well with him, either. Probably because his old man used to resort to money to solve all life's dilemmas.

Damn. He'd tried his best not to emulate his father, not to become just like him. But the similarity in their styles, in their problem solving skills, suddenly seemed a little too close for comfort.

This wasn't the same, he insisted.

He could tell himself that all he wanted. He just hoped that throwing money Elena's way hadn't created more problems for him.

Elena had nearly refused the extra money Braden had given her. She was a bargain shopper and knew how to stretch her cash. But that wasn't what bothered her the most.

Braden seemed to think that he could appease her with money. That he could dismiss her without guilt.

His words ran through her mind over and over again, yet she still couldn't figure out what was behind his offer. He might just be giving her the freedom to pursue her dream, but he could just as easily be trying to cut bait.

While she'd lain in his arms, awed by their lovemaking, she'd come to the conclusion that she loved him, but he hadn't given her any idea that he felt the same way. So, that being the case, how could she even think that they could have any kind of lasting relationship—long distance or otherwise?

While she hadn't made any immediate plans to leave for Houston, she was going to do so as soon as she'd fulfilled the one last promise she'd made to Braden and the twins—to take them shopping for ranch clothes and swimsuits.

Now, as she walked along the sidewalk in downtown Wexler, flanked by Bela and Beto, she held two big shopping bags in her hands. Both kids had insisted upon wearing their new boots out of the store. Bela, of course, was as cute as could be. And Beto seemed to have acquired the typical cowboy swagger.

It was already afternoon, so Elena asked, "Is any-one hungry yet?"

Beto, who'd been grinning nonstop ever since leav-ing the boot store, brightened. "I am!"

Bela's arm shot up. "Me, too!"

"Great. Then all we need to do is decide on what we want to eat. There's a café that serves hamburgers down the street."

"I want a cheeseburger," Beto said. "Can we get milkshakes, too? And French fries?"

"You bet. It isn't far from here. Maybe five or six blocks. Let's leave the car in the parking lot and walk."

They both agreed, something she still found refresh-ing. She loved her younger brothers and sisters—she really did. But if she'd been on a shopping trip with them, at least one of them would have complained about the heat or a broken shoelace or come up with some other objection. But Bela and Beto seemed happy just to be with her.

She liked being with them, too. How could she ever walk away from them without a backward glance? Then again, how could she walk away from Braden? And did she really want to?

Maybe what they really needed to do was to have a heart-to-heart.

"Look!" Bela said, pointing straight ahead.

When Elena gazed in the indicated direction, she spotted Lola Garcia walking out of a lingerie store, a bright pink shopping bag in her hands.

The attractive woman, who'd noticed Elena at the same time, brightened and gave her a whole-arm wave.

Great. Now that they'd seen each other, Elena

couldn't very well avoid her. So she feigned a smile as she approached her.

Lola wasn't dressed as sexy as she'd been yesterday, although her skinny black jeans molded to her curves. And she still wore a pair of spiked heels.

They greeted each other in Spanish and made small talk for a minute or two. Just as Elena was about to tell her goodbye, Lola stooped to address the kids. There wasn't anything out of the ordinary about her talking to them, but the words she spoke slammed Elena in the gut.

Lola was going to start work at the Bar M on Monday morning.

Seriously? There had to be a mistake. Braden had told Elena that he was going to ask Francisca to watch the kids.

And we can go horseback riding with Mr. Braden, Lola told the children in Spanish. *Won't that be fun?*

When Elena quizzed her, Lola explained that "Senor Braden" wanted her to come to work as soon as possible. So she'd gone shopping to pick up a few things she would need.

Like lingerie?

The words Braden had told Elena, the things she'd struggled with in her heart, began to repeat in her mind.

I'm not going to hold you back from leaving or try to convince you to stay… You don't have to wait until I find someone else to look after the kids. I can handle things until Mrs. Flores starts work.

But it wasn't Mrs. Flores he'd hired.

And he hadn't just told Elena she was free to go,

he'd actually encouraged her to leave—sooner, rather than later.

Had he offered her the extra money as a further incentive, hoping she'd take it and run? Had the thousand dollar "bonus" been his way of getting rid of one nanny so he could take up with the new one?

As the truth played out in her mind, Elena could hardly believe it. Nor could she understand how she'd misread Braden these past two weeks. The handsome cowboy was a womanizer, just like his father!

And Elena had slept with him! Had that been his game plan all along? To get her into his bed, then move to better pickings?

She wanted to argue otherwise, but what else was she supposed to think? Besides, she'd read that letter from Christina, the woman who'd wanted to hook up with him, even when he'd been with someone else. She had half a mind to call him on it, except she didn't want him to know she'd been a snoop.

She drew herself up tall and offered her congratulations to Lola on the new job, then she led the twins to the café. The only problem was, her stomach had twisted into a giant wad and her appetite had vanished.

Still, she couldn't disappoint the kids.

They might feel badly when she told them she was leaving the ranch later today, but she couldn't help that. She wasn't about to stand in Braden's way. After she took the twins home, she would give them each a kiss goodbye. If they were disappointed, Braden would have to deal with that. Well, Braden and Lola.

Elena's stomach twisted tighter. But it wasn't only her appetite that had been damaged. Her heart had cracked in two.

* * *

Braden had planned a special dinner for this evening, pulling out all the stops. He'd picked up a couple of steaks at the market, which he would grill, along with hotdogs for the kids, in case they'd rather have those. He even drove into town and picked up a chocolate fudge cake at Caroline's Diner.

He would consider it to be a celebration, as well as a bon voyage meal, but he still hoped that Elena would change her mind.

Letting her go was a lot harder than he'd thought it would be, although he got the feeling that she might be a bit reluctant to leave.

That's what he was counting on. That she'd realize on her own that she wanted to be with him and the kids. And speaking of the kids, he'd decided that he wanted them to live with him from now on. He had a feeling both Jason and Carly would agree with that plan. He just hoped Elena was okay with it, too.

It might be too much to hope for, especially for a guy like him, but maybe they could even become a family of sorts. Of course, he'd have to think long and hard about how he'd propose something like that to Elena. Right now, he'd be happy if she'd just agree to give him—and them—a chance.

By the time he arrived at the ranch with the groceries and the dessert, he realized Elena and the kids had beat him home. Not only had he seen Elena's car parked near the barn, but when he entered the living room, he spotted several shopping bags and a couple of shoe boxes strewn on the floor.

"Hey," he called out. "Where is everyone?"

"Getting dressed up like real cowboys," Beto hollered back.

Braden's heart warmed. It was going to be nice having his little brother around. He was looking forward to teaching him to rope and herd horses like the real cowboy he hoped to be.

He was going to like having Bela around, too. She tried hard to emulate her brother, but she was a girl, through and through.

There was no need in hanging out in the living room when he had groceries to put away, so he carried the reusable bags to the kitchen.

Twenty minutes later, he'd seasoned the meat, made a green salad and put four russet potatoes in to bake. Then he returned to the living room. But the kids hadn't turned up to show off their new boots and jeans.

Was Elena helping them dress?

While he waited, wondering what was keeping them, footsteps sounded on the stairs. He turned, eager to see what they'd bought.

But it wasn't the kids. It was only Elena. And when he spotted the suitcase in her hand, he realized what had been keeping her. She'd been packing.

His heart thudded, and the hope inside of him died.

"What's going on?" he asked.

"I'm leaving. You're on your own."

His brow furrowed as he tried to wrap his mind around what she was saying, what she was doing. Sure, he'd told her she could leave whenever she wanted to, but he hadn't actually expected her to go. And certainly not before dinner, not before he'd had a chance to offer a plan B—whatever that might be.

"Where are the kids?" he asked.

"They're in their room. I've already told them good-bye."

"Are they all right?" Hell, if her departure seemed as sudden to them as it did to him, they'd be…hurt. Dumbfounded. Speechless.

"They're feeling sad, but they'll be all right. I told them I'd come back to visit. However, I didn't tell them when."

"I don't know what to say."

"Goodbye is standard."

Damn. She was acting so…cold. And snappish. "Is something wrong?"

"No, you seem to have things all figured out."

He raked a hand through his hair, not at all in agreement with her. "I…uh… I guess I owe you some money."

"You can give it to my dad. Or you can mail it to him. It really doesn't matter at this point." Then she headed for the door.

"You're angry," he said, wondering why he hadn't seen through her clipped tone sooner. "Did I do something…?"

She turned and arched a single brow. Her gaze lanced his heart. "You lied to me. And you used me. That's about it in a nutshell. But it's my fault. I should have known better."

As she headed for the door, he said, "Wait a second. I'm not following you. Let's talk this over."

She turned. "I don't expect you to 'follow' me." Then she opened the door. "And if you want to talk it over with someone, I suggest you discuss it with your new nanny."

Before he could question her logic, the door slammed shut.

Chapter Twelve

Braden was at a complete loss. Nothing Elena had said made a lick of sense, but she was clearly upset. She'd also claimed that he'd lied to her. But about what? He didn't have a clue.

And what did the new nanny have to do with anything?

He was tempted to run after her and ask, but what would he say? What would he be forced to reveal?

He'd probably end up begging her to stay, which would only make things worse. It would certainly make him *feel* worse. He'd be damned if he'd act like a woeful pup that had been tied up in the yard while its littermates frolicked over hill and dale.

No, he couldn't do that.

His other option was to go upstairs and ask the kids if she'd said anything to them, although he doubted it. That wouldn't be cool. Besides, it wasn't her style.

Nevertheless, he was drawn to the big bay window. He looked out into the yard, hoping to spot her standing outside, having second thoughts. Instead, he watched her pull out of the driveway, her tires spinning up loose gravel.

When she was gone, he headed upstairs, where he found the kids in their room, sitting on their beds, talking to each other in soft voices. They wore their new Western finery and appeared to be ready for a day on the ranch.

He knocked on the doorjamb. When they both looked his way, he let out a long whistle. "Wow. Don't you look nice. Just like real cowboys."

Bela's lips formed a pout. "But I'm a cow*girl*." She pointed out the red ribbons that dangled from her pigtails. "See?"

"And you're a beautiful cowgirl," he said. "I'd never mistake you for a boy."

That seemed to appease her, because she smiled, her disappointment transforming into girlish pride.

He made his way into the bedroom. "I have a question for you. What did Elena tell you guys?"

"Just that she had to leave," Beto said. "And that she was going to miss us because she loves us to the moon."

"To the moon and *back*," his sister corrected.

"Yeah," Beto said. "I just wish she didn't have to go away. Me and Bela are going to miss her."

"I'm going to miss her, too," Braden said.

Maybe that was something he should have admitted to her. If he had, would she have been in such a hurry to leave? It was hard to say. The whole thing had him perplexed.

"Did she mention anything else?" he asked.

"Yes," Bela said. "She also told us to obey you. And Lola, too."

Lola? Braden never had the chance to tell Elena that Mrs. Flores couldn't work for him. Nor had he mentioned that he'd been forced to line up Miguel's sister.

"That's weird," he said, unable to help muttering his thoughts. "How did Elena know about Lola coming to work here?"

"Lola told us when we were shopping," Bela said.

Oh, crap. They'd run into Lola while they were in Wexler? He'd ever expected them to cross paths. Not that he'd planned to keep it a secret that Lola was going to work for him. He just hadn't had a chance to explain the reason for it to Elena.

Was that the lie she'd assumed he'd told? And was that why she'd taken off like a bronc with a burr under its saddle?

Probably. At least, that could be part of why she'd made such a speedy exit. But the more he thought about it, the more he realized something else must have been bothering her long before she'd talked to Lola.

"Elena promised to come and visit us," Beto said, drawing Braden from his thoughts. "And it won't matter where we're living, with you or with Jason or Carly. She said she'd find us."

"We also get to go to her store," Bela added. "And we won't even need money to buy stuff. She's going to let us have whatever we want."

Obviously the kids had taken her departure fairly well, but Braden was still struggling with it. Finding a solution was going to take some serious thought.

"Thanks," he said.

Leaving the kids in their room, he headed downstairs, crossed the living room and went out the front door. He did some of his best thinking when he was outside in the fresh air.

Elena had left in a huff, but he doubted she'd gone straight to Houston. At least, he hoped that was the case. If she went to her parents' house, he could go after her. He could explain how the Lola thing had come down.

But would it matter? She'd been planning to leave before he'd mentioned bringing in a nanny to replace her.

He walked to the edge of the porch and placed his hands on the wooden railing. As he sucked in a deep breath, relishing the country air and hoping it would help him move on, all he could think of was Elena. And that he missed her more than ever.

He came to an unsettling conclusion. He'd fallen in love for the first time in his life, only to have Elena leave him before he'd told her how he felt. But then again, revealing how he felt probably wouldn't have changed anything. She'd already made up her mind to leave.

His thoughts drifted to a memory, to a time when he'd been about twelve or thirteen.

It was summer, and he'd been required to spend two weeks with his dad. But as it often had come to pass, his dad had a business trip lined up, so Braden had been sent to the Leaning R to stay with Granny. Jason had been there, too.

Funny, but he could no longer remember what Jason had said to start it all, but Braden's temper had gotten the best of him. Even though his brother was two years older, four inches taller and about twenty pounds heavier, Braden had rushed at him, fists raised.

Granny had seen it all—the teasing, the first punch. She hadn't interfered until Jason had gotten Braden on the ground and began to let him have it. Then she stepped in and put a stop to it. She'd sent Jason to the barn to wait for her to come and talk to him, then she took Braden by the arm and addressed his temper.

"So what?" Braden had told her. "I hate Jason. He's a jerk."

"He's your brother," Granny had said.

"Not a real one. He's only half. And besides, he's my dad's favorite anyway. I don't count. I never have. But what do I care? I'm not like them."

She'd pondered that a moment, then said, "You boys are going to be great friends someday. So the sooner you realize what really matters in life, the better."

"Jason doesn't matter to me," Braden had said, swiping a hand at the blood that oozed from his split lip.

"You're wrong, Braden. The two of you have a lot more in common than you realize."

Braden had clucked his tongue at her crazy assumption.

Instead of snapping at him for his disrespect, Granny had stroked his back, offering comfort he hadn't been able to accept at the time. "The only thing that really matters in this world is love and family. But if you continue to have that tough-guy attitude, you'll find yourself all alone someday."

While Braden hadn't pulled away from her touch, he'd written off what she'd said. But he'd never forgotten it—or her closing advice. "You need to saddle your temper, son. And you need to open your heart to others, or you're going to grow up to be a very lonely and unhappy man."

Braden had taken at least some of her words seriously. He'd gotten his temper under control, something his mom had objected to, as well.

But now, the more he thought about it, all of Granny's advice seemed to make sense. He'd shut out his brother for years. But recently, after their father died, they'd been forced to talk, to work together. And if truth be told, he'd begun to really like Jason, to admire him.

He glanced in the direction Elena had driven and realized he'd never felt so alone in his life.

Or so much like his father. He'd refused to get emotionally involved with anyone for years. And he'd resorted to using money to fix whatever problem cropped up.

And while he'd convinced himself that he was different, that Charles Rayburn's influence and DNA hadn't gotten a hold on him, that wasn't true.

Open your heart, Granny had said.

His great-grandmother might have been right about that. But did he dare lay his heart on the line, even if Elena didn't care, even if she left anyway?

Yes, the old woman seemed to say in the late afternoon breeze.

Braden stood there for a few minutes, pondering his options. He'd have to talk to Elena, he supposed, but she was long gone.

I don't expect you to 'follow' me, she'd said. *And if you want to talk it over with someone, I suggest you discuss it with your new nanny.*

However, the only nanny Braden wanted or needed was the one who'd just left.

Elena had driven up one county road, then down another with no real destination in mind. All she'd wanted to do was to take time to get her thoughts together and to put some distance between her and Braden.

If she'd had an immediate game plan, she would have gone straight to Houston while it was still light. But the sun was now beginning to set. Besides, she couldn't leave town yet. She needed to talk to someone, and the only person she could depend on to give her sound advice was her father.

When she arrived at the house he shared with Laura and the kids, she left her suitcase in the car and strode up to the front door. After letting herself into the empty living room, she called out, "It's me. Is anyone home?"

"I am," her dad said, as he came out of the kitchen, wiping his hands on a dishtowel. But the moment his eyes met hers, he frowned. "You've been crying. What's wrong?"

As much as she'd like to keep her mistake, her foolishness to herself, she opened up and told him everything. Well, not the part about sleeping with Braden last night. That would be her secret.

"I'm sorry," he said. "So Braden turned out to be a ladies' man, like his father used to be?"

"Yes, that's the way it seems. He's certainly had his share of women." And, apparently, he still had them lined up, ready to take their turn in his bed.

At that thought, her heart ached.

"Did you tell him how you felt about him?" her father asked.

"Not exactly. But he knew." He had to have known.

Her father draped the dishtowel over the back of an easy chair and moved toward her. "I don't mean to sound critical, honey, but you've never been very expressive of your feelings. Even though I know you love me, as well as the rest of the family, you've never come out and told us."

There'd been a reason for that. She hadn't been sure that her love would be returned. Yet that wasn't the case, she admitted now. Her dad and Laura had always made their feelings clear. And she'd been accepted into the family from the first day she moved in.

Should she have been more honest with Braden? She doubted it. How badly would she have felt if she'd told him she loved him, only to have him throw it back in her face?

When the doorbell rang, her father answered it. "Well, look who's here."

Elena expected to see one of the neighbors. Margie, who worked as a waitress at Caroline's Diner and lived across the street, often stopped by to have coffee with Laura.

Oh, gosh. Margie also repeated things to the locals who frequented the diner. That's all Elena needed—to become fodder for gossip.

But it wasn't Margie standing on the stoop. It was Braden, his black Stetson in hand.

"Come on in," her father told him.

Elena stiffened. Would her father have been as welcoming if he'd known what she and Braden had done last night?

"What do you want?" she asked him.

"To talk to you. You left before I had a chance to tell you something."

"You were going to tell me about Lola?"

He nodded. "Yes, I was. It's not what you think. When I asked Francisca if she could start on Monday, she told me she'd already accepted another job. But at that point, I'd already told you that it was okay to leave whenever you wanted. So I called Miguel to contact Lola. But as soon as I can, I'm going to find someone more permanent—and more motherly."

She supposed she could believe that, but he'd still encouraged her to go to Houston, to spread her wings. So while his explanation made her feel better, she couldn't soften, couldn't allow him to break her heart further.

"I also wanted to tell you that I've…" He paused for a moment, as if reluctant to finish. "I've decided to keep the twins with me. I'm going to the district office tomorrow to enroll them in school."

"I'm glad to hear that." She'd been hopeful he'd come to that conclusion so Beto and Bela wouldn't be shuffled off to another home. Yet that did very little to ease the ragged pain in her heart.

"Speaking of the kids," she said, "Where are they?"

"I dropped them off with my mom and Erik. They're going to have dinner with them tonight."

She merely studied him, wondering what else he might have on his mind.

Braden glanced at her father, who stood with his arms crossed, his eyes narrowed and his brow furrowed. But Braden didn't seem ruffled. "I have the utmost respect for your daughter, Paco. I came here to let her know there was a big misunderstanding. And I'd like to rectify that."

Her father's expression gentled. "Would you like me to give you two some privacy?"

"That's not necessary. I don't have any secrets. Not anymore." Then Braden turned to Elena. "I'm sorry for being insensitive and holding back my thoughts and feelings. It won't happen again."

"Insensitive?" she asked. "In what way?"

"For teasing you about Lola in the first place. I knew she wasn't nanny material from the moment she stepped into the house."

Elena wanted to believe him, but she was unwilling to let that weaken her resolve. Still, if truth be told, it was already wavering because he'd decided to keep the kids.

"I've never lied to you," Braden said. "No, wait, I take that back. I wasn't exactly honest or forthcoming when I told you I could handle things without you. I probably can. But I don't want to."

So he came looking for her to ask her to remain his nanny. But there was no way she'd take that position again. Not when she'd hoped to be his... Well, she wouldn't even ponder what she'd once thought she wanted to be.

"I fully support your dream to open The Attic," he added. "In fact, I just signed a two-year lease on a store located in downtown Brighton Valley. It's the empty shop across the street from Caroline's Diner."

Surely, she hadn't heard him correctly. "You did *what*?"

He reached into his back pocket and pulled out a

rolled up sheet of paper. "Here's my copy—signed, sealed and delivered."

She took the lease and scanned the wording. It certainly appeared to be legitimate. She looked back at him. "What are you going to do with this?"

"Give it to you and hope that you'll use it, that it'll work as a good location for The Attic."

"That's crazy," she said. "What if I don't want to open the store in Brighton Valley? What are you going to do with a two-year lease?"

"You may think I've lost my mind." His lips quirked into a crooked grin. "But the craziest thing I've ever done is to fall in love with you—deeply and madly. And I'm sorry that I wasn't able to tell you outright. Instead, I kept that secret to myself. But it's not going to do me any good to keep it locked in my heart."

She couldn't believe what she was hearing. "You love me?"

His smile deepened. "To the moon and back. Isn't that the catch phrase these days?"

She nodded. It's what she'd told the kids.

He glanced at her father, tossed him a smile, then caught her gaze. "I want to marry you, Elena. But I'll wait until you decide whether you feel the same way about me."

She did feel the same way. Maybe she'd even take an extra orbit or two around the moon, making the distance a bit further, her love deeper still.

But could she trust Braden at his word? Could he make the kind of lifetime commitment she needed?

"What about Christina?" she asked.

His brow furrowed. "Who?"

"Now I have a confession to make," she admitted.

"That day Beto made a mess in the office, I started picking up those files and papers from the floor and noticed a letter from a woman named Christina. It was wrong of me to do it, but I read it. So I'm sorry."

Braden slowly shook his head. "Oh, that Christina. Don't worry about her. She never meant anything to me. I didn't even respond to that letter. In fact, I thought I'd thrown it away months ago. And for the record, Lola is as good as gone. I'll let her know that the kids and I don't need her. Then I'll look for a proper nanny or hire whoever you think would be the best candidate."

She was too stunned to speak. That woman meant nothing? Braden loved *her*? And he wanted to marry her? He must. He'd even taken out a lease for her store.

Could a shop like The Attic succeed in Brighton Valley? Possibly. The downtown shops were so quaint, the street so appealing, that it drew a lot of patrons from Wexler and beyond.

"That's all I can offer," Braden said. "That and my heart."

Elena glanced at her father, wishing now that he hadn't been privy to the conversation. But the grin stretching across his face told her he approved—of Braden, of the apology, of the proposal.

She turned back to Braden. "I love you, too. More than I'd ever expected. More than I'd ever dreamed it was possible to love a man. I accept your apology—and your proposal. At least, if you meant what you said."

"I meant every single word." Then he swept her into his arms and kissed her senseless.

If he had any thoughts about her father looking on, she'd never know it. And quite frankly, Elena didn't care. She'd fallen in love with him, too—deeply and madly. Wasn't that the catch phrase now?

When the kiss ended, he said, "So you don't mind marrying me, even if I'm a package deal?"

"Not at all. I want to help you make a home and family the kids deserve."

Before he could comment, the front door swung open, and her half siblings— Correction! Her siblings entered the house, followed by Laura.

When Elena announced her good news, Braden was swarmed by his future in-laws. When they'd been congratulated, Laura assigned jobs to her husband and to each of the children. Then she hurried to the kitchen to prepare a celebration meal, leaving Elena and Braden finally alone.

He pulled her close. "This is wild. Granny once told me that the most important things in life were love and family. And for the first time in my life, I know exactly what she meant."

"I feel that same way. Something tells me we're going to have an awesome family, Braden, with more love than you or I know what to do with."

He kissed her again, drawing it out until she thought she might collapse on the floor.

"Believe me," he said. "We'll know what to do with all that love. We'll shower it on each other and the twins. And speaking of the twins, let's go get them. Bela and Beto should be a part of this celebration."

He was right. And Granny had been right, too. Life was all about love and family.

She took her future husband by the hand. "What are we waiting for? Let's go get the kids."

Epilogue

When Thanksgiving rolled around, Carly, who'd just given birth to a baby girl she'd named Erin Marie, suggested the family gather at the Leaning R for dinner, and everyone agreed.

Jason and Juliana were seated in the living room, cooing to their new daughter, a precious little bundle who had a tuft of dark hair and big blue eyes. Jason's name was on her birth certificate as her father, not that anyone would ever doubt that. She looked just like him, something that made Braden think about the Horton book.

Carly's husband, Ian, had insisted on baking the turkey and making the stuffing, a family recipe he got from his grandma. Elena and Juliana had made the side dishes, and Jason had purchased the pies from Caroline's Diner.

Braden and Elena had a lot to be thankful for. First of all, they'd gotten married the previous month at the Wexler Community Church. Braden had never been happier than the day he and Elena had vowed to love each other forever. Both Bela and Beto had taken part in the ceremony as a bridesmaid and a groomsman.

Just last week, Braden and Elena had attended parent-teacher conferences at the elementary school and learned that both children were doing super work and had made a lot of friends. Best of all, their little family was both happy and healthy.

Elena had already stocked her new store on Main Street and was looking forward to the grand opening, which was scheduled for Monday, right in time for the holiday rush to begin.

So, yes. They had reasons to be grateful.

Now, as he stood in the living room of the home that Granny had once owned and now belonged to Ian and Carly, he studied the way his sister had decorated the old-style ranch house. For the most part, it boasted new paint and furniture, but she'd kept some of the pictures and plaques that their great-grandmother had once cherished. Granny, it seemed, would always be a part of the Leaning R.

In a corner of the room, Bela sat in an easy chair, holding little Erin Marie McAllister, Carly's newborn.

By the fireplace, Beto, who wore his boots and hat, looked at a photograph that Ian was showing him. It was an aged yellow photo of Clayton Rayburn, the man who'd first settled in Brighton Valley and built this ranch house. Their Rayburn ancestor, who wore chaps and spurs, as well as a hat, looked like a true cowboy, and Beto was impressed.

Yep. Granny had been right. Love and family were the only things that really mattered in life.

As Elena entered the room and approached Braden, he opened his arms, and she stepped into his embrace. On the day he'd proposed, he'd thought that he loved her more than was possible. But he'd been wrong. He'd come to find out that he loved her more with each passing day.

"Dinner's almost ready," Elena said. "Where's your mom and Erik? I thought they'd be here by now."

"So did I. Maybe I'd better give them a call." But before Braden could pull his cell phone from his pocket, the doorbell rang. "That must be them."

And it was. Braden welcomed them into the house, glad they were here. He was also glad his brother and sister had insisted that they be invited.

For as long as he could remember, his mother had reached out to both of his siblings, offering her love time and again, even though they'd been reluctant to accept it. But times, they were a changing. Both Jason and Carly had welcomed his mom and stepdad into the family fold.

Braden greeted his mother with a warm embrace. "I was getting worried about you."

"I…" Shannon glanced at her husband, her cheeks flushed. "Well, I wasn't feeling very well earlier. So I waited until…"

"Are you sick?" Braden asked. Damn, she must have been eager to be a part of the family holiday to come anyway.

"It's not contagious." A grinning Erik asked her, "Are you going to tell him?"

"I thought I'd wait until after dinner," his mother

said. "And then I was going to tell him and Elena in private."

"Tell us what?" Braden asked. If Erik hadn't been beaming, he'd be worried about her health.

"I'm going to have a baby," his mom said.

Braden's jaw must have dropped to the floor. "No kidding?"

She nodded. "I hope you're not upset by the news. I realize I'm a little old to be having a child. And you certainly didn't expect to have a little brother or sister at your age."

No, he hadn't. But then again, he'd been surprised before. He glanced at Beto, then at Bela. "Not to worry, Mom. I'm getting used to having younger siblings."

"I think it's wonderful," Elena said. "I know how much you love children."

"We couldn't be happier." Erik slipped his arm around Shannon and drew her close.

Braden had been surprised by the news. Shocked, actually. But his mom deserved to be happy. And nothing would please her more than having a child with the man she loved.

Beto, who must have sidled in beside them and overheard the news, said, "I'm happy, too. Does that mean I'm going to be an uncle again?"

Hell, Braden wasn't exactly sure what that would make him, either legally or officially. But that didn't matter to him.

"You're going to be a big brother," Braden told Beto.

"Cool," the boy said. "I'm going to tell Bela. She likes holding babies."

They chuckled at the boy's enthusiastic response. Then Braden stepped aside to allow his mom and

Erik—no, make that his *parents*—into the house. They might not be Rayburns, but they were definitely family.

As his parents entered the living room, Braden held Elena back. When she turned to face him, he cupped her cheeks with both hands. "I love you. More than you'll ever know."

Then he took her in his arms and kissed her with all the emotion that had been stored up in his heart, a feeling that grew stronger and more bountiful with each new family member who came into his life.

Yes, he and Elena had a lot to be thankful for—a home, a family and love that would last forever.

* * * * *